SHIGIDI

AND THE BRASS HEAD
OF OBALUFON

SHIGIDI

AND THE BRASS HEAD
OF OBALUFON

//////////////////////////////

WOLE TALABI

DAW BOOKS

Jacket design and illustration by Jim Tierney
Interior design by Fine Design
DAW Book Collectors No. 1945

DAW Books
An imprint of Astra Publishing House
dawbooks.com
DAW Books and its logo are registered trademarks of Astra Publishing House

Printed in the United States of America

ISBN 978-0-7564-1826-7 (Hardcover) | ISBN 978-0-7564-1827-4 (Ebook)

First edition: August 2023
10 9 8 7 6 5 4 3 2 1

For my mother, Sola, who left us too soon.

Thank you for your love and your words and for letting me help you with your theology studies all those years ago.

CHAPTER 1

So, there he was, barely conscious in the back of a black cab being driven down the Haymarket road on the spirit-side of London by a man who died seventy years ago, when Nneoma finally told Shigidi that she loved him.

He would have laughed if he wasn't already half past dead.

The driver downshifted gears and swerved the hackney carriage so sharply and violently that the two left-side tires lifted off the ground. Shigidi lost his balance on the plush leather seat and fell over into her thighs, pressing the open wound where one of his arms used to be and leaving a large, ugly red mark on her lovely blue dress. A smear of blood, clay, and spirit particles. The contact forced every muscle in his body to contract. He felt like his insides were being separated from each other, like he was being torn apart from within by an angry pain-shaped animal. He was forced to lift his head out of her lap to shout out some of the hurt. The sound that came out of him was strained, strident, and strange. It was a sound he didn't recognize, even though it was not the first time he had screamed out in agony.

The fog of pain cleared just enough for him to stop screaming. *I don't know how much longer I can hang on to what little consciousness I have left.*

Bright light was spilling in through the windows, accompanied by a sound like the beating of the old Oyo empire war drums. It was almost funny because he had once used those same fearsome sounds as inspiration a long time ago, when the Ooni of Ife had sent him to give nightmares to six of his enemies. He was no longer a nightmare god but he still remembered what it was like to weave the disparate myriad threads of deep-seated personal fears into a tapestry of terror and pain and uncertainty. And he still knew what it felt like to be caught inside such a web, in a nightmare, desperate to wake.

Everything about this feels like a nightmare.

In the blur of movement and disorientation, he caught a glimpse through the rear window. The sky was a maelstrom of thick, neon-edged clouds and constant flashes of electric-white lightning set against a pitch-black sky full of thick, dark clouds.

No god could hope to reign over such wild spirit-sky.

Down on the ground, four bronze horses with flames for eyes were galloping madly behind them, leaving a trail of broken asphalt, sparks, and fire in their wake. A large angry figure rode behind the horses, driving them forward with vicious purpose. A bronze rope that extended all the way to the horses' strained throats was wound tightly around the imposing figure's forearm as it rode the back half of a crudely bisected gray sedan, giving chase in a makeshift chariot.

Shigidi's vision swam. The glare from the horses' flaming eyes became nothing more than an afterimage superimposed on a million others that danced on his irises, but he could tell that their pursuers were fast—faster than any flesh-and-blood horses could ever hope to be—and drawing closer. But their cab driver was supposed to know the spirit-side of London better than anyone else, living or dead—or kind of both—and so Shigidi hoped that knowledge would be enough to get them to the rendezvous point before dawn, before the life leaked out of him completely.

I don't want to die in a foreign spirit land.

Just then, the driver swung the wheel madly again, forcing the car to swerve right, barely missing two ghosts in long gray frocks . The cab scrambled clumsily down a short flight of cobblestone stairs before reconnecting to actual road and accelerating again. He fell back down into his lover's lap, and his head bounced against the car door so hard he feared for a moment it had cracked open. His vision went blank, and he wasn't sure if it was because he had closed his eyes or if the impact had damaged something in his head, but he didn't really care. All he knew was, everything hurt.

"Careful!" She shouted at the driver as she pressed her hand into Shigidi's and pulled his head into her bloody bosom.

"Sorry! I'm doing my best here, luv," the driver called back, "but in case you haven't noticed, we are being chased by four living statues and one pissed-off giant."

She ignored the driver and whispered into Shigidi's ear, "Hold on, my darling. I love you. Do you hear me? I love you. Just hold on. Everything will be okay. We are almost there."

Stunned, he forced his lead-heavy eyelids open and looked up into her large, wet eyes shimmering with a glaze of tears and the reflection of bright yellow spirit particles. He wanted to embrace her and tell her he loved her too, the way he'd always imagined he would when she finally said the words to him, but he was short one arm and his mouth couldn't form the words. His tongue felt swollen and numb in his mouth, saturated with the sharp taste of iron and clay. He could still hear her; he was still mostly there, but her voice sounded woolly and far away, and the galaxy of blurry lights reflected and refracted around him were becoming too bright. He could barely feel his arm or his legs or his face or his anything anymore.

I guess my time is running out faster than I thought. He hacked out a bloodstained cough. *But it's not too bad. I suppose there are worse ways to die than in the arms of someone you love.*

A force slammed into the vehicle with a deafening sound like an explosion made of other explosions. The driver let out a primal scream that Shigidi could barely hear above the cacophonous violence of metal crunching against metal, the shattering of glass, the screeching of rubber on asphalt. In that moment, he was sure it was over. They were done for.

He focused on the thing that mattered most to him—her. His eyes remained fixed on her open mouth and her widening eyes as the world around them turned into a chaotic galaxy of smoke and metal and glass. And then, when he could barely see her anymore, he shut his eyes against the army of white light invading his consciousness and braced himself for what he was sure would be the final, endless fall into nothing.

I love you too.

And I'm sorry, for everything.

This is not how I thought things would end.

CHAPTER 2

Three Days Earlier.

Perhentian Kecil Island, Terengganu, Malaysia

JULY 2ND, 2017 | 08:47 AM.

In the beaming bright light of late morning, the beach was beautiful. Powdery white sand hugged the arc of the island, transforming through low surf into turquoise crystal where it kissed the water. A widely spaced succession of small, brightly colored boats—mostly fiberglass utility models and a few wooden long-tails with equally colorful sashes draped around their prows—rocked gently in the shallow water. They were tethered to the beach by a sparse web of colored synthetic fiber ropes and rusty metal anchors. A lovely sprinkle of reflected colors danced on the edge of the turquoise like it was bleeding rainbows. Behind the beach line, a lush green island rose.

An array of bold, brown wooden bungalows, perched on the elevated rocks, peeked out in places like curious children.

Up and down the beach, there was a smattering of young people; mostly tanned Europeans and quiet south-east Asians in their twenties and thirties, lying on plastic beach chairs under colorful parasols or exposed on the sand. Around them were the usual handfuls of seaweed, cigarettes, seashells, beer cans, and the charred remnants of a bonfire from the previous night's fire dance.

Shigidi and Nneoma stood out on the ribbon of beach, and he was keenly aware of it. They were a pair of sable-skinned specimens, their bodies sitting still, side-by-side in the sand as the white surf washed over their feet never going beyond their knees. It had taken him a while to get used to the looks that they often drew in this part of the world, but Nneoma always seemed comfortable everywhere. She was leaning back on the sand, in a red bikini, her torso elevated on her elbows. He was raised too, hugging his knees to his heavily muscled chest as he inhaled the salty smell of the water and watched it move in and out like the coral bay itself was breathing. The sound of surf licked at the brittle silence that had settled between them since they first camped out there, at dawn.

"She's been staring at you for fifteen minutes," Nneoma whispered. She glanced to her left without moving any other part of her body to indicate the direction of the person in question.

Shigidi grunted and swiveled his head, eyes hidden behind his sunglasses, to see a tall, toned, and tattooed woman who looked to be in her late thirties sitting on a pink beach towel and trying her best to pretend she wasn't looking at him.

"Maybe you should buy her a drink. Say hello. We could take her to our chalet later tonight and find out what her spirit tastes like," Nneoma said casually, like she was asking him what he would like for breakfast, her voice still low, but clear.

"Hmm. Maybe we should take it easy for a while," Shigidi said, remembering the blonde German man whose bold, adventurous spirit they'd just shared a few days ago, after a drawn-out seduction back in Hanoi, on their way back from Ha Long Bay. "Maybe we should just leave the mortals alone for a while and enjoy each other's company."

When they'd first started their partnership, Nneoma had indulged in human spirits sparingly, preferring to play games with potential prey for days or even weeks, and consuming them only when she needed to, or occasionally when she spotted someone being abusive or saying something she didn't like. She had her own arcane sense of justice and fairness which he was still figuring out. But ever since they had incurred a debt to Olorun, chairman of the board of the Orisha Spirit Company, for saving their lives, Nneoma had changed. She'd become insatiable. Reckless. She didn't need the spirits, but she was persistent in consuming them. Almost aggressively so. Like she was using the hunt and the high of spirit consumption to blunt the edge of something else that she didn't want reveal to him.

"Maybe we shouldn't become boring," Nneoma retorted.

Shigidi raised his head, surprised at her sudden sharpness. "Boring?"

Out of the corner of his eye, he noted that the tattooed woman, whose stare had started all this, was gone. Her beach towel was still on the sand, its pink flamingo patterns now creased.

She said, "Oh. You know what I mean. I am a succubus, you're a retired nightmare god. We are anything but normal. We need to keep doing things that keep the sparks in our spirit particles crackling, things that excite us."

"We already excite each other enough," Shigidi said, but deep down, he wasn't so sure. He was hoping she would agree, but she just sat up on the sand, straightened her back, and flipped her long, braided hair over her shoulder. So, he added a hesitant, "Don't we?"

"I'm just saying, I've been doing this much longer than you have, darling, and I know how easy it is to become bored when you have most of eternity to look forward to," she said. "And boredom can lead to obsession and attachment and bad decisions."

He looked down at the white sand, feeling the gentle heat of the rising sun against the dark surface of his perfectly smooth bald head, before responding. "Attachment isn't always bad. Besides, eternity with someone you love cannot be boring."

"Yes," she agreed, "sure. As long as things remain interesting. And to remain interesting, they have to keep changing, you know? I mean, think about the most enjoyable thing in the world. The thing you enjoy doing the most."

His eyes subconsciously drifted down to the place where her thighs met. She caught the motion, acknowledging it with a laugh.

"Even sex. Imagine sex with the same person, forever. No matter how wonderful it is, how compatible you are as partners, even if neither of you age, or change, after a while it will get boring. It may take a year or two or ten or a hundred, perhaps even a thousand if you're really creative, but it will, eventually. Unless you can find a way to make the sex different. Interesting. New every time. So that there is always something to look forward to. That's all I'm saying. The humans offer us endless possibilities and permutations in the ways we can play with them and then consume their spirits together. It's fun. It's exciting. It's interesting, isn't it?"

This was the third time she had made some variant of this

argument to him, but it was only a way of avoiding the real question. Even though she'd been the one to seek out his companionship, the one who'd made the offer and used so much of her power to make him her partner, she always held him at some emotional distance. First, she'd been preoccupied with teaching him the skills he needed to exist independently, as a freelance spirit, with her. And now she was diluting the time they spent together with seductions and consumptions. They were freelance spirit entities, free of the schedules and objectives and constraints that other deities in the employ of the larger spirit-companies had to deal with, but Nneoma seemed to be obsessively consuming a new spirit or two every other day, like she was a spirit company employee with unreasonably high quarterly or yearly targets to meet.

"It's fun, yes, but there has to be time and space for a couple to just be a couple. We can be interesting together," he said.

She rolled her eyes and waved at him with her perfectly manicured, long and slender fingers like artisanal knives. "This conversation is pointless, darling. We don't need to make this into more than it is. Do you want to have that girl's spirit or not?"

Shigidi clenched his jaw and scratched the top of his head. He suspected that since he had revealed the depth of his love for her, he had exposed something raw in their pairing, some deeper need or fear or something that she didn't want to confront. There was no other way to interpret her actions. She'd been avoiding his attempts to spend more time alone with her, obsessively focusing on the tasks they had to perform to pay off their debt to Olorun, or wildly throwing herself into feeding on spirits like they were about to go out of stock.

He blurted out the question before he could stop himself. "Do you love me, Nneoma?"

The line of her mouth tightened, and she glared as though she was almost angry at him for asking a question she did not want to answer. He held her gaze, a mounting fear growing in him that he'd overplayed his hand by pushing her, and that she'd say "no" just to regain control of the situation.

The lapping water continued to lick at the new strained silence between them. And then they heard a deep, low laughter. They turned together to see where it was coming from.

An old man in a flowing purple dashiki and matching trousers, who looked even more spectacularly out of place than they did, had replaced the tattooed woman on the pink flamingo pattern beach towel. He was laughing gently, deepening the crease lines that radiated from his eyes and bordered his broad nose and mouth. He watched them with a cool-eyed confidence that made it seem like the world around him would bend to his will as he toyed with a reddish-brown kolanut in his palm. His skin shone fiercely like polished iroko wood in the early sunlight, and the thick gray beard covering his chin was only a few inches longer than his perfectly groomed afro.

Shigidi lowered his head out of habit and sighed again, but deeper and more audibly now. Nneoma let out a gasp. The old man looked different from the last time they had seen him, but there was no doubt. They both knew exactly who had come looking for them.

"Olorun," Shigidi said as he looked up. "We were in the middle of a private discussion."

Olorun seemed to have drifted closer to them on the pink flamingo towel. Shigidi could have sworn that the tattooed woman wasn't nearly as close when he'd first seen her.

"I know, I know. I can see that you two are having a little, what do they call it, ehh . . . couple's spat *abi* lovers' quarrel," Olorun replied with a smile that constantly threatened to morph into a laugh. "Could it be the age difference? Dating older women is not easy my boy. Or maybe vacations are not so good for your love life, eh? Too much time to think about things instead of just doing them?"

"That's none of your business," Nneoma snapped.

Her candor shocked Shigidi. He would never get used to the way she spoke to elder gods, but he supposed it made sense, seeing how she had known most of them since they were little more than abstract concepts first made manifest. Shigidi, however, only came to know most of them long after, and some like Olorun, only as his boss's boss.

Still, the smile on the old god's face didn't change.

"Rude," Olorun said, "but true. Very true indeed. So, lovebirds, let's talk about my business then, eh. I have a special job that needs doing, urgently. You have both done very good work so far, in Singapore and Thailand, so when this opportunity came up, I just knew you were the ones I needed for it. You have the perfect skill sets and profiles for it. This is not about your debt to me. You have almost completely paid that off. No, this is something completely different. In fact, if you agree to do this special job, then consider that debt completely wiped out, in addition to what I am offering for this one: a substantial up-front payment and an even bigger bonus waiting for you at the end." He paused to take a bite of kola. "If the job actually gets done."

"Well, I don't know if we want to enter another contract with you when we are already so close to ending the current one—" Shigidi started.

"But we are not going to refuse an offer until we hear what it is," Nneoma cut in.

Olorun smiled. "I need you to retrieve something for me," he said between quick bites of the kola in his hand, "something I once gave to someone you might know." He turned to Shigidi who was salivating with memories of the kolanut's bitter stimulation. "It was part of a business deal long ago. It was stolen from its storage place, and I ignored that loss of ehh . . . intellectual property until now, since I was supposed to be retired and hands-off on spirit business matters. But now that I'm back, well . . . I need it back."

"What are you talking about?" Shigidi asked, clueless.

"Your friend Obalufon, you know he used to be human, don't you? Of course you do. Many of the minor orishas who worked at your grade level, and with whom you interacted in the spirit company, started their careers that way. He was the third Ooni of Ife, a long time ago. Back then, they called him Obalufon Alayemore, and he did fairly decently until he was ousted by his uncle Oranmiyan. That one was a crafty bastard. Anyway, in his exile, Obalufon made an interesting appeal to me, not unlike the one you made a while ago when you were in trouble." He nodded at them. "When some of Oranmiyan's assassins cornered him, he asked me to save his life and to give him power to take back his throne, and in return, he would unite the people and unify the belief system so that we, the orishas, could grow stronger in their combined and concentrated faith. It was a good deal, so I gave him the power he requested, and it paid the spirit company huge dividends for a long time. At least until the Christians and the Muslims *ati bebe lo* showed up and started aggressively seizing market share."

"And this power you gave him, someone took it?" Nneoma asked.

"Yes, in a manner of speaking." Olorun spat a red mass of masticated kola onto the sand. "They stole it."

She raised an eyebrow and kicked a spray of powdery sand off her feet. "Care to elaborate?"

"No, I don't care to actually," he replied, still smiling. "Not yet. All you need to know right now is that the power I gave Obalufon was contained in a physical form, a totem, which was buried with him when he died. A reasonable arrangement. I would have found it and retrieved it eventually, when I was ready. But it was dug up and taken away to a foreign land where, as you are well aware, I cannot freely operate thanks to current spirit trade regulations and their globalist bureaucratic nonsense. That is why I need you again, my two independent agents who owe me their lives." Olorun drew out the last few words of the sentence and winked at them playfully like it was all a game and not a matter of existence. "And it is why I am willing to forgive your existing debt and pay you with stock in the spirit company this time, guaranteeing you a virtually endless supply of spirits and even worship, if you want it."

Reading a guileful look in the old man's eye, Shigidi asked, "Is this going to be dangerous?"

Olorun smiled widely this time, showcasing unexpectedly perfect pearly white teeth before he took another bite of his kola. "Very much so. I am an old god returned to a position of power that I left long ago. Every move I make is dangerous. If you fail, you will almost certainly be destroyed, or worse, trapped forever."

He paused, broke what was left of the kolanut in his hand into three chunky pieces and placed them on the beach towel to form a triangle.

"But if you take the contract, it will be worth your while." He spread his hands and shrugged before he brought them back together in front of him and flicked his right hand along the surface of his left like he was spraying dollars on dancers at an owambe. "Worth even more than stock in the company. If you do this for me, I will end your exile and allow you to return to Yorubaland under my protection, despite the objections of your former boss."

Shigidi and Nneoma looked at each other, unsure of what the other was thinking exactly but knowing that neither of them would miss an opportunity at vengeance against the orisha of fire and lightning, Shango, the thunder god, who had once tried to kill them both and would probably try to do so again.

Shigidi liked the way Nneoma was looking at him, with a glint of excitement. He suspected that she had already decided to do it but was hesitating, waiting for him to show his hand. Perhaps the danger and unpredictability of a big risk like this would finally satisfy whatever instinct had been driving her to seek out the stimulation of ravenous spirit consumption, and he wanted to give her that. Perhaps once it was done, she'd be normal again. At least they would be able to do it together.

Shigidi nodded.

Nneoma smiled. "We'll do it."

"Very good. Then be in London by noon tomorrow." He stood up and approached them. Olorun didn't leave any footprints in the sand, and when he reached them, he leaned over and took Shigidi's arm, pulled it to him and turned his hand up so he could place a finger into Shigidi's palm. A crackling of bright white spirit particles erupted where he touched Shigidi's skin. They rearranged themselves into text that spelled out a number and an address as if he'd been tattooed with pure light.

When he was done, Olorun turned to Nneoma with another smile. "You know, succubus, I have had my eye on you ever since you started to operate around Lagos. I've always admired your ability to navigate situations to get what you want, even if, as I've told you before, I still find your methods distasteful. But I will admit, I'm looking forward to this."

"Err, thanks." She cocked her head. "But I don't think you're in a position to judge my methods or my life, old timer. How many times do I need to tell you? I am what I am. I am true to my nature. Get over it."

"Of course. No vex." He put up his hands. "We are all what we are. See you in London."

And then he was gone before she could respond, like he had evaporated into nothing, leaving only the three pieces of half-eaten kolanut on the beach towel and a faint metallic smell like burning wires in the salty air.

CHAPTER 3

The Afrika Shrine, Ikeja, Lagos, Nigeria

JUNE 20TH, 1977 | 11:46 PM.

Aadit Kumar was sitting on an uncomfortable metal chair close to the raised stage at the far end of the courtyard, surrounded by low buildings. Above, the sky was a dark purple, illuminated by a bright half-moon. The evening air was humid and full of smells: assorted foods, vaporized palm oil, perfume, sweat, cheap beer, and smoke. It all combined to saturate the air with a heady mix of lust, freedom, and marijuana.

He was at an unstable table carved of cheap wood and barely held together by rusty nails and the skill of a poor carpenter. A half-eaten bowl of pepper soup, a mostly eaten plate of suya, and three tall, brown, empty bottles of Gulder beer were sloppily spread in front of him like reluctant offerings. Everything around him vibrated, including his own head, pulsating with the loud music and the rising rush of alcohol. Up on the makeshift stage, where a yellow-painted board spelled out the words: *Fela Kuti and the Africa 70* in dark blue letters, a thin, shirtless man in tight trousers with chalk markings on his face sang into the microphone while simulating sex with a sweaty, skinny woman in a gold miniskirt and bra, cowrie shell bangles shaking around her ankles and wrists. Fela's voice strained as he sang in pidgin.

Aadit picked up a few words from the song. It was something about a woman who didn't like being called a "woman" and preferred to be addressed as a "lady".

An army of musicians played guitars, saxophones, drums, danced, and sang backing vocals that echoed Fela's voice. It all looked like chaos to Aadit but the resulting sounds were undeniably scintillating, and he unknowingly swayed his wooly, booze-addled head in time with it. He was glad he had taken his company driver's recommendation to come here, despite his initial reluctance at the idea of attending a concert in Lagos on his own. He'd even worn the protective gold chain and peacock feather that his mother, ever the religious woman, had given him at the airport before he left for this expat assignment, just in case. But his concerns had been unfounded. He was having a good time. The apparent musical mayhem on stage was mirrored all around him by the gathered audience, a few of whom were sitting and smoking around crowded, clumsy tables of their own, some of whom were standing behind him singing along and laughing. Many were dancing to the music and bumping into other swaying dancers in a veritable sea of dark, sweaty bodies.

Fela kept singing about the African woman who only wanted to be called a "lady" just as a woman extricated herself from the crowd and made her way over to Aadit's table. She sat next to him and smiled. He only stared back at her. His vision was not yet blurry enough from the booze to not immediately realize how stunningly beautiful she was. She had radiant ebony skin like polished midnight, and the edges of her frizzy afro refined the stray bits of light from the array of hanging bulbs to an eldritch fringe, like a halo. She seemed, in his mind, to be Africa made flesh—dark, mysterious, and just a little bit dangerous. She reached out to Aadit and started stroking his face with her long, sleek fingers, running them through his hair. Her touch sent a shiver down his spine.

The song hit a high note.

Stunned, Aadit tried to process what was happening. This beautiful woman had ignored everyone else at this gathering of young, nubile Nigerians and had come to sit by the hairy man with the straight, graying hair, gold chain, wedding ring, and an American accent. Aadit was wearing an ankara shirt with khaki bell-bottoms, and he was the most out-of-place person there. He thought, charitably, that she had to be a very beautiful prostitute. His driver had told him that this was a good place to relax and find women to help him ease his loneliness, and so he let her continue to stroke his beard and smile at him as the space around them buzzed with electric lust. Fela continued to grind his hips against the dancer on stage, singing, moaning, and laughing with fevered ebullience.

He kept singing, proclaiming that there was more to the woman who wanted to be called a "lady."

Aadit tried to avoid staring at her, but his eyes kept drifting to her face, down her cleavage, and further below her red tank top and leather miniskirt to her gleaming brown thighs. Sweat slicked his palms and forehead. What felt like a dozen eternities to him passed quickly, with her fingers constantly sliding along his chin, teasing him.

Aadit endured the aching in his loins until it became a mad pounding in the space behind his temples.

"Do you want to leave here?" A short, nervous laugh caught in Aadit's throat, as he tried to mask his embarrassment and the urgency of hot desire that had possessed him.

She leaned in closer, letting her puff of hair brush against his face while her leg pressed against his. "Don't be shy. Just tell me what you really want."

"I want you." He was unable to bear it any longer.

"And you are willing to pay the price?" she asked.

His guess must have been right. "Yes. I'll pay anything."

She cooed, "Say the words then."

"I will pay your price."

"Are you sure?"

"Yes."

She laughed sharply, then smiled again and stood as the song went into a loop. There was more to tell about the "lady", Fela kept singing energetically. But Aadit was not longer listening to the music.

He started for the entrance—the way he'd come in when his driver dropped him off—but she pulled him away and back, into the crowd. They pushed through the press of bodies until they were clear and entered a small building with crumbling and cracked walls behind the crowd. They navigated a maze of winding corridors until they exited through what looked like a kitchen where a group of sweaty, heavy-set women, wearing an array of assorted Ankara wrappers, turned large pots of rice, scooping up soft lumps of amala, and ladling out generous helpings of pepper soup into ceramic bowls. They gave Aadit and the woman dirty looks, but the woman pressed on, leading him away from the kitchen exit and down a dark, quiet alley behind the Afrika Shrine after she paused to slip a thin old security guard with glazed eyes a few naira notes to walk away from his post.

When they were alone, she leaned against the brick wall of the alley. "Do you want me to start?" The way she asked the question made him feel like he had been set on fire.

"What's your name?" he asked.

"Nneoma," she replied. "You can call me Nneoma."

He wanted to say her name but wasn't sure he could repeat the sounds correctly, so he took her face in his hands. Her lips were full and parted. Her breath was sweet, with a hint of the metallic on it. He drew her in for a kiss in the darkness, but she pulled back at the last moment, just as his lips were about to touch hers, and turned her head away. When she faced him again, she stared straight into his eyes, and he thought he saw a flash of yellow.

"Let's be quick. I know what you really want," she whispered breathily.

And with that, she turned around, thrust her hips back, and hiked up her leather skirt. She reached back and slid her fingers expertly down his loose trousers. She seized him. Aadit could barely breathe. When she drew him into her, it felt like every nerve in his body had been saturated with pure pleasure. He braced himself against the wall, closed his eyes, and let out a deep moan. She continued to thrust her hips back into him. Saxophone notes echoed around them.

Time seemed to disappear as he drowned in her. A cornucopia of sensations overran him as images flitted through his mind like butterflies in a field.

Birds. Lips. Music. Flowers. Wings. Skin.

He began to shake uncontrollably as an explosion of pleasure unlike anything he had ever experienced before erupted within him. The feeling intensified as she moved against him, constantly cresting. He was close to release. He tried to open his eyes, but he couldn't focus his vision on anything through the blur of sensations, and so he shut them again. It felt like he was convulsing as he neared the peak but then . . . their faces appeared in his mind, as clear as though they had been projected onto a screen behind his eyelids. His wife Sachika and their three-year-old son Ravin back in Mumbai, playing in the backyard of his family home, laughing, and calling for him. *Daddy, Daddy, come and play with us.* The vision flooded him with guilt more intense than the pleasure he was feeling.

Sachika.

Ravin.

No.

He crashed back down into himself as his mind crystallized around the shame and guilt that had brought him back to coherence.

"I'm sorry," he mumbled as he clumsily pulled out and away from her. She turned around and stared curiously at him. He started to struggle with his trousers as he withdrew a fist full of naira notes and thrust them out at her.

Nneoma looked first at the money, her lips curling with disgust, and then glared at him with eyes like dying coals. "What is this?"

"I'm sorry, I can't. I shouldn't have . . . I have a wife. This is your money. I have more, if you want, but I need to leave. I have a—"

Her voice took on the quality of an earthquake. "What is this? You think you can just stop now? You think this is the price? Your filthy money? Stupid man. There are things that money cannot buy.

Do you understand? You agreed to the price. My price. We had a deal."

Aadit's guilt was hastily replaced by fear of equal magnitude. Perhaps greater. He glanced at the ground and noticed that despite the faint light of the moon hitting them at the same angle, his shadow was alone.

"You must pay the price."

Aadit realized with all the abruptness of tropical rainfall that he had done something terribly wrong with something that was not quite human. Driven by a wild, mad need to escape, he snatched the gold chain hanging around his neck, removed the small peacock feather hanging from it that his mother had often told him would protect him from evil, and threw it at her. Nneoma hopped back to avoid it, but her back hit the wall, and she fell awkwardly. Aadit took his chance and fled for the entrance and the carpark beyond it.

A piercing scream came, followed by a tremulous cackling behind him, tainting the saxophone echoes in the air like black paint spilled on fine silk.

Aadit kept running.

He did not look back.

CHAPTER 4

Perhentian Kecil Island, Terengganu, Malaysia

JULY 2ND, 2017 | 12:52 PM.

About four hours after they'd accepted Olorun's offer, Shigidi and Nneoma were back in their private beachside villa. It was a large, white-walled open space with a queen-sized bed in the middle, pushed up against a stone divider with wide gaps on either side leading to the toilet and bathroom. Both were open to a grass-covered wall, through a glass barrier. There were no paintings on the walls, or any decoration, save for a couple of large, dried-out seashells that hung on the stone divider like charms. The aesthetic was obviously meant to invoke feelings of being close to nature, but Nneoma thought the place just looked pretentious, especially given the price they were paying per night.

Moving around rapidly in large strides, they folded, squeezed, and threw their few belongings into the large blue travel box they shared, which was at the center of the bed. All thoughts of taking the spirit of the curious, tattooed woman they'd seen on the beach were now gone.

They didn't speak much—they hadn't exchanged many words since they'd left the beach—but the tension in the room was building steadily, and Nneoma didn't like it. Every time they brushed past each other and he averted his eyes, her skin tingled.

When they eventually had all the things that mattered to them in the box, they both reached for the handle to close it at the same time. Their hands met on the cold plastic. They froze and looked at each other, finally locked in each other's orbit after drifting around for so long. She caught the querying look in his eyes and she knew what was coming next even before Shigidi squeezed her hand, making her feel like she was about to lose hold over her body and explode into a million fragments.

"You never answered," Shigidi said. Like an accusation.

"Answered what?"

"Nneoma, do you love me?" he asked again, his jaw clenched tight as it always did when he was stressed, even when he was asleep. It sometimes escalated to his grinding his teeth loud enough to wake her.

She sighed and closed her eyes. "Why do you keep asking this? Why does it matter so much?" And the moment she asked the question, she regretted it.

He withdrew his hand from hers and underneath the hard lines of his face and the dark brown surface of his skin, she thought she saw Shigidi redden.

"It's fine. I understand if you don't love me. This was always meant to be a business arrangement before it was anything else," he said. "But I think you feel more than you are letting on, and I just don't understand why, if you do love me, you won't say it, or say if you don't. *Abi* is that so complicated?"

The hairs all over her body stood on end. His words made her suddenly feel fragile. Too fragile. And she resented it.

"I love being with you, Shigidi," she blurted out hastily, sinking so that she sat on the bed. He was still standing, leaning forward with his hands on the box. She shifted her weight on the bed towards him. "You know that. I know that. You know it's more than just business between us. You say you don't understand why I won't say the words, but what I don't understand is why you keep asking the question, why any of this is so important to you, all of a sudden. Besides," she added, "you knew exactly what I was when you met me, when you agreed to this partnership."

She watched as Shigidi furrowed his brow and sat down, tilting his heavily muscled torso away from her without breaking his gaze. She ran her eyes along his frame, scanning and parsing his body language. It was a game she was used to playing and now, playing it with a body that she herself had given him. She knew when he would break the silence just a few moments before he actually did.

"Yes, I know what you are," he said, the timbre of his voice elevated with earnestness. "I know your nature. I heard of your kind since the very first time I was molded into shape and given the spark of life. But I have spent time with you, tasted spirits with you, listened to you. I sabi you now, personally. You may be a succubus, but you're also more than that. I know you, and I love you, but right now, I'm just not quite sure what we are to each other."

"We are partners," she said. "Partners. It's that simple really. Partners."

She hoped the purpose of the repetition was not lost on Shigidi. It was something she did sometimes, a habit she had developed and constantly applied during discussions, especially during negotiations. She used it as a verbal signpost to indicate that she had come as far as she was willing and would go no further without resistance. Shigidi should know that by now. She'd given him a signal that she wanted to end the conversation, and she hoped he had received it. Her full lips still pursed, she leaned back and pulled loose the elephant-print, sheer beach cloth around her waist as though she had filled up and expanded with emotion and needed more space.

Shigidi snorted, apparently acknowledging the impasse they had reached, but he said nothing to qualify his expression; he just sat there, scowling. Nneoma tried to assess his thoughts, she knew he was unsatisfied, that he didn't understand her reaction to his question. But he couldn't know. He couldn't know how steep the cost of romantic love between independent spirit entities could run. That it was stifling. Restrictive. Binding. He couldn't know that it had cost her a sister. But he should have known enough to stop asking. Love had almost cost him his life. She wondered if he regretted the day they met, regretted falling so deeply for such a beautiful and terrible creature as she. Silence settled between them, and she refused to break it. Time passed, slowly.

Finally, Shigidi stood up, peeled away his orange-and-blue swim trunks, and kicked them away to the far corner of the room near the bathroom, as if they had offended him.

"Partners." His voice was hoarse. "Yes. Partners. That's what we agreed to. In that case, let's finish packing. We need to get to London. We have a job to do."

He went to the couch where a soft white towel was draped, and Nneoma took in his nakedness, like an artist admiring her work. She took in the thick elevation of his pectorals, between which was engraved a scar the size of a man's hand. The row of elevated abdominal muscles around his torso were as chiseled and firm as his taut buttocks. She followed the rounded ends of his fingertips as he grasped the towel, as a solid beam of sunlight squeezed through the window and touched the hollow of his belly. Shigidi was beautiful. She had made him this way, remolding the clumsy, craftless work of the executive orisha into something—no, someone—spectacular. Someone who had now fallen hopelessly in love with her, endangering himself. Endangering them both.

She stood up, allowing her sheer beach cloth to pool around her legs.

"Shigidi, darling, are you really angry?" she asked, attempting to lighten the mood.

"I am not angry," he said, but she could see on his face the strain of damming all the emotions that had built up. "We are partners. We take and share spirits. We have sex sometimes. We take the contracts we need to pay our debts, and we generally get the job done. That's it. *Abi*? I get it. No wahala. It's all clear."

She raised her left hand and pointed a finger at him. "Then what's the point of all these questions, love?"

"I don't know, but right now I know that I don't want to argue with you anymore." He growled. "It's getting us nowhere, and we have a flight to catch."

She stepped forward until she was barely a breath away from him. "Is this going to affect our ability to work together?"

"Of course not. Like you said, we're partners, aren't we?"

"You're still angry," she said.

"Of course, I am," he started, his voice still low but carrying a caustic undercurrent. "Nneoma, this is the first time I have asked you for anything that wasn't part of our agreement since we met. I have opened myself up completely to you. I have literally been torn open for you. But you have never opened yourself up to me. Not even a little. Fine, I understand, you're a succubus. It's in your nature to play these games with sex and power and emotion and desire. I know all that, and yet here I am like a fool, like a mumu, willingly allowing myself to fall into your web. Fine, I love you, let me lay in that web. Na me do myself. But just this one, simple thing, I ask you, and you refuse to say either way." His fists had balled up while he spoke, his knuckles pale and crackling with barely restrained electric green spirit-particles.

Nneoma closed her eyes. She was filled with a confusing mix of emotions at his outpouring. It reminded her of a time that was now long past, a time when whole cultures had prayed to her and her sister, mistaking them for twin elemental goddesses, executives of some spirit company that had operated in their lands. There was something both frightening and intoxicating about Shigidi's need. It was a heady mix, and it induced in her a feeling she hadn't had in what felt like centuries. But it also brought back memories. Memories of her sister Lilith and what had happened to her when she fell in love. Nneoma didn't like the memories or the feeling like an embrace of emptiness. And so, she did the first thing that thousands of years of developed instinct drove her to do. She reached up for Shigidi, cradled his tense face in her hands, and on her tiptoes, shut him up with a kiss.

Shigidi didn't pull away, even though Nneoma suspected he wanted to. She could feel the vibration of his body under her touch, the tightening of his facial muscles. She projected her essence out into the room, manipulating the potent sexual desire he was emitting so that it resonated even more powerfully. They both knew what she was doing, she'd taught him most of her tricks, but she suspected he would be so intoxicated with the taste of her lips that it would erode all that was left of his resistance. He wouldn't be able to stop himself from allowing it to happen. He wouldn't want to. And so, when he fell into her, wrapping his arms around the soft exposed flesh of her waist with an intensity like hunger, she was not surprised. Their tongues wound together as though the kiss could tie them to each other completely again, bridge the space that his questions and her silence had opened between them. They sank to the floor slowly, Shigidi kissing her nape as they descended. On the floor, he wedged himself between her legs and righted his posture, leaning on her thighs. She pulled his head back down into her chest and held him there for a moment.

"Damn it, Nneoma," he whispered breathlessly into her bosom.

She wondered at how easily he had let her win this game. Perhaps it was why they had worked so well together thus far: his perpetual willingness to forgo the thing he wanted for the thing he needed. For her. And that, that willingness, was the essence of the danger of what he wanted from her.

I will not be my sister.

Their lovemaking was urgent, frenzied, and intense, like the beating of drums she'd heard at new yam festival in Awka. With every touch and thrust of his hips, she felt him trying to share all that he was with her, reconnect with her completely. It reminded her of their very first coupling through which she had transformed him so thoroughly, given him so much and birthed their partnership. But deep down she knew that the strain would remain until she gave him an answer. The fissure that had always existed between them had now opened wider and exposed all the need and doubt and fear beneath the veneer of their partnership. And now that it was exposed to the elements, it would continue to fester and grow until it was a chasm of unfulfilled needs and unrequited desires that could force them apart. And so, she closed her mind and focused on his body, doing everything to please him in all the ways she had learned he liked, playing the body she'd given him like it was an instrument, every spike of his own sensual joy reverberating with hers.

By the time they finished, his question had been pushed back into the recesses of her brain by the tidal wave of pleasure and contentment. Shigidi fell asleep first and she watched him with heavy eyes as the line of his jaw moved and he began to make a sound like the sawing of wood. He was grinding his teeth again. He's still bothered. *Stressed.* Nneoma gripped his jaw between her thumb and index finger, pulling downward to stop the sound. Shigidi turned away from her and tossed his head back and forth. She lay back in bed and closed her eyes. It was no use trying to stop his tossing or grinding. He'd fallen into another deep, deep sleep full of vivid memory-things that came to him like dreams even though she knew dreaming was impossible for a former nightmare god.

CHAPTER 5

Orisha Spirit Company Estate II, Orun (Spirit-space)

OCTOBER 31ST, 2016 | 06:41 PM.

The world was spinning around him when Shigidi woke up. His head was pulsing like a fearful heart. When he tried to open his eyelids, the light attacked his eyes like an army of sharp red needles as the hangover began to bloom in his head. He felt like he had been in an accident, or he had somehow become the living embodiment of an accident, and so he didn't try to move. He lay in place, eyes shut against the world, completely motionless, for what felt like hours, occasionally opening his eyes just enough to see if the world had stabilized. It never did.

Eventually, he decided that he needed to get moving or he would be unreasonably late for work, even by his own already abysmally low standards of performance. He elevated himself onto an elbow and managed to roll off the rough raffia mat that served as both bed and sitting area, before he vomited a good portion of the previous day's merriment and excess onto the red clay floor of his company-assigned hut. The mess was brown and viscous; it contained pieces of half-digested kolanuts, morsels of masticated meat, palm wine and blood. Lots of blood. Almost more than usual for a wild night out with his only drinking buddy Ososhi, the orisha of hunting, but not by much. He retched and threw up a second wave of vomit that left him feeling slightly less terrible, but only just. After that, the world seemed a little less unstable. He summoned the will to drag himself to his feet, stumble out of the creaking wooden door and past the brief brush of bush beside his brick hut, to the hole in the ground that served as a crude latrine. He was there for what felt to him like days even though it was only a few minutes, all of them spent heaving, retching, and spitting.

When the only thing that came after each burning retch was a clear and colorless liquid, and he felt like his insides had been scrubbed with a handful of freshly cut palm fronds, he lifted his head from the stink and darkness of the pit and looked up, towards the spirit-sky. The sun hung low and there were no clouds. Just a series of blue and red and yellow streaks, broad and blurring into and out of each other's edges, making it look like a silk sheet had been generously tied-and-dyed by an artist and spread out above them. On the horizon, though, where the spirit-sky met the ground beyond the forest that marked the company compound, a halo of blue ringed the spirit world. It was unique, Shigidi had to admit. Every day, the spirit-sky took on a new and unusual appearance, and this one was particularly impressive. He turned away and spat out a brown glob of phlegm one final time before standing on his small, unsteady feet and muttering under his breath, "If only Olorun spent half as much time paying attention to company business as he did playing games with the colors of the heavens, maybe the spirit company wouldn't be such a mess."

The orishas of the spirit company all knew that Olorun was vain, their aloof and leisurely sky god. But Shigidi had always felt an affinity with and admiration for Olorun. Even though he'd never met his creator, and his initial admiration was slowly morphing into resentment, he still desperately wished that the retired chairman of the board of what used to be one of the largest spirit-companies in existence would care enough about the organization he had left fallow to check in on them every once in a while. Instead, Olorun had allowed things to degenerate in his absence.

Shigidi felt unmotivated, uninterested in executing any of the tasks demanded as conditions of his godhood in the Orisha Spirit Company, but he had to go to work, else he would weaken and eventually die. Or, perhaps worse, he'd have to answer to the more powerful orisha that managed the company.

Godhood is overrated.

He staggered and stumbled his way to the back of his hut, where a crude clay enclosure with an entrance covered by palm fronds marked his bath area. He stripped off his filthy ankara print trousers and left them outside the enclosure. He then grabbed a half-cut calabash from atop the filmy surface of a bucket of water that had been sitting in place for more than two days. He dumped the water on his head and as it ran all over his body, he slowly began to feel like himself again. At least as much of himself as he could be with a terrible hangover. He rubbed his rough, callused hands over his skin, trying to make himself as clean as he needed to be, and wiped away most of the grime and dirt that had attached itself to him without his thinking too much about the pockmarks, rashes, scarification lines, and sores that he was always acutely aware of whenever he touched himself. Ugliness was part of his nature, an essential trait for his job, regardless of how it made him feel.

What use would a beautiful nightmare god be?

No, repulsiveness was a requirement for his position in the spirit company. And even though he desperately hated his job, the dreary, uninteresting, mundane, and occasionally traumatizing tasks he had to execute under the supervision of other gods he hated being around, for barely enough prayers and offerings to keep him in existence, every deity had to do what they could to survive in these hard times. Belief was scarce. Good offerings were few and far between, and almost every god he knew had already taken a prayer-cut, unless of course, they were friends with the CEO or in upper management.

When the bucket was empty, he went back into his hut, naked and dripping, enjoying the feel of the evening air on his wet skin. Inside, he ignored the rotten smell of the slimy mess on the floor and started to ready himself for work. He could clean up later. No one ever visited him anyway. He put on what he needed to quickly: another pair of cut-off ankara print trousers to fit his short and stocky legs, these ones orange and green, with hints of brown; a plain black cloak that sat on his shoulders and ran down to the back of his ankles, with cowrie shells and lizard skulls sewn into the fabric; and his face covered with black ash to complete his fearful appearance.

By the time he stepped out of the hut again, the sky was a deep and abiding black, shimmering with stars and a brightly beaming moon, like bedazzling. He sighed heavily. "Bloody waste of power."

It only took him a few minutes to walk to the end of the spirit company residential area and connect to the bush path that snaked through the spirit shadow of the now-defunct evil forest. He stepped off the moonlit road and into the darkness of the path. The wet, woody smell of the towering trees and fallen leaves and peaty soil wrapped itself around him as the underbrush crunched beneath his bare feet and loose twigs slapped against his ankles. The evil forest, diminished as it was, still greeted him in the ancient way—with a whisper of wind and the murmuring of wild creatures, its power significantly muted since most of the spirits it once housed had been displaced, its sacred deities long gone. He thought he saw a pair of cherubic abiku, their small child-shaped bodies silhouetted against the moon-polished stream that flowed at the far end of the forest. They were playing a game he did not recognize. They disappeared when he blinked, and he doubted his own perception, wondering just how drunk he still was.

"Shayo na bastard," he said out loud, and continued walking along the shortcut, remembering that Ososhi, the hunter orisha and one of the few gods he considered a friend, had told him over a calabash of palm wine that the Orisha Spirit Company board had voted to cut down the evil forest to make way for a shrine to cinema. It was a shame, but they must pander to what few customers were left, Ososhi had said. Shigidi understood. At least he thought he did. It was another depressing change. That was the way the spirit business was going.

Evil forests are out, Nollywood is in.

Faith is a funny thing.

Shigidi kept walking and didn't exit until the verdant curtain of forest finally gave way to a clearing at the end of the path. He stepped into the moonlight, only a few hundred meters away from the entrance of his office. Like many other minor orishas, he worked out of a satellite office. This one was a two-story red brick building older than he was, with six square windows facing out and a black sloping roof. Impossibly, he thought it looked even worse than he remembered it from just two days earlier when he had come to collect his last month's pray pay—most of which had been spent on the items he had thrown up earlier in the day. A new hole had appeared in the front wall just beside the door, and another wooden windowpane had slipped from its place to hang precariously over the overgrown grass that surrounded the entire compound like wild hair. The lights were out. Shigidi couldn't tell if it was because no one was there or if the power supply had been cut again. He sighed and his shoulders fell as he made his way to the door, sauntering through the curtain of hanging beads and into the reception area, standing in a thin sliver of moonlight that entered through a broken window.

"Shigidi." The shrill, high-pitched voice of Oya, the orisha of winds and his recently appointed supervisor, assaulted his ears with unexpected suddenness, and when it hit his still-hungover brain, he winced.

"You are late," she added, a bit less loudly.

He turned in the direction of her voice to see her broad outline, sitting in the darkness, planted in a weatherworn leather chair at the reception desk, like a tuber of yam in freshly turned soil.

"You this woman, why are you hiding in the shadows like a rat?" he asked, irritated.

She scoffed. "Everything will be darkness and shadows until one of you idiots gets a sacrifice or act of faith big enough for us to afford to pay Shango the cross-charge for power generation. You know how much effort it takes to passively control the flow of electrons?"

"No, I don't," Shigidi said truthfully as he scratched his head. He hated Oya's caustic way of distilling situations down to simplistic statements and projecting problems back onto him. Like he was the only reason the company couldn't afford to power the satellite offices for minor deities. He wanted to tell her that perhaps if headquarters took a slightly smaller percentage of the overall spirit company prayer revenue to keep themselves so powerful, perhaps the situation wouldn't be so dire. But he knew better than to say that, so instead, he decided he would try to appeal to her sentimentality. "But, well, I think it might help if you could speak to your husband about making an exception—"

"No." She stood up and stepped into the sliver of moonlight with him. "I won't." She was so close that he could smell her. Palm oil and rich earthy perfume. She smelled like someone had tried to fry a bouquet of muddy roses. She handed him a half-melted white wax candle and a box of matches as she took him in from head to toe, a look of scorn plastered on her face. "You are already an embarrassment—ugly, stupid, always late, always drunk. You barely bring in any worthwhile prayers, and now you want to turn me into a beggar on your behalf? Don't you have shame? You want me to go and beg in my own house." She hissed at him, like a snake. "If you ever even just mention my husband's name again, I will slap you, you hear?"

Shigidi balled his fists in anger. She was almost three times his height and significantly wider, with rolls of flesh around her arms, hips, and belly. Not just because she was that big, but because he was that small. Ugly and small. Those were the characteristics that made him perfectly suited for the job which he hated so much. Olorun had created him that way intentionally—large head, ugly face, small body, ashy, and pockmarked skin of unpolished clay. Every time he saw himself reflected, in a mirror or on a water surface, he craved the oblivion of alcohol. He had never even felt the touch of a woman— human or god or spirit. *How could I,* he thought, *looking the way I do?* He hated it, and because of it, he'd spent a significant amount of his existence hating himself. He had taken up the issue of his appearance with his spirit resources representative but had been told that his creation and appearance were both non-negotiable. Apparently, there were many non-negotiable aspects of his existence and of his contract with the spirit-company, including what Shango would do to him if he ever got into a fight with one of his wives.

So, he said, "Fine. You are lucky I don't want to give you any trouble today," hoping to end the issue there. The throbbing in his head was getting worse and there was an intense pressure along his jaw.

She hissed loudly again and rolled her eyes. "Let me hear word, please. You don't have anything to give. Not even trouble." She thrust her chin toward the stairs, indicating his office upstairs. "What you do have, is an assignment to get to. Someone sent in a client request and a made a sacrifice three hours ago. Small, as usual, but you people need it. I am amazed anyone still believes in you. Log-in to the human world and respond to them as soon as you can. You know you still have a lot of objectives to meet this quarter." She handed him a plain piece of white paper that crackled with green sparks when he touched it, as the spirit particles arranged themselves into a format he recognized: a standard work slip. He scanned it casually, taking note of a few key words and phrases. Business partner. Cheating. Hotel. Fear. Death. It looked like a standard *nightmare-and-kill* job.

Turning around to leave, Oya asked him if he had seen Ososhi, whose office on the ground floor was also dark and empty.

"No, I haven't. Not since yesterday," he said. Ososhi had seemed a bit less talkative and a bit more eager to drink than usual when they had met last night to celebrate the end of the month. At some point Ososhi had asked Shigidi what he thought of killing other gods and independent spirit entities that encroached into and operated in the spirit company territory without permission, competing for scarce business. Shigidi had laughed it off and made a joke about all being fair in love and spirit business. Ososhi hadn't laughed. It was possible that Ososhi was still in bed, as drunk as he had been not too long ago, but thinking back to that exchange and the way Oya had asked the question, out of the blue, something made Shigidi's skin suddenly turn cold with worry for his friend. "Why are you looking for him?"

Oya spun back around with more agility than Shigidi expected her to have, then bent down and poked a thick finger in his face. "Why are you asking me why I am looking for him? Is it your business? *Amebo*! Useless, lazy drunkard. Work you don't want to do, but when it's time to ask stupid questions, that is when your eyes will shine."

Fists clenched again, he muttered, "hag," under his breath and walked away, climbing up the uneven stairs with difficulty. Shango's second wife was rude and aggressive, but he knew he could not insult her to her face. Her husband—his boss, Shango—would punish him in ways that would boggle even the most macabre of minds in the spirit company. And his was already significantly macabre, being the god of nightmares. And even if Shango didn't retaliate, he knew Oya could easily defeat him in an altercation with her dominion over winds and storms.

Maybe she is right. Maybe I am useless.

In a fistfight, what good is the ability to manipulate dreams and conjure up nightmares?

He shook his head and continued to his office, huffing and breathing heavily.

I guess it's great if your enemy spontaneously falls asleep.

His office was a small, gray room farthest from the stairs at the front of the building, with a small bowl of water set in the middle of the bare floor. Several ancient charms hung on the walls. The basics of his trade: tortoise shell, cowries, palm fronds, dried frog skin, kolanuts, and one two-hundred-year-old gourd of palm wine that he had often considered drinking on days when the job didn't seem worth it anymore. Like in the days just after he'd been trapped and tortured by a girl wielding powerful bori magic, whose lover he'd killed as part of an assignment. That experience still haunted him, and he'd been drinking a lot more since it happened, but he needed the special palm wine to generate pure nightmare essence, and he was only ever resupplied once every ten years. Shigidi made his way to the bowl and knelt. He placed the piece of paper Oya had given him into it, whereupon the work slip dissolved, decrypting the message back into its essential spirit particles. The water in the bowl turned bright green. When it did, he placed his hand into it, up to his wrist. The scarification marks that formed the shape of a triangle on the back of his hand tingled. Each mark on his body served a function, and the one on his hand was a sigil, a log-in key of summoning for the wind between worlds when he had the right permissions. He broke into fevered incantation, repeating words lifelessly from memory.

The wonky system that untangled corporeal fundamental particles and the spirit particles of Orun took a few moments to identify him and approve his temporary pass to exit spirit space. When it came, it came suddenly. The wind between worlds wiped his office out of his consciousness like it had been painted out by an artist in one broad brushstroke. He was plunged into a familiar, absolute darkness, hurtling in some impossible-to-define direction.

Here I go again. Same shit. Different day. New nightmare.

House 22, Ibara Housing Estate, Government Residential Area, Abeokuta, Nigeria

OCTOBER 31ST, 2016 | 10:58 PM.

Shigidi reentered the world of men suddenly, gasping for sensation like he'd just surfaced from a tar-black ocean of nothingness. He immediately wished he was back in spirit-space, in Orun.

The air was hot and humid and smoky, like he was breathing exhaust fumes from a poorly maintained okada. It almost made him choke. He rose to his feet carefully and looked around the worksite. The wind between worlds had deposited him in front of a brown metal door in a spacious but largely empty room. Cold, hard linoleum flooring. No carpets. No pictures. Just one dresser with a mirror set into it. It looked old, like it had been hand-carved locally using fine, thick wood from one of the nearby forests that lined most of the highways in the southwest of the country. There was a low, similarly high-quality wood-framed bed nestled in the corner of the room, and a fan spun lazily, suspended in the center of the ceiling. Shigidi wondered briefly why the bed wasn't centered in the room too, instead of tucked away in the corner farthest away from the door and why there was a solitary sliding glass window which was open but had black metal bars running across it, slicing the evening moon like a series of parallel knives.

This looks like the home of a paranoid person.

And rightfully so.

There was someone sleeping in the bed. A man. Splayed out like he had collapsed backward onto the thick spring mattress and fallen asleep immediately. There was one thick-fingered hand pressed to his chest and a bright yellow-and-red ankara sleeping cloth pooled around his feet like he'd initially used to it cover himself and had slowly kicked it off as the heat mounted. Shigidi took a moment to acclimatize himself to the stuffy warmth and the constant metal groaning of what sounded like a diesel generator just outside the window, and then he approached the bed. The sleeping man was thick set and tall—his feet spilled over the footboard and his thinning salt-and-pepper hair was cropped low to match the stubble on his face. His skin was dark and clammy with sweat. There was what looked like a woman's hairnet hanging on one side of the dresser, but the man was alone. Shigidi was thankful for that. There was no risk of someone else waking and interrupting his work. Or worse, being traumatized enough by it to hunt him down and torture him as an act of vengeance. The man appeared to be in his late fifties or early sixties with a protruding pot belly that distended both the white singlet and the elastic of the boxer briefs he wore. According to the work slip Shigidi had received from Oya, the man was Shigidi's target for the evening.

Time to get this over with.

He climbed onto the bed in slow, careful movements, glad that the frame was low and that there were no side rails. He took one final look at the face of the man whose business partner wanted him dead for some vague personal reasons of his own—they did not matter to Shigidi. The reasons for what humans did or didn't do to each other didn't really matter to him. What mattered was that the business

partner in question still believed in Shigidi enough to make a prayer ,
and offer a sacrifice to the spirit company through an accredited
Orisha Spirit Company customer service agent—a babalawo. That
being done, Shigidi would do as his believer asked, be on his way, and
get paid. The quicker the better. Partly because he could sense that
the believer who had made the sacrifice was still awake somewhere,
unable to sleep until the job was completed, as was the ancient custom, even though it didn't matter to Shigidi either way. But mostly,
he wanted to get it over with quickly because he didn't enjoy the
work. Some ignorant humans considered him an evil entity, a carica-
ture villain that enjoyed manipulating fear and killing people in
their sleep. Once, during a job, he'd even been called a demon by a
woman as she tried to break out of the nightmare he'd woven in her
mind.

Can you imagine? Me? A demon?

If only they knew how far from the truth that was.

Shigidi put his hand out in front of him and spread out his fingers
so that his palm was pointed at the head of the sleeping man. He
closed his eyes and used his imagination, the core of all his power, to
picture the swirl of loose thoughts and memories and emotions in
the man's head as a mass of drifting, disparate, multicolored threads,
rendered visible to Shigidi by sleep. He projected his essence into the
mass in the man's mind, feeling, touching, assessing each of them.
Searching.

Red. A broad, beautiful woman in a towering gele, dancing at an
owambe, smiling at the man. *No.*

Orange. Six scrawny children in dirty uniforms laughing in a circle, pointing at the man. *No.*

Yellow. Two dark figures sitting at a table, one laughing and holding out a piece of paper, the other crying and holding out a golden pen, both waiting for the man. *Not quite.*

Shigidi worked the fingers of his projected mind, threading them through the mass of images and sensations and sounds, trying to the find the ones that held the most potential for primal fear. There was no resistance like he got sometimes when his target's Ori, their personal spirit, was particularly strong or if they were possessed by or held strong allegiance to another spirit entity, perhaps even one of the orishas. He pressed on.

Green. A sea of featureless faces, all sweaty underneath the hot sun, chanting, Jide. Vote Jide. They are cheering for the man. *No.*

Blue. A cloud of hot pounded yam floating in the sky, as it begins to rain dark green ewedu soup onto the man. *Definitely not.*

Black. A river of blood, overflowing its banks, rising, and rising and rising, and drowning the man. *There!*

Shigidi snatched the thread of dread he'd found and pulled at it with the full force of his imagination. It unspooled rapidly, and he exhaled as he began to see the full extent of it.

An incident in the man's childhood. A visit to see his grandparents in the village. A river where he played and bathed with his cousins when they went to fetch water to cook and bathe. A loose rock. A slip. Blood. A fall. And then drowning. Drowning. Almost. A hand, firm like a tree branch. Choking and vomiting and spitting. Fear. So much fear concentrated into just a few moments, embedded early in the mind when it was still young and unstructured, lacking the clarity of logic. *This should work.*

Shigidi held onto that thread of perfect fear made of memories and began to twist and weave it around his fingers, interconnecting the most intense parts of it in short loops so that it took on a new shape, like a net. When he was done, he imagined himself casting the net back into the mind of the man so that it enveloped all the other free-drifting thoughts.

The bed began to shake as the sleeping man tossed and turned, removing his hand from his chest and moving it to his head as if he could push away the nightmare.

Shigidi opened his eyes and watched the man twitch and shake for a moment, his breathing now quickened and short. Shigidi waited, allowing all the sensations of dream-drowning to build until at their peak, they sent a memory of pain lancing through the man's lungs, suffusing his subconscious with recycled threads of panic. When it did, the sleeping man moved his hands from his head and began to claw desperately at his throat.

It's time.

Shigidi took a deep breath and jumped onto the man's chest.

A high, tinny sound escaped the man's lips, and his long legs kicked against the footboard as he struggled to breathe against the real pressure on his chest and the imagined column of water throbbing in his throat.

This was the part of his job Shigidi hated the most. Waiting for them to die. Some struggled for a long time, resisting the pain and heat and oppression that his bulk spread from the pit of their stomachs to their chests. Some of them reached out, thrusting their minds in every direction, reaching for escape, for comfort, for salvation, for anything except the death hurtling towards them. Some, in the moments between dream and death, managed to wake and catch a glimpse of him sitting on their chest and even, in some cases managed to say a few words before they were gone.

The man turned out to be one of the latter. His eyes shot open like a bomb had gone off in his head. Curious. They were the same dark brown as the eyes of the woman all those years ago who had also fought to wake and called Shigidi a demon. The man's hands continued to claw at his throat, but they were less urgent, already drained of oxygen and energy. The man's pupils narrowed when he saw Shigidi and a cluster of white-hot thought threads suddenly appeared in his mind, but they, too, were contained within the nightmare net that Shigidi cast. Among them, Shigidi detected a flash of memories that culminated in something like understanding.

"Bu . . . Bu . . . Bukola?" The man croaked.

His business partner's name, probably.

Doesn't matter. At least he will die with some sense of understanding, even if it is false.

The threads were spontaneously cut. And the new threads of thought that entered the man's mind came frayed and short and lacking color.

Not much longer left.

Shigidi closed off his mind from the man's, leaving him to the privacy of his final moments. He felt every vibration of the man's body, every desperate spurt of his rapidly slowing pulse. The man's face arranged itself into a mask of terror as the last breath squeaked out of him and he was unmoored from life.

Shigidi exhaled deeply.

Finally. Job done. Time to go home and get a drink.

"Your work is not very elegant, is it?" a voice like an echo from a faraway place said, coming from behind him.

Shigidi started and lost his balance, falling off the dead man's chest. He bounced off the bed and onto the floor where he spun around quickly to see who had spoken to him.

It was Eshu-Elegba, divine messenger, trickster orisha of chance and fate, and head of communications at the spirit company. He was bare-chested and wearing red-and-black trousers with a straw hat. At first, Shigidi wondered why he looked unstable and then realized that Eshu-Elegba was floating, thin arms spread out to his sides and legs folded underneath him. He held an electronic tablet in one hand and a crackling spirit work slip in the other. Shigidi immediately bowed his head in respect.

"Egbon," Shigidi said, acknowledging the senior orisha. "No the work is not elegant, but it's my purpose."

Eshu-Elegba cocked his head. "Hmm."

"What brings you to my worksite?" Shigidi asked.

Eshu-Elegba held out the work slip. "It seems you are popular today, Shigidi. Two job requests in one night. It's been a while."

I thought I was done for tonight, but it seems wahala no dey finish. Shigidi stepped forward and took the work slip with another bow. He regarded it curiously and noticed that the spirit particles that bonded it were red and black, not his usual green.

Odd.

"I have already decrypted it for you," Eshu-Elegba explained.

Shigidi nodded, holding the work slip up so he could read it. It was another *nightmare-and-kill* job. Across state lines, over in Lagos. "Thank you. But you didn't have to. I was about to go back to the office, Oya would have passed it on."

"Yes, but this aspect of me was already on the way to an Ifa shrine nearby. And it seemed . . . urgent." A smile cut across Eshu-Elegba's face. The orisha of chance and communications always made Shigidi uncomfortable, partly because he was a board member with far more authority and power in the spirit company than Shigidi could imagine, but mostly because of his contradictory, capricious persona. Sometimes he was jocular, silly even, making light of everything and playing little practical jokes. Other times he was deathly serious, focused on critically important information. That in itself wasn't unusual, most gods had multiple sides to them, but the timeshifts between the aspects of Eshu-Elegba's personality changes was measured in milliseconds, not days.

Shigidi looked into the coal-black eyes of the wiry god and tried to read what this was, a trick or a true assignment. But he could not project into the waking mind of another spirit entity, much less a management level orisha. He couldn't tell anything. All he picked up was the smell of sulfur and ash. A thin layer of sweat appeared on Shigidi's upper lip. "Very kind of you," he said finally, deciding it would have been too much for Eshu-Elegba to have faked a sacrifice and prayer request in the spirit company system. It had to be real. "I will head to Lagos as soon as I get reentry permission."

"Ah. No need for all that permissions and approvals nonsense." Eshu-Elegba said, and quickly wrote something in his tablet. "Come. I will take you. I am always connected to the wind between worlds. It's the only way I am able to be in multiple places at once."

Shigidi hesitated a moment, then put out his hand, turning down his palm so that the triangular scarification marks on the back of his hand were visible to Eshu-Elegba, a point of contact. Eshu-Elegba's eyes rolled back in his head, leaving them stark white, and he reached out suddenly like he'd been shocked, enfolding Shigidi's hand in his own, tightly. Shigidi gasped at the sudden contact. His entire body felt cold, his clay skin tightening as the familiar sensation spirit particle transfer began to spread.

"Good luck." Eshu-Elegba's voice echoed.

And then suddenly, it came. Eshu-Elegba, the brown door, the barred windows, the dead man on the bed, the dissected moon, all disappeared as Shigidi was thrust into darkness, carried on the wind between worlds. A constant, faint rattling accompanied him; it sounded like an opele being thrown. He did not close his eyes, but the darkness invited itself. The journey only lasted a moment before he came to an abrupt halt, the world inserting itself back into his vision with a blur.

Blue River Hotel, Victoria Island, Lagos, Nigeria

OCTOBER 31ST, 2016 | 11:24 PM.

Shigidi found himself in what looked like a lavish hotel room, dimly lit by a solitary, bulbous sodium vapor lamp in the corner, like a miniature setting sun. He was standing beside a king-size bed where two naked women lay vined together, sleeping quietly on what looked like thousand thread-count sheets. Smooth and lustrous. A mess of clothes, papers, bottles, and a vibrator that looked like a purple bullet were strewn on the carpeted floor. When he caught his own ugly reflection in a large rectangular mirror set in an old mahogany frame, carved with leaf and flower designs, he hastily looked away and focused back on the couple in the bed.

The first woman, the one closest to him was shorter, thinner, and looked older—deep lines ran along her plump skin like the surface of a dried pond. Her face was long and oval, her hair was done up into thin braids, held together with a red band. Wedding ring on finger, slight and slender, she appeared to be in her late fifties or early sixties. She was good looking; athletic, like a distance runner or a triathlete.

According to the work slip, she was Shigidi's target for the evening, courtesy of a jealous husband. Jealous enough to want his cheating wife dead. He'd made a significant sacrifice. Perhaps that was why Eshu-Elegba had brought it himself. So often it was family and friends that engaged his services.

There was something about the other woman, however, that drew Shigidi's attention so intensely he could not resist. His eyes slid from the object of his task to her, and the first thing he noticed about her was just how sleek her fingers were, resting on the older woman's abdomen. They were svelte and finely crafted, like cigarettes. She had radiant ebony skin that gleamed in the faint light, and on her head was a corona of long black curls splayed about her on the pillow. Her eyes were closed, and her lips were full and blood-red.

She is spectacularly beautiful.

It occurred to Shigidi that she was the kind of woman some of the pettier and more vindictive orishas in the company would have used to torment a king or a prideful man, who had offended them with lust and madness, before fully destroying him, back when people still believed in the orishas enough for them to take such an active role in human lives.

"Focus," he mouthed when he realized he had been staring for more than a minute.

Focus Shigidi. You have work to do.

He stepped toward the bed, readying himself to press out the breath from the woman whose husband wanted her dead. He wondered briefly if it was really just the fact that she was cheating on him that had driven him to contact a babalawo and ask for her death or if there was something else to it. He'd observed that human men generally had fragile egos when it came to women, and Nigerian men particularly so. It was probably the fact that she was cheating on him with another woman that had done it.

Ah. Focus. What do I know about woman wahala anyway? All this is none of my business. Just finish the job and go.

Shigidi clambered onto the bed, using the bedside table for support, and almost exclaimed at how enjoyable the smooth feel of the sheets was on his skin. Luxurious indeed. Nothing like the rough touch of his raffia mat and wrapper or even the plain unremarkable feel of the bedding in the Abeokuta house he'd just visited. A flash of memory hit him, and he felt a tinge of pity for the other woman because she would have to wake up in such delightful surroundings right next to the corpse of someone she loved or at least liked enough to sleep with. It was pity almost strong enough to become familiar guilt. But he pushed that out of his mind. It wasn't personal, just spirit business.

He reached for the gorgeous woman's hand to move it from the older woman's abdomen so that he could sit on it and slowly crush her lungs while he wove her deepest fears into vivid visions of terror. That was when he noticed that her chest did not rise and fall steadily, as one would expect of a sleeping person. The older, athletic woman was barely breathing. Shigidi took a closer look at her face and saw that it was frozen in a rictus of pleasure. A sense of wrongness settled upon him.

That's not right. Something is not right.

He held still for a second, hesitating, as he scanned the room again. Nothing particularly strange jumped out at him and eventually, urgency overtook his caution. He needed to get the job done and get out. He continued, making to move the woman's hand.

When his hand made contact with it, she shot up out of the bed and into the air suddenly like an erupting volcano: hot, naked and with unexpected force.

What?

Shigidi lost his balance, fell back into the silken sheets, and slid off the bed. The woman latched onto the ceiling with claws that had extruded out of her long, slender fingers, which, like the rest of her body, were now covered in razor thin scales that reflected the dim light. Shigidi stared up in horror as long, membranous wings sprouted out of her bare back, seamlessly obscuring her contorted spine. Her neck twisted at an impossible angle as she stared back down at him, smiling.

"You must be Shigidi," she rumbled, her voice abrasive, like sandpaper in his ears.

"Shit!" he exclaimed, once he'd finally processed the situation and realized what—even if he still didn't know who, exactly—she was. A succubus.

A bloody succubus.

He knew her kind—they were freelancers not affiliated with any spirit company, one of several independent spirit entities. They did not trade in belief or prayers or offerings. They directly obtained spirits from humans and used them for their own sustenance. Some of them, like succubae, used seduction and exploited the temporary exposure of the spirit at the peak of sexual pleasure to siphon it out of the unsuspecting humans. Others used verbal trickery and deceptive marketing to get vulnerable humans to hand over their spirits willingly in private contracts and arrangements. Some simply took the spirits by force. Whatever form they came in, independent spirit entities were reviled by the spirit company management and by most of Shigidi's own colleagues. He was indifferent to them, but in that moment, the only thing he could think was that he absolutely did not want one of them undercutting his job.

"You know my name. Fine. What is yours then?" he asked the thing that had been the woman on the bed. It still was, in many ways. The creature had retained all her voluptuousness, despite the wings and the scales and the piercing yellow eyes. She was a vision of corrupted beauty, both alluring and terrifying.

"Nneoma," she said in a voice that vibrated violently like the ground beneath a besieged city. "My real name is Naamah. But I prefer to be called Nneoma."

Ah, she was one of them then—one of the originals of her kind. Those that had been cast out.

A small measure of fear crept up on him like a touch of ice to his spine.

I've been mistaken for a demon, now here I am, face to face with one. Life is funny sometimes.

"Nneoma." He jutted his chin to indicate the woman on the bed barely breathing. "This woman's life is mine." He raised his scarred and tattooed hand and waved his palm through the air, displaying the message that had appeared in his work slip in bold, green spirit particles.

She laughed with a sound like a burning city. Shigidi lowered his hand and furrowed his brow.

"Those documents mean nothing to me, nightmare god. Organized spirit company nonsense. My ways are older and much simpler. She has lain with me. She has enjoyed the pleasure between my thighs. We had an agreement. Her spirit belongs to me now. I was just about to claim it," she said.

"You cannot do that," Shigidi protested. "My job requires me to kill her so that her spirit can be claimed by the company. Please don't make this difficult."

Nneoma twisted again on the ceiling to allow her upper body hang low, her taut muscles rippling underneath the scales. Staring directly at him, she smiled and let out a sound somewhere between a laugh and a growl, like she was both amused and annoyed at the same time.

"Can't you find someone else to feed on tonight?" he asked, hopeful.

"No," she said. "I told you we had an agreement and I've already invested myself. Fulfilled my part of the bargain." She glanced at the woman's face, frozen smile of ecstasy still in place. "I always collect what's owed to me."

"I see."

Her ever-present smile made Shigidi uneasy. He shuffled his feet awkwardly.

"But I can't let you do that."

"Then it seems we have a problem, little nightmare god," she added.

"Yes. We do," he confirmed, sighing heavily as he mentally prepared himself for a fight he suspected he would lose. He had only a few powers that would be useful against her kind, and none of them possessed sufficient potency to do any real damage to her physical or spiritual configuration. His was the realm of dreams and nightmares, not the hard and tangible world around them where physical and spirit particles held their forms steadily. He was at his most powerful and complete in the in-between places of the minds of men and gods, in the subconscious where he could project his imagination into un-supervised thoughts and rearrange them. But it seemed that she was leaving him no choice, so he looked around the room for a good location from which he could deal his best strike at the beautiful, evil creature that confronted him. Finding none, he began to back away from the bed, into the corner where, at least, he could avoid an attack from behind. He wondered what the chances were of an aspect of Eshu-Elegba coming back to check on him.

Close to zero. Probably.

Shigidi kept his eyes trained on Nneoma and as he did, he noticed that there was something strange about her, beyond her horrific beauty or the fact that she was perched on the ceiling, her pupils trained on him with an amused intensity. No, he had seen stranger than her familiar form. The leathery wings and haunting yellow eyes were elements he had played with in constructing many nightmares to terrify people on behalf of his clients or even to conjure in the minds of other orishas for a drunken laugh at the spirit company's annual end-of-season parties. No, there was something else, something subtler. It was the look in her eyes behind the false mask of amusement. It was a look intimately familiar to him; one he'd seen in mirrors and reflective surfaces since he'd first been created. It was . . .

Sadness? Loneliness?

Her eyes still glowed bright and danced in their sockets frantically like the flames of a bizarre forest fire but as he continued to look at them, he started to see it more clearly. There was a kind of turmoil beneath the depths of those fiery eyes even though he wasn't entirely sure what it was except that it was the same look he saw in his own eyes every time he caught his reflection.

They stared at each other.

And then, Nneoma blinked twice. She fanned her wings gently, the motion so slow and deliberate it was almost imperceptible except for the sight of it pulsing through her hair.

"You're not happy, are you?" Her voice was no longer harsh and trembling; it had suddenly gone soft and genteel. "With your life I mean."

"No." He answered rapidly and honestly, surprising himself. He stopped retreating but continued to hold her in his gaze.

So, she's seen it too.

If you gaze long enough into the eyes of the succubus, the succubus gazes back into you.

"I understand. And it only makes what comes next even harder," she said, closing her eyes slowly like she was sliding them shut. And then, "I'm sorry, little nightmare god."

She moved so quickly that following the yellow trace of her gave Shigidi an instant headache. She dropped down from the ceiling, used a short pulse of her wings to catch the air and lift her body back up as she arched her back and thrust out her legs like a gymnast. It almost looked like a dance. And then, she shot straight at him like a flesh and spirit missile, feet first. Shigidi had never seen anything like it outside of an errant dream.

Shit.

He only had enough time to tense before she crashed into him. Her feet clutched to his shoulders with sharp claws as he was pushed back into the wall. Shigidi struggled, grabbing onto her ankles, but it was futile. He could feel blood and loose clay-flesh dripping down into his armpits, and his arms began to stiffen. He only realized what she was doing when he heard buzzing and saw the cluster of bright yellow lights that surrounded her begin to accumulate around the claws of her feet.

Is she . . . physically manipulating her own spirit particles?

"What are you doing?" Shigidi asked. She did not respond, so he tried to push harder, but by then it was too late. The pressure on his limbs had grown beyond his ability to resist. He was too small, too weak, too unskilled.

I can't fight her like this. There must be another way.

He could barely move, and the buzzing was loud in his ears. He closed his eyes and tried to tune it out, to listen instead to the faded breaths of the woman on the bed as he projected his imagination toward her. Her thoughts were a jumble of still, lifeless threads resonating only one emotion. The woman was still sleeping, but not the normal slumber of mortals. No, she seemed to be in a kind of suspended state, her consciousness perched precariously on the peak of pleasure Nneoma had taken her to and left her on, her spirit loose and easy to pry out at the Succubus's convenience. Shigidi listened to the woman's breathing, trying to catch the flow of it and use it as an entry point into her mind. Nneoma detached her claws from his shoulders but he barely noticed. He was completely focused on his task, searching for something, anything in the woman's subconscious that he could use to gain an advantage.

I might not be able to beat the predator, but I can steal her prey.

He found what he was looking for. *Grey.* The color of a half-forgotten memory. A memory of sitting in the back of a room while a man in a frayed navy-blue suit drew something on a dusty chalkboard and wagged his finger. Astral projection. He was telling them something about astral projection, that it was an evil practiced by witches and agents of Satan. It was a memory of church. Sunday school. The man in her memory described the loosening of the bond between body and spirit. Quoting from the Bible. The silver cord be loosed . . . *Ecclesiastes?* It didn't matter. Just more Christian doctrine used to reinforce their dominant market share. What mattered was she believed. Shigidi sensed a faint hint of faith in the concept. It was a long shot, something he'd never done before, but he was willing to try. The sleeping woman believed that her spirit could be untethered from her body. That could be enough. It would have to be enough.

Shigidi focused on that thin thread in the woman's mind as Nneoma turned her back to him and drifted confidently back to the bed, puffing her wings slightly. Shigidi twisted the thread of belief and memory in the woman's mind, wrapping it around itself to reinforce it until it felt strong enough to carry the weight of a nightmare. And then Shigidi wrapped it around her subconscious mind, and he opened his eyes. The woman twitched on the bed as she slipped out of her lust-induced fugue and began to dream vividly of being a young woman back in that classroom, trying to project her spirit out of her body to see if the pastor's words were true and realizing, in terror that they were. Dreams can be very convincing, especially when woven from faith. Nneoma saw the twitch and the flicker of eyelids. She stopped in her tracks and spun around to face Shigidi, "What are you doing, nightmare god?"

In her dream, the terrified woman on the bed tried to pull her hovering spirit back but it was too late, Shigidi smiled as he used his imagination to seize it and pull it into a cage he had constructed in his own mind, an illusion of a clearing in the evil forest that bordered Orun. Her nightmare merged with his subconscious. Her spirit was now fully encased in his realm, out of Nneoma's reach, as long as he kept his focus enough to keep up the illusion.

Nneoma stared at him curiously. "Impressive trick. What was that?"

"She was asleep. Dreaming. So, I induced a spirit-body decoupling," Shigidi said, holding back a smile.

She relaxed her shoulders and folded her wings. "I see. How exactly?"

"She already believed it was possible. I just encouraged it."

"Right. But it's not real. I could slit her throat and end the nightmare."

"Maybe. But our dreams are now interlinked. I don't know what will happen if you abruptly cut the connection from one end. Her spirit may be caught in one of the in-between places. Or destroyed. Or just stay in my imagination, part of me forever. I don't know. I've never done this before. But desperate times, desperate measures, *abi*? Do you want to risk it? My body may be small and weak, but my imagination is persistent."

Nneoma smiled. "Hmm."

The woman began to convulse on the bed as Shigidi sensed fear expanding to fill the void in her.

"All right," Nneoma said. "Let's assume I don't just kill her and then kill you and see what happens. Let's say we truly are at a stalemate. What do you want to happen next?"

"Let's make a deal," Shigidi said.

"What kind of deal?"

"Let me take her spirit and complete my job, and I won't report your activities to the spirit company."

Nneoma laughed. "You may be clever with your little nightmare tricks but you're not a great bargainer, are you? Because that's a terrible offer. Surely you know I can't accept it."

"That's the best I can do. I need her spirit. I need to complete my job."

"No, you don't." Nneoma spat out and flared her wings out again like she was expanding. "Your job. Your job. You keep talking about your job. The job that you so clearly hate, that gives you no joy." She paused and fanned her wings just enough to drift herself slowly back up to the ceiling. Shigidi followed her eyes with his, trying to maintain focus on both the dream of the woman's spirit in his head, and the balletic movement before him. She turned just before her head touched the ceiling and latched back on with her claws, as if she felt more comfortable there, or perhaps, was preparing for another attack. "Have you ever had sex, Shigidi?" she asked. Her voice was low.

"What does that have to do with anything?" he retorted, confused.

But she didn't reply immediately. Time passed in silence as though she were weighing her answer carefully on a scale before she gave it to him. Shigidi's eyes, which had been so riveted to hers, slipped free to take in the arch of her naked spine, now angled so that the dim light of the bulb hit her forehead and shoulders and breasts.

When she spoke, her words surprised him even more. "I can break your contract," she said quietly. "I can free you from your connection to the Orisha Spirit Company."

Shigidi tilted his head to the side, feeling the strain of her binding his shoulders. "What do you mean?"

She smiled again, the smile not reaching her eyes, "Exactly what I said. I can break your contract with your spirit company and make us alike, little nightmare god. You're clever and sad and creative and reckless and you have potential. If you lay with me, I can transform you. You will no longer be as you are now. You should already know I possess powers of both extraction and transformation, given the right spirit particle stimulation. Or don't they tell you that about us in your stupid company meetings? I have turned angels into demons, men into gods."

"Living into dead." Shigidi added with another jut of his jaw.

"Yes, that too. Same as you. We aren't so different, and you know it." She continued: "It is costly, but it can be done. So, give me her spirit and lay with me. You will take on a new form. One I can guarantee you will actually like."

Suspicion and curiosity rumbled in Shigidi, trapped inside his earthen flesh like two warring animals. He couldn't believe what he was hearing. It seemed too good to be true, and he had lived long enough to know that in the spirit business, nothing truly good came without a steep price.

"Is this a trick, Nneoma?" he asked.

"Not at all. It is an honest offer. You let me have this woman's spirit and in return, I will change you and free you of your obligations. We don't need to keep fighting over it." Her body rippled as the protective scales on her flesh receded and the bulk of her aggressive and fearsome persona regressed, leaving the supple skin and the perfect nakedness that Shigidi had first seen when he saw her on the bed. She freed the claws of a hand from the ceiling, leaving a deep dark gash in it and pointed her finger at him. "Once you are free, we can even work together. It's not so different from what you do now, you know. You will still take human spirits, but you can do whatever you want with them first, not just sit on them till they suffocate, which is a bit uncreative, if I may say so, given what I've seen you do. And you will work for yourself, not for that corporate sociopath, Shango, or that absentee manager, Olorun. You can travel beyond these shores too—there is so much more variety to spirits in the rest of Africa and beyond. Have you ever been to Egypt? Mozambique? Algeria? Norway?"

Shigidi shook his head. The blood dripping down his shoulders was cold and sticky and uncomfortable.

"Oh, there's so much more than this." She drew a circle in the air with her finger. "A whole world of spirits to enjoy. And you will no longer be ugly. You can take on a new form. The form I'm sure you've so potently imagined and tried to make real. Handsome, tall, hulking, admired by all who set their eyes upon you. Tell me you haven't dreamed it."

Shigidi's eyes widened in his head, inflated with imagination. "I have," he whispered.

Nneoma waited, watching her words sink into him like fishhooks. She pursed her lips, allowing them to curl just at the edges, so it looked like a pout, and then she said, "I don't want to hurt you anymore. I don't want to risk destroying one so skilled at manipulating emotions just as I do merely for this meagre mortal's spirit. No need for waste. You already said you wanted a deal so let's make a good one. I see something in you. And I think you see something in me too. Lust is not that different from fear, you know. So, let us both gain something from this . . . encounter. Lay with me, Shigidi."

He considered her proposal as he took in her polished ebony skin, long neck and gracile arms that seemed like they had been carved by the hands of a particularly precise god. He wondered if he too could ever be viewed with such awe, with such intense desire. Perhaps if he believed her. If he lay with her. Gave up the spirit he was holding hostage in his imagination and abandoned his job. Or he could keep trying to fight her and probably lose. If she knocked him unconscious or did enough damage to him, he would probably lose the bond between his mind and that of the woman lying on the bed. Then he'd be dead, or worse, forced to return to the office with an assortment of injuries to face the bite of Oya's caustic insults. There was no way he would meet his quarterly spirit-collection objectives and the company would probably dock his pray-pay for the next six months or year. He'd have to continue to work while being starved of sustenance, without even the sweet oblivion of alcohol. The thought of it all saturated him with exhaustion. He shook his head. The sensible thing to do was to take her offer, but he suspected that there was something else at play, some ulterior motive. He'd seen the querying sadness in her eyes even before she'd attacked him. Was it a ploy? A trick to get him to open up? Or even an elaborate test of his loyalty by the spirit-company? Eshu-Elegba had brought him here after all. He didn't know but he wasn't going to allow himself to be used in a anyone's games so easily.

Besides, she already said I wasn't a great bargainer.

"No," he said, refusing.

Her pout widened into an ear-to-ear grin that couldn't quite mask her surprise. "No?" she asked, slightly tilting her head so the light accentuated her cheekbones. She seemed unruffled by his initial refusal. He could not tell if she was just amused by it, given that he was trapped, or was she simply unused to being denied.

"No. I will not lie with you. I will not accept your offer. Not until you tell me what's really in it for you."

"What's in it for me?" she repeated as the mask slowly fell from her face. "Honestly, I . . . I don't . . ." And then she seemed to gather her thoughts. "I told you, you're not like the other spirit company gods. That trick you're using to hold her spirit, it's unusual. It should be impossible really. A corporate god would never have even thought to try it. You wanted honesty, here it is. I think you have . . . potential. You're molded from Olorun's spirit-clay, unlike the others. You could be far more successful than any of them if you were unshackled. You could be so much more than what you are now. And we could do great things together. Of course, I want that, if I can have it." She swiped her hand through the air. "I think you know, deep down, you're more like me than you are like them, your colleagues in the company. You're an outcast. Unconventional. Look, even if you don't believe me, if you don't believe any of that, don't you want to be beautiful? The spirit market isn't what it used to be. Faith has been falling for a long time and of all the spirit companies I have encountered, your company is one of the worst performing right now. Wasteful, disorganized, mismanaged. You aren't a priority there, and you know it. I can see it in your eyes. At least if you are one of us you will feed directly from the source. The more of us freelancers and the less of them there are, the better. There is safety in numbers. It's that simple. Come on now, make the smart choice."

So, *there it was*, Shigidi thought. *Safety*. Behind all the looks and the words and the violence, she wanted a capable partner because she was scared. Alone. Shigidi understood that. Fear. What she really needed was a glorified bodyguard or an attending companion. Still, given that, he couldn't resist the allure of a chance to no longer be ugly.

A freshly harvested spirit was worth the faith of a dozen believers, but the consumption of spirits was tightly regulated within the companies. It could only be done when requested by a human prayer or summoning. If he took her offer, he would be free of all that. He barely had enough adherents who still believed in him to get by, and what few he had were generally vengeful, petty creatures. Like the greedy business partner whose bidding had taken him to Abeokuta, or the jealous husband whose offering had brought him to this hotel. The days when kings and great rulers had prayed to him to strike fear into the minds of their enemies were long gone. Now he had to rely on his share of whatever spirits he and the other minor gods reaped with the rest of the company. The times had indeed changed and perhaps it was time for him to change along with them.

My options are limited anyway.

Take a risk for beauty and freedom or take the certainty of pain and continued unhappiness? In the end, the choice really was, as she said, a simple one to make.

"Can you really make me handsome?" he asked.

Nneoma snapped her fingers and a burst of yellow spirit particles followed like sparks from a lighter. They hung in the air like fireflies. She pointed down at the supine body of the woman whose projected spirit Shigidi was still holding in his mind. The particles streamed down onto her face. When they touched her lips, they disappeared, leaving her face strange and mouthless.

"I can remake anyone," she said, "once they have established a bond with me."

That was all the push he needed. Shigidi nodded his head, "Then yes, I accept your offer."

Her grin disappeared and the pout returned. Shigidi's skin tightened.

She retracted the claws of her other hand and her feet, allowing her body to descend slowly downwards from her perch on the ceiling with gentle pulses of her wings, gracefully, like a grand butterfly. She landed on the other side of the bed and sat with her back to him. Her wings folded and collapsed into what seemed like slits which had appeared in her back and disappeared once the wings were gone. "Release her from the nightmare. Let her spirit come back."

Shigidi forced out a smile, trying his best to sound confident even though he didn't feel it. "Release me first."

"Ha! We need to trust each other for this deal to work."

"Exactly," he replied. "We both need to demonstrate trust. Ladies first."

It was her turn to smile then. "Fine."

She raised her right hand and snapped her fingers. The yellow spirit particles that bound Shigidi to the wall retreated and agglomerated into a ball with a crinkling sound, swirling around an invisible nexus, like a miniature galaxy. The weight of his body settled back onto the floor, and he exhaled deeply, ignoring the pain in his shoulders and upper arms. He kept his eyes on her, amazed as the mass of her spirit particles recoiled back into her hand and settled into her body with a shimmer as though they had been absorbed through her pores.

I've never seen anyone, human or god, manipulate spirit particles like that before.

Nneoma thrust her head back and lay onto her side, crossing her legs in front of her so that the line of her thigh rose over the sleeping woman's spiritless body. She placed a finger on the place where the woman's mouth used to be. "Your turn."

Shigidi nodded. He opened his mouth to relieve the tension in his face and adjusted the focus of his mind so that the nightmare of the sleeping woman was foregrounded, and Nneoma's visage blurred ever so slightly. The woman believed that her spirit was in the shadow of the evil forest in Orun, running sweatily and silently in circles around a clearing she could not escape because Shigidi had imagined a solid boundary into their shared dream. There was a look of panic in her spirit's eyes, manifesting the state of her consciousness as she slept fitfully on the bed. Shigidi withdrew the fingers of his imagination, allowing the handshake of their consciousnesses to loosen. The barriers of the forest disappeared, and the woman dreamed her spirit back into her body.

On the bed in front of Nneoma, the woman's body twitched. "There we go," she said.

Nneoma beckoned to him, again with a finger. Shigidi angled his head, the supple clay-flesh of his shoulders yawing to accept the motion as he stepped forward, trembling with both fear and desire.

He only paused for a half-step when he saw the mouthless woman he had been sent to kill start to char and evaporate on the bed, the bright red and black ash of her spirit absorbed into Nneoma's skin in wide geometric arcs like a magnetic field.

Too late to turn back now.

Shigidi's eyes were fixed on Nneoma's hills and crevices, and how the dim light seemed to bend to her body's whims.

He climbed onto the bed ignoring the ash and the faint smell of smoke.

She reached out and put her hands into his trousers with authority. Her touch was wonderful. He had never experienced anything like it, not in all the hundreds of years that had passed since he had been created. She pulled him close so that her lips touched his right ear, filling him with an alien heat and desire. He felt volcanic. Ready to erupt.

Olorun almighty, how can any creature be so beautiful and terrifying at the same time?

"Tell me, Nneoma, what is it like to be with a woman like you?" he asked in a breathless, eager whisper, betraying himself.

Her laughter was genuine, wild and all encompassing. It almost made him want to laugh too, to validate her mirth, but all he could do was take in short, sharp breaths.

She pushed him back onto the bed and scooped a handful of ash from behind him, letting it fall through her fingers like sand, "You insult me, nightmare god."

The ash continued to fall.

"Haven't you seen? I am not a woman," she said, placing her hand on his chest. "I'm so much more. And when it comes to sex and the power it possesses, there is absolutely no one like me."

He could barely contain himself as she dragged his trousers down and sat astride him, lowering herself in a slow, gentle motion. He felt his reality bifurcate, separated clearly into all the moments before her and all the moments after her by a single stroke of unbelievable pleasure. He gasped.

Ahh!

His consciousness had become a tornado and he was caught in it, spinning madly and losing his ability to tell the difference between flesh and spirit, dream and reality. The world spun around him and blurred into a greyish nothingness that pushed against him from all sides. And then, his body started to disintegrate and smear into the grey haze that was all-encompassing, leaving only the green, him-shaped clump of spirit particles. At that, something like fear spiked inside him, but it was subsumed so far below all else that it barely registered. Instead, as Nneoma continued to ride him, there was an intensifying mix of joy and wonder and pleasure and so much more than could possibly be coming from his own body that he began to think that he was getting a glimpse of omniscience. It was pure unadulterated freedom. He moaned.

Suddenly, he was all at once the smoke-filled air of Obalende and the verdant hills of Idanre, the fresh sea salt air of Victoria Island and the whitish-yellow kaolin craters of Ilorin, the swampy fog of Ogun water side, and the frigid metallic din of Apapa. The spread of him engulfed every spirit he had ever encountered, experienced every dream he had ever constructed, inhaled every breath he had ever pressed out, and loved with every heart he had ever extinguished, until it stopped. He had unfolded completely over Yorubaland like a cloud.

Just as he began to understand the scope and the cost of the gift Nneoma was giving him, he was suddenly withdrawn, dragged back to himself with the violent efficiency of a recoiling whip. He could not contain it anymore. He let out a guttural shriek as he peaked in a corybantic explosion of sensations and light. So much light.

The light became unbearably bright, and the urge to cover his face overwhelmed him. But he had no body in that instant, he was all spirit. Exposed. Enlightened. Afraid.

I can sense my own fear.

His body slowly reconstituted itself, scaffolding around the green core of his spirit particles into a form that was familiar but not quite, in a world that was now no longer expansive and abstract and nebulous but as firm as consequences. Swiftly, with his eyes still closed, his hands flew to his face and travelled down, collating organs, limbs, and features, making sure all the pieces were intact and where they should be. He was the same, still made of Olorun's familiar clay, but better. Much better. No longer the squat legs and arms, but sleek, muscular limbs and a chiseled jawline that even the most artistic hands in ancient Ile-Ife would have envied. Nneoma had remade him in her image, manipulated his body the way she manipulated her own spirit particles and given him the fundamental uniform of the succubitic independent spirit agent—beauty. He opened one resculpted eye, and then another before removing his lengthened, broadened arms from his face to unveil Nneoma, standing naked by the window overlooking the lagoon and smoking a cigarette. A diffuse line of orange light smeared upwards into the dark sky above. It was dawn.

"Did you enjoy that?" she asked quietly, turning to face him. She looked pale, her cheeks sunken and drained. Her skin was wrinkled and lined. Streaks of white that hadn't been there before ran through her hair.

This cost her. It cost her a lot.

Shigidi sat up naked in the pile of fine ash. He opened his mouth to speak but the unfamiliar vocal cords failed him, so he sat, jaw bobbing with croaks and wheezes, trying to wrangle words he couldn't seem to herd together. He simply nodded his head.

"Good," she said, flicking the cigarette ash through the window without looking. "I'm glad."

The upper rim of the sun appeared on the horizon, splaying bright white into the sky and casting Nneoma in a silhouette.

She took a long drag of the cigarette and exhaled a wide, swirling plume of smoke before continuing. "It isn't easy, being a freelancer in this business. It's dangerous being alone. And ever since my sister . . . I have . . ." She stopped and took another drag of the cigarette so that the burning end flared bright crimson and accelerated toward her fingers. "I haven't had a partner for a long time. But tonight, something seemed right. *You* seemed right. So, I took the chance. I hope I was right. We could achieve so much together if we work together. I hope you will stay with me."

She threw the cigarette away and walked unsteadily toward him. "Will you?"

Her hips had lost some of their swing, but he still thought she looked beautiful, if more vulnerable. She was lessened, having given so much of herself to his transformation. The familiar look of loneliness he'd seen in her eyes was still there, perhaps even enhanced now by the hollow circles surrounding them, and he was drawn to that loneliness even more because it finally seemed like she was being completely honest with him. No artifice, no games.

Shigidi did not want to be alone either, being so newly reformed. He wanted to be with her. To learn from her how to navigate the world in this new form. How could he not? She was powerful and beautiful and free, all the things he had longed to be. But she was lonely and afraid too, just like he was. She needed him as much as he needed her.

He wanted to say *Yes* but the words wouldn't come. He looked down between his legs at the ash that had been landscaped all over the bed, and using his fingers—still shimmering green with recently rearranged spirit particles—scrawled into the ash in big, ungainly letters:

"YES."

CHAPTER 6

The Montague Gardens Hotel, London, England

JULY 4TH, 2017 | 02:03 PM.

Shigidi turned away from the verdant expanse of garden at the sound of a plate being set on their table near the open terrace of the restaurant. He'd been lost in thought, his mind dreamily sifting through recent memories, from the lush white beaches of Thailand and Malaysia to the grey streets of Lagos where he'd first met Nneoma, drifting everywhere, except for his immediate surroundings.

Nneoma was seated next to him, nursing a cool glass of Malbec in her right hand, and staring at a steak salad which had just arrived—red and wet and green and glistening, like an offering. The restaurant was full of older men and women with tufts of snow white or greying hair seated on the woven cane chairs, drinking leisurely from tea-pots, and eating off dainty porcelain plates. They were surrounded by greenery outside and inside; a variety of potted plants set in corners like household gods, and vines eagerly climbing along white wood trellises. There was one gentleman in a business suit eating by him-self at a table near the door but no young couples or teenagers or even children. Olorun sat across from Shigidi, drawing very little atten-tion from the other guests, which was not unusual given Olorun's uncanny ability to blend into a variety of backgrounds. But the old god was lavishly dressed and should have turned a few heads. He was wearing a white, embroidered agbada with its loose sleeves bundled up around his shoulders, a long leaning fila that covered the top of his afro, and an assortment of colorful beads around his neck. But, and perhaps more importantly, he was aglow, radiating electric white spirit particles from his entire body like there was a star burning beneath the surface of his skin.

"Kaabiyesi," Shigidi started, using Olorun's royal title out of habit as he finally broke the silence. "Err. Why are you shining?"

"Oh, good, you're back with us," Olorun responded, smiling as he took a sip of water from a thick tall glass.

Shigidi grunted. "Sorry. Blame jetlag."

"No actually, I won't," he said, slowly waving a glowing finger in the air like he was admonishing a child. "You're still an orisha funda-mentally, we don't get jetlag. Especially not after Nneoma rearranged your physical form. So no, I'll blame whatever problem you and your lovergirl have been desperately trying to avoid talking about since you got here." He leaned back into his chair. "Anyway, that one is none of my concern. Just don't let it get in the way of our business. And yes, I am glowing but only you and others like you can see it. It's part of my diplomatic arrangement with the British Spirit Bureau. I, just like every other employee of a foreign spirit company, must openly declare myself as a foreign spirit company representative whenever I am within the UK's borders so that they can identify and track me if they need to. Therefore, I glow."

"Oshey, shine, shine bobo. And I assume their spirit entities also have to do the same when they are in your territory?" Nneoma asked, with a smirk.

"You already know that they don't." Olorun rolled his eyes. "You've been around enough. Europe isn't like Asia or Africa. Border restrictions are a function of power, not security or fairness. Even spiritual borders. But I choose my battles, and I have my ways."

"Of course, you do," Nneoma said, crossing her legs.

"But this is exactly why I am so grateful that you two are erm, how do these oyibo people say it again . . . ? Off-the-books. You can move freely between territories, undeclared, untraced, undetected. Unless you mess something up and get caught. You don't need to carry this glow," he added, circling a finger around his head. "But it's fine. These regular people around us just see me as a bespectacled small old man with a beer belly and a snow-white afro. They can't see my true form unless I allow them. They probably think I'm your father. Or father in-law."

Nneoma scoffed.

"By the way, have you always done that, Shigidi or it is new?" Olorun asked.

"Done what?"

"Grind your teeth. You were doing it just now."

"Oh. That. Only when I'm stressed," Shigidi answered, mildly embarrassed. "Sorry. I don't always realize when I'm doing it."

"It's called bruxism and yes, he does it a lot, especially in his sleep," Nneoma added.

A server appeared and set a steaming cup of coffee in front of Shigidi. The smell hit him like he was inhaling pure, vaporized energy.

"I ordered it for you. You need it." Nneoma offered by way of explaining without looking directly at him.

"Anything else for you?" the server asked Olorun, cheerily. She was a short, frail-looking woman with wrinkled skin, who looked close to retirement herself. She was generous with her smile, her face framed by a shock of grey hair.

"No thanks, that will be all for now, unless you have some kola?" Olorun asked, coyly.

"Cola?" the woman asked, her eyes widened with confusion but the smile still in place. "Umm. We have Coca Cola and Pepsi. Would you like me to get you one of those?"

"No. Forget it, we have all we need. Thank you."

Nneoma rolled her eyes. "Very funny."

They both knew that Olorun's request was facetious.

Shigidi took a sip of his coffee and the caffeine flowed into his system like wild electricity. Since Nneoma had transformed him into an independent spirit agent, he hardly ever ate or drank anything anymore, especially not alcohol, but he still loved kolanuts and coffee. The former because they stimulated his latent powers, making him feel like he could completely manipulate raw subconscious fear if there was someone asleep anywhere close to him, and the latter because it did something to the other, newer power lodged in his chest, making him feel more alert and capable, even in small amounts.

He caught Nneoma watching him out of the corner of her eye, but she turned away to her food when he met her gaze. She had reshaped him and given him so much. They made great partners—he had even almost given up his life for her, but she was still withholding some part of herself, and the fact of it bothered him greatly because he didn't know or understand why.

"So, now that we are all here, can we finally focus on business?" Olorun asked.

"Yes," Shigidi said.

Nneoma nodded, her mouth full.

"Good. Then let's go over the job." The colored beads on his wrist dangled noisily as Olorun reached for an ornate woven briefcase that he'd set on the floor beside him. He pulled out a sheaf of documents then unfolded one of them to reveal a blue and white schematic drawing and spread it on the table in front of them, using Nneoma's wineglass to weight one of the edges. The schematic showed three floors of a building and had markings and symbols that Shigidi was sure were ancient runes, inscribed all around it.

Celtic? German? Anglo-Saxon? Norse? I can't tell but Nneoma probably knows.

"This," Olorun said, smoothing his hand across the drawing, "is the British Museum. It's right behind us, more or less, and it is one of the largest museums in the world. Four wings, taking up more than ninety-two thousand square meters of space and almost a hundred galleries which display over fifty thousand items, most of them stolen. Some of those stolen items rightfully belong to me or, at least, to my people, those who worship and believe in me. But one of those items is of particular significance to me right now." He looked up and swept his eyes from Shigidi to Nneoma. "So, you are going to help me get it back."

They looked at each other, and then back to the old orisha.

"What exactly is it?" Shigidi asked.

Olorun leaned back again, pulled from the briefcase a piece of paper with a full color image printed on it, and set it on the table on top of the schematic. "This is what I need you to get for me."

The image showed a sculpted brass head of a man with bold eyes, wide nose, hard mouth, and a beaded headdress like a crown, which encircled the head in a three-layer composition and from which a vertical, somewhat phallic plume extended, slightly bent. Parallel lines ran from where the headdress met the forehead to the base of the jaw. Small holes circled the mouth. The head appeared to be just a little under life size, symmetric, naturalistic, and obviously the result of exquisite craftsmanship despite the patina and green-grey discoloration that betrayed its age.

Shigidi nodded. He knew the image well.

Nneoma shifted her glass slightly to the left and stared at it. "It's beautiful."

"Yes, it is." Olorun pushed the image aside and pointed to a circled area on the schematic, which highlighted the upper section of the Museum's lower floor. "Here. It's held in the African Galleries on lower level two, right opposite the Center for Education."

"What about security?" Nneoma asked.

Olorun pulled out another piece of paper that had lists and numbers printed on it. He tossed it to Nneoma who scanned it quickly, running her long, red lacquered nails down its length as she did.

She said, "It all looks fairly standard. Almost boring. Basic scanners and bag checks before entry. The shifts rotate but seem predictable. About one guard per gallery. Cameras everywhere so I suppose we'd need to be a bit careful to avoid being spotted if we want to get out of the country easily later. I mean, I could just temporarily change our appearance, with some effort. Or we can just disable the cameras and avoid all that bother. Well, *I* can anyway." She put the paper down and looked directly at Olorun, holding his wrinkle-framed gaze. "We are not thieves. And even if we were, there is nothing here that a good human crew of experienced robbers cannot handle. They could sneak in, subdue the guards, snatch this and be out in a few minutes, I imagine. You could even do this yourself if you really wanted to, despite the spirit bureau tracker. So, what do you need us for? What are you not telling us?"

Olorun smiled, deepening the lines of his face. "Yes, you're right of course. It's a little more complicated than it seems initially. Physical security isn't the problem as you've rightly pointed out. The museum is protected by a special branch of the Royal British Spirit Bureau called Section Six. They are very secretive and unfortunately my people on the ground here don't know much about them except that they have ties to the very oldest spirits of this land, the ones that ran the spirit business here before the Christian takeover, and they are fiercely protective of what's left of the British Empire."

"Sounds like they would be fun at an owambe," Nneoma rejoined sarcastically as she took another forkful of steak salad.

"Indeed. They are not party people at all. In fact, I don't think they even enjoy their work, but they do take it very seriously. However, I did manage to find out two interesting things courtesy of Teju Odewunmi-Smith, new deputy commissioner at the Nigeria High Commission. These runes here and here," he said, pointing at two of the largest symbols along the edge of the building schematic. Together they looked like an H with the connecting line sloping downward. "They indicate an alarm for disruption," he continued. "The moment any item is moved outside its exhibition space by more than five meters without the curator-priest's pre-approval, the building will be automatically locked down by a Section Six sealing ritual. Once locked, the doors won't open without fingerprint, retinal, and spirit particle authorization from the curator-priest himself."

"Meaning, if we try to move the brass head of Obalufon, we'll be trapped inside." Nneoma clarified.

"Yes."

Shigidi grunted, "I can break us out of any barriers they put up. I've destroyed four shrines and killed two minor gods already."

Olorun nodded towards Shigidi's chest as though he was trying to see through to Shigidi's core, to the power wrapped around his heart. The glow from Olorun's head left a trail of light. "Yes, yes, I know you are eager to exercise your new abilities, Shigidi, but as you can imagine, most of the artefacts taken from other places and cultures hold great power, psychologically, politically, and spiritually, even if not directly to the British people, but to the people they were stolen from and to the gods that feed on their belief."

"Like yourself?" Nneoma asked, before taking another sip of her wine.

"Like myself. Exactly. And as long as the British hold them, they still hold considerable leverage and influence over those they subjugated long ago. This is the principle of the Commonwealth of Nations and all that jagbajantis, even though the only thing the member nations have in common is that their wealth was plundered by the British." He scrunched his nose with scorn. "Anyway, the point is that this leverage and influence is valuable, and it is something I am sure they do not want to lose. Couple that with the fact that this is being handled by Section Six and, well, it may take more than a few well-placed punches or a blast of stolen lightning to get past that sealing spell. You should not underestimate the challenge this could pose and understand the fact that once the alarm is activated, you may not be able to escape."

Nneoma curled her lips and nodded, "Okay. Fair enough, so how do we make sure we don't get trapped inside once we get the item for you?"

"By being smart and using information." He pointed back to the schematic, "According to Teju, the rune placement here means you will have a small window of time, exactly one minute, before the sealing spell's enchantment takes complete hold of the building. Which is where the good news comes in."

Shigidi chimed in, "Good news?"

"Yes," Olorun said. He pulled out another piece of paper crackling with spirit particles and placed it on the table. It showed another schematic, this one a vertical cross-section through all three floors of the museum and what seemed to be a small substructure below it, linked by an upward sloping tunnel to an exit through the first floor of a large nearby building.

"There is a hidden structure below the lower floor of the museum. It's an old conference room for processing sacrifices, performing negotiation rituals, and conducting business meetings with the various spirit companies that used to control the faith of people in this region thousands of years ago. Apparently, it used to be called the Pendragon Room. If you can get to it in time, then you can take this tunnel all the way to the building next door and exit there. Once you're out, make your way to the Nigeria High Commission on Northumberland Avenue as quickly and quietly as you can. That's the meeting place, *abi* rendezvous point."

"Why the High Commission?" Nneoma asked.

"That doesn't concern you, just meet me there," Olorun responded curtly.

Nneoma nodded her head, mouth curled at the edges. "Let me guess. Somewhere in the High Commission there is a secret room with something symbolic, some air or some soil or maybe even a tree from Ile-Ife that you can use as a back-door portal to the Orisha Spirit Company system to sneak in and out of the UK when things get diplomatically tricky?"

"You're not stupid, Nneoma, but you're not nearly as smart as you think you are either." Olorun leaned back in his chair again and folded his arms in front of him. "Stop asking about things that don't concern you. Just meet me there once the job is done and you will receive your promised payment, understood?"

Nneoma raised an eyebrow. "Hmm. So sensitive. If it's none of our concern, why don't you just go get the brass head yourself then?"

Olorun's eyes flared wide. "Can you even imagine what would happen to the spirit company and all the other orishas if I got trapped and caught by the spirit bureau here, arrested for violating spirit trade and border control laws? No, you don't. You can't even imagine what kind of repercussions it would have on all of Yoruba reality. You only have yourself to think about. I can assure that it's absolutely not worth the risk for me. I'll take my chances if you refuse or if you fail. But you shouldn't because for you, well, the risk should be worth it. I've made it worth it by offering you company stock, free passage back to all Orisha-held territories despite Shango wanting to murder you on sight. Isn't that enough for you?"

Nneoma stabbed another forkful of salad. "Sure. It is. Okay. Relax, Mr. Lecturer. You don't want to risk yourself and you think we are expendable in case things go wrong. Got it. Now, how do we get into the substructure? I assume there is a passage that this Teju person has told you about," she said before putting the fork in her mouth.

"There used to be, but it was sealed off in September of 1945. It's all concrete floor now."

Nneoma swallowed. "I see."

Shigidi gulped down the last dregs of his coffee and focused on the schematic in front of him. As he considered it, his expression hardened. Something about it seemed wrong to him, even though he couldn't immediately place a reason for it.

It doesn't look right.

For much of his existence as a nightmare god in the spirit company, Shigidi could always clearly tell the difference between the nightmares he created and the reality of both flesh and spirit worlds around him, no matter how much palm wine he'd had, or how elaborate any competing conjuration was. He could even carry on conversations in both real and dreamspace simultaneously, if he had to. That aptitude came from a well-calibrated internal sense of *wrongness*, knowing when the things presented to his senses were not as they should be. A sense which was in overdrive right now. He stared until it finally came to him with sudden clarity.

"Wait. Are the dimensions here to scale?" he asked, directing his question at Olorun without looking up at him.

"They are."

Shigidi grunted and said, "Then this building can't possibly be here, can it? There can't be another structure of this size so close to the museum. It would overlap with the museum itself."

Olorun pulled up his agbada sleeves, leaving trails of light on either side of him like wings, and flashed another broad, pearly smile,

"Ah yes Shigidi, you have good eyes. Ermm, let us just say that half of the substructure, the half connected to the tunnel and the exit door in that building opposite the museum, is not located in this reality."

Nneoma shook her head. "What do you mean it's not located in this reality?"

"I mean it's on the spirit-side of London," Olorun said.

Nneoma and Shigidi looked at each other uneasily. They each knew exactly what the other was thinking. They both knew that there were only three types of entities that could possibly gain access to the spirit-side of any city: one, official employees and immigration-approved contractors of the operating spirit company of the city; two, the spirits of humans who had died in the city and were not allowed to proceed to the designated final resting place of their chosen faith, or had no faith at all; and three, people who knew how to manipulate and rewrite the space-time coordinates of localized spirit particles, people also known as *magicians*.

Nneoma smirked and took another sip of her wine. "All right, so the only viable exit is in spirit space. Cool. Is there anything else of critical importance that you haven't told us yet, or are we just supposed to keep peeling this onion until we find a rotten core?"

Still smiling, Olorun said, "Yes, now that you mention it, Teju did say that the exit door can only be opened from the outside."

Nneoma started laughing hysterically, a genuine, wild, and all-encompassing laugh that shook the entire table and drew disapproving looks from other patrons. Shigidi stared at her in puzzlement, unsure of what to do. Finally, after coughing and half-choking on her own mirth, she recomposed herself and said, "Right, so if I understand all this correctly, we need to sneak into the British Museum, get past the guards and cameras, enter a sealed gallery, snatch the brass head of Obalufon which triggers a magic seal, break through—what?—six-to-eight inches of solid concrete floor in under a minute, then enter a supposedly secret substructure, transpose ourselves onto the spirit-side of London using magick that we don't have access to, and then escape through a door that can only be opened from the other side. Do I have all that right?"

Olorun smiled again, "Yes, that sounds almost all right."

"Almost?" Shigidi asked, cocking his head.

"I need it done tonight. There's an important spirit company board meeting tomorrow, and I'll need it before then."

Nneoma laughed again, this time leaning over and burying her head in the crook of Shigidi's arm.

"No wonder you don't want to do it yourself. It's almost impossible, even for you." She howled as she paused for breath before surrendering to fits of hysterical laughter again.

Shigidi gave Olorun a severe look as they both waited out the storm of mirth.

When it was over, Nneoma sat up, whistled, stabbed at the last piece of medium rare meat on her plate, swallowed, and put her fork down before turning to her brooding lover as she wiped a gleeful tear from one eye. "What do you think, Shigidi darling? Do you think we have a chance of pulling this off? Or does this old timer just want us to die in a foreign land with this elaborate ruse? Maybe it's his way of trying to tie up all the loose ends and cover up all the dirty work we've been doing for him?"

Shigidi contemplated her question. He knew that Olorun liked to play games, but he didn't believe this was one of them. There was an unfamiliar tension in the elder orisha's smile, an alien unease that Shigidi hadn't seen in Olorun before. It was something like fear, but not quite of the right texture. And that, in turn, made Shigidi un-comfortable. But they had already agreed to do the job, and they had come all the way to London, so he said in the calmest tone he could muster, "It's a tricky job, but it's not a suicide mission. We have a chance. But this is obviously a three-person job. Nneoma, you can easily use your charms to sneak us into the museum tonight and ensure the cameras are turned off when we need them to be. A little spirit particle manipulation should do it. Once we get the head, and the museum is sealed, I can break through the floor and handle any additional security they have. The third person needs to be a local magician, someone intimately familiar with the spirit-side of Lon-don. Someone who knows how to get us there and back again fast. Someone who will be waiting on the other side of that door to let us out. Do you know anyone like that?"

Nneoma tilted her head as she rummaged through her memory.

"Yes actually," she said after a few seconds. She picked up her wineglass and emptied it before setting it back down firmly on the table, rolling the thin stem between her thumb and index fingers. A smile slowly expanded across her face, "I think I do."

CHAPTER 7

Bou Saâda, M'Sila Province, Algeria

NOVEMBER 14TH, 1909 | 03:32 PM.

The desert spread out before the three travelers like a silk sheet. Pale waves crested and dipped across the sunbaked sea of sand, perfectly still beneath a cloudless blue sky. Every breath he took through the indigo tagelmust wrapped around his face filled Aleister Crowley's lungs with hot air. His vision blurred with heat shimmer. Yet, he was sure he could just start to make out a small dot in the distance that, according to the map and the trail they were following, should be the town of Bou Saâda, the oasis where they could recuperate. Their guide, a hardy and reserved Tuareg man named Wararni, slowed the pace of his camel and pointed ahead with a thin, dark-skinned hand covered in colorful protective amulets and bangles inscribed with verses from the Quran. It had to be the place. Excited, he shifted his weight on the saddle to turn to his companion, Victor Neuberg.

"We are close to rest. Let's try one more time," he said, adjusting the tagelmust to free his chapped lips. He was rewarded with the abrasive taste of fine desert dust.

Victor was naturally skinny, with a hooked nose, a kind face and a clean-shaven head, though none of those were visible under his own black tagelmust, except perhaps his skinniness. His clothing billowed around his frame like an array of flags on a flagpole, and he swayed with every motion of his plodding camel. He looked like he was about to slump and fall off at any moment.

"We've read the aethyrs six times already," Victor croaked out. "Are you sure this will work?"

Aleister, still bouncing forward on his own camel, slowed so that they were side by side, and then said to him, "Of course it will work. Don't you want to find enlightenment with me?"

"Of course, I do," Victor said hastily, and Aleister could immediately tell from his tone that Victor was trying to sound more eager than he truly felt.

"Then you must have more faith," Aleister admonished. They were on a quest after all, a pilgrimage of sorts, to summon a demon that was a personification of the wild and churning forces of the abyss, the formless plane in which no spirits dwelled. At least, that was what Aleister believed. He continued, trying to revive some of the enthusiasm of his companion which had evidently been evaporated by the desert heat. "Remember, the abyss is filled with all possible forms, swirling endlessly like the dust devils of this desert. In that endless swirling, every form is equally possible. All potential exists.

To create. To destroy. To remake. To revive. Think of it, Victor. Imagine it. It is the essence of evil. But it is evil only in the truest sense of the word—that is, meaningless but malignant, because it has desire. The abyss itself craves to become real. To manifest." He coughed and licked his dry, cracked lips, "Once we commune with these swirling forms and convince them to aggregate and assert themselves, we will finally meet the demon Choronzon, then we can subdue it and have dominion over it and all its potential. We will have the final alchemy. We will gain access to the highest magick. We will be gods among men. Remember that in these difficult moments."

Victor squeezed out a smile. Aleister knew that he had heard variants of this speech several dozen times but he enjoyed the way Victor listened, enraptured despite the familiarity. When they first met, Aleister had been studying the principles of Enochian magick which he believed would help him achieve this feat of demon conquest, and so, in a sense their love had come into being at the same time as Aleister's need to perform this magickal operation. Both desires were birthed together. Victor had joined with him and focused on recording his operations, participating where he could. Now, they were in the desert and close to their goal. Not only the summoning, but also the conquering of the demon that represented all that potential. Sometimes he wondered if Victor was truly enraptured by the magickal concept itself and its vast potential or by him and his words, the words of a man with whom he was completely in love with and whom in the moments when they lay together, he'd sworn he would follow anywhere, for whom he'd sworn he would do anything. Aleister hoped he could lean on that faith because even his own deep-rooted faith in Enochian magick was wearing thin after six failed attempts at the summoning.

"Yes, we will access true magick. Once we manage to make this work," Victor said.

"It will work." Aleister declared, bartering a laugh for Victor's smile. "It will," he repeated, trying to convince himself, too, with his own words.

"Yes, Aleister. We will do it together."

"And once it does, even Samuel Dell's achievements will pale in comparison," Aleister muttered under his breath.

Victor blinked away dust and angled his head. "What was that my love?".

Aleister bit back his tongue, drawing the thin taste of iron. He was annoyed and a bit ashamed that he'd let the mention of his old mentor in magick slip. The writings he had studied which had brought them so far, taught that to have true dominion over Choronzon was to destroy one's ego and thus overcome the final obstacle to ultimate enlightenment, to access the infinite plane. Deep down, Aleister was worried that that one of the primary motivations driving him to seek this very enlightenment in the sweltering North African desert was his ego, his need to surpass his former teacher in the ways of magick. He didn't want to admit it, but part of him believed that it was the mental block preventing him from connecting to this higher plane.

"Nothing," Aleister said, trying to refocus as he spun around and whistled to signal to their guide that they were making one more stop. Wararni turned gracefully on his camel, like it was an extension of his own body and nodded acknowledgment. He continued riding ahead, swaying rhythmically.

"All right, let us read again. Here. Right here," Aleister said, pointing at a spot in the space of hot sand between the feet of their camels.

Wararni rode some distance before dismounting near the shaded base of a low dune slip face. He pulled out a small burlap rug, lay it atop the sand, and sat, leaning against his camel which had folded its legs beneath it and was sitting compact, giving him additional shade with its wide, sinewy body. Wararni faced away from them, gazing west into the horizon where the arc of the sun was already dipping. Aleister wasn't sure if he did that to give them privacy, or just to distance himself from whatever unholy activity he imagined they were conducting. It didn't matter though; they had paid him extra to keep his eyes and opinions to himself, and he was doing a good job of it so far.

Aleister and Victor descended from their own camels carefully, their thin leather boots sinking slightly into the warm, shallow sand. Victor extracted a large yellow topaz and a thin, leather-bound book on which was written in embossed, faded lettering, *The Grand Enochian Aethyrs*. He handed the book to Aleister, who turned rapidly to the worn and faded page he sought.

Great Nuit, Hadit, Ra-Hoor, please give me guidance and open my eyes.

He began to recite from it softly, trying to make his voice loud enough to be clear but not enough to carry on the desert air. He read the thirtieth of the aethyrs, as he had during the previous six attempts. They were the words needed to invoke the powers of angel magick that lay closest to the physical plane, the ones he believed he could access most easily, so that once he received his vision, he could work his way up to the first and final aethyr, gaining new wisdoms and powers along the way.

His lips worked frantically as they wrapped around the words and spat them out, repeating them over and over again, waiting for the feeling of power that was meant to follow a connection with a higher plane. Instead, there was nothing but the heat of the desert on his shoulders and thirst in his throat and the self-consciousness of Victor, staring at him intensely and of course, the sense of nothing, absolutely nothing happening. The now-familiar sense of another failure.

After he had repeated the thirtieth aethyr for the fourth time, his voice began to shake. Victor mercifully put an arm around his shoulder.

"We should get going if we want to make it to Bou Saâda before nightfall," Victor said. "We can try again tomorrow."

Aleister closed his eyes to hide the words from himself. He let out a deep breath and silently handed over the book and the stone. Victor kissed Aleister on the cheek before but even that warm gesture felt cold and lifeless. He didn't know if he had enough faith to keep trying, to keep failing. He needed to figure something out. Perhaps he wasn't ready, his mind not humbled enough for this kind of magick. Or perhaps the problem was the magick itself, its operations not properly described. Whatever it was, he needed to figure it out.

They remounted their camels and exchanged a look of exhaustion and disappointment before Aleister remembered to try to encourage his lover with a strained smile. Victor wrapped the end of the tagelmust back around his face. They tugged at the ropes attached to their camels' necks, awkwardly guiding them back into steady, pendulous motion. Ahead, Wararni had already observed their approach and was back atop his own camel, his feet crossed on top of its neck. He waved at them and then turned, exiting the shadowy base of the dune and leading the stone-faced and exhausted pair toward the town where they could finally get some much-needed rest.

Bou Saâda, which the locals referred to as *the place of happiness*, was an ancient town that had once been the site of a bishopric in the twilight of the Roman empire, and through shifting fates and seasons, had evolved into a small, yet bustling town. But with all its changing fortunes through the centuries, one thing had remained constant: it was always a nexus of trade. Nomads, poets, migrants, soldiers, and conquering kings; everyone stopped at its oasis when making their way across the Sahara. It was natural that a town had sprung up around the oasis, just like the ribbon of date palm groves that ringed it. The mélange of people that made it to and through the town traded jewelry, art, guns, carpets, books, knives and anything of value that could be desired. Like a cold beer at the end of a long day in the desert.

Aleister and Victor had gotten directions to the local watering hole from Wararni and arrived as the sun hovered over the horizon, staining the sky a stark orange. It was a small stone building in the new French quarter of the town, away from the high arches of the Ksar, where the local population preferred the people and the things— those they did not like to be reminded of—be located. Things like rowdy French soldiers, and opium, and prostitutes, and beer. Wararni had stayed back at the guest house with the camels.

Aleister and Victor entered and found a place for themselves in a corner of the stone house, sitting face-to-face on a mass of colorful carpets, a flagon of cold beer sweating on a stone slab between them. The room was saturated with burning tobacco and lit by smoky candles.

"I don't know what's wrong," Aleister said after taking a long sip of the beer, exhaling the words like a burden or perhaps, a belch. "I have made the call of the aethyr and concentrated on the shew stone. This is what is required, we know that. But my mind-state remains in this plane. I don't know what else to do."

"Maybe this is the wrong place, the wrong desert." Victor offered.

"No, no, you've read the writings. This is the ideal place. We are just . . . I don't know." He threw his hands up in the air. "I just don't know."

Victor brought the beer to his own lips as if to avoid saying anything. Aleister turned away, taking in the room again hoping for something to distract him from thoughts of his failure while the alcohol took its time blunting the hard edges of his disappointment.

And that was when he saw her for the first time.

She was seated alone on the floor to their right, legs tucked beneath her. The first thing he noticed about her was the sleekness of her fingers, wrapped around a short, clear glass. They were long, and thin, and smooth. Her lips were full and red, and every one of her movements was measured, graceful, sensual, like a dance. She didn't drink from the glass so much as kiss the liquid from it. The exposed ebony skin of her forearms and face seemed to radiate a glow and her curly hair peeked out of the front of a dark red headscarf that looked like it had been woven from dried blood. The flowing red dress she wore was loose but seemed to bend to her body's whims where it encountered her curves. Large hoop earrings hung from her ears like chandeliers. She looked incredibly out of place, like a queen in a farmhouse.

Aleister didn't realize he was staring until she turned to face him. He found himself under the regard of strange eyes that were like flickering yellow jewels set in orbs of white marble. They held a look he recognized clearly. The same look his mother had in the days after his father's passing. Aleister began to feel weightless and woolly-headed, like he was floating in an ocean of thick yellow sorrow.

A man dressed in simple but well-made brown and blue robes came over and stood beside the woman, breaking the spell her eyes had cast on Aleister. The man was dark-skinned too, though his skin was lighter than hers, and he had curly black hair, cut short and packed tightly around his head, from its having been wrapped under a turban for much of the day. His nose was slim, and his limbs were slender, like stalks. When he put down on the table a silver tray piled with grilled lamb's feet, zviti, olives, al-shetitha, and fish cured in spices, Aleister saw the ring he wore on his right finger. It was a broad gold band with inscriptions and a circlet of bright blue lapis lazuli set in it that seemed to almost bleed its color into the air around it as his hand moved. It was a faint effect but one Aleister was used to seeing. *Magick.* It was magick.

As he settled onto the cushioned floor beside her, the man addressed her in formal Arabic, which Aleister did not understand fluently.

"Eat, Nneoma," the man said. "We still have a long way to go."

"Yes," she said, her manner cool and direct. And that, Aleister understood.

She picked up an olive without breaking eye contact with Aleister and slipped it between her lips.

The man looked up and across the room, following the line of her sight. When he saw Aleister staring at them, his face scrunched, deep frown-lines appearing. He grabbed Nneoma's arm forcefully, with his ringed hand, and she turned to face him, her eyes full of venom but her apparent anger blunted by . . . something. *Pain?* Aleister thought he could see a faint array of helices rising like smoke from the place where the man's hand had made contact with her flesh. The helices wrapped themselves around her shoulders and throat, but he wasn't sure if he was just imagining it.

"Stop it Riyad," she said through gritted teeth, before adding, "Please!"

Aleister looked away, back to Victor who, he realized by the widened look of his eyes, had also seen the last part of the exchange.

"There is something strange going on with those two," Aleister said as he took another sip of beer.

Victor nodded. "Yes. But it is none of our business."

"I suppose it isn't," Aleister replied, searching his pockets for the topaz shew stone he had been trying and failing to use as a key to the aethyrs and take the next step in his evolution as a magician. "But what if there is magick involved? What if someone is using magick to hold another person hostage, do we not have an obligation to help, as members of the order?"

He could almost see the gears turning behind Victor's eyes as he thought about the question for a moment. "If it was, then yes, according to the teachings, we are under some obligation," Victor said. "But I don't see any evidence of magick, only abuse. Besides, she may be his servant, by evidence of her skin. That is not uncommon here. We are strangers in this place. I don't think it is wise to get involved."

"I don't care much for the woman," Aleister lied, his mind still full of her image and the deep abiding sadness her eyes had flooded him with. "Do you see the ring on the man's finger?"

Victor stole a quick glance and said, "Yes."

Aleister continued. "Focus. Unlock your first mindgate and watch the air around it closely. Tell me if you observe anything."

Victor muttered a hushed incantation and his eyes narrowed as he focused on the man's hand. Aleister joined him, looking more intently than he had the first time, to confirm what he had seen before, and he did. As she continued eating gingerly, her eyes cast down, they could see that the woman—who they heard addressed as "Nneoma"—was bound tightly by the thin streaks of light emanating from the blue and brown of the lapis lazuli as it radiated like a powerful lamp.

"Do you see?" Aleister asked.

"Is it some kind of binding magick?" Victor whispered, his voice trembling.

"Yes. Exactly," Aleister said, already thinking about the magickal operations he could perform with a shew stone powerful enough to passively run binding magick. He wondered if he could use it to finally establish a connection to the aethyrs and perhaps to control the demon Choronzon when they finally unlocked the final aethyr. Victor would oppose stealing it, he knew that, but perhaps he could be convinced that it was a charitable act to save the woman.

"Victor, look at her. Her clothes, her manner, her eyes. She is no servant. She has clearly been abducted using magick. We have an obligation to help. We can set her free."

"I don't know, Aleister, this could be dangerous."

"What good thing can be achieved without some risk?"

Victor hesitated for a moment, put his palm to his head and asked, "How?"

Aleister reached for the nearly empty flagon of beer between them. "It is simple. He is using binding magick. Channeling it through that stone on his finger. So, we take the ring," he said, smiling. He poured the dregs of beer down his throat and wiped his brow. "There are two of us. If we do it at the right time, employing the element of surprise, there does not need to be any violence. We can subdue him and free the woman."

Victor looked at Aleister and then he said, "Fine. We wait until they leave, then we follow and take it from him once we find an isolated area. We don't want to be arrested as thieves here. There is no telling what they would do to us."

"Agreed," Aleister said. He raised his hand to order another beer, and they fell into watchful silence.

When Nneoma finished her meal and Riyad finished his drink, they left money on the table and exited, moving so smoothly across the tavern floor that it seemed they were floating.

Victor and Aleister hastily paid for their own beers and followed.

When they emerged from the stone building, the sun that had held so much sway over the land during the day was gone and in its place was an open sky full of stars, like a sparkle of fireflies frozen against a perfect blue ribbon that wrapped across the world.

Aleister and Victor followed the pair at some distance, through the chaotic streets of the French quarter, winding through narrow alleyways that offered glimpses of the inhabitants' lives through open windows, like a living mosaic. Children playing. Women cooking. Men smoking. Families eating. But they swept past them too quickly for Aleister to make any detailed observations. They were focused on the man and woman from the tavern.

When the pair turned to enter a dark and windowless alley, Victor and Aleister nodded at each other to acknowledge the opportunity.

Victor sprinted ahead and ran until he crashed shoulder first into the man's back. The transfer of momentum knocked Riyad off balance and as he tried to stabilize himself, Victor engulfed him and wrapped his thin arms around Riyad in a bodylock, gripping his own fingers so that he completely pinned Riyad's arms to his sides.

"What—!" Riyad exclaimed just as Aleister caught up to them, snatched the lapis lazuli ring from his finger and wrapped his palm across Riyad's mouth in one smooth motion.

Riyad's eyes widened with anger as he struggled against Victor's pressure. He was about to pry apart Victor's bony grip, but when Aleister began to recite a Latin incantation, the look on Riyad's face turned to shock and then finally, to resignation as the binding magick took hold of his muscles.

Nneoma stood off to the side, watching. A smile slowly spread across her face.

"It is done," Aleister said, when he finished his operation and was sure it had worked. With the ring in his hand, he could already feel the increased potency of his words. Everything had worked out perfectly. In fact, it had all happened quite fast and easily. Perhaps too easily. He kept his guard up.

Victor released his hold, but there was no change in Riyad's posture save a tightening around his eyes and lips, and a straining in the tendons of his neck as he struggled against the invisible restraints that held him and kept his mouth closed.

"It is binding magick. You are familiar with it, aren't you? Of course you are. What goes around, comes around. You should know you cannot escape it." Aleister told him before turning to Nneoma. "Are you all right?"

She walked up to Riyad in smooth long strides and slapped him viciously, twice across the face. One strike with the palm and the other a swift return with the backhand. Victor flinched at the sound of it. Riyad remained rigid and continued to vibrate with impotent lividity.

"I am now," she said, folding her arms to her chest. "But you need to give me the ring."

Aleister was a bit surprised at her perfect English, spoken without a hint of the Arabic, French, or even any of the hacking desert tongues accenting the words of most of the people they'd encountered so far in their journey. He thought she sounded vaguely Egyptian or even West African; he couldn't be sure. But he was most surprised by her apparent lack of gratitude. She wasn't acting like a woman in distress who had just been rescued. Nor did she show the signs of someone just delivered from peril. No, she was projecting . . . arrogance, and it both irritated and unnerved him.

"Why should we give it to you? And how did you come to be held prisoner by this man?" Victor asked.

"Magician," she corrected. "He is a magician. Like you, I see." She snorted and walked around Riyad's sessile body in a tight circle, her eyes roving with scorn. "I don't like magicians."

Aleister raised an annoyed eyebrow. "Well maybe we shouldn't have helped you then."

She ignored his remark, which only angered him more. "He and I had an agreement, but he lied to me, and he caught me in a moment of weakness. He tricked me and has held me hostage for months with that ring and its binding magick."

"Well, you are free now, ungrateful as you are," Aleister said. "So, go. But I am not going to give you the ring. It is a powerful totem.". He fingered the smooth surface of the lapis lazuli ring in his palm. His lips trembled with anticipation of uttering the incantations again in the dry desert air, hopeful that this time they would work.

"Oh!" She stopped mid-step and raised an eyebrow. "Just because I don't like you and I haven't thanked you yet, that doesn't mean I am not grateful. I owe you a debt and I am going to repay it. Once you give me that ring."

"Why did he hold you? You were kidnapped for a ransom?" Victor asked.

Aleister nodded, equally curious. He knew Victor was only asking for his conscience's sake, hoping they had done the right thing, but Aleister was more interested in knowing more about the woman who so causally made him feel so many emotions at once.

"In a manner of speaking," she said, waving a delicate hand in the air. "It doesn't matter. What matters now is that I am free, and we can make an arrangement of our own. I overheard some of your conversation in the tavern, and I will tell you this for free: Your summoning magick is not working because you have not yet invoked the right kind of magickal power."

At that Victor's jaw dropped open, and it took Aleister a moment to notice that his had too. They were both stunned.

"Stop staring like that," she said with a smile as she placed a hand on Riyad's rigid shoulder and leaned in close, breathing down his neck. She was apparently enjoying the reversal of fortunes.

"How do you know what we were talking about?" Aleister asked finally.

"Like I said, I overheard," she replied. "You were not very discreet."

Victor shook his head. "What do you know of magick?"

She brushed a strand of hair from her face and looked up to the star-dappled sky. "I was there when magick was first brought into this world," she said. And then she laughed a soft laugh like a tremor. "In a manner of speaking anyway. And I have known more magicians than I care to remember."

Aleister was even more stunned than before. He gaped, more observant now, watching the flow of her robes, the surface of her skin, the glow in her eyes. As he did, he slowly became aware of a deep longing, like lust, growing in him like a creature in his belly. There was something animal-like about her manner and graceful movements that was intoxicating, inspiring images of pale and dark flesh rubbing against each other, of wetness and kisses and moans and the firm grip of fingers around mounds of smooth skin. So many feelings had coursed through him since he first saw her. Curiosity. Repulsion. Sympathy. Fear. Annoyance. Unease. And now overwhelming desire. Victor, wide-eyed with fear, touched him on the shoulder and said, "I think we should leave. Now."

Instinctively, Aleister tightened his grip on the ring and raised it up to his chest, holding it in front of him like a shield. Frown lines appeared around Nneoma's eyes and her lips tightened.

Aleister saw Riyad's eyes glow with delight. Perhaps he could sense the shift in the air, could see the fear that was growing in theirs. He may be trapped in his own body, but Riyad wasn't the only one afraid of Nneoma.

"What are you?" Aleister asked. His voice now hoarse, even to his own hearing.

She stood straight up now and returned his gaze, almost mesmerizing Aleister with her deep brown eyes as she said, "That doesn't matter. I want that ring. Give it to me and I will tell you what you need to know to invoke the aethyrs."

Aleister felt like a fly in a spider's web trying to negotiate his way out of being eaten. But the temptation of her offer was too great so he ignored Victor's tightening grasp on his shoulder and asked, "And you will help us with the summoning?"

"No. Magickal operations are not my area of expertise."

Aleister tried to hide the contours of disappointment that appeared on his face but he failed.

"What then is your area of expertise?" Victor whispered with a trembling voice like he was almost afraid to ask.

"Sexual revelations."

Aleister's simmering annoyance flared, pushing back all the other emotions. "Ah. I should have known. You are nothing but a sharp-tongued, black, desert whore!" He felt angry with himself for being lured in and almost aroused by this dark-skinned woman who carried herself so regally, but who—he was sure—wouldn't even be worthy of cleaning his bedchamber back in London.

"Not quite," she said, staring at him as though she were boring into his soul. "And I don't appreciate the insult. Especially coming from someone like you."

Despite his confidence in his ability to use the ring in his hand and the many years of believing in the superiority of his skin, his mind was still stirring with a heady mix of lust and fear. He felt unstable, like there was a tremor in the ground beneath him.

"What do you mean *someone like me*?" he asked.

A blast of cool nighttime desert wind rushed past them. Aleister looked beyond Nneoma, suddenly concerned that someone could come by any minute, and they would have a lot of explaining to do. The moonlight had painted the stone and timber of the entrance to the alleyway behind her in sharp silver, like it was a gate, an opportunity to escape the darkness and the allure and the strangeness and the danger of the woman before him. This woman that he was so powerfully drawn to. But there was no one at the head of the alley. In fact, no one had walked past the alleyway since they had entered. It was then he realized how silent the town seemed to have become. The silence was abiding. Earlier, when they had exited the tavern, the air of the French quarter had been full of dogs barking, people laughing in the streets and stumbling home. In the bubble of the alley, there were no laughs, no calls, no windows opening, no footfalls, no coughs, no whispers: nothing pierced the silence.

Nneoma touched an index finger to rigid Riyad's temple like he was an illustrative dummy, "You know exactly what I mean you childish and conflicted man. Perpetually rebelling against the Christian morality of your upbringing like a teenage brat. Driven by anger at world over your father's death. I know more about you," she turned to Victor briefly, "and your partner here, than you can imagine." She brought her hand in front of her and waved it in front of her face like she was driving away invisible flies. "So much of your essence leaks out through your eyes and your skin and your heart. I can smell your history on you and let me tell you, you are not special. Neither of you. I've met more men like you than you can imagine. But I'm bored with this now. Just give me the ring and I will tell you what you need to know. It is a simple trade. You keep thinking you need *more*. More totems. More incantations. More attempts. You don't need *more* of anything. You just need the right *kind* of thing. The right kind of invocation. This is key. Once I show you what I mean, you will understand. And then you will be able to figure out the summoning on your own . . . if you're not stupid. So, no point risking more heatstroke for nothing. Give me the ring and your quest can end."

Aleister stepped back, suddenly feeling faint. His hand was trembling. How could she know these things about him? It was impossible, unless . . . was this goddess Nuit herself, lady of the stars, as had been revealed to him when he visited Egypt and had been given the book of the law?

The manifestation of Nuit? The unveiling of the company of heaven?

No. Nuit could not be bound by another magician. Unless this was only some limited aspect of her sent to him, to bring him this experience. No. She could not be. He didn't want to believe it and yet, deep down, he wanted it to be true. Desired it. That desire took over his body. Desire for knowledge, for deeper magick, and for the sexual revelation that she promised with her body and her words. He turned to face Victor who seemed to have been shocked into silence and took his hand. It was shaking too.

"I apologize," Aleister said, looking back to Nneoma. "I mean, we apologize. We did not mean to offend. My name is Aleister Crowley, and this is Victor Neuberg, although I suppose you may know that already."

She smiled at that.

A confirmation. Is that truly you Nuit, made flesh?

"And Riyad called you Nneoma? Is that your true name?" he asked.

"Yes. I have many names, but you can call me Nneoma."

It is as the book says. *"Therefore, I am known by my name Nuit, and by a secret name which I will give him when at last he knoweth me."* Perhaps it was her.

"Are you a djinn?" Victor asked, his hand trembling. He did not yet understand.

"No, I'm something better." Her gaze softened, and Aleister thought he saw a flash of amber. He also saw his opportunity.

His eyes brightened. "Nneoma," he started, stumbling all over her name like it was a crooked staircase, "We will give you the ring. Even though it's ours to claim for helping you. Consider it a gesture of goodwill and perhaps, one day, you will be in a position to help us."

She smiled and said, "I like you, Crowley. You're almost clever. Almost."

He was about to smile himself but something about the way that she spoke gave him pause.

He considered his own words carefully before he continued. "All we ask is that if such a day comes, that perhaps you will return the favor. Consider it a kind of loosely defined debt. To be claimed later."

She laughed again, sending new vibrations through the bodies of both men, and for a moment Aleister thought that he had overplayed his hand. But then she suddenly stopped laughing and said, "Fine. I accept your terms. We have a bargain."

Aleister could not contain his excitement. "So then tell us, what is the right *kind* of power to access the aethyrs?"

She laughed again. "That's not how this works. You have been playing at petty little magick all your life. There is a whole world of spirit-business you have no clue about. If you want to know how to access true magick, then first, give me the ring. Only then will I truly be in your debt."

Aleister stretched his hand out and opened his palm, offering the ring to her. Its faint blue aura waxed and waned in the evening air. She drifted toward him in slow, deliberate strides and plucked it out of his hand like it was a delicate fruit. She stared at it for a moment, turning from side to side the thing that had been used to bind her as if she was admiring the way the moonlight pooled in thin bright streaks against the gold band and in small ellipses against the surface of the inset gem.

And then suddenly, she kissed her teeth, making a prolonged scornful sound, before dropping the ring on the ground and stomping on it with the flat heel of her shoes. Every time her foot made contact with it, a shower of blue and yellow sparks exploded, like miniature fireworks. Victor and Aleister drew closer to each other as they watched the helix of binding light that had wrapped its way around her body flare up again into the air, like a sculpture of light, and break before falling off in pieces that dissipated before they could hit the ground.

When she was done, there was nothing left on the dusty ground but ash and a faint blue afterglow. She lifted her face up to the sky and let out a deep breath.

Aleister sensed the change in the atmosphere like a prickly heat all over his skin. He interlocked his fingers with Victor's. They had gambled and now would come the moment of truth. Nuit or not, they had made their move.

"That's so much better. I hate being bound to anything . . . or anyone," Nneoma said. She snapped her fingers and they crackled with yellow and orange sparks that illuminated her face. "Thank you."

"The aethyrs," Aleister said. "How do we—?"

"I already told you. Sex. Sex magick," she interrupted. "It is the most powerful tool available to your kind after your imagination. The closest you can come to the divine. You recite the incantations in the right place, and you hold your totems in the right way, and you think you have opened your mind to the right channels, but you are wrong. You can manipulate loose spirit particles, and you may overhear the ramblings of a few careless spirit entities, but your minds are not made to contain or manipulate the chaos of pure magickal potential until they have been fully opened," she paused, looking deeply into Aleister's eyes, "at the moment of orgasm."

"Orgasm?" Victor echoed. He sounded confused.

"Yes," she said. "There is a temporary blurring of the barrier between worlds, an exposure of your spirits at the peak of sexual pleasure. It can be manipulated in both directions, to draw power into your spirit or to have your spirits taken out of you—so you need to know what you are doing." She smiled and put her hands on her hips, accentuating the curve of them. "I can show you."

Is this what the revelations in the book meant then? "I give unimaginable joys on earth: certainty, not faith, while in life, upon death; peace unutterable, rest, ecstasy."

Another burst of lust hit Aleister like a tornado. His skin tingled and his mind was overrun with images of naked brown bodies writhing, tongues licking, mouths open mid-moan. He licked his dry lips as a kind of revulsion and desire wrestled each other within him. He blinked twice and shook his head as though the motion would force the images to shake loose and fall to the sandy ground, but they persisted. Looking to Victor, he wondered if his companion felt the same surge of desires that had hit him. But the clear and concerned look in the whites of his eyes indicated otherwise.

"Just you," she said to Aleister as though she had read his mind.

Great Nuit. It had to be her.

"Why?" he asked.

"Something I sense in you. Something stupid. I'm going to toy with it. Correct it. Or make it worse. It is a matter of skin," she replied enigmatically, even though he knew that she knew that he knew what she meant. He wanted her and yet hated himself for that desire. He began to tremble. He was terrified and tantalized so thoroughly that he felt like he was being put into a trance. "Is this part of our bargain?"

"No," she said, still smiling, "It's just fun for me." She seemed to be thoroughly enjoying his conflict but he didn't care. He would have his revelation this night, from Nuit or whatever this woman was, and the more he thought about it, the more certain he felt that he was ready to risk it.

"Go back to the inn," Aleister said to Victor, keeping his eyes and focus on Nneoma. He wasn't sure what most propelled him to his decision—pride, desire, or wisdom, but he had played his hand and he was prepared to see it through. "I will return with the knowledge we need."

Victor turned to him and opened his mouth but the protest Aleister expected did not come. Victor just stood there like the words were stuck in his throat, choking him.

Finally, the words came out in an unclear, inarticulate stream: "Don't go. Don't go. Don't go. There is an inhuman hunger in her eyes. Surely you can see it if I can. This is dangerous." He squeezed Aleister's hand tighter, but it was too late, Aleister had already made up his mind.

"Don't worry, Victor, I won't bite," Nneoma said with a smile.

Aleister took Victor into his arms and held him in an embrace.

"This is an opportunity," he whispered into Victor's ear. "Another revelation."

Victor shook his head. "This is no revelation Aleister, this is not like Egypt. This is manipulation, maybe something worse."

"You don't understand. I need to do this." And then he kissed Victor before letting go of his hand and stepping away, toward Nneoma.

It is as the book says, "He, my prophet, hath chosen."

"What about him?" Aleister asked as he walked toward her, indicating the frozen and frightened Riyad with a nod of his head.

"Ah yes, him." Her expression darkened, "We have unfinished business. He owes me something. And I always collect what is owed to me."

She turned to regard her erstwhile captor with a threatening smile. Aleister was not expecting it when she turned gracefully, like a ballerina, and grabbed Riyad's head with one hand. Aleister froze mid-step. She attacked Riyad with a kiss like a dagger against his lips as she slid her free hand down his torso, navigating her fingers between his robes and into his loose trousers. She manipulated him with quick movements of her wrist. Aleister watched, too stunned to speak but he heard Victor making a sound like a whimper. After what seemed like only a few moments, Riyad's face contracted into the familiar mask of orgasm as he convulsed under the binding magick restraints. A bright orange light erupted where her lips met his and expanded to engulf his body, dappling him like a shimmer of stars. The skin of Riyad's face began to shrink and desiccate before their eyes, Riyad's own eyes wide with a look of terrified pleasure. His locks of curly hair shook loose and fell over his forehead, and his skin took on a bright, translucent quality, as if his blood was fuel set ablaze from within. His clothing started to loosen with the rapid reduction of skin and muscle, as he contracted to a cadaverous version of himself. And then, in an instant, the light was snuffed from his eyes and his skin turned wet-ash grey. What was left of his body fell to the ground with a thud and crumbled into a puff of ash and dust.

The sound of the body hitting the ground ended Victor's whimpering. Aleister looked back and saw his companion's eyes filled with a singular instinct. Victor turned and ran, his feet pounding into the ground with loud thuds as he sprinted farther into the alley until he reached a place where it connected to a narrow space between two houses. It didn't look like it was meant to be a passage, but Victor squeezed into it and was swallowed by the darkness.

"Forgive me Victor," Aleister muttered, as the sounds of his companion's escape faded. He turned back to face Nneoma and saw that she was changing. Subtly, but definitely. Her dark skin rippled like the surface of a lake at night and became even more smooth and supple. Her hair gained luster and her red lips became fuller.

Aleister stared in awe.

I can see it now, great Nuit. I understand the revelations. I know what you mean when you said "I am the naked brilliance of the voluptuous night-sky."

His skin prickled, as if her aura had expanded and engulfed him, intensifying his desire for her and all she promised. It was intoxicating. He knew he should be afraid, and a part of him was, but it was subsumed by desire. She reached out to him, beckoning with her finger, and said, "Come."

At the sound of her voice, Aleister remembered to continue walking.

"Where are we going?" he asked as he continued to approach her; the woman, the creature, the temptress, the darkness, the manifestation of Nuit that promised so much and terrified him in so many ways. He advanced steadily with small steps until he was close enough to take her hand. The feel of her skin against his palm sent a wave of desire through him that was so intense it made him gasp.

She looked at him with flame-filled eyes that constantly shimmered in a translucence of yellow hues. "Into the desert."

Netherwoods Guest House, Hastings, England

DECEMBER 1ST, 1947 | 06:06 PM.

Room thirteen of the old stone guest house was dimly illuminated by the embers of a dying fire. It was a gloomy room with a single leaded windowpane and heavy brown cotton curtains that smelled of smoke, fish, heroin, curry, saliva, and damp. Aged and grey, Aleister Crowley sat alone in a chair by the fireplace smoking a wood pipe and blankly regarding the bright orange coals. He'd been sitting there, like that, for hours.

"Well, I never expected the great beast to end up like this," a sultry voice came to him from across the room, "old, penniless, powerless and worst of all, alone."

He hadn't heard the door or window swing open.

"How did you get in here?" He asked, speaking in the direction of the voice as he set his pipe down and turned to regard the intruder, his bulging midsection straining against his shirt as he leaned forward.

A woman-shaped figure approached him, but it took several seconds for his eyes to adjust and resolve what was in front of them.

The memory of her hit him like a punch to the chest as soon as he saw her standing there in a short-sleeved white dress with chartreuse, pink, and white patterns. Her long sleek fingers that sat on her hips, her glowing dark skin, her long, pressed and now curled hair, her full red lips. It all came back to him in a rush of erotic memory. Full moon. Algerian Sahara. The night he had learned the profound and secret power of sex magick. And yet somehow, in some way, she hadn't aged.

Great Nuit.

"Nneoma?" Aleister gasped and the pipe fell out of his hands, hitting the ground with a thudding sound. "Is that really you?"

"In the flesh," she said, revealing perfect white teeth.

His eyes widened with surprise, "It has been so long."

"Yes, it has," she said, glancing at the glowing fireplace he had been mesmerized by for so many hours. "You know I really do not like your kind. Magicians, I mean. But I will admit you can be useful, under the right circumstances. And I have never forgotten what you did for me."

He shook his head, trying to make sure he wasn't dreaming. "Is that why you are here? You have come to repay your debt?"

"Yes and no," she said, strutting in front of him. There was a feral aspect to her movements, like a predator stalking prey. It reminded him of the way she had walked around Riyad, all those years ago. Right before she turned him to ash "Yes," she continued, "because I always pay what I owe. But no, because I've decided that I'm going to invest in you, Aleister. I'm going to offer you something so special that you will be indebted to me for the rest of your . . . life."

"I don't have much life left to live," he croaked out, realizing that even if she offered him anything new or even the same experiences and knowledge as she had that night so many years ago, he would barely be able to withstand it enough to enjoy it. He looked down at his liver-spotted hands. They were trembling. "And I am not the man I once was. I can barely perform even the simplest magickal operations anymore or even muster the will for . . ." His voice trailed off.

"But you want more, don't you?" she asked. "More life? Another life?"

"Of course," he said, speaking so quickly that he started to cough a deep hacking cough. He spat out accumulated phlegm before continuing. "I would give anything to be young again, to travel the world and relive the pleasures of my youth, to conjure up new magicks, but I am weak and spent. My days are exhausted."

"Oh, let's see about that." Her eyes flashed bright yellow in the dim light of the room, and she peeled off her dress, slipping out of it like she was discarding old skin to reveal the smooth skin and voluptuous body beneath. She stepped toward him and ran the claws that had extended from her slender, long fingers down his face and along his shoulder, holding him captive with her gaze. His mind filled with memories and feelings and images of dust and wind and flesh and pleasure. So much pleasure. He found himself stirring again, a sensation he had not felt in almost a decade. It had been so long; he was almost afraid of it.

"I have two spirits I have just taken, from young and foolish men, wild and conflicted and full of desire, just like you were once. But I have had my fill of wild young English men who hate themselves for secretly lusting after other men or after women with skin like mine." Her face was so close to his that he could inhale her breath. "Do you want them? These foolish young spirits that remind me so much of you?"

"Yes," he rasped, almost breathless at the thought of being young again, despite his embarrassment at being called out, exposed.

"I knew you would. Then you will get two lifetimes. Consider the first spirit as payment for what I owe you, to conclude our decades-old bargain."

Her body rippled and spasmed in bursts as her polished, supple skin became hard and scaly and the long arch of her spine twisted. The flesh of her back folded and tore as long, dark bat-like wings, the same rich color as her skin, emerged and spread to either side. They were so long they almost touched the walls of the small room.

"And the second, well, since we both like bargains so much, once I give you this, *you* will be in *my* debt. A debt to be claimed later." She smiled.

Aleister nodded his head rapidly, stunned by her image, by memories, by fear, by mad desire, by the chance to live again . . . and again.

She sat astride him, her wings lifted, and her thighs parted as she worked his trousers. "Consider it a long-term investment I'm making in you. Payable upon request."

"Yes," he croaked.

She took him into her, and he let out a moan like an exhalation of soul.

CHAPTER 8

Cocolove Club, London, England

JULY 5TH, 2017 | 01:25 AM.

Shigidi and Nneoma arrived in a black cab and glided out onto the cold cobblestone streets, strolling past the winding queue of would-be partiers braving the chill for some promise of excitement. They went right up to the dark, leather-padded entrance that looked like a fleshy orifice. Thick, thumping bass like the unsteady heartbeat of a decadent god seeped out from inside, punctuated by an occasional rhythmic chant too dull to hear clearly. Nneoma looked around, a sparkle developing in her eyes. This was her kind of place. Cave, palace, tent, village square, it didn't matter, as long as there was darkness, people, music, intoxicants, and desire, she felt at home. Shigidi was wearing a blue, fitted blazer over a white shirt and matching pocket square with trim black pants. The blazer barely contained his arm when he flexed it. His clean-shaven head gleamed when the light from the ubiquitous array of bulbs hit it. Nneoma had chosen a blue, straight neck bodycon dress that fit her like a second skin and matching Louboutin shoes. Her hair flowed over her shoulders like silk. They were, as usual, dressed dangerously. Tonight, they needed to be. Nneoma noticed how many looks they drew and held with a kind of prodigious visual magnetism as they drifted past the queue. At the entrance, she slipped the burly bouncer four fifty-pound notes and a seductive smile as they made their way in without being stamped or searched. Through a narrow dark corridor was the main hall attended by a hostess in a short spandex dress, clipboard in hand.

"Reservation?" the hostess asked.

Nneoma simply held out two fifty-pound notes by way of reply.

The hostess took the money, smiled, and stepped to the side, "Welcome to Cocolove."

Nneoma nodded to her, and they pushed through the thick, padded door.

It was like entering a fever dream. The music exploded from a faint consistent thumping into a rhythmic booming. There was movement everywhere and it was difficult to tell just how big the place was or how many people were there, because of the ceiling-high panels of reflective glass that multiplied and reflected every image they caught. A woman in a leather skirt and fishnet top swept past them, her nipples visible and hard in the air-conditioning. Shadowy people-shapes gyrated sensually against each other in the dimly lit and least reflected corners of the club. Small groups of four to five shouted and laughed and swayed in place around tables populated with brightly colored bottles. A train of smiling hostesses in short skirts delivered even more expensive and brightly colored bottles crowned with bright sparklers to an especially large VIP table, one of the few things that was bright enough to see. At the heart of the club, bathed in strobing lights, a large mass of bodies pressed together, writhed, bent, and twisted on the dance floor, sensations running over, their disparate movements all timed to the afrobeat sounds played by a DJ on an elevated daïs near the bar.

There, in the club's loudest and busiest corner where everyone was hustling for the bartender's attention and everything was jouncing to the beat, Nneoma found the man they were looking for.

She could only see him from behind, but his blond head of short hair stood out in the sea of waist-length weaves, afros, braids, blowouts, buzzcuts, and shaved heads. Besides, her skin had started to tingle the moment she turned in his direction; the spirit particles that had once been held within her had sent a kind of vibration through her, as though they had sensed the proximity of their previous place, a kind of spirit compass. She thought it was almost funny how even now, after so many years, she was still connected to him—this man she both liked and despised at the same time. She nodded in the man's direction and twirled her index finger, giving Shigidi the signal they had agreed upon, and he responded in kind to acknowledge it. Shigidi made his move, circling around a cluster of low crowded tables to flank the man from the right. He positioned himself at the end of the bar, by a bright neon-green sign that indicated the way to the restrooms. It was a good vantage point. From there he could survey the entire club, especially the people jostling for drinks right in front of him, and he was within leaping distance to their target, if things went badly, although Nneoma had already assured him they wouldn't.

When she saw that Shigidi was firmly in place, Nneoma advanced toward the man they'd come for. He was talking to a young girl with glistening skin and short dreadlocks who wore a black mini skirt and white crop top. She had come to the bar to buy a drink but had apparently been distracted by the blond stranger who looked so out of place, and who, Nneoma could see, was offering to pay for her drink. Nneoma stood close to them, just a half step behind him, amusing herself with their clumsy, flirtatious conversation as they took turns shouting into each other's ears.

When a thick-necked and even more thickly bearded bartender placed two glasses in front of the couple, Nneoma saw her chance. In one smooth movement, perfectly timed, she stepped around and slid her hand into the space between the man and the girl, took one of their newly delivered glasses full of what looked like whiskey and downed it in one gulp.

"Hey!"

Surprised, they both turned to look at her and she stared right back at the young girl, eyes full of a fierce glare above a smiling mouth. She couldn't have been more than twenty. Maybe twenty-one. Nneoma snarled. The girl wilted, snatched the other drink, and squeezed her way away from them, scurrying back to her friends like a frightened animal.

Nneoma turned to the man she hadn't seen in seventy years, "Aleister Crowley, the Great Beast six six six. Or should I call you Alix Black now?"

"Nneoma?" he asked, eyes wide with shock.

"Live and in the flesh that you lust after so deeply." She brushed a strand of loose hair behind her ear. "How are you, Alix? That is the name you go by these days, isn't it? Alix?"

"Oh, wow it really is you." Aleister exclaimed.

"Yes, it is. So how are you, Alix?"

He blushed visibly. "You know you don't have to call me that, luv."

"Oh. Don't I? I saw you on the cover of *Teen Now* or *Seventeen* or some other children's magazine that kept fawning all over the sexy, brooding, lead singer of Britain's hottest up-and-coming rock band—what is it called? Equinox?" She threw her head back and laughed.

"Yes, Equinox. Right. Yeah. It's just a cover."

"Yes, I know but it's not a very good one. Couldn't you find something less cringey? And you know what else? I don't like your new name . . . Alix. It's a silly name. Now, Aleister, what's a nice young hundred-year-old white boy like you doing in an African den of sin like this?" She looked around the room. "Have you finally fully embraced the desires that you used to try so pitifully to hide from yourself and your racist friends, back in the day?"

He shook his head rapidly, immediately defensive. "That was a long time ago, luv. I'm a different man now. You helped see to that. The times have changed and so have I."

"I can see that."

"Besides it's been so long since I saw you, I thought I never would again. Figured something had happened to you."

Nneoma laughed. "Of course, you were always going to see me again." She placed the bright red nail of her index finger against his neck. "You still owe me a favor. I always pay my debts, and I always collect what's owed to me. You should know that by now."

Nneoma leaned in close to him, so that her breath flowed against his neck. His own breathing became rapid and heavy. She found that she was enjoying the effect she had on him. It had been a while since anyone besides Shigidi had desired her so intensely without her manipulating them.

She turned around quickly to catch a glimpse of Shigidi, watching from the end of the bar. His face was blank, but she could tell he was simmering. Jealous. She pushed his knees apart and pressed closer into Aleister. He shifted uncomfortably on the barstool.

"Have you enjoyed the gifts I gave to you?" She had lowered her voice but was so close to him that it still carried over the noise of the club. "Have the lives you gained from them been full of pleasure?"

"Yeah. Yes, they have," he replied, blinking rapidly as though he was trying to recall all that had happened since the last time he saw her, loading up memories like film. "The first got me all the way from the fifties to the nineties. Wild times, truly. Special. I kept wondering where you were. You probably enjoyed every minute of those years."

"I was in Lagos, mostly. San Francisco, occasionally. Cairo, once or twice," she said quickly. "And yes, I did. Enjoy it. Mostly, anyway."

"Now I'm on my second of the lives you gave me and it's all a bit of the same as before but more so. You know—new music. More sex. Different drugs. Wilder parties. New tech. Signs and wonders, babe. You know how it is. But none like the pleasure we shared that night in the desert. That first time." He looked into her eyes and she returned his gaze with a steel smile.

"You know, when it comes to you," he continued, "I have always wondered why. Why did you choose me that night and not Victor or some other random traveler? Why did you come back for me all those years later with the gifts? I've had a long time to think about it, a few lifetimes worth, but I've never really come to a conclusion." He paused and then he asked, "Am I special to you in some way? I mean, have any other men besides me been given these wonderful gifts?" His voice had thinned out into a rasp.

Nneoma's smile folded back into itself as she pursed her lips and leaned in even closer until they were nearly ear to ear. And then she said, "No. There have been no other men. Only gods."

She felt him tremble with a familiar excitement and then she pulled back like a whip and stared him in the eyes, "But don't get it twisted. That doesn't make you special to me darling. Just interesting. And potentially useful."

The blood drained from Aleister's face, and his shoulders sank. Nneoma knew then that she still held sway over him, completely and truly. She didn't even need to use her power to manipulate his desires anymore.

"Speaking of being useful, do you still have friends in Third Dawn?" she asked before he could recompose himself.

Aleister nodded in time with the music, indicating his agreement.

"Good, very good." She slid her long, delicate finger up Aleister's inner thigh, leaned in and whispered. "To be honest, over the years I had imagined so many things you could do for me to pay your debt, but I never expected that it would be what I am about to ask now."

"Ask. Anything. I'll do anything for you," he said.

He sounded so eager, Nneoma was not sure which he wanted more, to be with her again just to reexperience the heights of pleasure she had shown him or to see if she would eventually give him another stolen spirit to extend his life.

"Oh, I know you will," Nneoma said.

She took in a deep breath, enjoying the feeling of being so desperately desired, the sense of absolute power. The moment seemed to swell, making her feel light and weightless and liberated. There was something about it all converging—the music, the DJ, the crowd, the worshipful man before her—that magnified it, refracting the moment into a thousand small memories of other, older moments in the beginning just after the after The Fall, when it had just been her and her sister banding together in the embryonic new world, completely in control of their own lives, free to do as they wished, unbound to anything except the temporary arrangements they made with the people and gods and spirit entities they chose without fear or thought for any other. And they had been so similar, almost always wanting the same thing that there was hardly ever any disagreement between them. The world had been young then, when they'd been cast into it. Young and pliable. They were free to satisfy themselves whenever they wanted to. Nneoma had been free to take souls and spirits where and when she wanted. Free to do with them as she wished. Once, in the great rift valley, she'd even been worshipped as a kind of savage goddess. And later, as a twin goddess with her sister in Sumer. She'd been a poet's muse. She'd been consort to a queen. She'd been so much and more back when she was truly free. Long before the gods had resolved themselves into rigid spirit-companies and created rules to manage the new artificial borders. Long before men had learned to manipulate spirit particles and made themselves dangerous to her kind. Long before her sister had made the wrong choice and become lost. Long before she'd become afraid. Before she'd learned to negotiate her continued existence. She wasn't free to do as she pleased anymore, not really. Not without feeling like she was constantly in danger. She'd traded her independence and fear for partnership and security but sometimes, in moments like the one in which she found herself, when she was reminded of what it was like to be unbound, she wondered if the trade had been worth it.

She grasped Aleister's thin hand with a sudden motion and jerked him up to his feet.

"But before we get down to business, let's just . . . get down."

He stared at her quizzically.

"Dance with me, for old times' sake," she said, looking back over her shoulder at a stone-faced Shigidi before turning away to look ahead into the murky, strobed depths of the dance floor like it was an inviting womb.

"Just like our last night together, in Algiers," Aleister said, smiling faintly with what she recognized as a sliver of renewed hope.

"Yes. Sure," she said. "Just like Algiers."

Aleister fished out a twenty-pound note from his wallet and put it on the counter. He stood there for a moment, like he was going to wait for his change, but she wasn't patient. She put her arm into the crook of his elbow and pulled him away and through the mass of bodies, onto the dance floor. When they were near the center of the rhythmic chaos, she wrapped her arms around his neck and began to twist her hips to the tune of Mr Eazi's *Leg Over*, pulsing though the speakers. His breath shortened, and she felt him slowly become turgid as she rubbed her hips against his groin. When he put his hands around the curve of her waist and pulled her in closer, she didn't resist.

Nneoma emptied her mind and allowed herself to drift into a wheeling kaleidoscope of sweat, emotions, faces, perfumes, bodies, whispers, and desires, flowing in a current of the things she was so used to manipulating. There was no more thought of Olorun or Shango or Murugan or the British museum. There was only an intense sense of being. She felt Aleister's hands roving her waist and thighs, but she couldn't distinguish it from all the other sensations she was allowing to flow into her.

She didn't know how long she remained in that state, but in the space between instants, she momentarily emerged from the clouds her head floated over the sea of shoulders and her eyes made contact with Shigidi's from across the room. She gave him a smile and held his gaze, enjoying the flavor that his jealousy added to the taste of sensations.

It took almost a minute of watching but when Shigidi finally stood up, the taste of the anger in him threatened to overwhelm the emotional cocktail of the room. She could see the stress-induced bulge in his lower jaw and a paleness in his knuckles that made her think that anger could burst through his hands in wild streaks of lightning. But he remained calm as he closed his fists and walked steadily across the dance floor toward her without breaking eye contact, his impressive bulk pushing merrymakers to the side like he was a bulldozer.

When he reached them, Nneoma had a thin sheen of sweat on her forehead, a mischievous grin on her face. Aleister withdrew from her and stopped moving instantly, like he'd been frozen solid.

"Who are you?" Aleister asked, barely audible above the heartbeat of the club.

Shigidi ignored him and kept his eyes on Nneoma.

"We need to go," he insisted, his voice loud and firm. "You've found him, he's agreed, so enough of this."

"Enough of what?" Nneoma asked, raising an eyebrow as she allowed herself to regain control of the emotional space.

"Enough of what?" Aleister echoed, sounding confused and scared.

Shigidi turned to face Aleister who took a step back, bumping into a group of gyrating girls. They assaulted him with their eyes, stabbing at him with vicious looks, but turned away quickly before he could begin to apologize.

"Enough of this time-wasting. You agreed to what she asked, yes?" Aleister nodded.

"So, let's go. We don't have time. There is a job we need you to help us pull off," Shigidi said, before wrapping his arm firmly around Nneoma's waist and turning to pull her toward the door. She resisted him a bit, but not enough to make him believe she really wanted to.

Shigidi spoke over his shoulder, almost shouting to Aleister over the booming bass. "Follow us. Now. And from this moment on, if you ever touch her like that again, I'll crush you into fine powder and feed your secondhand spirit to those filthy pigeons in Trafalgar Square. You understand?"

For the second time that night, Nneoma watched Aleister nod in time with the music to agree to something, even though she was sure he had no idea what was happening. But she knew that he was smart enough to recognize a powerful independent spirit entity when he saw one, so she wasn't surprised he didn't argue. Still, she wanted to make a point, so she stopped moving and resisted Shigidi enough to force him to stop, too.

"I'll let whoever I want to touch me, Shigidi. That isn't up to you. Do you understand?"

Shigidi looked at her with fire in his eyes but calm in his voice. "Yes. I understand."

"Good. Let's go."

They continued, and Aleister followed.

They passed the table where the girl Aleister had tried to pick up earlier was sitting and laughing with her friends. Nneoma looked back and caught Aleister hiding his face from them. The girl's exposed thigh gleamed in the light and was reflected in a dozen surfaces around the room as she pointed at him and the gaggle of girls erupted into a giggle.

"Fuck," Aleister muttered under his breath as he awkwardly pressed down the tented front of his trousers.

Poor Aleister. His night had definitely not gone the way he'd hoped. Not even a little bit. Nneoma almost felt guilty. Almost.

They exited the club the way they had come, through the dark corridor and past the hostess in the spandex dress, brushing past a steady trickle of new patrons, glossy young people constantly talking to each other and laughing in excited hilarity.

Outside, when the cool wind returned and the noise receded, Aleister found his tongue again. "Nneoma, please tell me what's going on. What is this job?"

She slowly turned to face him but didn't answer his question, she just asked, "Where is your car?"

"Across the street," he said.

"Good. Take us to it. I'll tell you on the way."

"On the way where?"

"Third Dawn," she replied.

His face was suddenly suffused with a kind of dismayed confusion but Nneoma was sure the threatening look on Shigidi's face would be enough to convince Aleister not to ask any more questions for now.

"Fine," Aleister said.

They crossed the road and navigated their way along a stream of parked vehicles until they came to his car, a black SUV.

Aleister opened the driver side door, sat down and keyed the current address of the Anubis-Urania Temple of the Hermetic Order of the Third Dawn into the GPS system. Shigidi sat in the front passenger seat, visibly maximizing his already high level of discomfort while Nneoma slipped into the center of the backseat, smiling and enjoying her position as the object of shared, if unbalanced, desire of both man and god alike.

Aleister adjusted the rear-view mirror, and Nneoma caught the flash of confusion and expectation in his eyes.

"So," she began, as he started the engine and gently swung the car out onto the road, "Let me tell you what you need to know. This is my partner, Shigidi. He used to be a kind of nightmare god back in Nigeria, with the Orisha Spirit Company. We're freelance now. Contractors, if you like. And the job he was talking about is this: We need your help to get something for an elder god with whom, I guess you could say, we have become professionally entangled. And we need to get it tonight."

Aleister shook his head, "Get what? And what do you mean 'professionally entangled'?"

Nneoma sighed. "It's a long story."

CHAPTER 9

Parkview Estate, Ikoyi, Lagos, Nigeria

NOVEMBER 20TH, 2016 | 10:28 PM.

The champagne-colored, ombré sequin dress clung tightly to Nneoma's body and glimmered sharply under the bright bulbs of the chandelier, lending an almost spectral quality to her figure. It had been only a few weeks since they had first met and become partners, but thanks to a steady diet of spirits, she was almost back to her full health and strength, as she'd been when Shigidi first saw her on that hotel room bed: her skin supple and full, her hair lustrous, now styled in a cascade of dark curls, and her eyes full of orange fire. She always looked good whenever they went out but, *tonight*, Shigidi thought, when she finally emerged from the master bedroom, *Nneoma is truly dressed to kill.*

"You look amazing," he said.

"Thank you," Nneoma replied, smoothing her dress with her hands. The night was young, but the day had aged quickly.

They had spent much of it in bed, making love and talking. Mostly talking. The conversation was largely carried by Nneoma, naturally, because she had become his teacher of sorts, his guide in the ways of freelance spirit life. She'd kept reminding him that in their new partnership, she needed him to watch out for her, as she would for him and in order to do that effectively, he needed to learn quickly. He needed to learn how to be independent as a spirit entity and how to avoid the maze of rules and barriers and controls that the major multi-national spirit companies had put in place to manage their existences and prevent conflicts; rules that were designed to limit people like her. Like them. Rules designed to prevent things from returning to the way they used to be, in the beginning. Sometimes she told him stories of adventures she'd had and people she'd encountered, and those stories filled his already potent imagination, even though she never told him any stories about the true beginning—her beginning—before the event that she only ever referred to as The Fall. And although she mentioned her sister often and said that she was gone, Nneoma never told him any details and he never asked why. He let her tell him what she wanted, and he absorbed it all, as much as he could. She showed him things too. Mostly, how to manipulate his own spirit particles in multiple ways, to control his own body and use its inherently pliable nature to his advantage—a skill she was extremely adept at.

That evening, as the sun set behind the closed curtains, she'd showed him again how to loosen himself. The first time she'd tried to show him how it to do it was just after they'd made love in his new form, after her hands had examined every inch of his body. She'd told him to try to separate his spirit particles from the physical elements of the clay that bound his body together. She'd taken him through the steps she used to manipulate things, showing him how she'd first ignite a spark by willing her body to release pheromones, maximizing any latent sexual desires in the area, and then project that, gathering it and using it to direct the movement of her own spirit particles. She'd told him that in order to do it, since his own divine strengths lay in the illusory, not the sexual, he would need to use his imagination. He would need to visualize himself as he wanted to be, to believe that loosened version of himself into existence the same way he used to find and mold human fears and terrors into manifesting in his victims' minds. He'd nodded gently, accepting Nneoma's wisdom without question, but the first time he attempted to change his form his head felt like it would split in two. It felt unnatural, trying to manipulate his own body, trying to manipulate something that wasn't a dream. He had put his hand up in front of him as he lay on the bed staring through his fingers at the ceiling. He'd started with his fingers so he could see if it would work. That first time, his body had resisted the effort as he imagined the thick unfamiliar fingers of his new form expanding, spreading out. His head had begun to throb like his mind was a taut drumskin that someone was banging with a large stick every time he'd visualized the expansion. But he had pushed through the pain until he felt like his head would simply burst, and then he had to stop. He'd vomited then, rolling off to the side and falling off the bed onto the carpeted floor of the bedroom. Nneoma hadn't reacted much. She simply regarded him without judgment, the soft curls of her hair falling over her face as she leaned over the edge of the bed and told him to get up and try again.

"Everyone fails the first time," she said. And so, he did, still failing, but no longer throwing up or falling over. And he'd started to notice his body change in response to his efforts.

And as he tried again that evening under her instruction, he'd finally seen some results.

"It is like training a muscle," she explained to him. "The more you do it, the more your muscles develop and the less exertion it requires. So just keep trying."

"Hmm."

"You are made of divine spirit-clay. You know that already, and you know much of what it is capable of, and you know how to do this, you just need to break past the threshold, the belief barrier in your own mind," she'd told him, as she propped herself up on an elbow. "You will get there."

Shigidi had repeated the sequence of actions as before: lay back, raise hand, focus on fingers, but this time, he'd closed his eyes to prevent the visual stimulation of reality from interfering with his internal vision. He'd pictured his fingers loosening and spreading out from his fist like snails. He'd drifted into something like sleep, but not quite. It had been a heightened state of awareness. There he felt the flowering within him of a potential for expansion, for reshaping, for reforming, for all the things Nneoma had told him he could do and so much . . . more. And there was no pain. No headaches or nausea. He'd continued, imagining his fingers spreading out like thick, wet ropes, reaching up toward the ceiling. He'd pressed on, imagining heavily and intentionally, until he felt like the image in his mind had taken form, had developed physical weight like something from one of his constructed nightmares.

When he'd opened his eyes, he saw it. His fingers had extruded.

He turned his hand from side to side, staring at the appendage like it didn't belong to him. The skin was drawn tight, and the flesh was thin. A cluster of bright green spirit particles hovered around it at a short distance. Something twisted in the pit of his stomach: excitement and fear. This was no dream; he could reshape himself. He didn't stop. He pressed on, his mind swelling with imagination as he pictured more of his hand loosening, expanding. It got easier and easier, just as she'd said it would, his imagination pressing his body out farther and farther. He hadn't even noticed that saliva was collecting in the corners of his mouth as he continued to loosen himself, changing the form of his physical body through the power of his imagination. It had been exhilarating.

"That's enough expanding," she'd said quietly, pulling his attention back. "Don't overdo it. You need to collect yourself again."

He'd closed his eyes again then, clearing it of all thought, all imagination. He contracted.

"Good." Nneoma had said. "Very good."

He'd opened his eyes again and his hand was back to its usual form, stable and solid. He'd still felt the residual high of the experience, like all the nerve endings in his body had been overstimulated and were still excited with sensation. He'd sat up and kissed her and they'd made love again.

When they were spent, they lay in bed quietly. They hadn't noticed it when the curtain of night started to fall. It was only a sense of *need*, like a bone-deep hunger, and a realization of the late hour that finally made them move and begin to plan the evenings activities. They were eager to find a spirit to consume before the dawn brought the wild Lagos city nighttime revelers, so desperate to destress, back to their cautious senses.

Shigidi was glad to be free of schedules and work hours and targets and the demands of the higher ranked orisha in his former company, but he had learned from Nneoma that independence required its own flavor of self-awareness and responsibility. Like knowing that they still needed to collect enough spirits to heal Nneoma back to her full strength and keep themselves satiated without drawing the attention of the operating spirit company. Rich, fun-seeking Lagosians were good, generally godless prey.

Finally, they were both dressed up and ready for the night's hunt.

Shigidi took her hand and they hurried down the winding stairs of the stately Ikoyi town house they had *inherited* from their last victims three weeks ago. They got into a waiting Range Rover in the driveway, one of three cars that had come with the house. Shigidi started the vehicle and eased it out of the compound through the automated gate, tires crunching loose gravel. Before long, the house was a speck in the mirror, too small to distinguish from the dozens of other houses that lined the street like cloned soldiers.

Cool wind blew in through the partially open windows as they drove down the uncharacteristically traffic-free Gerrard Road, navigating around potholes. Shigidi looked up through the window to see a bright beaming full moon hanging above a patchwork of thick silver-edged clouds, like a blanket. There were no stars.

"Olorun is playing games again tonight," he said out of habit, his lips barely parting.

Nneoma turned to him, with a look of confusion on her face. Her eyes shifted around sharply but only briefly. Then she seemed to understand, and she relaxed.

"This isn't spirit space, darling. There, the orishas may have their games, but here, we have ours," she replied with a smile.

"Yes, but their actions are reflected here," he said.

"True," she conceded.

"I wonder what spirit sky looks like now."

She squeezed his left hand which sat atop the gearstick. "Forget about your previous life, Shigidi."

"I know. I just need time," he said. "It was all I knew before you."

She kissed his cheek and turned away, eyes searching the road ahead.

He pushed a button in the armrest and fully let down the open window of the sleek, black vehicle, savoring the titillating scent of the city. Smoke and dried fish and kerosene and ripe fruit mingled with the sweat of the ubiquitous hawkers, many of whom were still out, late as it was. Lagos was an olfactory mélange. Shigidi only now realized he had never before truly smelled the city he had frequented so much, back when he still had his poorly formed, small, squat body. With his new, carefully sculpted shell, he saw and smelled and felt so much more. It was intoxicating. Despite the occasional hankering and stray memory of good things from the time gone by in the spirit company, he knew he would never trade this new life with Nneoma for his old one. Ever.

"You look so handsome," Nneoma said, her eyes still on the road and her voice thick with a rasp.

"Thank you," he replied, wondering why the compliment had come so long after his.

He was wearing a grey suit, purple shirt and matching pocket square—an outfit she had chosen for him. He glanced at his own reflection in the rearview mirror as if to verify what she had said. The image staring back at him was truly handsome, like a work of art. His clean-shaven head gleamed whenever the bright beams of oncoming headlights hit it. He was still almost unrecognizable to himself, sometimes feeling like he was piloting someone else's body. She had molded his clumsy clay body into something exquisite. He wondered if her praise was more for her handiwork than for his benefit. Or if it was just a diversion to distract him from thoughts of Olorun, and the sky, and the past.

He drove past a trio of rat-eyed and potbellied policemen at a broken checkpoint shed painted white and red with the colors of the bank that had sponsored their presence. Then he slid the vehicle onto Falomo Bridge. All along the raised concrete curb, a stream of pedestrians and hawkers milled about.

"Look at them," she said, placing a hand on his shoulder. "All these people, standing, selling, walking, all of them looking without seeing anything. At the mercy of the elements and the gods and whims of other, more powerful people like them. They will never know what it is like to be . . ." she hesitated, "to be free . . . free to do as you please, to prowl for faith and spirit sustenance when you need it. To answer to no one but yourself and the partners you've chosen. To not be tied down. It's wonderful, isn't it?"

He said, "Yes, it is." Mostly because that was what he was supposed to say, but also because he thought it was mostly true.

He was about to complicate his answer with a question when, just as the traffic forced them to slow, a skinny young boy in tattered clothes pressed himself into the side of their car and started trying to clean the windscreen with an ugly makeshift squeegee that was nothing more than a cut-up piece of old mattress foam and a broken mop handle.

"Hey!" Shigidi shouted at him through the open window before dismissing him with a short but violent wave of his hand.

The boy wiped the smear of soapy water he had applied and started to turn away when Nneoma stretched out her hand to offer him a crisp new hundred naira note.

The boy sprinted around to her side, took the money, and thanked her effusively before disappearing through the tight spaces between the crawling vehicles, back to the sea of roadside bodies.

"Why did you do that?" Shigidi asked.

Unexpectedly she responded to his question with a question of her own, "Were you ever human, Shigidi? Even temporarily?"

Nneoma's eyes were still firmly on the road ahead. She seemed to be in a strange mood.

"No. Never," he replied.

He had friends that had once been human. Kings like Obalufon. But Shigidi was molded right from spirit clay and given life by Olorun himself. Some spirit entities were allowed short-term assignments in human bodies, but these were restricted to high-value performers in the spirit company—the real faith-makers and spirit reapers and those minor deities who kissed Shango's ass. He considered telling her that such assignments were tightly restricted because the spirit company was desperately worried that one of them would impregnate a human woman and create an abiku. And abiku were hard to control.

"I see," Nneoma said.

"Were you?"

"No. But when I was first cast out, after The Fall, I lost my memory for a while. I thought I was one of them. Human. It was my sister who found me and reminded me of who I was." She sighed her way through a pause. "In some way, I think . . . I pity them. Without them we wouldn't exist, and yet . . ." She went quiet.

Confused, Shigidi said nothing.

A few silent minutes later, they reached their destination.

Oriental Crowne Hotel, Lekki—Epe Express Way, Lagos, Nigeria

The massive metal gate remained shut as though regarding them with suspicion. They waited while one of the thin and balding guards on duty inspected the trunk of the car, ran an inspection mirror under their vehicle, and took the number of their license plates. When he was done, he signaled to his colleague on the other side of the gate to pull its maw open. Shigidi slowly slid the car through and drove to the right as indicated by the frantic waving of another skinny and much more animated guard with considerably more hair. Shigidi parked the car in a convenient and compact space, a few meters from the front of the main foyer.

"Let's get some food," Nneoma said as she put her hand into the crook of his arm.

Determined to make the most of the night, they walked up the stairs and into the building briskly, to the clicking metronome of Nneoma's heels on the marble floor. The hotel lobby was a well-furnished and well-decorated womb of conditioned air and artificial light. An array of bulbs beamed down white and yellow and orange light that bounced off the reflective floors and pillars and walls, giving the entire space an ethereal glow. On the far wall ahead of the entrance stood a framed explosion of colors, the images it depicted all bounded by a spinous network of thick black ink that made the entire piece look like a divine coloring book. "Dreamscape." It looked like a kind of mind map, with a shape like a vulva at the center, a woman's figure below, and a face and hands above, all connected to depictions and images representing an assortment of things and ideas—dense iconography from religion, politics, technology, sexuality, history, music, biology, and so much more, all connected and layered and almost overwhelming. It was art, early afromysterics style. According to the manager—a smooth talking Lebanese man with slick black hair who spoke fluent pidgin, it was the largest free-hanging, oil-on-canvas painting in public display in Lagos. Shigidi knew Nneoma would want some time with it again. It was one of her favorite things in the city and admiring it had become a sort of pre-feeding ritual for her whenever they came to the Oriental. She always took her time with it, studying the intricate pattern of networked lines that connected the disparate images. They ambled up to it until they were within touching distance. Nneoma rested her head on Shigidi's shoulder. They lingered.

"Magnificent, isn't it?"

The voice came from behind them. It was gentle and melodious, like the music that came from the slow dance of fingers on a finely tuned goje. They turned around slowly to face its owner—a tall, shapely woman in a royal blue bodycon dress. She had coffee-and-cream-colored skin that was too even and smooth to have been bleached that way; and thick, dark, braided hair. Her green eyes caught the lights frequently, revealing a different color each time as though it were a trick being performed by both her body and the building. She wore the kind of smile that was reserved for women that often went by *big madam*. The kind of smile that, when coupled with the right quantity of naira notes, could make anything happen in Lagos. Shigidi thought the whole woman an improbable mosaic. She was too beautiful, her voice too euphonic, her manner too forward. A mami-wata working independently? A human with a particularly powerful protective spirit? Or just a woman whom wealth and circumstance had given an appearance of the near-divine? A tingle ran through his spine, and he instantly grew suspicious. But not suspicious enough to be uninterested.

"It is a Sebanjo." The woman said to them, still smiling her Lagos lubricant smile.

"Yes, the manager told me that it cost them a fortune," Nneoma said to the woman, smiling too. "A million dollars he said. I know he is lying but it doesn't matter, it is still a pleasure to see such a beautiful thing in such an ugly place."

Nneoma spoke with the kind of warmth typically reserved for old friends even though Shigidi was sure she had never met this woman before. He had seen her use the same *old-friend* tone on other people who soon became lovers or prey. She had used it on him too. At first. Nneoma could be consumingly charming. It was part of her work philosophy, as she liked to remind him, and she seemed to instantly like the improbable woman, perhaps because of her confidence.

So will she be lover or prey or both?

"Yes, a pleasure indeed." The woman said, extending her hand to Nneoma. "My name is Omolara and this is my husband, Rotimi."

The man she gestured to with a tilt of her head, was about seven strides away, looking at another less-impressive painting. He was dressed as glamorously as his wife, in an embroidered white kaftan and matching trousers, but lacked the same brilliance in his eyes or confidence in his smile. The kind of man Lagos would eat alive if he stumbled into the wrong corner of the city. He turned to address the group and raised his hands, mildly amused by the interaction his wife had orchestrated. He came up to them, kissed Nneoma's hand and shook Shigidi's as Nneoma introduced herself to them.

"Nneoma," the woman echoed. "I've always thought that was a beautiful name. Did you mean what you said? You really think this hotel is an ugly place?"

"No, not the hotel," Nneoma corrected. "The hotel is nice enough. I meant Lagos. Lagos is an ugly city."

"Ah, so you are not from here. I should have known. And not because of your name. I don't like to guess these things based on tribal names, since you know Lagos belongs to all of us now, but from your attitude, you don't seem like a Lagosian."

"Well, no, I'm not from Lagos," Nneoma said. "But I like it here. I always have. Even before it became this bustling messy metropolis. I like its ugliness. It's a real kind of ugliness that I appreciate. Besides, it's always in the ugly and in-between places that you find the most pleasurable things." She flashed Omolara a smile like a knife's edge.

"I can't disagree with that," Omolara replied, drawing nearer to them. "Nneoma, can my husband and I buy you and your—" She paused, waiting for Nneoma to introduce Shigidi since he had chosen to remain silent throughout their exchange.

"Partner." Nneoma obliged.

The woman and Shigidi regarded each other briefly.

"Yes, of course, your partner. Can we buy you and your partner a drink?"

Nneoma nodded at Shigidi and, before replying, twirled her index finger, the signal that marked them as their first targets for the night. "Only if you join us upstairs at the bar," she said. "I hear there is an excellent live band playing Fela classics tonight."

Prey it is then.

"Of course," Omolara agreed, and the curve of her smile compressed into a ringed pout. The light caught her eyes and flashed hazel. She was making it clear that she knew Nneoma was flirting with her and that she welcomed it.

They walked to the elevator at the end of the lobby hall briskly—a powerful quartet of beauty, flamboyance and sensuality drawing stares from passing staff and patrons like a four-sided magnet.

Once they were in the claustrophobic embrace of the elevator, Omolara, without warning, turned to Nneoma and pulled her in for a kiss. It was a hasty thing. There was no artifice to it, just raw, frenzied need. Nneoma kissed her back fervently and they clung together like a compound name.

Her husband, Rotimi, pressed himself against Nneoma from behind and started to kiss her neck. She threw her head back, surfacing from Omolara's lips and laughed, enjoying their attentions. She turned and flashed Shigidi a look of disapproval which slowly morphed into invitation. She reached out, holding his lower jaw between her and thumb and index finger, and she shook his head like she was trying to loosen him up and get him to join in. But he was still uncomfortable with his new body and with the blatant and sometimes unexpected eruptions of desire that Nneoma seemed to be able to elicit from humans like these. There was also an architecture of *wrongness* to the situation which he could sense, that kept him at bay. But at the insistence of her eyes, he finally relented and joined the three bodies with a small step forward, slipping a hand between Nneoma and Omolara to cup a full breast. The overabundance of heat and lust in that small space threatened to overwhelm him. Shigidi could tell that Nneoma was not manipulating the emotional energy around them because she had taught him how to recognize the faint yellow-and-orange aura of her influences as well as the feeling of vibration in the air that followed whenever she exerted her power. Shigidi was no longer sure if they were the seducers or the seduced, but once his hand contacted Omolara's flesh, he could not bring himself to pull away. Not with Nneoma's encouraging hand on his, egging him on, obviously eager to claim the two lusty, beautiful spirits that had come to them so willingly.

The four of them never reached the bar. They arrived instead on the ninth floor where Omolara and Rotimi had booked a penthouse suite. A fluid mass of heavy breaths, roving limbs and wet kisses, they spilled out of the elevator and flowed into the expansive luxury suite.

They all fell into the bed like it was an ocean, and Shigidi watched as Nneoma yielded herself to Omolara and Rotimi's hands. There was a learned aspect to their manipulations, especially Omolara's. Hands that seemed just as fluent in the language of pleasure as Nneoma's. Omolara buried her face in Nneoma's bosom and Rotimi undressed, rolled off onto the other side of the bed, lifted Nneoma's dress until it bunched up around her waist, and eased himself into her with one smooth and deliberate thrust. She gasped.

Shigidi let his mind drift as her moans and pleasure intensified, hypnotically drawing him deeper into the tangle of flesh, into that mire of mad desire. He threw off his suit jacket and slid forward on the bed. Omolara reached for him, cupping his face, and expertly guiding it to her mouth for a kiss as steady and intense as the nighttime crashing of waves along Bar beach. Shigidi was suddenly thrown into a haze of his own pleasure. His eyes rolled back behind shut eyelids as he let himself relax and allowed Omolara's mouth to work its magic, reminding him of the night he had first met Nneoma.

The kiss held.

It held for so long, he began to feel like he was drowning.

And then, as in a nightmare, he realized he was.

He could not breathe, the clay of his lungs felt swollen and thick, like there was an invisible hand inside his throat, squeezing his windpipe. He began to struggle, pushing against her and kicking out as he tried to wrestle his mouth away from Omolara's but he could not. Increasingly desperate, he threw a panicked punch right into her abdomen. She detached from him with a muted whimper, rolled backwards off the bed and onto her feet, snarling. The sense of discomfort and wrongness that he had felt since he first laid eyes on her magnified tenfold, as he realized that something had gone very wrong with the night's business. He scrambled backwards on his hands and butt until he was off the bed; eyes still trained on Omolara.

Shit. Shit. Shit.

This was what they used to call—back when he was in the spirit company—an "unforeseen process deviation."

Nneoma had jerked her head up, at the sound of the scuffle, eyes widened and cleared of all passions. When she saw Shigidi and Omolara roll off on opposite sides of the bed, she grabbed the headboard and tried to pull herself out from under Rotimi, enscaling her skin as she did. But her body barely budged. Shigidi saw her struggling and failing to get out from underneath Rotimi. She let her wings loose, ripping the sheets and bedding beneath her as well as what was left of her dress as she tried to rise into the air, but she was unable to elevate herself more than half a foot, unable to detach herself from the slumped bulk of Rotimi who had stopped thrusting and now lay atop her, still as a statue, his tongue lolling from the side of his head like a dead lizard.

Realization hit Shigidi like a bucket of cold water to his face. It had to be magun. One of the oldest and most powerful categories of juju. Special binding magick which was effective against humans, gods, and spirits alike. It was most often invoked to bind the bodies of cheating spouses to their adulterous partners but its core function, an ability to entangle fundamental physical and spirit particles to each other, was one that had been taken advantage of by the orishas and babalawos alike for centuries. He could not believe they had fallen for it.

Magun. Fucking magun.

"Nneoma," Shigidi shouted to his pinned-down partner without taking his eyes off Omolara. "Listen to me, you've been locked to that . . ." he glanced at the hardened, still figure on top of her, ". . . thing."

Nneoma's throat strained, and her mouth opened like she was trying to scream, but her voice trailed off into silence. She kept trying and even though her mouth was still moving, lips trembling as they resisted the force that was rigidifying her from within, no sound came. The magun had not only fixed her to the creature, it was locking down her entire body. Even her wings barely moved anymore, and she slowly settled into bottom position, sinking back into the softness of the bed. Shigidi knew that she would not be able to move or talk to use her powers or do anything until he broke the magun and separated her from Rotimi. He tensed as he tried to think of his next move.

Omolara kept her red eyes locked on him. She started to expand like she was being inflated or pumped full of some kind of thick fluid. Her creamy skin started to desiccate and flake away.

"Shigidi," Omolara started, glaring at him. The gentleness of her voice, like her skin, was melting away and now hit him like the roar of flooding rivers. "What made you think you could just break your contract and run away with this demon whore?" Her raging river voice carried an undercurrent of scorn.

She had almost completely shed her skin, and beneath it he could see she was not at all the Omolara woman she had claimed to be, if such a person ever existed. The figure molting out from the false shell was corpulent, grounded by a round, heavy belly that tumbled down to her thick, dimpled thighs. Thighs that sank into the ground like banana tree stalks. Grand rolls of fat hung loosely from her back and sides and arms like fleshy drapes. Her ears had been cut off, leaving jagged, scarred edges and her hair was woven into tight corn rows that ran parallel to each other, meeting at the center of her head from which rose a solid spike of plaited hair that rose high above her like a failed attempt to stab the ceiling. It was Oba, first wife of Shango, and head of spirit-resources at the spirit company he had called home for so long.

Beads of sweat seeped out of the pores of his face and forehead, bringing with them cold realization.

His former employers had come for him.

They had tricked them with an elaborate disguise juju and a golem-like puppet, which Shigidi suspected was made from the same clay as he was but only animated temporarily and by a less potent force. The magun had probably been kneaded directly into the clay, embedded deeply in the elementary spirit particles of what had become Rotimi and concealed with the same juju that Oba had used to present herself to them. Shigidi was surprised that neither he nor Nneoma had perceived it. Every manipulation of spirit particles leaves a faint trace of its influence, and he should have at the very least been able to sense the imprint of magun on the Rotimi-thing, and the cloak of concealment on the Omolara disguise, like a whiff of perfume riding the sea breeze. No one can touch or make a thing without leaving a fingerprint; this is true even of spirits. But they had missed it. It had to be cutting-edge juju, something unfamiliar. He had sensed something unusual about Omolara and Rotimi from the moment they had met but his discomfort had not been enough, and Nneoma was still in a diminished state so they had ended up in a precarious position, their undoing at hand. Still, he had tasted exquisite freedom and desire and pleasure and beauty, all the things that had been denied him for so long. Shigidi was not about to give them up without a fight.

"You weren't treating me very well," he said, shifting his feet to blade his body toward Oba, his left foot sliding forward into a stable stance. "So, I found an alternative way to make a living, to survive."

"With this foreign demon?" Oba snapped. "Business is bad for everyone. You got a fair share."

Shigidi shook his head and forced out a laugh, using the opportunity to take a sweeping look around the room and through the sliding glass panels that opened to the balcony below, where the filthy water of the Lagos lagoon lay like a lovely, lazy child, undulating softly. He didn't see anything, but he had a growing feeling that there were more of them nearby. Waiting, watching. Protecting Oba. Shango would never send his wife without backup, especially after anything that was not human.

"Fair?" Shigidi asked, reflecting her scorn. "We must have very different definitions of fair if you think it was fair for your husband to take more than half of all the spirits and faith we brought in for himself."

"It is company policy."

"Of course, you'd say that. Monkey dey work, baboon dey chop. And who made that policy again? You and your husband *abi*? You can't possibly think we were okay with that."

Oba shook her head. "You can't question Shango. You should have known there would be consequences for your actions."

"So, what are you going to do?" Shigidi asked, jutting out his jaw. "Force me to come back to work for you or what?"

Oba, naked and unashamed, simply smiled. "No, we are going to kill you."

A rope woven of wind wrapped itself around Shigidi's left ankle at the speed of a malicious thought. Before he could even look down to see it, he was dragged to the ground and pulled toward the balcony. He swept past Oba's feet in a flash, his hands flailing and clawing at air, her laughter ringing in his ears. The glass panel of the sliding door and the steel frame of the balcony exploded with a crash when he hit them on his way out of the room. Everything was a blur. When he finally stopped moving, he was face down and staring into the dark surface of a body of water, shimmering waveforms shimmering like ghosts where they caught the moonlight as they flitted on its surface. He was hovering over the Lagos lagoon, buffeted on an invisible, flowing barrier, like a cushion of wind.

He tried to calm down and slow his breathing as he struggled to his feet, balancing awkwardly on the invisible wind-floor. Standing, he scanned around and saw Oya—the orisha of winds and storms, his former direct supervisor and sister-wife to the corpulent and deceitful Oba. She stood suspended in the air across from him, a few meters away. She had a plain, powder blue wrapper wound tightly around her body, tied off just above her breasts and red beads on her hands, neck and ankles. With the new body Nneoma had given Shigidi, he knew he could have taken her out with one clean strike, if only he could manage to close the distance between them enough to land it.

Oya gestured with her hands and the carpet of wind beneath him spread out and folded up. It formed an invisible box of dynamic air and spirit particles, trapping Shigidi. He threw himself at the barrier, shoulder first, but it didn't work. He only bounced back, falling to his knees as he struggled for balance. The box of wind around him warped and reshaped its surface, extruding out an array of barely visible fists and palms and oddly shaped appendages that came at him from everywhere. Punching, slapping, hitting.

Shigidi was buffeted on all sides. He blocked Oya's ferocious assault with his forearms, using all the speed and grace his new body afforded him until suddenly, mid-motion, he felt a flare of pain, sharp and hot, unlike anything he had ever felt before. He screamed. Oba's laughter coming all the way from the balcony of the room pierced through the wall of wind and the fog of pain as he looked down to see a vicious arrowhead crackling with bright cerise spirit particles sprouting from his abdomen. A bloodstain began to blossom across his shirt like an evil flower. And then he saw another evil flower appear. And another.

Fuck.

There was no more pain, or less, with each flower of blood that bloomed on his torso. He had reached his threshold after the second hit. There was only surprise. Surprise because he recognized the precise cut of the hard-edged arrowheads, the signature color of the malicious juju that had guided them along their paths to him, the careful craftsmanship of their wooden shafts. He turned around to see the

Ososhi, hunter-orisha he had once called his friend, dressed in his sleeveless black war-attire, festooned with red and white ivory and wood-carved charms, his bow lowered. He was naturally tall and thin, but with his back bent and his face gaunt, as he stood beside the cackling Oba, he seemed even thinner than the last time they had been drinking together. Ososhi looked away when Shigidi made eye contact with him.

Ah!

I cannot believe this bastard ever shared palm wine with me.

Fucking spineless. . .

Another fist of wind smashed into Shigidi's head, spinning his jaw before he could complete the thought. His vision smeared. He closed his eyes, but flickering flowers of light appeared beneath his eyelids, dancing. A woolen echo filled his head, silencing much of the world and he fell face-first onto the carpet of wind beneath him.

Lying there with three arrows in his chest, every nerve of his body conducting its own unique orchestra of agony, he drifted into something like a dream as time itself seemed to disappear. Barely holding on, he searched his mind for something that his consciousness could hold on to.

Nneoma.

I must help Nneoma.

We are supposed to watch out for each other.

He ruminated on the things she had taught him, things he had only recently come to understand. One of the first was that working for yourself, you needed to know your strengths and weaknesses. So, they had made a list together, highlighting their unique divinities, and she had made notes for him, helping him understand himself better, bringing him to new realizations even as she taught him new skills. Now, engulfed by pain, he searched and screened and indexed and collected and organized the relevant realizations in his mind and repeated them to himself.

I am made of spirit-clay and animated by Olorun's breath.

Spirit-clay is a fine-grained material that allows spirit-particles to bind with metal oxides and organic matter.

I have dominion over the subconscious, the imaginary, the formless.

All clays, on every side of reality, are plastic due to their water content and can become hard and brittle when dry.

I can manipulate fear, even my own.

Spirit-clay, like all other clays has remarkable absorption capacity.

Clay. Plastic. Absorption. He repeated the words in his mind like a mantra until they were crystalized. He reached deeper into his own mind, probing at the threads of his fear—fear of pain, fear of death, fear of losing what Nneoma had given him. He seized each one when he found it and began to rearrange his fear into something new. He reimagined himself as strong, bold, standing tall, immune to pain, and he remolded his fear until it matched that vision in his mind. When the structure of his new mental state felt solid, he opened his eyes, and felt a rush of cold, clear constructed confidence. In a sudden surge, sound returned to the world. He knew exactly what he was capable of enduring. And he knew what he needed to do.

I need to free Nneoma.

And that meant he either needed to destroy the wielder of the magun or the puppet through which it had been applied.

Battered and wounded, Shigidi rose again. First to a single knee and then back up to his feet, arms spread out for stability on the carpet of wind. He tensed his body and, using the trick Nneoma had taught him, he imagined himself rock solid, the spirit particles extracting the water from his body and turning his malleable clay flesh hard as stone. He punched a hole in Oya's wall of wind, creating a vortex that spun out toward the hotel balcony. Ososhi's eyes widened, and Oba stopped laughing. A trio of arrows came in quick succession, whizzing past his head and shoulders. Shigidi slipped, ducked, and then used the spring from the motion to launch himself through the hole in the wind-box before it could close, sailing through the air gracefully, like a gazelle, tattered shirt, arrows, blood, and all. Ososhi and Oba retreated clumsily, staggering backward into the room. Shigidi landed on his feet in front of them, hitting the balcony with a force that sent a spiderweb of cracks through the floor.

Back in the room with Nneoma still pinned to the bed, Shigidi took Oba by the throat and squeezed desperately, the blood vessels on his arms bulging, the now-solid muscles straining. He was unwilling to yield even as Ososhi recomposed himself and stabbed at Shigidi's sweaty and bloody back with an arrow. It broke on impact. Shigidi's will, like his body, was rock. Oya followed him into the room, seized his feet with a tempest of ropes and even threw a whirlwind noose around his neck but he had hardened himself, completely prepared for it all and against the multitude of powers, he did not yield. Oba's eyes bulged in her head as he squeezed tighter. The whites of the naked river goddess's eyes began to turn red as they filled with the blood from burst vessels and the horrible realization that she was going to die.

Suddenly, there was an incredibly loud sound as a bolt of lightning broader than a man pounded into Shigidi. He collapsed onto the floor and rolled away, his body spasming as Shango materialized before them, encased in a column of white-hot light.

The orisha of thunder, and CEO of the spirit company was drawn to full height and brimming with rage.

Shango was wearing a brown agbada, made of aso-oke with vermillion flame and azure lightning embroidered onto it. The stitching danced electric. His fila drooped lazily to one side. He held a broad machete with a translucent blade, its hilt carved to resemble a tiger, and his eyes burned as white as the light around him. Of course, he was upset at the way this whole business had turned out. Especially the attempted murder of his first wife.

"Shigidi!" Shango bellowed, as Oba coughed and gasped for breath, kneeling on the floor behind him. "What is the meaning of this madness?"

"Madness?" Shigidi pointed an accusing finger out at his former boss as he rose to his feet hastily and scrambled to the edge of the bed where Nneoma lay, eyes straining, still locked in her own body. Shigidi's heart threatened to burst out of his chest, but he had already started to reweave the new fear that had manifested in his mind. His thoughts were racing almost as rapidly as his heart was beating but even in the chaos and in the process of weaving, an idea was starting to coalesce in his mind. "Is it madness because I didn't just lie down and allow your deceitful wives and their traitorous lackey to kill me? Or is it madness because I took an opportunity for a better life? Tell me, which one is the madness?"

The aura around Shango surged in intensity. "Look at this small god of yesterday talking to me like I am his agemate. Madness. Insolence. What happened to you, Shigidi?"

"Abeg! You think say I be mumu?" Shigidi shouted back, fear and excitement causing his Yoruba to momentarily slip into pidgin English, a potent tongue for protest, "Nothing has happened to me. I am just no longer the stupid minor orisha you used to take advantage of. I have become my true self. I have become what I always had the potential to be. You took advantage of my ugliness, but I am now beautiful. You made me think I was weak, but I have now learned my own strengths. You treated me like I was stupid, but I know so much more now. You treated me like a slave in the company, working for a pittance, now I feed on spirits for myself and to my own satisfaction. The real madness was when I still worked for you. My head is now correct."

"You tried to kill my wife," Shango bellowed, billowing the sheets on the bed with his rage. He swung the machete in his hand backwards and forwards like a deadly pendulum. As an idea took shape in his thoughts, Shigidi followed the motion, watching the anger build up in the thunder god's expansive frame. That anger could be just what he needed to free Nneoma.

"Ehn. I am sure it doesn't matter that she tried to kill me first. I was defending myself. And if I had the chance, I would do it again."

The swinging motion stopped as Shango's grip on the machete tightened. "Okay. All right. I can see that you have lost your mind. I will relieve you of your head. But first I will show you suffering unlike any that has ever existed."

"Well," Shigidi glanced down at Nneoma who was still prone on the bed, and twirled his index finger, hoping that their signal would let her know he had a plan. He lifted his eyes back up to Shango. "Do your worst. Just don't expect me to take it without a fight."

The angle seems about right.

"Ah. Look at this fool. You overestimate your new self, Shigidi. But this nonsense, it ends now."

Shigidi forced out another laugh as he hastily wove the terror that was coursing through him around his vision of success, of winning. He said, "Look, oga, all this is fucking talk. Talk. Talk. Talk. Too much talk. If you want to kill me then stop talking and do it. Come and kill me."

Oba, Ososhi and Oya gasped from behind Shango whose eyes had fully rounded into saucers. Shigidi knew that Shango had probably never been spoken to that way before, by anyone or anything in all of creation, and it was driving him visibly mad. Which is exactly what Shigidi wanted him to be for this to work. Angry. Careless.

"If you can," Shigidi added, the challenge issued with scorn.

Shango let out a wild bellow and hoisted the machete high above his head, his power instantly turning the blade to an intense, blinding white. He swung the machete down in one clean motion. Shigidi kicked the foot of the bed so that it spun at a right angle and pulled the sheets so that Nneoma and Rotimi rolled onto their sides, just as he completely relaxed his clay flesh, loosening himself and sinking down to the hotel room carpet like a puddle of thick mud. Shango's machete cut through the empty space where he had been. Momentum carried it down until it hacked cleanly into the side of the body that had been Rotimi. The solid faux-human frame split in two and became a deflated contortion, its entrails spilling onto the bed and the floor in a mangled mess of severed flesh, tubes and clear fluid.

Finally free, Nneoma leapt up from the bed and took to the air, ready to join the fight.

"No!" Oba cried out as Shigidi reconstituted himself, just in time to evade another one of Shango's vicious downward strikes with the retrieved machete.

There was an explosion of wood, fabric, and concrete beside Shigidi as the machete crashed into the ground beside him like a bomb had gone off. His ears rang and his heart thumped as he danced away from another sweeping slice, amazed by the width of the white trail the blade left in its wake.

He caught a glimpse of Oba, Oya and Ososhi forming a line behind Shango, as they watched the fight play out, apparently too afraid to be hit by an errant strike or too unwilling to do anything unless they were explicitly told to, not even help their lord and master.

Which works just fine for us.

Two on one is better than two on four.

Nneoma let out a feral scream and scudded down from behind Shigidi with her wings spread and her claws extended. She tackled Shango, grabbing onto his hand and using it for leverage to launch a kick into his chest. He barely budged. But she managed to knock the machete out of his right hand. It fell to the floor with a clang, throwing wild streaks of electric discharge into the air and burning a hole through the carpet and the wood and the concrete, filling the room with the smell of ionized oxygen and acrid smoke. Shango swung the hand Nneoma had latched onto in a wide arc, tossing her away as though she weighed no more than a butterfly. She crashed into the door headfirst and slumped, stunned.

"Hey!" Shigidi shouted.

The thunder orisha raised his head and his eyes met Shigidi's briefly. Shigidi stiffened, momentarily losing control of the fear in his mind, its threads loose and flailing. Shango smiled, his brown teeth like stones. Shigidi knew then, in that moment of mental clumsiness, that Shango had seen past his bravado and apparent fearlessness. Had seen what he was most afraid of. A cold, horrific realization settled over him.

Nneoma!

Shango leapt across the room, sailing over the bed with the grace his size should not have permitted, his hand full of a bright and crackling azure energy.

For the second time that night, time seemed to slow for Shigidi. An exotic flood of emotions surged through him, a cocktail of the panicky urge to flee what he knew was coming and a blinding need to protect Nneoma all swirled into a white daze that blotted out his every conscious thought. His limbs moved of their own accord, and he jumped, as Shango's body converged towards Nneoma's, led by the dastardly power in his right hand that was aimed straight for her heart. Shigidi loosened his clay body with a single focused thought, allowing everything that was him to become thick and fluid just as he intercepted Shango's handful of lightning. The hand sank into Shigidi's viscid chest. Nneoma gasped from behind him as she scrambled to her feet. Before the pain could fully set in, Shigidi hardened himself again and shut his eyes, face scrunched in readiness for what was sure to come as the cold power of the thunder god's hand touched his core and became locked within it.

Shango jerked and pulled his arm, trying to wrest his hand from Shigidi's chest. The hotel room floor cracked and gave under his feet, exposing the metal reinforcement rods beneath. Shigidi gagged and coughed and convulsed as he resisted the yanking motion. Nneoma's hand touched the small of his back, and he heard her voice break into a fevered and unfamiliar incantation. She was doing something. He could sense the shift in the air but only barely, and he had no idea what it was. His mind was fixed on the two things he had become certain of in that moment. The first, that he was going to die. And second, that he loved Nneoma.

Olorun, I'm returning to you.

"Insolent creature!" Shango bellowed, cursing as an azure stream of pure plasma tore through Shigidi.

I only wish I'd found Nneoma sooner in the time you gave me.

Pain bloomed inside him. The stream of his consciousness overflowed like water spilled from a calabash and the spark of intelligence that animated him spread thin, unable to process what was happening to him anymore. Visions and images flew though his mind like uncaged birds, an eddy of unconstrained nightmares. He saw a ship made of fingernails, six babalawos wearing white flowing robes, a six-armed woman riding a peacock, a black and red rooster at a dusty crossroads, a throne of thunder bolts, two dogs eating a hailstorm, a pale woman wearing a purple ankh, a man wearing a dress made of evening sky, red earth being poured out of a white shell into water, a train made of chains, a crocodile eating a hurricane, an old man in bright silver armor sitting on two clouds gripping the sun. He saw. He saw. And then, suddenly he did not see anymore. He heard whispering. Shouting. A scream.

His last conscious thought was this: *Nneoma, I love you.*

Then he heard nothing.

He was nothing.

Nothing.

///////////

White light dissolved the darkness and the nothingness that had consumed him. He opened his eyes and saw sky. So much sky. Blue and white clouds whizzed past him like memories being forgotten.

Mere inches away from his, were Nneoma's smiling lips.

"You're awake," she said.

"I'm alive?" he asked, finally realizing that she was cradling him in her arms and that she was flying. The air streaming past his bare chest was cold and his heartbeat seemed erratic inside it, but he didn't mind, he was grateful to be feeling anything at all.

Her smile dimmed and she sighed. "Yes. You are," she said quietly.

"How did I . . . what hap . . . how did we survive that?"

She looked off into the clouds ahead and said, "I made a deal."

Shigidi tried to take in as much as he could of her naked body, which was no longer covered in scales, and her broad wings in their slow and constant up-and-down motion. As far as he could see, she was unharmed, but he knew that she must have traded away something of significant value to purchase their lives. Shango would not have let them go quietly, or at all.

"What deal?" he asked.

"It doesn't matter," she replied, the curve of her neck strained. And then she added, "You shouldn't have done that. You really shouldn't."

Shigidi was confused, "I shouldn't have done what? Saved your life?"

"No, not that. I mean, thank you," she corrected hastily. "But I told you to let go of your old bonds. To forget your old life. I was trying to find us an escape, to open a channel to the domain of an older power as last resort, someone I know from The Fall, but you . . . you called out to Olorun, you reached for him in the darkness and it corrupted my call. Your appeal brought him to us, instead of my contact."

Shigidi paused for a moment trying to remember. "Him? You mean Olorun came?"

She stiffened briefly and then relaxed. "Yes. He intervened."

Shigidi's mouth opened.

"Olorun is still chairman of your former spirit company, with veto powers and significant influence," she continued. "When you called out to him, he answered. He . . . saved us. I don't know why; he usually doesn't get involved in these things. But he chose to come this time. He wanted something. I guess he remains a businessman above all else. So, I had to negotiate."

Shigidi was still confused. Who was this friend, the higher power from The Fall? Could this friend have truly saved them? But most of all why did Olorun come for him? Olorun no longer got involved in spirit company affairs. But all he could muster out was: "Negotiate?"

"Yes. I had to offer him something that no one in your former spirit company could. It was the only way he would agree to make Shango and his cronies let us go."

She stopped flapping her left wing and banked, turning down at an angle in the direction of the rising sun. The clouds around them exploded with wild, new colors as the sun's light hit them, scattering and reflecting and refracting in a multitude of ways and wavelengths that made everything around them look soft and impossible.

He opened his mouth to ask her exactly what it was that she had traded to Olorun for their lives but stopped halfway, his mouth frozen in a querying O. He decided to leave the question for later, so he closed it, pressing his lips tightly together, keeping his worrying tongue caged behind his teeth.

A few silent moments passed before Nneoma smiled a strained smile at him again and said, "It's fine. What's done is done. We'll make it work. Besides, I'm not sure Lucifer would have actually come to my aid in time to save you anyway, so perhaps it's for the best.

Olorun did his part." She paused. "Shango wasn't happy about losing his hand though."

Shigidi cocked his head at that.

Within his chest, he felt something new, something that beat with the steadiness of a heart but was cold and thunderous and alien and immensely powerful and felt like it had once been a part of someone much more powerful than he was.

He closed his fist and was shocked when he felt the crackle of lightning on his skin.

1-Altitude Bar, Singapore

FEBRUARY 13TH, 2017 | 01:54 AM.

The strobe lights danced lazily in the periphery of his vision as Aadit Kumar downed an oversweet Singapore Sling, only mildly aware of how clichéd he was being. The live band in the corner was playing a decent rendition of "Don't Stop Believin'" and although the bass was a bit too heavy and the singer's accent a bit too forced, it still managed to be enjoyable. Aadit suspected that anything would, sitting at a bar on the 67th floor, overlooking the precise electric order of the city-state.

Aadit raised his empty glass in the direction of a thin and tattooed bartender with rolled-up sleeves, a beard, and a ponytail to indicate he wanted another of the same drink. When the bartender acknowledged him with a nod, he set down the glass and scanned the open-air rooftop bar, resting his hands on his bulging pot belly. Around him sat a slew of expats smoking slim cigarettes, svelte local sex kittens in short skirts and even shorter dresses with barely existent necklines, the odd drunken corporate yuppie group here and there in their boring white shirts and loosened ties, an old Black man with a thick white beard, wearing a blue robe and sitting alone, just like he was, but at a private table with a look of boredom plastered across his face. *Typical late bar crowd.* There was an imposing tower of a man nestled in a corner near the entrance, whose dark loamy skin and glimmering green eyes made him seem even more out of place than the old man. *Looks like a bodyguard.* Aadit rotated his stool and fixed his gaze beyond the crowd, on the array of partially lit buildings in the distance that looked like microprocessors in a computer. He liked to drink alone.

When he straightened his back, Aadit was cruelly reminded of his age. He tried to ignore the smarting bolts of pain that lingered from his having borne Kavadi—an offering made during a pilgrimage to the Batu Caves temple of Murugan, the deity his parents had taught him to worship—three days earlier when he had visited Malaysia for the twenty-ninth time. Pain radiated from the wounds in his back where hooks attached to bright gold-plated bells had been looped in. The pain brought with it memories of the overwhelming density of the Thaipusam crowd. He had been a tiny drop of water in a veritable river of humanity that flowed along the fifteen-kilometer trek, each bearing their own Kavadi. There had been so many more people than usual this year. He'd stumbled along the path, despite the crowds and the pain. He'd trudged step by step, one in a sea of heads, some of which had been shaven clean and daubed with yellow sandalwood like his, while others had been dreadlocked. Some bodies had been clad in saffron robes and white cloth like his but many had been tourists in sweat-stained, t-shirts and shorts, lining the streets. Some had carried silver pails of milk and heavy wood and metal constructs attached to their bodies with wicked braces while others, mostly the tourists, had carried cameras and took pictures. Some of the most devout, he had seen with spikes through their faces or hooks through their backs or their sides pierced with needles the length of a giant's forearm. Aadit had borne all three. The rekindling of his relationship with Murugan, god of war, for saving his life back in Lagos, had demanded great pain as payment, every year since.

He touched his hand to his lower back and felt another scar. He was glad to be done with it, for the year at least. Glad to be back home.

The bartender returned with his drink in a sweaty glass; pink, packed with ice and topped with a lemon slice.

"There you go sir," the young bartender said. "Enjoy. And let me know if you want another. Last call in five minutes."

"Thanks," he replied.

He lifted it to his lips and was about to take a sip when a dark, luscious thigh appeared on the vacant stool beside him, anchored to a body sheathed in a white dress so tight, it could have been a condom.

"Need some company?"

The voice was vaguely familiar.

He immediately assumed she was a prostitute so he started to say, "Not tonight honey. I'm . . ." And then his breath caught when he saw her taut, polished-ebony skin and impeccably sculpted face. Her hair was different, it was long and curly now and the afro was gone but in forty years she had not aged a single day. No wrinkles. No sagging flesh, no greying of hair. Nothing. There was no doubt about it. It was her. Nneoma. She had haunted his dreams for decades, and now, here she was, real and beside him, halfway across the world. His first words were an explosive excrement of exclamations. "Shit. Shit. Fuck!"

"Oh, don't be crass." Her smile was a full red slash that revealed perfect piano-key teeth.

Aadit's shoulders sank, and his hands started shaking, "How . . . ? Why are you here?"

"Why did you run away?" she snapped back, .

The live band segued from Journey's "Don't Stop Believin'" into Bon Jovi's "Livin' On a Prayer."

Aadit had always feared that this moment would come ever since the night in the dingy Lagos alley all those years ago even though it had been so long ago that he had started to allow himself hope that it wouldn't. But even then, he had never forgotten who had saved him that night and who he believed could save him again. He pushed his glass away with trembling fingers and stood up to his feet as Nneoma watched, amused.

"You . . . you cannot h . . . harm me," he said, his voice shaking. "I . . . I call upon the protection of Lord Murugan."

A chill blew through the open space as a man in a striped black and white sherwani suit with a mandarin collar appeared beside them as though he had been painted into the scene in one smooth brushstroke. Aadit swallowed air as he stepped back and almost tripped on the stool behind him. He had seen so many images of Lord Murugan since he was a child, but he was still shocked at seeing him made flesh. Murugan wore a peacock feather in his breast pocket, and his silk trousers were puffed around his ankles. His sherwani was embroidered with images depicting weapons from myth and legend.

He had ashy, dark skin and long wavy hair that sat in a tangle on his shoulders like the plunge pool of a waterfall. Aadit began to feverishly mumble the words to a prayer his mother had taught him as Murugan stepped into the space between him and Nneoma.

"What is your name, foul spirit?" Murugan's voice sounded gravelly and distant, like a broadcast from a faraway place.

"Naamah," Nneoma replied as she snatched up Aadit's drink and sipped it lazily, apparently unperturbed by the appearance of the hindu god of war, "But you can call me Nneoma."

"Naamah, you and your kind are not allowed to operate here. Leave now," Murugan commanded. "And leave this man alone, he is under my protection. Go and find another mortal with whom to satisfy your perverse hunger."

Her laughter was wild and all encompassing, a tropical rainstorm of mirth that made Murugan's face furrow with rage and sent a chill down Aadit's spine.

Why is she not running?

Aadit continued to pray, the words clattering out of his mouth clumsily like stones.

"Did I say something funny?" Murugan asked, clasping his hands in front of him.

"No. Not at all. You're humorless. Absolutely humorless. I doubt you could make me laugh if you tried. No. It's the situation that's funny," she replied through spurts of laughter. "It's funny because there was a time when I would have actually been scared of you, Murugan. A time when I would have fled just because you or your influence were near." All the humor evaporated from her face suddenly. "But that time is gone."

Murugan grabbed her forearm and said, "Then you should learn to fear again, succubus."

"No, *you* should learn to fear. I will make sure you never put your hands on me again," Nneoma licked her lips and called out, "Shigidi!"

A bolt of bizarrely precise lightning shot through the bar, striking Murugan square in the chest. It was trailed by a hulking body that gleamed like glazed wood, moving with grace and speed that should have been impossible for its size. It was the imposing man with green eyes Aadit had seen in the corner near the entrance. *But how? Is that the Shigidi?* The man took three hefty steps, a short sprint and then a vault in such quick movements that Aadit barely tracked them all.

1-Altitude was bathed in brilliant blue, green and white lights as Shigidi's form met violently with Murugan's.

The two potencies crashed into the reinforced steel and glass barrier at the edge of the bar, and fell, plummeting toward the ground in a flurry of fists. The skies above turned turbulent. Lightning struck indiscriminately without the courtesy of thunder. The patrons at the bar screamed and ran for the exits. Their addled brains were probably unable to process what they had just witnessed in the bar at the top of the city. Aadit could barely believe it himself. He saw the bartender with the ponytail push a thin waitress out of the way as he sprinted toward the back room. Glass shattered everywhere. Everyone had fled except the bearded old Black man in the blue robe who'd sat up in his cushioned chair, who seemed finally interested in what was going on.

Aadit kept trying to pray but the words, the words were no longer coming. He was praying to a god he'd just seen tackled off a rooftop by someone working with a woman who hadn't aged in forty years. Nothing made sense to him anymore. Nneoma stood up and cupped his face in her cold hands and pulled him in close. Her breath was sickly sweet, like old wine. "Come on," she said, "Smile. Finally, after all these years, we are alone together again."

Falling, Shigidi engaged Murugan. He grabbed onto a fistful of Murugan's sherwani, just below the collar, to keep him in place as he tried to hit the war god, the cool air rushing past Shigidi's face and shaven head. He was impressed by how nimbly Murugan rolled his shoulders to evade three of Shigidi's rapid lightning-wrapped punches as they plunged down the side of the building blazing a luminous trail against the night sky. On the third roll he saw Murugan summon his vel—a vicious short spear that materialized from thin air right into his hand as if it had always been part of him. Murugan turned his elbow and thrust the vel into Shigidi's side. But Shigidi was ready. He had researched this. He knew that the spear which had slain many demons, felled many gods, and won many wars, was Murugan's ultimate weapon, and he had prepared for it. Shigidi had already begun to imagine his body as solid, impenetrable rock, dehydrated and rigidified by his own spirit particles. He hardened himself. When the vel made contact, he felt only a thudding sensation and then a short vibration as the vel snapped on impact, like a toothpick, without even piercing his solid clay flank.

Murugan's eyes widened with surprise.

You didn't see that coming, did you?

Shigidi pressed the advantage created by the shock of the failed strike and rammed a powerful punch into Murugan's solar plexus. The god of war let out a whimper as the wind was knocked out of him. Shigidi didn't give him a chance to recover. He pulled Muru-gan's head up toward him as he swung the top of his own head down to land a vicious head-butt just as they finally crashed into the ground below. The impact pushed away everything near the hypocentre of their impact. Shigidi felt the rush of a powerful wave of dust, debris, lightning and compressed air blow out, making the air thin around them in a fraction of an instant.

Temporary low-pressure point.

He braced himself as the implosion hit and all the debris folded back in on itself like an empire being invaded by its own army. Car alarms wailed in protest. People ran way screaming.

Murugan lay pinioned beneath Shigidi, his suit now in tatters, his spear broken, and his face bloodied, with a deep cut above his eye-brow and a broken nose.

"Beast, you cannot kill me, I am the son of Shiva." Murugan's bloodstained lips barely moved but the sound came to Shigidi from everywhere at once. "This is our company territory. These people pray to us. They are under our protection. You cannot do business here!"

"Shut up." Shigidi growled above the din of the disrupted city.

He raised his hand, and it became a thing of solid rock, gloved in harsh blue and white lightning. Shigidi saw realization surge into Murugan's eyes, but it came too late. He didn't give him enough time to disassemble his spirit particles in a hasty retreat. Shigidi's lightning-gloved fist pounded into Murugan's face, collapsing it with a sickening crunch and an explosion of white spirit particles.

Shigidi continued hitting him, pummeling his head until it was an incongruous glowing mass of carmine blood, dark flesh, and off-white bone. When the glow of the dead god's essence dimmed, the fractured, gory remains of his body disintegrated into a swirl of fading red spirit particles like a nebula of dying stars.

So, this is what it's like to have real power, power enough to kill other gods.

Shigidi straightened his back and threw back his head to inhale a lungful of debris-laden air.

//////////

Aadit couldn't stop shaking. Nneoma's voice was terrifyingly calm. "Aadit, it's over. You must complete the transaction. I told you all those years ago; no one tastes my pleasures and shirks the price. No one. Not men. Not gods. Not the ancient ones. Not the Endless. Not even Lucifer himself. I always get what is owed to me, eventually."

Hot tears ran down his cheeks. "Please . . ." His voice, like his soul, was broken as he realized that Murugan was not coming back to save him after all his years of sacrifice, of Kavadi. It had all been for nothing.

She tilted her head to the left and her features softened as she stood up and pulled his head down into her bosom. "Aww, poor baby. Poor, poor baby. Come here. It's not personal, it's just business, okay? Don't be afraid. Let me make it all stop."

Aadit wanted to fight her embrace, but he couldn't summon the will to resist. He felt numb, and his thoughts became hazy, the connection between his mind and body was muddled and unclear. His limbs hung limply by his side as he allowed her to unzip his corduroy trousers. He was devoid of desire but at the touch of her fingers, he found himself turgid. She hiked her dress up. There was nothing but smooth skin underneath.

No. Please.

She pushed him back down onto the barstool. He sat and she straddled him, wrapping her arms around his neck. He sucked in a deep breath as his mind was flooded with pleasure that blotted out the numbness and despair. She rode him, gently at first and then fiercely, in great big crests and troughs of hip and thigh. His orgasm came quickly, and when he was done, it all washed over him again like a wave. His body was racked with sobs as more tears followed.

Sachika. Ravi. I'm sorry. I'm so sorry.

She kissed him on the cheek, disengaged herself and whispered in his ear, "Now we're done. Don't cry. Don't beg. It will be over soon."

Aadit remained tearful, his body still shaking on the barstool as she pulled down her dress. He still couldn't move his hands or feet, so he sat there, head lolling forward and tears dripping down onto his laps like drops of distilled despair.

"Goodbye Aadit."

Panic filled his mind when he was seized by a sudden heat deep in his bones. He watched incredulously as a network of bright orange sparks expanded out from his groin to cover his body, like a kind of luminescent infection. He wanted to scream but he could no longer feel his tongue in his mouth.

No. I don't want to die. I don't want to die. I don't . . .

His skin turned dry and translucent, and his body began to shrink. Like he was desiccating. A burning sensation flared deep within him, like something had bitten into his soul with flame-teeth. It filled him with a pain unlike anything he had ever felt; sudden and sharp and rich and fully textured with notes of every other kind of pain he had ever felt in his life. Aadit kept trying to scream until there was no more consciousness left in him.

//////////

Nneoma watched as Aadit's now-empty shell greyed rapidly and fell off the stool, disintegrating into fine ash-like particles as it did. The tiny pieces of what he had been were carried on the wind like pollen. She waited until she felt the surge of his extracted spirt entering her, entangling with her own spirit particles. It made her skin shimmer. She exhaled. When it was over, she turned around and walked toward the seated Olorun—the old Black man in the blue robe—emphasizing the feline swing of her hips with every step.

"Did you enjoy the show?" she asked, taking up a plush seat beside him. She could hear the faint trill of approaching sirens in the distance.

Olorun combed his fingers through his beard. His flowing blue robe had turned a deep purple and masqueraded as black in the dim light. "Yes actually, I did. Although I could have done without your little sex game at the end. Your methods are . . . crude."

She snorted with scorn. "Please. You males are all the same. Both human and god alike. You love sex, you're all obsessed with it even, but you like to pretend you aren't and you especially hate it when we use it as a weapon against you. You use words like crude and shameful and whore and temptress. Whatever. I've heard it all before. It's my power, I'll use it as I like."

"Don't start. It's the power you were given. So be it. I will say no more about it. But yes, besides that, it was a good show. The people who needed to see something, saw it. Shigidi barreling into Murugan, now *that* was a sight." He leaned forward. "And you have your man's spirit. The one that got away. Two birds, one stone, as they say."

"Yes. As they say," she repeated dryly, still irritated by his 'crude' remark. "So, what next?"

Olorun crossed his legs and was silent for a moment, as though he was trying to decide how much to tell her. "The witnesses are the key. There were at least twelve of weak mind who will begin to worship the image of Shigidi without even knowing who or what he truly is. Such is human nature. Such is the nature of belief. They will draw images and write words, they will start rumors and conspiracy theories about what really happened here today, they will seek out each other and reinforce their belief, create a new mythology of the event." He smiled. "They could be the seeds of a new Orisha Company cult here. Let's give them time to germinate. When the seeds have taken hold, I will ask you to visit again. There is nothing like a good, personal revelation to kickstart a new branch of the spirit company."

Nneoma shook her head. "Fine. But this isn't exactly what I had in mind when I offered to help you expand your business to new territory. The Mahādevas will not just let you establish a new Orisha Spirit Company branch here. Especially not after they find out you had Murugan, Shiva's son killed."

Olorun frowned, uncrossed his legs and leaned forward in his chair. "Ehn, and what do you know of spirit company business, Nneoma?" He curled his lips and waved a dismissive hand like he was swatting at invisible flies. "Of course, they will oppose our setting up a new branch here. We organized and made rules for a reason. But as long as rules have existed, there have always been ways to bend them. Killing Murugan was just an advance negotiation tactic. Besides, they have enough followers to reincarnate him eventually. Business evolves. Jihads and Crusades and missionary expeditions are little more than hostile takeovers, but not all of us can afford such open avarice anymore, sacrificing thousands of believers to gain new ones. Especially not in this day and age. When Yeshua's believers stole thousands of my worshippers and took them westward to work their fields and converted them to a new belief, did I go to war? No. I negotiated a new joint venture with them. Today, our Santería franchise operations are a thriving million prayer-a-year company." He paused and his suit changed color again, shifting through a series of tonal gradations from purple to deep blue with streaks of light dancing across it like shooting stars. "Everyone that matters in this business knows that we must ensure business continuity, above all else. If I did not understand this, Shango would have your head hanging on a wall by now. Love, death, family, sex, pride, rules, and laws; they are nothing but tools to further belief, the core of our existence. You of all people should understand that."

"Fine. Yes, I understand," Nneoma said as she closed her eyes under the weight of memories, memories of her sister and the mistake that had taken her when she allowed herself get caught up in a spirit business war. "We do it your way."

Olorun sank back into his chair and began to fade away like a man-shaped fog in rising heat. "Of course, you will. We have a deal, *abi*?"

Nneoma nodded without opening her eyes.

"Good," Olorun said. "I will let you and Shigidi know when you are needed again."

Nneoma rose to her feet and watched as Olorun faded away, into nothing.

When he was gone, she turned and walked to the broken barrier at the edge of the rooftop where Shigidi and Murugan had gone over. The sirens had grown louder, filling the air with their incessant howl.

Nneoma let out a guttural, piercing scream full of frustration that blotted out the sound of the sirens for a few seconds. She hated the feeling of being boxed in by Olorun's machinations, of having to do as she was told like some spirit company employee, of being caught in spirit company politics. And all this because of Shigidi. Because she had sensed something in him.

Was it even worth it? Am I repeating my sister's mistake?

Fear seized Nneoma's spine like a frozen hand, and she stopped screaming. She listened to the thin echo of her own scream coming back to her and then took three deep breaths to clear her mind.

No. What's done is done. We will see it through to the end.

Her back rippled and the skin began to shred as she sprouted and unfurled her long, thin wings, spreading them wide to feel the wind caress them for a moment before she reeled them back in tight. She used her claws to hastily rip off what was left of her white dress, and then launched herself off the edge. Nneoma fell, cutting through the air like an arrow in a straight and graceful dive down to the streets where she decelerated rapidly and embraced waiting Shigidi, engulfing him with her arms, her wings, her perfect nakedness.

Together, they took to the velvet blue sky, moonlight beckoning at their heels.

CHAPTER 10

The Anubis-Urania Temple of the Hermetic Order of
The Third Dawn, London, England

JULY 5TH, 2017 | 03:04 AM.

At a few minutes past the witching hour, Shigidi, Nneoma, and Aleister arrived at the unassuming brown brick townhouse in West London's Chelsea area, which served as the home of Third Dawn. A bolt of pale moonlight peeked through the curtain of dark sky. Aleister snorted as he slowed the vehicle down to a crawl and saw the bright green numbers of the clock on the dashboard console.

Perfect time for making an unexpected visit to a cult of mystics in the company of a demon I haven't seen in decades and a dodgy god who seems eager to kill me.

He parked right in front of the house and killed the engine.

Silence invaded the space around them. Third Dawn was one of the few consistent things across Aleister's three lives. It was an occult society and magickal order he had belonged to as a young man during his first life, long before he had met Nneoma or even his beloved Victor. It was there, in that townhouse, that he had first found people like himself, curious to see and to understand the world beyond the corporeal and eager to learn how to manipulate it through magick. Every time he visited; echoes of emotions from those first days came to him like whispers. Even though Third Dawn was largely underground now, and they'd become more like a new-age cult than the esoteric secret society they'd been when he was a member, he still maintained contact with some of its members because he considered them friends, and he didn't have many of those anymore. Besides, they possessed a rich library of magickal works, even though many of the current members didn't know how to use them. They barely knew any magick at all. That library included the only copy of the Wærlan-Drýlic, a book he used to access to the spirit-side of London, where he could still commune with his old friends and lovers long lost to the ravages of time and nature, which he'd temporarily escaped. He'd told Nneoma about it when they'd first met in Algeria. Now he almost regretted it because she wanted him to use it to help her steal something from the British Museum. If he didn't owe her two of his three lives, and wasn't still so desperately attracted to her, he would have refused.

"All right, let's go," Shigidi said to him when Aleister had taken a few too many seconds to stare into the dark road ahead without moving.

Past, present, future, it's all overlapping, cycling.

Aleister exited the SUV, climbed the stone steps, and knocked on the door, the supernatural couple following closely behind him. He twice pushed a bronze doorbell that was shaped like a cluster of three rising suns twice and looked up, staring into the narrow red eye of the security camera that he knew was recording them. There was no response. He pushed it again. Still nothing.

"I told you there might not be anyone in the temple at this time. And if there are, they are probably deep in sleep," Aleister said. "It really is an unfortunate time to show up at someone's house unannounced, isn't it? Maybe we should come back when the sun is up?"

Shigidi shook his head, "Weren't you listening to what she told you? That's not an option. If they don't respond in three minutes, I'm going to kick that door in. So, if you have a phone number or any other method of getting in or getting attention, I suggest you start using it."

Aleister threw up his hands. "This is an old and special building. It may not be what it once was, there is still powerful magick protecting these walls, you can't just barge in."

"Actually," Shigidi rotated his neck with a sharp crack, "I think I can."

"Wait." Nneoma stepped forward and up the steps to stare up at the camera. She held her left hand in front of her and snapped the fingers of her right three times. Bright yellow sparks appeared with each snap, depositing something like a fine ash or powder onto her skin when they settled. She pursed her lips and blew into the spirit particle residue. The ash lifted and danced in the air, wafting its way onto the glass eye of the camera with sensual, erratic movements, like cigarette smoke. When it hit the lens, she closed her eyes.

"There is a broad man with balding, wispy grey hair, seated at a table in a blue and white housecoat on the other side," she said as the images came to her. "He is wide awake, holding a hunting rifle and staring at us on the security monitor like we are some kind of scientific specimen."

"Shit. It's George," Aleister muttered under his breath, recognizing her description of the temple custodian and deputy high priest who had been his friend for a long time. George was one of the few members of Third Dawn still willing to break temple rules and allow him access to the sacred manuscripts on the odd occasion, but he knew that showing up at this time of day, with strangers no less, would have set off every alarm bell in the paranoid old man's mind.

Nneoma smiled as she turned to Shigidi and said, "Not every time hammer, sometimes scalpel."

Shigidi nodded and quietly held out his hand to help her down the steps even though Aleister couldn't see what she needed his help for. Perhaps it was his way of acknowledging her cleverness. There was something strained about the way they interacted, and it bothered Aleister, but he didn't want to think about it. There was more than enough to be worried about.

"All right. So, it seems George is in there and he's awake. He's probably just scared of you lot," Aleister said. He pushed the doorbell again and spoke in a calm but insistent tone. "Hey, Old George, it's me. I know you're up there. I apologize about the time but there's no danger here. These are my friends, umm . . . please let us in. It's an urgent matter. George?"

There was no response. The red unblinking eye of the camera stared back at him accusingly. Aleister's pulse quickened as he tried to think of something that could possibly convince his friend that it was safe to let him into the temple with two unfamiliar people at three in the morning, or at the very least, something that would make George think the situation was important enough to take the risk.

Once the idea manifested itself, he spoke before his conscience could stop him. "Hey George, listen, please. I need to see Evelyn. She called out to me."

"Ah," Nneoma said.

Aleister turned to her. "What?"

"He just leaned forward. Looks like you got his attention."

Aleister choked back the feeling of shame that was welling up inside him at using Evelyn's name and memory this way. She was George's grandmother, and Aleister knew she was the one who had first introduced George to the occult and inducted him into Third Dawn. He knew because she'd also been a close friend of his. That was how he'd first met George as a chubby and eager young boy before rediscovering him by chance, as an airy young man in the small, dimly lit basement of a Soho club on Regent Street in the 1960s. They'd spent a few years partying together and one night, drunk on sloe gin, he'd told George who he really was, when he'd first met George as a boy holding tightly onto Grandma Evelyn's hand, how he'd summoned Choronzon and learned the keys to higher magicks, and how a beautiful woman he'd met in the desert had given him another life, another soul. George had laughed at his stories then, assuming them to be drunken exaggerations. They'd parted ways when Aleister moved to Argentina in 1965 but rediscovered each other again one cloudy afternoon in the corner of the King's Head pub, three days before the new millennium, when Aleister had returned to London, ageless, strange, and wearing a different name like new clothes. George believed his stories then. George had never doubted him since.

"Please. Evelyn needs me," Aleister said as he stared into the camera, trying to project all the depth of their shared history forward, hoping it would be enough to make his old friend ignore whatever instinct was making him suspicious. After a few moments that seemed like hours, there was a clicking sound at the door, announcing that it was open. The three of them filed inside.

The temple consisted of a small living room that had been converted to a waiting area full of frayed and ugly brown plush seats; two bedrooms that had been converted to a meeting room with a large table at its center and rows of books stocked in massive shelves; and a small room upstairs where George lived with an array of monitors and his own bathroom and kitchen. It was all old and worn but neat and clean. When they rounded the corner of the waiting room, George was standing there at the foot of the stairs, the barrel of his Winchester magnum rifle trained on them.

"What's happened with Evelyn's spirit, Al?" the old man asked, his voice shaky.

"I don't know. I need to go over and find out, but it's urgent," Aleister said, feeling another twinge of guilt for the lie he had told and—if George didn't put the gun down—for what Aleister suspected was about to happen to the man he'd considered a friend for almost eighty years.

"And who are these people with you?" George asked.

"They're old friends. They were with me when she reached out. No need to worry, they mean no harm. We will leave you in peace soon. I'm just here to see Evelyn, spirit side, and they're accompanying me to my place after."

His words didn't seem to do much to allay George's suspicions. In fact, his suspicions seem to have spiked because his hands began to shake, and his finger trembled tantalizingly close to the trigger.

"Is that so, Al?"

"Yes, George, it is," Aleister said, trying for a smile.

"Then why didn't you just ask them to wait outside?"

Aleister glanced at Shigidi, who had already begun to adjust his feet. He gave a small shake of his head, but it seemed that Shigidi had already decided. Aleister was just about to shout *Wait!* but Shigidi leaped forward and to the side at an impossible speed. He left only a trail of electrical discharge in the space where he had been. George didn't even have enough time to convince himself that he needed to pull the trigger before Shigidi's fingers wrapped themselves around his throat, choking back a cry, while another arm twisted the rifle out of his grasp in one smooth motion.

Shigidi released George, who stumbled backward, tripped on the bottom step of the staircase, and fell to the floor with a whimper.

"Stay down," Shigidi said softly. "I don't want to hurt you."

The old man sat up and seemed to be on the verge of trying to fight back, with nothing but foolish pride propelling him to take on the younger, stronger, and more confident attacker who had moved like lightning. But then he glanced at Aleister, who shook his head before saying, "I'm sorry, I really am."

George spat in his direction and quietly sank back down on the carpeted floor as if it were a bed, his chest heaving with labored breaths.

Aleister hung his head and said, "You didn't really have to do that did you?"

Shigidi glared back at him with green-tinted eyes that made his skin crawl. "We don't have time for games. Let's get what we came for and get out of here."

Nneoma placed a hand on Aleister's shoulder and said, striking a consolatory note, "Look Aleister, don't worry about your friend. Shigidi didn't do any damage." She offered him a smile. "The book?"

"Yeah," Aleister said, feeling powerless. "The book."

He led them through the beaded screen that separated the waiting area from the meeting room. No photographs or paintings or decorative items hung on the walls, but there were a lot of old books on assorted subjects arranged neatly onto an array of shelves, primarily on mythology, folklore, and the occult. He walked right to a shelf in the corner of the room and pulled out a red leather-bound volume. On its cover was what looked like a map embossed and foil-stamped in gold.

"There. Let's go," he said.

They turned to exit the house, taking care to avoid George who was now sitting on the bottom step of the stairs with his eyes closed, either asleep or just unwilling to acknowledge them. Aleister was tempted to stop and check which but Nneoma put her arm in his and pulled him out of the house and into the dark of premature morning.

When they piled back into the SUV, Aleister set the book down on the center console. As Shigidi adjusted his seatbelt, his elbow brushed against the book and he withdrew rapidly like he had touched a hot stove. *Ow!* He looked up with utter surprise and saw an amused Aleister, his neck strained with the effort of resisting the urge to laugh.

"What's so funny?" Shigidi asked.

"It repelled you," Aleister replied still trying to hide his amusement at seeing the large and imposing god react in such a childlike manner to the touch of a book.

Shigidi remained deadpan. "What does that mean?"

"It not actually a book, per se. That's just a guise, the result of some clever containment magick. Its true name is the Wærlan-Drýlic and it is really just a cluster of entangled spirit particles from London's flesh-side and spirit sides. Naturally, they would repel each other and separate, but someone with access to much more powerful magick than I know of originally bound them to each other, permanently," Aleister explained. He'd first learned of the nature and power of the Wærlan-Drýlic from his mentor and the founder of Third Dawn, Samuel Albus Dell, back in 1904 when the spiteful and ailing old man had reluctantly given it to him, describing all the necessary steps and drawings to execute binding magickal operations. It was only after Aleister gained dominion over Choronzon that he understood enough to be able to set up markers for which particles belonged to what side and map out the right-shifted spiritual tension sites where they could be socketed in on either side of reality to create a working Swedenborg-Heindel bridge or, as Samuel Dell had called it, a spirit portal.

"But the spirit side particles embedded in it will resist unauthorized spirit entities like you," Aleister turned and adjusted the front mirror to bring her into focus, "and like Nneoma."

It occurred to him that in a sense, if he had never met Nneoma, the Wærlan-Drýlic would probably have just been another book gathering dust on the shelf of the Third Dawn meeting room, with no one able to use it. Still, he would have never guessed that he would one day need to use it to help her.

She smiled at him and asked, "But not you?"

"No," Aleister said, picking the book up again and holding it up in front of Shigidi like it was a trophy. "Not me. I'm a London man."

What he didn't add was that he'd taken advantage of the growing regional spiritual enterprise systems of the late 1940's to hard code his access to the spirit-side using the Wærlan-Drýlic.

"Right," she said. "And you will use it to get us spirit side, right? You know the right spells to use?"

Aleister put down the book and started the car. The headlights came on, piercing the darkness of early London morning. He idled the engine as he turned back to look at Nneoma, enjoying the chance to be in control of the situation for the first time that night. "You know we don't like to call them spells luv, they're magickal operations. And yes, I will. A debt is a debt. It's why you came looking for me isn't it?"

"Yes, it is," she confirmed. "And thank you."

"You're welcome. But once tonight is done, perhaps you'll be the one in my debt again?"

She snorted. "That worked once. It won't work again so don't push your luck too far, Aleister."

"Fine, fine," he acquiesced. "I get it."

"Good. Then drive. We have a job to do," Shigidi said impatiently.

Aleister stared ahead, his brow furrowed with thought as he put the SUV in gear and entered the road again, this time headed for Bloomsbury. He was sure that no one flesh-side had visited the spirit-side as often as he had, seeking knowledge and the counsel of the dead in a bid to escape their fate. Even now, he visited often to see and speak to old friends. It wasn't likely that anyone on this side of reality knew the spirit side of London better than he did, except perhaps people that worked for the spirit departments of the government. He was sure he could help them get in and out like they had described, and he was sure that the Wærlan-Drýlic was by far the most reliable way.

Shit. The memory hit him like punch to the gut. *I am as attached to it as it is to the temple.* His grip on the steering wheel tightened until his knuckles turned white.

"Hey, are you okay?" Nneoma asked. She must have noticed the change in his demeanor.

Fuck.

He had almost forgotten that the Wærlan-Drýlic had been bonded to the Temple of the Third Dawn by Samuel Dell after they had fallen out and he'd been excommunicated from the group. It was a bond Aleister was yet to break despite decades of effort—efforts he had almost forgotten about because he had stopped trying to break the bond more than a lifetime ago and simply used the book as it was, limitations and all. That meant he never took it out for more than an hour or two at a time for his visits to the spirit-side, and usually in the mornings after sunrise or late afternoons. But this was different, and the timing was unfortunate. Very unfortunate.

"Umm, are you sure we need to do this right now, luv?"

"Yes," Nneoma replied. "I already told you that."

"Then there is something I think you should know," he said, exhaling deeply and stretching out his tense fingers. "Whatever you want to do spirit-side, you need to do quickly because if the Wærlan-Drýlic isn't back on this side of reality by sunrise, it will be summoned back to the temple, and any bridge or portal I have opened will be shut, and we will probably be trapped on London's spirit-side forever. If we postpone till tomorrow we can give ourselves more time to get back."

Shigidi gave him a sharp look, but Aleister kept his eyes on the road, not wanting to focus on what radiated from the perpetually pissed-off god's eyes.

"You're joking right?" Shigidi asked, finally.

"I'm afraid not."

From the back, Nneoma started laughing. Aleister stared at her in the mirror as Shigidi turned to face her too, looking puzzled.

"This evening just keeps on getting more and more interesting, doesn't it?" She said.

"Interesting isn't the word I'd used to describe it," Shigidi responded.

"Yes, well I am not sure what other word to use. Because there is no way we can postpone. Olorun said this needs to be done today or the deal is off. Board meeting, remember? So, what do you think Aleister? You think we can make it back by sunrise?"

He thought for a moment and said, "Yes," then added after a pause: "It should be fine as long as we don't have any hiccups or stay too long. I've been using it this way for years. Just move quickly once you get inside. Shouldn't take you more than a few minutes to grab an item, should it?"

"No, it shouldn't. Assuming there are no surprises," she said, closing her eyes. "I'm starting to wonder what will happen if we fail and don't make it out in time. Or at all."

"We will make it," Shigidi said firmly. But even Aleister, his eyes back on the road, could tell that Shigidi was not so certain.

CHAPTER 11

*OAU Conference Center, Obafemi Awolowo University,
Ile-Ife, Nigeria*

JULY 1ST, 2017 | 02:15 A.M.

I t only took Olorun a minor effort, as minor as a passing thought, to collect and reshape himself. First, into a sudden sheet of heavy rain through which he descended onto the soil of Ile-Ife from his comfortable throne of cloud-pocked sky, without any accompanying thunder or lightning. And then, when all of him had accumulated in the land of the people who first believed in him, changed shape again into his preferred and familiar form, that of an elderly man. He manifested fully garbed in his formal white agbada, which was embroidered with silver and gold around his neck and chest, and a pair of polished brown leather shoes that shone like mirrors when the returning sunlight kissed their surface. A rainbow array of beads and bangles adorned his wrists and neck: precious stones, colored glass, dried nuts, carved wood, and worked metals that he had received as tribute or taken from long-defeated enemies and effusive devotees over the years. The Chairman of the Board and former CEO of the Orisha Spirit Company raised his head to take in the flat, grey, three-story building in front of him, the markers of his prime godhood on full and necessary display as he made his first official return to active duty. The time had finally come to confront Shango and retake control of his spirit business. He took one step forward before pausing and squaring his shoulders as he remembered his custom. He put out a palm, as though pressing it to an invisible wall in front of him, and released a small pulse of pure primordial power, of his elemental divine energy, his ashe. It was a final herald to let the other orishas gathered inside, who made up the spirit company executive board, know: Olorun had arrived.

He continued, entering the building in long strides, his gait steady with divine resolve. He swept up the short flight of stairs and past two pot-bellied security guards in ugly brown uniforms, their hands suspended in the air and their lips caught open mid-sentence. Stuck, like insects in amber. They were in a frozen bubble of spacetime while the orishas made use of the facilities they were supposed to be guarding; facilities that stood over the spot where the orishas had first been believed into existence and made contact with the reality of mortals. Olorun smiled at the ancient memory as he rounded the main foyer and entered a hallway at the end of which stood a large mahogany door. Beside it, his son Obatala stood, waiting.

"Kaabiyesi." Obatala greeted using Olorun's formal title, kneeling, and bowing so low that his flowing white wrapper pooled around his feet on the ugly brown carpet. "Welcome back."

Obatala's shock-white, dreadlocked hair draped around his head and sat on the carpet like mangrove roots. He held up thin, cowrie-shell covered hands that emerged from the sleeves of his white dashiki like branches on a skin-colored tree of bones. He was pale under the fluorescent lights.

Protocol had always demanded that Obatala meet and greet Olorun first, at any company meetings when he deemed fit to attend. And so, even though the sight of him had grown unfamiliar due to centuries-long absence, Olorun was unsurprised to see Obatala attending to it. It was a duty that Obatala, the orisha of light, had never neglected, partly out of guilt for failing to execute his assignment as one of the very first members of the Orisha Spirit Company: the creation of myth-bodies for the Yoruba people. He'd gotten drunk on the job, his head filled with palm wine. It was the ultimate career-limiting event. Its effect essentially eternal, the shame was so great. It was the primary reason, when Olorun had decided to retire from the position so many centuries ago, that he had chosen Shango as CEO of the company instead of Obatala.

An error on my part.

He took Obatala's extended hands in his and pulled him back up to his feet. "Thank you," he said.

They exchanged a look of knowing. It was the rueful look of a father to the son that failed him and had spent, would spend, the rest of his existence seeking to regain favor. It was not easy for Olorun to see his first son like that, so shrunken, bent, his position in the spirit company stagnant. Before Obatala's drunkenness and the subsequent usurping of his duty by the more cunning orisha, Oduduwa, Olorun had held high hopes for his first son, a vision that he would manage the spirit company carefully and with consideration. But

Obatala had shown himself to be weak of mind and will. How could he have left a weak-minded god to manage the spirit business in his absence? Even after that failure, and Obatala's struggles with Oduduwa to regain some sense of pride, he had been temperamental, uncalculated, ineffective.

Perhaps now that the soul of the company hangs in the balance, he will finally live up to his potential.

It remained to be seen. But in that moment, the knowing look held between them, he wanted his first son to feel acknowledged, empowered. He squeezed Obatala's hands and pulled him in for an embrace. The warmth of their bodies and the crackling sting of their spirit particles suffused the space between them, and they both allowed themselves to luxuriate in it. Olorun took in the smell of his son's dreadlocked hair, the urticating roughness of his skin, the unnatural thinness of his arms.

"It's good to see you again, my son. Please, lead the way," Olorun said, when he finally pulled away.

Obatala's face displayed his surprise as he nodded and turned to open the door. He entered, Olorun following closely behind, scanning the room full of waiting gods, most of whom were his own children, taking a quick mental roll call as they all rose to their feet.

Eshu-Elegba, trickster god, the orisha of fate and chance, who served as head of communications at the spirit company was standing and smiling in the farthest corner as always, wearing a patchwork red-and-black trousers and matching vest that left his chest bare. Oduduwa, orisha of ambition and creativity, stood tall in his own red aso-oke agbada, shoulders proud, smiling an oily, satisfied smile that Olorun had come to dislike hundreds of years ago—a dislike that only grew with the ages. Yemoja, goddess of rivers and streams, the first female orisha. She had plaited her hair to her head in thick undulating lines, like a sequence of endlessly cresting waves. It matched the elaborate blue wrapper she had tied just above her bosom and the array of shells that adorned her neck. She looked more regal than Olorun had seen her in a long time, and he gave her a short nod which she acknowledged with a bow. Olokun, the orisha least like him but whose name was most like his own, held dominion over the oceans and seas. Almost as if trying to outwardly reconcile an internally fluid gender identity, their face bore a more unusual mix of features than he ever remembered them having. They presented an interesting, heady image and, headier still, for the first time in what seemed like forever, their eyes seemed to be avoiding his. And finally, Shango, orisha of fire, lightning, and rock, who he'd placed in charge of the company. Shango was flanked by his three wives: Oya, the annoying one who talked too much and carried his armor; Oshun, the slender and quiet one who was always carrying his bow; and Oba, his first and most corpulent wife, who carried his machete and who he had nepotically appointed head of spirit resources in the company.

When Shango and Olorun locked eyes, the entire room seemed to shrink to nothing beyond the space between them. There was a clashing intensity of wills that sucked all the air out of the room. Eventually, after what seemed like minutes, Shango broke their gaze, as Olorun knew he would have to, and lowered his eyes, bowing ever so slightly. Olorun nodded to acknowledge him but noted the open defiance.

Good. At least we all know what must happen now. There should not be much pretense. This was always going to be a fraught affair.

Olorun made his way to one of the brown-cushioned chairs at the head of the long mahogany table so that he was flanked by the loyal

Obatala on his right, and the insolent Shango on his left. He raised his right hand and said, "Yes. Ehn, thank you all for allowing me to join you again for this scheduled board meeting to discuss the state and future of our company. I hope it will be a fruitful session indeed. I know I am not usually present at these meetings and Obatala typically manages the agenda," he shot a glance to the orisha of light, encouraging him with a smile. "You know me I don't like to interfere or disrupt things too much, so I'd like that to continue. Please, proceed as usual."

With that, he took a seat, sinking into the soft, yielding Oyo leather. The other gods followed suit.

Olorun watched as Obatala placed a small, scarred calabash half-filled with water atop the table and quickly passed his hand over it three times. The water rippled each time and kept rippling after the last pass of his hand until he spoke a single word and the water stilled suddenly. His reflection in it faded away, and the water turned bright and diffuse, like liquid light. The light rearranged itself into an array of luminous symbols that signified all the information he needed to present. When the meeting agenda written in light and water was stable and clear, Obatala gave a single clap of his hands and said, "May our deliberation bring clarity."

"For we have willed it so," they all chorused.

And thus, another annual Orisha Spirit Company board meeting officially began.

For practical reasons, the Orisha Spirit Company board no longer convened spirit-side, in Orun, as it once had. Orun enhanced the CEO's already considerable executive authority, making it too easy to influence and, in effect, to control the others, potentially coercing them into agreement and silencing dissent through fear of potent repercussions. And so, long ago, when Olorun was still in charge, Obatala had put forward a motion to have the meetings held in Ile-Ife, where each orisha had dominion over some aspect of the corporeal world and could, if it came to it, put up a decent fight or at least escape one if it came to that. It was a wise suggestion and seemed fair to Olorun, so he had joined the majority in passing it. In retrospect, it was a provision that Olorun was grateful for because without it, what he was about to attempt would be more difficult than it already was. And it was significantly difficult indeed.

"The first item on the agenda, as usual, is the decline in faith," Obatala started, after clearing his throat. "We have all seen the final performance reports diligently compiled by Eshu-Elegba. We have seen another significant decrease in believers and worshippers, a trend that has continued for almost three centuries despite our attempts to stop it. Most recently, the pivot from the direct faith market to the indirect market, feeding from imagination and subconscious faith, promoting ourselves through film and books and television, the, erm, Nollywood strategy," he shot a quick look at Olokun whose idea it had been in the first place, "has not made much difference. So, we need to determine how to address this and take action again before the market dries up completely."

Yemoja was the first to speak, her animated speech making the array of shells around her neck dance. "I think that all of us can see that these small-small adjustments *ati* rebranding efforts are pointless. All of us know that the global faith market has changed. This so-called Nollywood strategy is like pouring good palm oil on burnt yam. At the end of the day, it still tastes like burnt yam."

"Ehn, so what is your own suggestion?" Olokun spat out the question without looking at their sister. They had put on heavy make-up:

blue lipstick, eye shadow, highlighter, and heavy mascara, and their skin was light, much lighter than Olorun remembered it being, almost like it had been bleached. They were also wearing a blue western-style suit made of ankara cloth with an elaborate, matching gele tied tightly around their crown, which made their face stretch as they spoke. "Do you even have one? Or are we just going to spend the rest of today complaining and making stupid yam metaphors?"

Yemoja ignored them. "Sometimes the simple answer is the correct answer. A return to the old ways. Have any of you in this room today asked yourselves why it is that the human population is increasing exponentially, especially right here in our own core territory where we first appeared and where we have the largest market share, yet our belief-income keeps reducing so rapidly? The fact of the matter is that we need more direct focus on the worshippers we *do* have, the true believers and those connected to us by history and blood, instead of desperately appealing to those outside, trying to expand in different ways. We lose more of our core believers with each generation because their children wander from the ways of their ancestors. We need to bring them back. Their faith will sustain us and give us access to their future generations as long as we continue to manifest in their lives."

Olorun smiled at that. He was enjoying her spirited rant, glad to see that Shango hadn't crushed the spark that animated everyone in the company. Besides, she was making some points he agreed with even though he still wanted to expand.

Manifest in their lives.

Exactly what I have in mind.

"She has come again. Mama old-school," Olokun said following a short, clipped hiss as they looked around the room for support. When their eyes met Olorun's he noticed that they were both the same color—a pale blue. Another change. Olokun used to have one forest green and one a deep blue. They looked away quickly, and he felt the pang of incoming betrayal in his chest. Olokun had never been good at hiding their emotions.

Yemoja ignored the insult and continued. "These other things are distractions. Nobody takes these films and television programs seriously. You are getting their attention but not their faith. Haven't you understood that by now? Most of those depictions are wildly inaccurate to the point of silliness. We can't rely on those. Look, even you must have noticed how many more young people are seeking us out. Not because of some silly comic book or TV show but because they need something higher in their lives. Even though they lack faith they have curiosity, they want something they can believe in. Not just here but in the diaspora. They are tired of the illusions and transience of a world filled with unfamiliar foreign gods and inconclusive realities. They want guidance. With a little investment of our power, we can nurture their faith and it will yield dividends down the line. At the very least we need to analyze the situation again and come up with a new approach. The pittance we get from all this media nonsense can barely be called belief."

"But you can't deny some of it is working, can you?" Shango interjected finally, as a smile like a dagger cut across his face. "You mentioned the curiosity. Some of it is coming from the stories, comics, the movies, we have more visibility than ever. We shouldn't give up so easily. We can't just keep turning left and right anyhow because someone doesn't like the way things are going. Consistency is good. Stability. We should continue this and see how far it takes us, shouldn't we?"

His sentence ended in a tone that Olorun recognized. It was the tone of a question that did not seek to be paired with an answer. A tone that warned the person being asked that they were debating a point which had already been decided upon. His eyes settled on Yemoja to see how she would respond.

"Yes," she said, the rattling of her shells subdued. "I suppose we should continue. But . . ."

"But your points are well noted," Shango said, cutting her off as his wives tittered mockingly from behind him. They shouldn't even have been allowed to attend the meeting, technically. Only one of them was a member of the board. But Shango had insisted on appearing with his three wives at all formal events, another one of his ego-driven decisions that had slowly turned the company from what had been: a mostly loose, mostly family-managed spirit business, to what it was now: an almost cult-like, rigid, and hierarchal corporation run by a bully.

Yemoja looked away, and Olorun caught her eyes in motion. They were large black orbs set in aquamarine. Behind them though, he saw a flash of tempest, of a barely restrained flood. He knew that she was livid, but he also knew that she was too clever to show it without assurances that she could resist the potential consequences if she did. Even if Shango could not openly attack her on this side of reality, he could make her life in the spirit company difficult.

She has chosen to be clever. Let me help her choose to be brave.

"If I may," Olorun started, nodding at Obatala who was staring at him now, curious. "Perhaps we shouldn't just continue."

He waited for the other gods to fully take in his words, almost enjoying the range of reactions he received. Some furrowed their brows, some frowned. Some shook their heads and Eshu-Elegba simply continued watching and writing in the corner of the room, the sound of his lightpen on the slate loud against the sudden wall of silence as he took notes to ensure that the record of whatever happened was documented and the message passed along to the rest of the spirit company employees.

After a brief pause, Olorun continued, leaning forward and placing his hands on the smooth melamine-finished surface of the conference table. "Perhaps we should stop doing things that aren't working and, as Yemoja said, analyze the situation again. We can begin by looking inward."

"Inward?" Shango queried, visibly annoyed at having his attempt to move past the agenda item quickly, stalled. His biceps twitched and his eyes narrowed. He looked concerned as he folded his arms in front of him. Olorun noted that Shango's right hand, the one that was now locked away in Shigidi's chest, had been replaced with an elaborate bronze prosthetic that looked like a metal glove. The craftwork was impeccable, clearly the handiwork of Ogun himself, the retired orisha of war and metalwork. It almost made Olorun break the stare they were locked in just to admire it more closely. He didn't.

"Inward," Olorun repeated. "Yes. Inward. The way we appear to others when we go out must reflect the way we are at home, must it not? Or how is it those oyibo people like to say? Charity begins at home. So, look inward. Our own gods and deities and principalities within the company are dissatisfied and unmotivated to carry out the prayer requests of their believers or to even take actions to convince new converts. They do not *manifest* in their lives as they should."

"Are you referring to all that wahala with Shigidi?" Oduduwa blurted out, a bit too excitedly. The orisha of ambition and creativity raised his eyebrows, his annoying smile widening. It was a confident curl of his lips that seemed to appear whenever Oduduwa sensed that there was a situation he could potentially manipulate to his benefit. Like the one that was unfolding. Olorun did not like him or his ways but didn't fail to notice the twitch beneath Shango's eyes at the mention of Shigidi.

"Yes, I am talking about the Shigidi incident, and more," Olorun said, also crossing his hands in front of him.

"That has nothing to do with the company's performance," Shango said, his voice taking on an edge. "Besides, you are the one that allowed yourself to be dragged into that matter when that filthy succubus shamelessly threw herself at you, groveling for his life. I had it under control until you interfered."

Olorun almost flinched at the accusation. It was true that in Shigidi's case he had chosen to interfere, but only because if he hadn't, his backup plan for the future of the company would have been lost, and he couldn't have that. Shigidi was far too important, even if no one else knew except for Eshu-Elegba who'd been diligent in his secrecy, despite his penchant for games. Besides, the series of incidents that led to that situation and to Nneoma's offer, was what had piqued his interest enough for him to become curious about goings-on in the company. But once he had taken a close look into the situation, he knew he needed to get involved again or all his plans would have been for nothing. Shango would run the company into the ground if things continued unchecked. Shigidi and Nneoma's actions had been nothing more than a catalyst, accelerating his plans and forcing his decision to return sooner than he'd wanted to.

"Under control. I see," Olorun nodded in mock understanding. "Since when do we kill our fellow orishas in acts of vengeance for leaving? I don't remember instituting or deliberating that part of the company policy. And not just Shigidi, but what about Shopona and Aroni and others who have left or filed multiple complaints about being forced to do things that they do not want to do, just to ensure they receive their pray-pay. Were these situations also under control?"

The question lingered.

"Hmm." Shango's three wives interjected and shook their heads in unison like a kind of gele-wearing hydra to show their disapproval of the question, while Yemoja gently nodded her own. Olokun looked down at the table, angling their eyes up to Shango. Oduduwa kept his face stoic and Obatala leaned in. In the corner, Eshu-Elegba continued writing, his eyes focused. All around him, the orishas had concentrated their sights on Shango who sat, listening and visibly simmering.

Olorun continued, "It is clear that the rot runs deep. A widening inequality in the distribution of pray-pay and faith has woven itself into the structure of our company. The reports show a decline in income, yes, but they also detail wastefulness, a lack of restraint, lack of focus on the overall health of the company. Even if there has been a fall in faith, there is no reason for some to starve while others enjoy whatever they desire. There must be balance. That way, everyone is motivated to drive for growth. For the collective good. That is why you all exist as you are. And now that balance has been lost. There has been a significant failure of leadership. It is clear to me that the problem comes from within. Even if we were to make progress as a company, we must first correct this."

Shango's eyes began to glower an angry hot white. "Hmm. If you want to say something to me, say it directly," he demanded.

Olorun smiled as he said, "I left you in charge, to lead this company. There has been a failure of leadership. I don't believe I can be more direct than that."

Shango pounded on the table with a bronze fist adorned with red bead shells, causing a crack. "I failed? Me? You are the one that has been leisurely amusing himself above us all while the world changed. Now you want to come back here and tell me I did poorly? I have done the best I could under the circumstances."

"Yes. The best you could," Olorun echoed, keeping his voice steady. "And your best includes hoarding all the prayers and faith for yourself, your wives, and your loyalists?"

"We took what we needed. I have been doing my best. What don't you understand about that?" Shango thundered.

"Yes. Of course. Your best. I almost forgot." Olorun made no effort to conceal the mockery in his voice. "By the way, tell us, what *exactly* happened to Shopona?"

The question about the fate of the orisha of disease and health seemed to hit Shango like a bucketful of cold water to the face. A moment of hesitation, and then he said: "He died of course. Smallpox was his primary source of prayers, and when the new medicines and vaccines came, they eradicated his worshippers, so he died. *Abi* you want to blame me for that too?"

"No. No, I just want to clarify something," Olorun went on. "So, what you are telling the members of this board is that you definitely *didn't* ask Ososhi the hunter orisha to kill him when he was at his weakest so you wouldn't have to spend any more prayers to keep him alive?"

Shango quickly swiveled his head, peering around the table to scan the faces of his fellow gods, as if he were trying to evaluate their thoughts before responding to the accusation. He was met with an array of avoided gazes.

"You are playing a dangerous game, Kaabiyesi," he said, deliberately drawing out the syllables of each word so that everyone in the room could hear them drip with venom as they left his lips.

Perhaps, but you didn't answer the question.

That is your mistake.

"I think you are the one that has been playing a dangerous game, Shango. And the time for games has come to an end. Your time at the helm of this organization is over. I am taking back control of the spirit company."

Shango leaned back in his chair and clapped his hands in mockery. "Ah! I knew it. So that was your plan all along? To take control. You allowed that bastard Shigidi to weaken me when you refused to let me take back my hand and kill him. You made an evil covenant with that succubus. You sowed dissent among my subordinates and now you have shown your true colors. I see through you. Pretending to care about the company you abandoned for years. You just want back the power you handed over willingly long ago. Talking about balance and fairness and unfortunate things from the past. Liar. You still have so much authority and yet you want more, you want what I have now, the executive powers, the access to worship and the respect. Now who is the greedy one?"

"There is no greed in this," Olorun replied. "And I am not going to force you out, even though I could."

"What are you going to do?"

"This," the elder god sat up in his chair and said firmly, "I move for a vote of no-confidence to relieve Shango of his position as chief executive officer of this spirit company immediately."

The seated gods took up a roar around the table.

"*No!*"

"*No-confidence?!*"

"*Hmm.*"

"*It has never been done.*"

"*This cannot be!*"

And Shango, under his breath, "You wouldn't dare."

Olorun held up his right hand and the clamor started to die down. Through the tumult, he had been taking note of who said what and to whom, who was surprised and who was prepared, who was excited and who was afraid, whose voices and words and looks betrayed their intent. He catalogued all the observations as they quieted down and by the time silence settled, he'd weighed them against all he had expected, using his divine connection to each of them to extrapolate. And he knew exactly where he stood, save one.

"It is now a matter of procedure." Eshu-Elegba, who held sway over crossroads and was the steward of change, chimed in from the corner as though on cue. Olorun turned to the trickster orisha. He had finally stopped writing, and his hand hovered over a tablet like a hammer while he kept a steady querulous look on the visibly harried Obatala whose role it was to manage internal processes. "A motion for a vote has been tabled," Eshu-Elegba said. "It must be resolved."

Olorun smiled. Eshu-Elegba had always been an astute observer of both spirit and humankind, expertly navigating the churning sea of circumstance like an old fishing boat captain would. He had naturally recognized his role in a pivotal moment and had spoken the right words to the right person because he knew that even though Olorun had not chosen Obatala to be company CEO, he was still the orisha of light, spiritual purity, and moral uprightness, a perfect fit to be company secretary, responsible for ensuring that the rules of the spirit company charter were followed. Perhaps he lacked in will, in strength, in resolve, but he was not known to lack in procedural strictness. It was this reputation Eshu-Elegba had appealed to at precisely the right time, and Olorun was grateful.

Obatala looked from Eshu-Elegba to Olorun to Shango and finally back to Eshu-Elegba who kept laser focus on him, as though challenging him to do his duty.

Duty. Loyalty. Fear. Obatala's eyes frantically danced as though the three competing drivers were planets orbiting his mind, each with its own gravitational pull. After some time, he closed his eyes and rose to his feet, placing his palms on the table. Directly across from him, Shango was already shaking his head.

"The motion has been moved. The board must vote. This is the divine law," Obatala said. He exhaled deeply and then, "All in favor of removing Shango from the position of CEO of the Orisha Spirit Company, raise your hands."

Hands went up to join Olorun's, one by one. Yemoja's first. Then, surprisingly, Eshu-Elegba's. And finally, Obatala's. They all confirmed their vote with a verbal, "Yes."

Four.

"All not in favor, raise your hands."

Another set of hands flew up hastily as the previous four went down. As expected, Shango's, Oduduwa's, and Oya's. A chorus of "No"s followed.

Olokun seemed to have shrunk into their chair, hesitating, but Olorun knew it was only a matter of time. He had known where their allegiance lay from the moment he walked into the conference room. Besides, they had not voted Yes.

If you are not with me, you are against me.

Eventually, after a few awkward moments, they raised their hand, keeping their pale blue eyes trained on the floor.

Four in favor and four against.

Another silence expanded in the room as the gods took in the implication of this. All of them except Shango's attending wives who began to whisper to each other.

"It seems we have a tie," Eshu-Elegba said, laughing as he finally dropped his hand and continued to write on his tablet like he was documenting some curious new scientific observation, "How rare . . . and interesting."

Ties were indeed rare, but only because there were usually only seven board members in attendance, Olorun often being absent.

"Ehn so what now?" Oba asked finally, before her husband could stop her, "does that mean the motion is denied or how?"

"No, it is not denied," Obatala replied, exhaling another deep breath. He stood up straight and folded his arms in front of him, apparently gaining confidence as the moments went by.

Olorun allowed a smile to make its way across his face. He wondered if that burst of confidence was because Obatala relished his role as company secretary so much or if it was because he had finally realized that everything had gone exactly as Olorun had planned.

"In the case of a tie," Obatala started.

"Then the Chairman of the Board has the deciding vote," Olorun finished the sentence for him.

All the gods looked to Obatala for confirmation, and he nodded his head to give it.

Oba's eyes widened in shock.

"Well played," Olokun muttered under their breath, eyes still firmly downward. "Well played."

"No!" Shango's entire body flared white as he shot to his feet so quickly that cap almost fell off. Gritting his teeth until the thick tendons of his jaw became strained and severe, he stabbed his bronze fist toward Olorun. "You think you are clever? You think you are smart? Enough of these games. You have been lazing around for centuries while I have been here doing the work. I will not let you remove me from my place with dirty bureaucratic tricks."

Olorun tilted his head to the side and said, "In case you didn't notice, Shango, I already have."

Shango's face took on a reddish-brown color, and his mouth tightened further. Anger started to burn its way across his face in a familiar pattern. Olorun had seen it before and knew exactly what it preceded. He had suspected that narcissistic, vain, and hot-tempered Shango would not be able to contain himself, would think that centuries of retirement had taken their toll, would act on impulse and overplay his hand, even though Olorun had hoped he wouldn't. When the enraged thunder god reached back to snatch his dangling machete from his shocked wife's hands, Olorun made his move.

He let out a pulse of power that warped reality so that, to the other gods gathered, time appeared to come to a standstill. With that, he moved faster than they could perceive—even Shango, who was frozen in front of him like a statue. Olorun moved like a vicious wind, swift and invisible. As he moved, a streak of pure white light shafted its way into existence ahead of him, and he seized it with a firm fist. He swept behind Shango and stabbed the fistful of solid light into the narrow space between his bulging shoulder blades. The light spear cut through Shango effortlessly, erupting from his chest to pierce the table and the ground beneath where its tip pooled into a kind of circle, impaling him to the ground like a pillar. Shango cried out, first with surprise and then from the pain that Olorun knew was racking his entire body as the warped reality receded and time corrected itself. Yemoja leaned back in her chair as though avoiding the sound. Oya screamed. Olokun let out a gasp. Even Obatala took a step back, bumping into the chair behind him. The cry of a god was a terrible thing to hear.

They all watched breathlessly as Shango's body slid down the pillar of light in his chest, and he crumpled to his knees, head and chest on the table, mouth open in a constant paroxysm of pain. Hacking coughs cut their way through his shouts as he started to wave his arms around like he was drowning. Drowning in a sea of raw power. After a few moments, he stopped screaming but kept trying to stand up, to resist the vast wall of spirit particle pressure that Olorun was channeling through the light spear.

You must have forgotten.

It has been a long time, but I am still the most powerful of the orishas. I am the source. The font from which you all came.

And yet, Shango continued to struggle, a look of determination plastered on his face. Wild streaks of lightning wrapped themselves around the spear.

What are you doing Shango?

Suddenly Shango stopped as though he had felt something new or just come to a realization. His eyes narrowed.

Ah. Shit.

Shango took hold of the beam of light with his good hand, braced his weight against it with the other, for leverage, and pulled. The room shook with the force of Shango's resistance and shocked silence returned. Olorun watched but did not react even though he knew that Shango had found the crack in the wall of his power. It was only when he saw the first fissure appear in the spear, a dark zigzag that ran through the shaft of light like black lightning, that he moved again. He stepped forward so that he was at Shango's side, grabbed the orisha of lightning by the throat, and pulled him up just as the light spear shattered into bright spirit particles, like stardust. He was surprised when Shango's fingers wrapped around his own and began to peel them away, one by one.

"Is something wrong, old man?" Shango croaked out when he finally freed his neck enough from Olorun's vice-like grip to speak. He was smiling through bloody teeth. "You're still very fast, but you're not as strong as you used to be."

"Kaabiyesi, please stop," Obatala said.

"If we were still spirit-side, in Orun, I would unmake you," Olorun said to Shango, straining against the resistance.

Shango slowly twisted his hands away, "I'm not sure, Kaabiyesi. Even here, on this side of reality, I think I can hold my own against you now. I should never have let your threats force me to lose my hand. I was right. Leisure has made you soft. Lack of action has made you weak. You are spread thin. I felt it when I felt your power. I don't think you can kill me. Besides, what was it you said? We are not in the business of killing our own?"

"Please let us stop this, it is shameful to attempt violence at a board meeting," Obatala said.

"Shameful indeed," Eshu-Elegba echoed.

Olorun could feel the eyes of the other gods upon him like lasers, burning into his skin. He had gambled on the fact that Shango, like many of the others, had forgotten about the magnitude of his power. Power to make and unmake. Power that they needed to be reminded of. He had expected immediate capitulation once that reminder lesson was given. He had not expected Shango to resist so much, to push back with so much effort that despite the intensity of pain that had flooded his body, making every single one of his spirit particles vibrate at a frequency he had never experienced, he had still found the incompleteness in that power and exposed it. Olorun knew then that his return to the head of the company would be challenged, because as much as the orishas followed law, they only did so because they had agreed to. In any major disagreement, the highest and final law was and would always be power.

He released the tension in his hands and pulled them away from Shango before moving just as rapidly as he had advanced, back to his chair, a blur of motion and trailing light. "My apologies, but he brought that upon himself," he said, gathering the loose sleeves of his agbada back onto his shoulders. "He was the one who broke protocol and attempted the first strike." Olorun focused on his first son, Obatala, who no longer had that confident look in his eye.

Shango sat back heavily into his chair and his three attending wives moved to comfort him, kneeling at his side, rubbing the area around his wounded chest, and stroking his chin as they helped him adjust his cap. "My apologies to the board," he said, even though it was obvious he did not mean it. He kept his gaze firmly on Olorun as he rubbed his flesh and bronze hands together.

"Shango, by lawful vote of this board you have been removed from your position as CEO and all special privileges accorded you are hereby rescinded." Obatala paused to glance at Oduduwa whose chief ally was now no longer in charge. "Given your actions today and the accusations of past behavior, your place as a board member will need to be reviewed," Obatala added.

"Of course, it will," Shango agreed, still staring at Olorun.

"Let us convene again in three days. I will collect the evidence," Obatala said.

"Fine. Do what you will." Shango didn't even look at him.

"I move for another vote," Obatala declared. "I move for a vote to have Olorun take over the now vacant position of CEO." There was another uproar, but this one was more muted and didn't last as long. When the room had settled, Obatala added, "All in favor raise their hands."

Olorun watched as the hands went up, more hesitantly than he would have liked. But in the end, all of them rose, even Shango's, placing his bronze left hand to his chest as he raised his right. But he was smiling and licking his lips like a hyena that had smelled blood. It was a smile that was meant to let Olorun know what he was thinking: he had sensed the weakness, and he was going to reinforce himself. It was a smile that broadcast a message loud and clear.

This isn't over.

Olorun took in the array of raised hands, without completely removing his gaze from Shango's, refusing to concede even the staring battle. He adjusted his agbada again, lifted his cap and patted his salt-and-pepper afro down. "It will be an honor to lead you all again, my children," he said, and it was true. But his mind was filled with a single thought that he didn't share.

I have to consolidate my power.

CHAPTER 12

JULY 5TH, 2017 | 03:42 AM.

Aleister parked the SUV as he was instructed, just in front of a bus stop where a homeless woman swaddled in tattered brown rags and a blanket lay sleeping, her breathing labored. They were close to their hotel, just a few meters away from the brightly lit, Greek-temple inspired columns and stone steps of the main South Entrance of the British Museum. Aleister held the sacred text of the Wærlan-Drýlic close to his chest like a newborn child as they exited. Shigidi circled the vehicle and looked around and into the distance to make sure they were not being watched. Nothing caught his eye but the empty roads, stolid walls, and ugly red advertising along the glass barriers of the bus stop sitting area. A solitary streetlight illuminated the reflective white marks and lettering on the ground. They were still checked in to their hotel, but Shigidi had a feeling that they would not be checking out, even though he would have appreciated the chance to have one more cup of their excellent coffee. He could use the stimulation.

He took off his jacket, draping it over the passenger seat through the window, and rolled up his shirt sleeves. It was time to get to work. Nneoma walked up to him, her red-soled high heels unusually silent against the stone sidewalk. She stopped at just about an embrace away from him. Shigidi knew without asking, that she was using spirit particles to pad her footsteps. She stared at the streetlight until it flared bright orange, started to blink and then finally burned out under her concentrated spirit-particle pressure, leaving the three of them in a pool of near-darkness. Another overt display of her skill. Or perhaps just practice. He couldn't tell but he could see from the twinkle in her eye that she was enjoying herself. Or at least pretending to. She walked past him, brushing his arm lightly and spoke directly to Aleister.

"I'll take care of the CCTV cameras. You know where to go and you know what to do. So, let's do it. We don't have much time."

Aleister nodded, set the Wærlan-Drýlic down on the driver's seat and reached through the open door into the back seat of the vehicle where he retrieved a black, leather-bound briefcase as Nneoma stood still, faint trails of orange spiraling out from her body, seeking, probing for the city's ubiquitous electronic eyes. He quickly spun the combination locks on either side of the briefcase to the three-digit code and pulled out what he needed—a wood-carved mask painted forest-green with holes for mouth and eyes cut out under gold painted eyebrows. From the chin of the mask, extended a solid black three-inch beard with a series of rings painted in gold around it. When he put it on, Nneoma covered her mouth with her hands, trying to keep back a chuckle. She looked like she'd been sprayed with gold dust. "A mask of Osiris?" she asked, barely keeping her composure. "Really?"

"Yes, really," Aleister countered. "Do you want me to access London's spirit side or not?"

"You magicians are funny. But yeah, whatever works for you," Nneoma said, giving a conciliatory shrug of the shoulders as she snickered then turned back to Shigidi, "At least this doesn't require sex magick. Does it? That would really be awkward."

Shigidi almost burst out laughing himself but managed to choke it back to little more than a smile.

We are about to risk our lives and she's still amusing herself.

Aleister ignored the mockery, took out his smartphone and extracted its stylus with a gentle push. He turned up the screen brightness and used the stylus to draw out a shape in swift, smooth strokes. He chanted words that sounded like a mishmash of Latin, Arabic, and Hebrew to Shigidi's untrained ears, and as Aleister chanted, the white light from the phone screen began to pulse. Once it had established a sort of rhythm, he moved so quickly that Shigidi didn't see what he had drawn on the screen. He placed the phone on the asphalt road and covered it with the bulky Wærlan-Drýlic. The book also began to glow and pulse with a low white light of its own, as if it had become translucent and, after a few pulses, a ring of light rapidly irised out from its center before contracting back into the shape of an eye. The eye of light blinked at them twice, then stared.

"Okay. Operation complete. This isn't exactly the best tension site, but I found a few good sockets nearby for anchoring the corporeal and spirit particles. I think it will hold." Aleister took off the mask and cleared his throat. "Give me your phone."

Shigidi pulled his phone out of his left pocket, unlocked it with his fingerprint and passed it to Aleister, staring him down. He still half-expected him to try something that would give him a reason to punch him in the face. In some ways, magicians were a lot like babalawos, they were humans who had established connections to spirit entities and learned how to manipulate spirit particles. The key difference was, babalawos knew that they served those spirits. Magicians sought to have dominion over them.

I don't trust him.

Aleister simply took the phone, opened the voice recorder app, and spoke in the same bizarre macaronic mishmash language he'd used earlier which Shigidi still couldn't understand except for the phrase "abyssus abyssum invocat," which he'd heard before when one of his regular customers at the Orisha Spirit Company had been converted to Christianity. *Deep calls unto the deep.* Whatever that means.

"Now the two devices are tethered to the same portal through a secure back channel," Aleister announced when he was done. "Call my number once you're in position to establish the remote connection, and I will perform the operation to pull you spirit-side."

He passed the phone back to Shigidi who took it without a word. "Just make sure you're holding on to each other when you make the call. I need direct physical contact to be able to pull both of you in with the same operation, and I doubt we will have time to do it twice."

"Thank you, Aleister," Nneoma said.

"A deal is a deal luv," he responded, checking for Shigidi, who still watched him closely. "I'm going in now. Not sure how long it will take you to get what you need but we won't have much time before sunrise, before the Wærlan-Drýlic is summoned back to the temple, breaking the connection, so I'll grab us a ride spirit-side just in case. This is a heist after all, so no harm in having a getaway driver, is there?"

"I suppose not," Nneoma agreed, "if it's not too difficult to get one."

"You'd be surprised how easy it is to get a taxi in London once you're dead."

"Sounds good," Nneoma said.

Shigidi gave a reluctant thumbs up. "Great."

In the distance, the homeless woman's labored breaths turned into deep rolling snores that erupted periodically. Shigidi wondered briefly if she would survive till daylight or if someone would come for her before whatever illness she was clearly suffering from did.

I wonder if we will survive till daylight.

Staring into the eye-shaped portal, he distinguished a faint sound like wind blowing steadily behind the blinding radiance despite the background noise of snoring. The memory of what it was like to slip from the spirit world to the corporeal back in Lagos, when he was still a working nightmare god, before he had chosen this strange new life and gone freelance with Nneoma. It had been so long since he'd been to Orun, he found himself missing it, eager to cross to the spirit-side again even though this time he would be in a land of foreign spirits. And then he remembered just how dangerous their task was and how high the risk of being permanently trapped in a foreign spirit-place. All the sense of excitement drained from him and fear started to mount in his mind.

"You better be there to open that door like we told you. Don't mess this up," he said to Aleister as he reached into his own mind and seized control of his own fears, weaving them into something more like caution.

"Umm. I won't," the magician responded, looking at Nneoma as though seeking her final permission or blessing. Shigidi acknowledged that it was she who was owed the favor after all and this was the point of no return, so he wanted to be certain.

She nodded and smiled.

Shigidi just scratched his head.

"See you on the other side then." Aleister stepped forward confidently, into the eye of unnatural brightness. It rippled but remained stable.

Shigidi and Nneoma watched him sink slowly into the shining space between realities until his face was only about half a breath away from the eye of light. He winked nervously at them and then, just like that, he was gone; a traveler between the two irreconcilable sides of the ancient city. The eye closed and the light from it disappeared.

They were alone again.

Neither of them said anything for a second that felt flexible enough to be an hour, as the cool air of early London morning licked at them. The tower of unanswered questions, that had built up in Shigidi's mind since they'd left Malaysia, suddenly loomed large in that moment of silence as he considered all that had happened and all that could happen to them once they entered the museum. He needed to know. He tried to hold his tongue, but the words came out almost of their own volition.

"Nneoma . . ."

She looked up curiously at him. "Yes?"

"Why were you flirting with Aleister back in the club?"

She shook her head as though she were physically rearranging the words of his question in her mind. "I felt like dancing. I don't know why you got so upset about it. It wasn't a big deal."

He frowned. "We didn't have time for it. And you know you were doing more than just dancing. You were teasing him. I've seen you do it enough times to know. And you were enjoying it. I could feel you . . . projecting."

"Projecting what?" she shot back.

"I don't know," he admitted, consciously trying to keep his mouth partly open so that he didn't clench his jaw. "But it was not just sexual energy, it was an emotional state you have never projected around me."

It was Nneoma's turn to frown then, her lips curled in an annoyed line as she folded her hands in front of her. "Shigidi, we don't have time for this. You said it yourself, we have a job to do."

He ignored her statement even though he knew it was true, but he felt like he couldn't stop. "You're happy dancing in a club with your ex, or whatever Aleister is to you. You're happy fighting other gods and taking their market share for Olorun. You're happy seducing humans and taking their spirits, but you're not happy just being with me and I want to know why. I have a right to know why."

"Because I don't want to feel like I need anyone!" she shouted.

There, she's finally allowed herself to admit it.

"Okay? I don't like feeling like this. I don't like what my life has become, constantly having to make deals and trade favors and hide in the shadows and run errands for gods I don't like. I don't like having these stupid arguments about how I feel, whether I love you or not, and I don't like the fact that my sister is dead because . . ."

She stopped herself before saying it, but he could sense where she was going, the current of her words flowed strong, and he wanted to follow it to some sense of clarity.

"Finish it," he said, lowering his voice. "Because what?"

"Because she made a stupid mistake. She fell in love with someone, someone who was meant to be a partner but destroyed what we had. Destroyed herself because of it." She looked down at the asphalt.

"So, you don't want to love me because you think it will compromise you somehow?"

"I don't know," she said.

"You are not your sister. Do you really think you will make whatever mistake she made just because you fall in love? How do you know you're not in love already?"

"I don't know." She shook her head as she looked back up to meet his gaze. "I just know that I don't like where we are now. This is not what I wanted when I decided to make you my partner." She threw up her hands. "I didn't want to be lonely anymore. That's true. I saw what you could do, and I knew your potential, I knew it could benefit us both. I wanted that safety. But above all, eventually, I wanted freedom. Real freedom. And I don't feel like I have that now."

There can be both pleasure and pain in knowing someone truly, he thought. Knowing someone so completely that you know how their face looks when they are about to fall asleep or laugh or cry or orgasm or lie or try to hide something from you. Shigidi felt the pain of her incoming response hit him before he even asked the question.

"Nneoma, just tell me the truth, do you love me?"

She wiped at her eyes like she was clearing them of the emotion she'd let bubble to the surface, looked away and shrugged. "Why does it matter anyway?"

And at that she started to walk away, crossing the road. "It is what it is. We are partners in this enterprise, and we need to focus on what is in front of us now. We can pay our debts and live forever if we play our cards right. We will no longer be beholden to Olorun or any other gods or spirit companies or magicians. We can continue to get as many spirits as we need, when we need them. And no matter how we feel, the truth is that we are good partners, and right now, we have no one else but each other." She gave him a wry smile that didn't reach her eyes. "Shigidi, we are in the middle of a job that could reward us with vengeance against Shango, so I don't understand why my feelings matter at all. At all. And I am tired of being interrogated about it."

She didn't say it. She didn't say she loves me.

In that moment, Shigidi accepted it. Perhaps because he already suspected, deep down, that she didn't love him and even if she did, it was possible she would never admit it. She wouldn't allow herself. He suspected that she loved the idea of him. Perhaps as much as she loved the memory of her sister. She loved the idea of a partner. Someone as beautiful and potentially as powerful as she was, to eat and drink and make love and share eternity with. It was probably why she had spent so much of her power to remake him, remold him. He could have been any other lowly and pathetic minor god that she had come across in Lagos with the same desperate look in their eyes and the potential of Olorun's clay written on their skin. Maybe. It could have been anyone and it just happened to be him. So, he accepted it quietly and resolved not to let his emotions overwhelm him again like they did the night he had jumped in front of Shango's fist to save her life, or like they were doing again, overwhelming him in that very moment, causing him to endanger a mission in the hope of hearing those three words from her lips.

"Fine," he said finally, walking up to her and embracing her tightly from behind. "It doesn't matter. As you say, it is what it is. Let's get to work."

He only tensed for a second before pushing his foot down with explosive power and launching them up and over the row of buildings bordering the museum in a smooth leap, a weak sliver of summer moon behind them.

CHAPTER 13

Aksum, Tigray Region, Aksumite Kingdom of Ethiopia

FEBRUARY 14TH, 1021 | 04:38 PM.

The moon was swollen full and sharp as it slowly cut a dark crescent into the brightness of the sun. Like an evil omen in the sky, the eclipse cast a growing shadow on the world.

It was quiet. Most of the capital city's inhabitants had huddled themselves together indoors, hiding from both the omnipresent wrath of their new witch-queen and the foreboding sky that had heralded her.

Nneoma's sandals slapped loudly against the ground as she made her way hastily through the dusty, abandoned streets, her braided hair and face covered with a thin linen veil. She could still smell the smoke in the air through the soft fabric. Smoke that was carried on a persistent wind blowing eastward from the chapel where the witch-queen Gudit had locked in the last of the towns priests and elders before commanding her soldiers to set the building ablaze. Nneoma had watched it all from a distance, heard the crackle of flame taking to tinder and the first muffled cries of defiance that had quickly turned to desperate screams. She could no longer hear the screams but the howling wind grew louder as the sky grew darker.

Her heart was pounding, banging a drum of concern, but it was not concern for those whom Gudit was burning alive for no other crime than being in positions of power during the reign of the recently captured emperor Dil Na'od. No, she was only concerned about her sister, Lilith, and what could happen to her when the witch-queen discovered that Lilith's lover, Samael was bound to Dil Na'od by contract. Or worse, if Samael in some act of insanity, attempted to honor that contract and go on the offensive against her. No. Nneoma wanted no part of that. They needed to get out of the city and head anywhere, perhaps North to Kush, where they still had friends and contacts, or West to Wagadou where they knew no one but could trade their services to the warrior-kings they had heard of from salt and gold caravan traders. Whatever it was, they needed to leave immediately. Gudit was fleet with a bow, powerful with a sword and had mastered the manipulation of spirit particles. Worst of all, she was ruthless. As ruthless as any human Nneoma had ever come across, perhaps more so, judging by the stories the travelers had told. The most talkative of them said that she had seduced an evil spirit, Busha Ayyaana, with her beauty and ambition, inviting the spirit to possess her and share a body with her. That this was what gave her the power she used for conquest. To many of these people, those stories were only rumors, but Nneoma had been in the crowd when Gudit first entered the conquered city. She had looked into the witch-queen's eyes and sensed the projection of dark spirit particles entangled with her flesh when she rode past on a mare with skin and hair the color of midnight. Nneoma knew the stories were more than just rumors. Gudit was not a woman Nneoma wanted to take on. She wasn't even entirely sure she could if it came to it.

Nneoma's pulse became a steady beating in her head that grew louder with every step she took. She wanted to fly to her sister, but to do so would risk exposure.

Lilith, Lilith, Lilith. Why did we ever agree to come here?

It was that one question that stabbed at her heart most viciously as she rounded the end of the street and passed by a towering stone obelisk with Ge'ez script—which she could not read—inscribed on it. It was a hawulti, a monument to mark the location of a dead emperor's burial chamber. It occurred to her that if she and her sister died here, no one would erect a hawulti or even place a stone to mark their memory. They would go from being cast-out angels to less-than-nothings. From once feared and worshipped to destroyed and forgotten in what had been a long running sequence of poor choices.

Poor choices. Like choosing to side with Lucifer. Like following Samael here. If Lilith had not fallen for Samael; if they had remained in the shadows, avoiding the affairs of power-hungry men, ambitious women and organized gods, simply taking small sips of sustenance where they could; if Samael had not entered a contract with a doomed emperor; if they had made different choices, she would not be running down the darkening street, afraid for her life, while a hungry moon swallowed the sun.

She sped past the obelisk and turned left at a four-way intersection. Stone-paved roads gave way to packed dirt paths and smaller buildings. After another minute of panicked running, she came to the place where they had taken refuge. It was a small circular stone house with two street-facing windows like suspicious eyes and a thatch roof sloping at a sharp angle. It was usually a kind of tan, sandy brown, but in the daytime darkness of the eclipse, it looked grey and disquieting.

Nneoma ran up to the stocky door made of a stack of crudely cut pieces of wood attached to each other, her pulse still pounding in her ears. She knocked twice and the door swung open just as the moon began to slide past the face of the sun, lifting the edge of the curtain of shadows.

Samael stood there, a bronze-skinned tower of a man with an aquiline nose and a puff of curly, black Levantine hair. He was wearing leather armor, as though he had just returned from a battle or was about to go to one. He was so tall that he had to bend his neck so that she could see the top half of his head, see his eyes. Smiling. He was smiling at her. It was a thin, hard smile and he did not look at all surprised to see her. There was something about the falseness of that smile and the strangeness of the returning light making the grey walls of the house begin to turn brown again, that made Nneoma even more uncomfortable than she already was.

"Samael," she said in her best Amharic, trying not to scream. "Where is she? Where is Lilith?"

"You are agitated." He straightened and took a step to the side, clearing the doorway. "Come in."

Nneoma took a deep breath and slowed her heart rate down as she entered the open space of the house. It was clean, too clean, with its hard-packed floor recently swept. Of the furniture that used to sit in every corner none remained except for a single stool in a corner. A woven thatch screen farthest from the door separated the sleeping area from the rest of the house. A smell like animal fat hung heavy in the air. She stopped in the center of the space and spun around to face Samael. He seemed too calm, given the chaos that had overrun the city in the last few hours. It was true that he was older than her and her sister by some measure of time she couldn't name. She just knew he'd been created before they were. A minute or several millennia, no one could tell. And even though he consumed souls as frequently as they did, his age was starting to show. His pitch-black hair had a faint silver streak running through it, from his left ear to the back of his neck. And the lines of his face were few, but deep. In the right light, his eyes hinted at his power, their deep, unnatural green reflecting the intensity of his spirit particle potency. His lips were thick and his jaw solid. He was handsome in a rugged way, a warrior's way. She understood why Lilith found him attractive, but she didn't want to talk to him, she wanted to speak with Lilith.

"Where is she?" Nneoma asked again.

"Naamah, relax" he sighed. "She is over there. Getting ready."

"Ready for what?" Nneoma asked as her heart began to pound again.

"You know what," he said, folding his arms in front of him. "We had an agreement with Dil Na'od. We must go to his aid now."

Nneoma's knees suddenly felt weak and unsteady as her worst fear deposited itself into reality. There was a prickling sensation on her forehead as the fear turned to anger. "No! I knew you would say that. I knew it. You've always been too stubborn and impractical for your own good. That's why you stuck with Lucifer even through The Fall. This is foolishness. Go and rescue your stupid emperor if you like but leave my sister out of it."

"I am not asking her to do anything," he said. "My contract. My agreement. I am the one that is bound by honor. She offered to help me."

Even before she had taken the cover of the eclipse to come here, Nneoma knew that this was what Lilith would do. Since they had fled Egypt together, she'd known that Lilith had become too tightly bound to her lover. It had become more than a business arrangement, as she often claimed whenever Nneoma asked about their relationship. Nneoma had often asked jokingly about what would happen if Samael did something stupid, like jump off a cliff, would Lilith jump too? And now suddenly witch-queen Gudit had come, and the joke had flipped into a deadly sharp reality that was slowly stabbing its way into her heart.

"Lily!" Nneoma shouted, turning as she made for the thatch screen. "Lily! Answer me!"

"Naa?" The high-pitched voice of her sister.

Nneoma tore at the screen to reveal Lilith staring at her, mouth open with surprise, her hands suspended in her partially braided hair. She was wearing a black leather tunic cinched around her waist, an array of sharp daggers suspended from it. The contrast of the dark leather and her fair, milk-white skin mirrored the contrast of Nneoma's dark skin on her own flowing white robe and veil. They had always been different, Naamah and Lilith, both superficially and internally, but they remained together despite it. Perhaps even because of it. Because they were different in complementary ways, all their differences fit into each other like two halves of the same thing and perhaps because in the end, they were the same in the one way that mattered—they knew how to use what they had, to get what they wanted. At least Nneoma thought so. She wasn't so sure anymore.

"We need to get out of the city now, Lily," she said, taking her sister's hand. It was slippery with animal oils and herby fragrances. "It's not safe for us here anymore. If we leave now, we can make it to Kush in a day or two. We can fly over the desert."

"I'm not leaving, Naa," Lilith said casually, as though she were telling her about the weather or the harvest and not making a statement that would ruin them both. Nneoma took a step back. She heard the slushing glug of something being poured from a jar and was suddenly reminded of Samael's presence behind her.

"Let's go outside and talk about this," she said, half whispering, but Lilith simply shook her head and pulled Nneoma's closer to her so that they were almost in an embrace. It was a familiar position, one they used often in difficult moments that demanded sincerity and clarity.

"I know what you want to say, and there is no need to hide it," Lilith began. "There is no need to hide anything from him. I know what I am doing. You don't have to stay with us. Go. We will complete our contract and come find you in Kush when it is done."

Nneoma examined her sister for a moment, searching the deep ocean blue of her eyes for doubt, for some crack in Lilith's confidence that she could exploit and convince her to change her mind. But there was none.

"Gudit isn't just another power-hungry human conqueror," she said, rubbing Lilith's hands and pulling them to her bosom. "Did you not see how she moved the moon to herald her takeover? She has merged with a spirit, some ancient, primal entity, an elder god of this land and these people that holds a lot more power than anything I've sensed since The Fall. It's something so old, I've never heard of it, I don't even know its name. No one does. They just call it Busha

Ayyaana—the bad spirit. I could not see it, only sense the intensity of its spirit particles, and it is not that different from the one that made us. Do you understand? She is now a vessel for something much more powerful than we are used to dealing with." Nneoma turned sharply to look at Samael who was holding a brown ceramic bowl full of a liquid that smelled sickly sweet.

"I know that," Samael said as he took a sip of the drink. "And so does she."

"Then you know your patron emperor is as good as dead already. There is no point in trying to rescue him," Nneoma said.

"That is not true, we can get him back," Samael said. "It will be difficult but not impossible. Besides, we once rebelled against the ancient one himself, we can handle this witch-queen. A contract is a contract. Honor demands that I help him."

"You are a fool," Nneoma spat out, as her anger returned, leaking out of her in a cluster of bitter words. "You stood by your friend Lucifer in his rebellion against the ancient one and how did that turn out for you? Hmm?"

He scoffed. "You talk like you weren't with us."

"I rebelled because I believed in the cause. In the message. I wanted freedom. I still do. But you, with all this talk of honor but no talk of what makes sense; did you even understand why we rebelled? Our philosophy? Why we wanted to be free? Or were you just standing by your friend because you promised him that you would?"

"I didn't," Samael said, suddenly pensive. "I didn't stand by him at the end, in the final battle."

Nneoma stared, confused. "What?"

"Sam, you don't have to . . ." Lilith began, but he stopped her with a look and a raised hand. "Please. Let me explain."

He looked down at the ground. "You're right, Nneoma. I never truly believed in the cause. I never wanted to rebel. But I had made a promise to a friend. So, I fought with him. But when Michael and his army blocked our advance at the gates, and I saw just how vastly outnumbered we were, I was afraid. I was a coward." Samael's voice was trembling as though each word that came out of him was a thorn, its removal full of pain. "I abandoned him when he needed me most and that moment of betrayal has haunted every moment of my existence since."

Samael shook his head, took another sip of his drink, and wiped his lips. His confident smile returned but he could not hide the filmy wetness in his eyes. "I . . . I cannot do that again. I will not do that again. Ever."

Nneoma stared at him. She finally understood some of his obsessiveness with honor and keeping his word. But she didn't care. She didn't want to allow herself care. She only wanted to leave with Lilith. "Fine. Whatever. But you can't let the past drive you into stupid actions in the present. Things change, reality is fluid, we all make choices as we need to, and survival is the most important thing. It might have been a good idea to enter into a contract with Dil Na'od at the time, but you are a fool for trying to honor it now when it is no longer worth it. You're an even bigger fool for roping my sister into it. I curse the day Lilith and I agreed to form a partnership with you."

"Stop it, Naa!" Lilith shouted, and the shock of her raised voice forced Nneoma into silence. Lilith's pale face was flushed deep pink, and her eyes were wet globes of sadness. "We were created together, and we've been together for thousands of years; we've shared wine and food and men and spirits and pain and everything that is possible to share between two people. We have a bond built into us, and I love you as much as it is possible to love another, but I also love Samael. I want you to know that. I love Samael as much as I love you. It's a different kind of love, it's a love I chose. It may have started as a partnership, but it's much more than that now, and I am no longer afraid to admit it. He understands me, not because we were created alike but because he has chosen to. And I have chosen to stay with him because I cannot live without him now."

Nneoma let go of her sister's hand and stepped back. The admission cut her like a knife, because she knew what it meant.

I've lost my sister.

She started sobbing.

Lilith tried pull her back into their embrace, but Nneoma pushed her away again.

"Why would you choose to stay with him over me, especially now when you are in danger?" Nneoma asked, her voice trembling, "Why can't it be the way it used to be? Just you and me again, like it was in the beginning, sisters, partners, protecting each other. We may have needed Samael in Jerusalem, but we don't need him anymore. We can seduce any man or spirit or god we want. He may feel he has to do this, but you don't need to choose this with him. You don't need to. I know you feel attached to him, and I will admit I do too, but that too will pass."

"Stop please," Lilith croaked. Her eyes fell to the ground. "You still don't understand."

"Of course, I understand." Nneoma blurted out, desperate, as she wiped away a stray tear. "You love him. I understand. I'm sorry I suggested you leave him. I'm sorry. You can be together again. We can continue the way we have. But just come with me to Kush and let him complete his contract himself. You don't need to fight this battle with him. We are not warriors, we are free spirits. You don't need to be there. He can meet us in Kush when he is done. Isn't that right Samael? You love her and you don't want her taking this unnecessary risk, do you? You can—"

"Stop," Lilith repeated, louder, and she went over to Samael's side leaving Nneoma standing alone by the thatch screen. "Please don't say anymore," she started. "I really hoped you would understand but I knew you wouldn't. Maybe you can't. Maybe in this, we are truly different. Please, Naa, just go. We will do what we need to and then come and find you in Kush."

Nneoma wanted to say so much more to Lilith in that moment, to remind her of the past, to entice her with the future, to plead with her not to leave her alone, to tell her again and again that they had no real reason to stay and fight. But under the confident blue gaze of her sister's eyes, and the echo of the word *stop* in her head, all her own words seemed to remain stuck in her throat because she knew using them was pointless.

The three of them jerked suddenly when they heard it.

Insistent knocking at the door.

Nneoma's eyes shot to it first. Could the witch-queen's soldiers have found them? Could Dil Na'od have been broken so easily and given up Samael so soon? Her mind filled with horrible images of arrest and torture and execution, of slow and painful death, of unmaking by some strange and ancient spirit, of having their flesh cut up into pieces and their spirit particles unwoven from each other until they could not hold their consciousness together.

"I will see who it is," Samael said with far more confidence than Nneoma thought was appropriate. "Be prepared. In case."

The knocking continued and Nneoma looked at her sister, unsaid words hanging in the space between them like a raincloud. Lilith snapped her fingers and a burst of bright blue spirit particles exploded into the air. She moved her fingers in a tight circle and the particles assembled in a kind of orbit around her wrist as she turned to face the door, ready to counter an attack.

Nneoma spread her arms on either side, her own yellow spirit particles shimmering on the surface of her skin like glitter. She took a deep breath, bracing herself, as Samael opened the door.

A man stood in the doorway hunched over and wearing nothing but a piece of cloth tied around his waist. He was pressing bloodied hands to his belly.

Nneoma recognized him from the palace. She'd seen him the first day they had come to this city. It was Bes'ad, the emperor's head guard.

"Demon! The emperor demands your services now!" he shouted as he stumbled across the threshold, leaving a trail of blood.

"Were you followed?" Samael asked, still infuriatingly calm.

"No," Bes'ad said. "No one followed me. I used the eclipse as cover to escape."

"Of course," Nneoma muttered under her breath, as Samael closed the door and she allowed herself to relax.

Bes'ad grimaced. His skin was dark with fallen ash, and his curly hair was a sponge matted to his head, clumps of dirt and soot and grass embedded in it. His skin was covered in cuts, burns, and abrasions. "I was with the emperor when he was captured, but he tasked me with a duty: to ensure you fulfill your bargain with him."

"I don't think you are in a state to ensure anything," Nneoma remarked, and Lilith shot her a look.

Samael took the brown bowl and finished his drink in one gulp.

When he was done, he asked the injured man: "Her soldiers, did they use magick?"

"Yes. Our weapons could not pierce them," Bes'ad said, coughing.

"Then she has enchanted her army," Samael said to Lilith quietly.

"It will be a bit more difficult to enter the palace," Lilith said. Her voice was gentle too. "So, we enter from above."

"Yes." Samael agreed with a nod.

"No," Nneoma said, annoyed at their calm and casual way of speaking, as though they had already agreed before the words came. The way she and Lilith used to talk to each other. "Please don't do this, Lily. It's suicide."

"No, it isn't," Lilith shot back. "And even if it is, it's my choice. I choose to be with Samael in this. In all things." Her eyes were hard. Crystalized with resolve.

"You're making a mistake," Nneoma said and looked away.

Lilith said nothing in reply.

Nneoma took a deep breath before she spoke again. "I am asking you one more time, I am begging you Lily, come to Kush with me now."

"No, Naa." She shook her head. "I think you are scared, and it's okay. It's all right to be scared. You're scared for me because you care, and I love you for it. But I also love Samael, and I am not afraid of this witch-queen. We will fulfill our bargain, and we will live in this land just like we planned."

"This is wrong. Wrong. This isn't how we operate Lily. We don't engage large forces like this. We move in the shadows and we negotiate, and we take what we need, nothing more. This isn't our way."

"I know it isn't, but it is Samael's way, so I will go with him."

"Why?" Nneoma asked, exasperated.

"Because I love him."

"It's really that simple?"

"It is," Lilith replied.

A few seconds passed. "I don't want to lose you," Nneoma said finally, and the words hurt as they came out of her because they meant she had accepted this, and she hated herself for it.

"You won't lose me."

"Then promise. Promise me that I won't lose you because of this . . . because of him." She glanced over at Samael who was helping Bes'ad to drink from his bowl.

"I promise" Lilith smiled, and it was a sad smile that didn't reach all the way to her eyes. "You won't lose me."

As Nneoma took in those words, memories flashed through her mind. Memories of things they had done together—there were so many that she could barely remember any events in her life that did not involve Lilith. Dangerous things, yes. And pleasurable things too. And through them all, she'd always had the comfort of knowing she wasn't alone, that Lilith was there beside her or would be. That they were always there for each other. And as much as she wanted to believe that Lilith would keep her promise, she didn't believe it, she felt angry because she didn't think they needed to be in that position, and she felt guilty because she felt she was abandoning her sister. "Then fine. Do what you want here. But come back to me." She wanted to sound stern, but she only sounded sad and tired and scared, even to herself. She didn't like it.

Lilith stepped toward her and engulfed her in an embrace. Nneoma accepted it, allowing the warmth to suffuse her senses. She took in the smell of scented oils in her hair, the softness of her neck, the firmness of her shoulders.

"I'll meet you in Kush, Naa," Lilith said, when she finally pulled away.

"You better." Nneoma swept out of the house as quickly as she had entered, reattaching her veil.

"See you soon," Samael called to her, his voice rich and gravelly and calm. Always so calm.

She glanced back at him and shook her head.

When Nneoma stepped out of the stone house, the now-unobstructed sun was still high in the sky. She looked up at it and it stared back at her from behind a smattering of silver clouds, tracing its path across the sky slowly and quietly. She considered staying for a moment, a warm rush of excitement filling her mind as she imagined fighting side by side with Lilith against an army of enchanted enemies, their wings spread out and their claws extended, tearing at flesh and drawing blood in bright spurts until they won or were finally cut down and lying together on the ground, holding hands. They could die together. Or they could save Dil Na'od and raise an army, come back, and defeat the witch-queen possessed by Busha Ayyaana in a glorious battle, perhaps even become living deities in Aksum, together. Twin goddesses, as they once had been. The rush of excitement drained from her. She looked back down at the earth.

No. The world had changed. And Lilith had Samael now. Things would never be the same between them. Not even death.

All she could hope for now was that she would see her sister again.

Her eyes full of tears and her heart full of guilt and anger, Nneoma sprinted away. She ran and ran until the cluster of stone houses gave way to sparse patches of thatch huts and the wide dirt road of the city narrowed, becoming a path, then gave way to thick untraveled bush. In a single, piercing scream, Nneoma let out all the emotions that were swirling inside her as she ripped away her robes and her veil. Scales covered her skin like armor and wings shot out of her back, spreading wide and high as she took to the sky, turning her back to the sun.

CHAPTER 14

The British Museum, Bloomsbury, London, England

JULY 5TH, 2017 | 03:58 AM.

They hit the roof of the building, a pulsing shimmer of yellow spirit particles padding their landing. Shigidi let go of Nneoma and shuffled forward on the sloping roof until he was at the edge. Reaching down, his fingers found the triangular boundary of the tympanum that was filled with an array of sculpted images in a pediment above the Museum's main entrance. He held onto the edge of its recessed stone center with his left hand and slid off, letting himself dangle precariously in front of the graven image of a crowned woman in long drapes holding a globe and a spear. She stared back at him with empty stone eyes.

The images here are so lifeless and colorless.

He reached up with his right hand to see Nneoma waiting for him, a halo of moonlight behind her, highlighting the edges of her hair with ghostly flair. She took his hand and hopped off the roof in one fluid movement, dangling beneath him and checking around quickly to ensure they still hadn't been seen. When she was sure they were clear, she signaled him with a finger tap to his forearm, and he let go. They dropped down to the ground between two pillars in front of the main door, and onto the solid stone, still silent and upright, without needing to bend their knees. Nneoma's skintight dress didn't even ride up. They stepped, with one coordinated movement like a dance, behind the columns for cover.

Nneoma held her left hand up to her lips and kissed her palm, producing a cluster of yellow sparks. She blew the fiery kiss into the air. The particles floated, wispy, like living embers, into the museum, seeping through spaces between the hinges of the doors and windows to all the cameras and lock system locations she'd memorized that afternoon in their hotel room while Shigidi had tracked down Aleister. They waited for almost a minute, and then she smiled.

Shigidi allowed himself to relax a little, unable to completely push back his feelings of admiration, fascination even. He adjusted his rolled-up sleeves, pushing them up above his elbows. Together, they slid out from behind the columns and walked confidently into the museum like it belonged to them, the twin wood and glass doors opening smoothly like the welcoming wings of a hulking butterfly.

They went briskly past the narrow foyer and into a quadrangular room with a high tessellated blue glass roof and a circular central column large enough to be a room of its own, flanked by two staircases that ringed it like romantic suitors.

There, in the expansive great court, they saw a thickly bearded security guard with a pot belly and sunken, sleepy eyes wearing a navy-blue uniform two sizes too tight for him. He was pacing in front of the stairs. The sight of the two of them approaching at such a late hour must have confused him so much that he didn't know how to react at first, because he completely froze, as if every nerve in his body had been overloaded.

Then he muttered a bewildered, "What in the . . ."

He trailed off like his own words had jarred his thoughts, violently throwing his eyes wide open in a spike of panic.

But before he could reach for his radio, Nneoma fixed him with a look. Her eyes flared yellow and then narrowed. The security guard froze in place, and his eyes glazed over. Shigidi watched Nneoma as she focused her aura at him. He knew what she was doing because he'd seen her do it once in Hanoi—fill a man's mind with desire like newfound madness until it was soft and pliable. He would do anything she commanded him to do, like stay in place. Shigidi knew that the guard was not *unable* to move, he was just *unwilling* to. His mind was probably completely suffused with a desire to please her and could think of nothing else but staying exactly where he was until she told him to move again. It was one of her more impressive tricks, though it only worked on certain kinds of people, like this guard. He stayed still, just like one of the statues he was meant to watch over.

They didn't even miss a step, their shoes still silent against the polished marble floor.

They turned right and cleared some distance before descending the stairs that led to the lower floor. Winding along the stone and marble passageways, they ignored the splendid displays all around them. They were not exactly in a rush but conscious of the time. It was not long till sunrise.

When they arrived in front of a large, plain, white composite door beside a wide-framed display of Nsibidi symbols in black and white, Nneoma whispered, "We're here."

Shigidi first pulled the doors open and then pushed the secondary glass doors to gain access. They both yielded without resistance. A smell like vaporized bleach scraped at his nose, and there was a faint humming sound that made his spirit particles vibrate like an itch. The gallery walls were painfully white and sterile, arrayed with an assortment of colorful masks, cloths, pottery, weapons, and all manner of items displayed atop plinths, in transparent cases. Some of the items were works of art but some of them he recognized as totems of gods, deities, and spirit-entities from his and other spirit companies he had worked with in the past, now all displayed—hung, bound, or in locked glass boxes like prisoners. He stood still and stared.

"Are you okay?" Nneoma asked when she noticed that he had stopped moving.

"Yes," he replied quickly, remembering where he was. But he stayed still.

"Shigidi?"

He only started moving again when he realized that he could hear his teeth grating against each other for the first time. "Yes. I'm fine. Let's just get what we came for."

Despite his words, something had started to bubble beneath his skin, carrying a feeling like fire through his blood and filling him with heat at the sight before him and what it represented. He'd never cared much about these kinds of things when he'd been in the spirit company. He'd been far too concerned with the matter of his own happiness and survival then. Besides, things like totems and relics and idols and masks and shrines were commonplace; just the background elements of existence, the rigorously religious tools of worship in the lives of men. They may have been made, charmed, used, broken, reclaimed, forgotten, but they always mattered to someone. It was a certain kind of savagery to keep these once purposeful items for no other purpose than display, as trophies in memoriam of a colonizer's self-given right to take. To Shigidi, it felt wrong, and that wrongness ran bone deep.

They proceeded deeper into the gallery, past an elaborate case that caught his eye because it displayed a trio of masquerades from a mass hysteria project that he'd coordinated more than three hundred years ago with Okpolodo, the fearful Kalabari god of war and headhunting. Past a long, wooden opambata spear that Shigidi remembered from his time constructing the nightmares of a young boy who had seen his father killed with it at the hands of a cruel king. Past a rack of swords that included the ceremonial alligator sword wielded by Oba Orompoto herself, the first female Alaafin of the Oyo empire, in her conquest of Nupe. It was a sword that had once inspired so, so much fear in the hearts of so, so many men. The rush of memories from seeing the items reminded Shigidi of the early times, when the Orisha Spirit Company had been an exciting place to work, before everything changed. It all conflated to stoke the fire in him and set his bones ablaze with anger. He wanted to break all the glass cages and liberate everything, all these relics from his past life and from the lives of so many other gods he'd known, some of whom were now dead, starved of worship.

He wanted to bring it all down, but he restrained himself. They had a job to do.

Finally, they came to it, the brass head of Obalufon, in a raised glass cage of its own, atop a marble plinth and set against a wall, with a dim light over it giving its bold and lined features a sinister slant. They could see the discolored headdress and a spot where someone had tried to smooth a crack in the base but had not quite achieved the same level of craftsmanship as the rest of it.

"It's not as impressive up close," Nneoma said, staring, "not the way it appeared in the images Olorun showed us. It's not quite life-size, you know. It's just a little bit too small to be an average adult human head."

"Hmm." Shigidi grunted. He thought it looked spectacular. But that was because he was used to the disproportionate. He used to *be* disproportionate. And just like him, it was a vessel. A vessel crafted by a knowing, skilled hand. A vessel far away from the place where it had been first crafted and given purpose. A vessel that now contained a piece of someone more powerful.

We have it.

Now, we need to get out of this place.

Nneoma placed a long, svelte finger on the glass in front of them, the tip of her sharpened red nail making a delicate, yet insistent contact. She began to move her finger in a circular motion. The precision of the motion was uncanny as she cut into the glass smoothly and silently like she was made of pure diamond, leaving only a trail of faint yellow light and ash residue.

"The substructure," she said by way of reminder, never looking away from her work.

He nodded, leaving her to finish her task. A choking sensation seized his throat, and his skin tingled as though his spirit particles were vibrating their way out of him as he stepped between a row of three tall glass displays of iron, ivory, and bronze busts. They had been violently looted during the sacking of Benin City in 1897 as punishment for successfully repelling a previous British attack. He closed his eyes and took a series of short sharp breaths.

Focus.

It occurred to him that the angry fire that threatened to consume him from within was not just a matter of memory and regret for things lost, it could concern the present as well. Perhaps the brass head was not the only artefact in the building that still contained essences of its former creators, owners, and patrons. He was overcome with temptation to take more of them with him. To rescue them. Perhaps the mask of Queen Idia, the sight of which called to him like a siren song, reminding him of the long history between the Yoruba and Edo people written in shared blood.

He exhaled a long breath and shook his head to dispel his thoughts and refocus. Refocus on the task at hand. He was no longer a god in a spirit company. He was just an independent contractor doing a job. The past was the past, and he was standing in a monument to that fact, no matter how much he disliked it.

He resumed his short trek to the center of the gallery and knelt on the cold, hardwood floor in the clear space, placing his right palm on it. A chill ran through him not unlike the one he had felt when he'd first touched the Wærlan-Drýlic, but much less potent. Sealing magick. He braced himself, took in a deep breath and, without moving the rest of his body, pressed against the floor. Hard. A streak of quiet lightning shot out of his hand with such force that the wood and underlayment exploded out, leaving only cracked and blackened concrete and a small haze of white smoke. When it cleared, he lifted his hand up only a little way off the ground to keep the incoming impact limited, balled it into a fist and drove it down into the exposed concrete with one smooth movement. The impact instantly sent a tight, circular concave spider's web of cracks spilling across the concrete. The bonds that held the composite material together at the impact site yielded and deformed before giving and falling apart in large solid slabs, that dropped down into the empty space of the substructure below. The glass displays all around him had barely been disturbed. Shigidi rose and took one rapid step back to avoid falling as a chunk of concrete at the edge of the break fell, completing the hole that was big enough for three people to fall through. A damp, wet smell wafted up through it, and the dust tickled his nose. He smiled as he admired the precision of his handwork. Contained chaos. He had learned to control the power he'd absorbed from Shango. That was another gift he was eternally grateful to Nneoma for. She'd taught him so much about taking advantage of his form, using his own pliable nature to manipulate spirit particles, controlling his own fear, absorbing other energies. Skills that all proved extremely useful. He turned to see her smiling and cradling the head of Obalufon in her arms like it was a breastfeeding child.

He was about to say, "Let's go," when he saw her eyes widen and her face contort into the shape of an incoming scream. Before the sound of it could hit him, his entire body was compressed by what seemed like a vice made of rough skin, and then he was jerked backward violently. The world accelerated. His breath snagged, and his neck bent at an unnatural angle. There was a flash of pain when his head and right shoulder hit the angry edges of the hole he had just created, and he fell into its darkness, arms and legs flailing up at its receding maw. His blurred vision focused on the hole as it narrowed to a point in the abyss. He fell for what seemed like eternity before he finally slammed into hard, unforgiving floor, peppered with concrete debris, knocking the wind out of him. He almost blacked out on impact but the sounds of something like sinister laughter and loud, explosive footsteps inspired him to hold on to his consciousness aggressively.

There is something dangerous here.

Ignoring the pain shooting from his back, he rolled onto his belly and blinked rapidly until he could see again. There was some light, but it was faint and unevenly distributed. He assessed his surroundings. High stone walls up to at least fifty feet above, maybe more. They were strangely muraled and leaning at angles to the floor as though the room had funneled down. The wall right behind him offering no space to retreat. Shadows everywhere. A bloodstained, elevated stone slab ahead of him in what appeared to be the center. A small heap of bones, cloth, and yellowed papers right next to it. Dust, debris, dried blood all over the upward-sloping floor. Rows of black kerosene lamps that couldn't possibly have been burning actual kerosene hanging high up on the walls except at the farthest corner where there was a curtain of darkness where he was sure whoever or whatever had attacked him had retreated. He could still hear the heavy breathing and trailing snickers echoing around.

He scrambled up onto one knee just as Nneoma dropped down onto the floor beside him, her heels aspark with yellow and the brass head in her hands. She'd sprouted her wings; the back of her dress was torn, and her hair was wild with the rush of air.

"Are you okay?" she asked with wide eyes.

"I'm fine, I think," he said, even though his entire body ached.

"I saw a hand grab you and pull you down here. What was it? Section Six?" she asked, referring to the secretive branch of the Royal British Spirit Bureau that protected the museum.

"Maybe. But Olorun didn't say there would be anything *or anyone* here," Shigidi replied, before calling out into the darkness: "Show yourself, coward!"

No response. Just constant, heavy breathing and the laughter. The constant, infuriating laughter.

"Show yourself!" He shouted into the looming void.

The darkness gained an unusual border as two shapes appeared at the edge of the lamplit shadows on the ground. Mustiness pervaded the air.

"I don't know what that is, but I am not sure we want to wait to find out," Nneoma said.

"Yes. Let's get out of here now," he agreed. His body didn't like the memory of being gripped by whatever was out there. And his mind didn't like the games it was playing now.

The shadows continued to lengthen.

"Should we go back up? We can make the jump. Or I can carry you if you don't feel up to it." Nneoma suggested.

"And then what? We already moved the brass head from its place. That means the museum is sealed off now, so there's no exit that way. We can't go back. But we do need to get away from whatever this is. We're already in the chamber so we just have to get spirit-side."

"The phone," Nneoma said, nodding.

Shigidi reached into his pocket and when his fingers touched it, he felt the rough tickle of shattered glass and he could immediately tell that the screen was cracked.

"Shit," he muttered under his breath, feeling the ground start to vibrate beneath them. "Wahala no dey finish."

The shapes finally stepped out of the darkness and into the light resolving themselves into two hulking figures, at least three times Shigidi's own already impressive size. They were both thickly bearded and sported matching outfits: old and stained black shirts, brown trousers, and brown wingtip shoes. But one of them was a bit stockier, wore plain black suspenders and a frayed black porkpie hat that almost scraped the bottom of the hanging lamps. The other was wiry, long-limbed, and wore a grey ascot cap and a bowtie.

"Who the hell are you two?" Shigidi asked.

There was no response for a few seconds, and then the two giants looked at each other.

"We've got intruders, Gog," the stocky one said, pounding his right fist into his left palm.

"Intruders indeed, Magog. We don't like intruders, do we?"

Their voices were mirrored. Both deep and harsh and guttural like the sound of rocks being ground against each other.

Shigidi instinctively took a step back. "What are these things?" he asked, holding out the phone they needed to get spirit-side to Nneoma.

"They just told us. Gog and Magog," she said, taking it before adding, "the twin guardians of Albion."

"You know them?" Shigidi asked, eyes still trained ahead.

"I think so," she replied, retreating in step with him to assess the damage to the phone. "But I'm not sure, because if they are actually the twin guardians of Albion, then they are supposed to be dead. Killed in a wrestling match near Plymouth hundreds of years ago. At least, that's what an English spirit agent I met in Constantinople told me. But they don't look dead to me."

Shigidi grunted.

The two giants advanced slowly, like predators, grinning at them with large brown teeth like boulders.

Nneoma was furiously pressing the passcode into the crazed surface of the phone screen. All the while, the two giants continued to approach them, mouths, and eyes wide and full of malicious intent.

Shigidi kept his hand on the ground and his eyes on the twin giants.

"It's working!" Nneoma cried out when the screen finally unlocked.

And then the stocky giant to Shigidi's left took a leaping stride forward, coming at him fist-first. But Shigidi had already felt the ground shift and knew what was coming. He was ready. He rolled out of the way, feeling a rush of displaced air against his ribs as the fist went by and the giant lurched forward, head too far tilted over his center of gravity. Using the negative momentum of his roll to change direction, Shigidi sprang to his feet, and threw himself into the giant's bulk at a sideways angle, hitting him square in the chest and sending him crashing into a wall.

"Magog!" his brother cried out, kicking Shigidi mid-air just before he could regain a solid footing. Shigidi held on to the tree-trunk leg as all the air was forced out of him. His grip was tenuous, but it held, and it prevented him from being launched across the room into the back wall. It also gave him time to think because once Gog's foot yielded to gravity and was back down on the ground, Shigidi scrambled behind it and threw a vicious punch into the back of the knee, forcing the giant to crouch and bring his massive head down to Shigidi's level. Shigidi did not give Gog any time to react; he leaped up and wrapped his arms around the giant's thick neck in a choke that was more like an aggressive embrace, because the neck was the size of large man's torso and he could only manage to secure the choke by interlocking his fingers. He squeezed with everything he had but it felt like hugging a steel mountain. There was barely any give. Out of the corner of his vision, he saw Nneoma preparing to join the fight. Her wings were flared out to their full span, and her skin was taking on its hard, scaly form, morphing quickly like it was being folded from the inside out. She kicked off her high heels and pushed her hair back. Her eyes burned bright yellow and long claws extruded from her fingers which were still wrapped around the brass head they'd come for. Shigidi hardened his clay flesh, imagined himself as an un-yielding statue, and anchored his feet on two large ribs, pushing his hips into the giant's shoulder blades to torque the choke.

Immovable object, meet impossible force.

He grinned when he heard the gurgling sound of air and saliva being restricted by the pressure. He squeezed tighter but could only hold on for a few seconds before Magog seized his left leg and yanked him off. Shigidi slid down, and his face smashed into the ground before he could manipulate his form and loosen his body. The iron and ash taste of his own blood and spirit particles filled his mouth.

Shigidi rolled to a crouch behind the stone slab at the center of the chamber and looked up just in time to see Nneoma fly at the at-tacking Magog like a crazed arrow. Just as he was about to hit Shigidi, she rotated her body on its axis, like a gymnast, so that her feet made contact with Magog's face. She followed through, slashing at his face and forearms with her feet and wings in wild arcs of bright yellow, still cradling the precious brass head of Obalufon in her arms.

She's beautiful, even in the middle of battle. She's beautiful.

Shigidi took the opening she gave him to tackle the still coughing and retching Gog before he could fully rise to his feet, and they fell together, with Shigidi in the mount position, his knees digging into the giant's belly. On the ground, so close together and with gravity now on Shigidi's side, some of the giant's advantage was neutralized. Punch for punch and dodge for dodge, they matched each other. The hand of Shango around Shigidi's heart drove him like an engine as he squeezed out bursts of lightning with each strike, enhancing the damage. The giant was strong, and each wild, windmill blow that landed in retaliation threatened to send Shigidi flying. But he had hardened his clay body, and he held on to the giant's suspenders. He couldn't exactly match the giant's raw strength and so he returned each punch with precision and calibrated power, sending out flashes of white light through the room as if it were full of eager photographers. It was like riding a bull made of perpetual assault, but Shigidi took to it quickly. He targeted the weakest areas: the neck, the eye socket, the bridge of the nose, with downward pounding strikes and hammer fists that could have fractured mountains, but there seemed to be little impact, little damage. Always, still, there was that grin. That horrible grin. Shigidi glanced up as he twisted his torso to avoid a hook punch and saw that, despite using her spirit particles to edge her wings, Nneoma hadn't so much as cut the skin of the other giant.

We can't make a dent. They're strong and resilient. Too resilient.

The realization hit him fully that even assuming they could beat these monsters guarding the Pendragon room, it was possible that they would not be able to do it in time. They needed to get to the spirit-side of London before it was too late.

As his core musculature recoiled, he rotated back into a blow to his exposed chest, and he found himself airborne.

Shit.

He was still spinning mid-air, trying to stabilize himself by spreading his arms and lifting his chest, when a second blow caught him. Everything churned as if he'd been seized by a tornado. He tried to loosen his body, but the centrifugal force was too great, and he felt like he was spinning out, scattering away from his center, and so he stopped trying and just held his form. When he hit the ground, he landed on his back and pain lanced through his spine. A constellation of stars and sparks danced across his vision when he tried to open his eyes, so he shut them again, rolling away from the vibration of the ground just before a foot crashed into the place on the ground where he had been. His blood quickened, and he opened his eyes, willing the invading pain and darkness back with clenched fists.

He called out to Nneoma, "Let's get away. Make the call, now!"

She nodded and flew backward at a hard angle, retreating from Magog as she pressed her fingers to the screen, searching for the number that Aleister had keyed in. The distraction cost her. Magog's large hand shot forward faster than she could fly, wrapped itself around her like a hostile blanket and slammed her into the wall. The back of her head bounced against unforgiving stone.

"Nneoma!"

When he saw her pinned against the wall, Magog's bone-sickle grin next to her head, and his ugly giant fist raised in the air to strike her, Shigidi's heart froze. A memory as sharp and quick as a blade cut through his mind of the night they'd met, when she'd pinned him to the wall of the hotel room, and he'd had to attempt something he'd never done before. *If we can't beat them physically, there may be another way.*

He stretched out his hand and closed his eyes, using one of his old nightmare god tricks to feel for the giant's thoughts, even though he was still awake. A mass of foreign memories and thoughts and feelings and sensations hit Shigidi all at once like a truck. Boulders. Men with swords. Rage. A kiss. A fish. Lovemaking near a bonfire.

Gnawing on bone marrow. An embrace. Men in blood-red robes. Chains. It was too much. Too much. It was like being caught in a flood of feeling. And not every feeling was the giant's. He could see flashes of Nneoma in some of them, and even flashes of himself. He was no longer sure which thoughts were his and which were theirs.

I'm blurring the boundaries of nightmare and reality.

No. Focus.

Shigidi stood firm against the subconscious tide, sifting rapidly through it all until he caught a memory of falling down the side of a cliff. Embedded in that memory, he felt a flash of fear, raw and primal. It had to be the giant's. Shigidi's eyes shot open, and he seized it.

The giant's body froze, his fist just a few meters from Nneoma's face as he was caught in a waking nightmare of falling. A never-ending falling.

Got you.

Nneoma pushed against the massive hand, using both her hands and a concentrated beam of spirit particles. It budged the giant's grasp just enough for her to wrench herself out and smile at him. He was about to smile back when the look on her face changed, and she launched herself at him.

Nneoma, this is our chance make the call what are you doin... Gog!

He'd been so focused on stopping Magog that he'd almost forgotten about the other giant. Shigidi spun around just in time to see the sole of a large shoe approaching his face. He put out his arms to protect himself but Nneoma got there first, a defensive arc of spirit particles assembled in front of her like a shield.

When she intercepted Gog's kick, there was an explosion like a bomb and the impact sent all of them flying. Shigidi couldn't tell if he hit a wall of the ground, all he knew was that it was stone and it hurt.

Coughing, he stumbled to his feet and saw Nneoma lying at the feet of the frozen Magog, the cracked phone and the brass head in each of her hands.

She . . . saved me.

His eyes went wide when he saw it. Magog's fist was still moving. Slowly, but it was moving. It wasn't working. His body was resisting the waking nightmare, and he was going right for Nneoma.

No.

No more.

Instinct took over. Shigidi's chest tightened, and he felt an intense pressure in his chest like the hand of Shango was squeezing his heart harder than it ever had. The sensation filled him up with so much raw power, his skin strained against the pressure like an inflating balloon. A gate had opened in his mind, and he couldn't consciously control it. His entire right hand ignited with electric fire, radiating harsh blue and white streaks of light, and throwing strange new shadows along the walls. His arm felt like it was burning with a familiar fire but beneath that, he could feel a strange new sensation, like he was actually being consumed; like the very clay that bonded his spirit particles and delineated the boundaries of his body was being destroyed. He thought his body into rigidity, trying to mentally hold on to his body as lightning leaked from him in unexpected places. The magnitude of power he had summoned in that moment surprised him, and he could no longer keep it concentrated in his fist. It overflowed as he launched himself right past Gog and into the air like a missile, aimed straight for the monster that would do Nneoma harm. When he struck his target, he felt a mass of flesh and clay and spirit-particles cleave to him as he stabbed his turbulent fist into the giant's exposed neck. It exploded. Blood and light bathed the chamber. A shockwave flung them apart and sent Shigidi reeling in a direction he couldn't tell. Loose stone fell and dust rose. At first there was silence, then a hollow cry of pain and then a scream.

It was Nneoma. Nneoma was screaming. Shigidi forced himself to look up, to make sure she was okay, but when he saw her, she was staring back at him, eyes full of terror and hands over her mouth, choking back the scream that had initially escaped her when she first saw what had happened to him. He was kneeling in a pile of scattered chunks of brain matter, large skull fragments like ancient pottery, pools of thick blood that appeared black in the harsh light. He was covered in it all. It took him a moment to realize that his right arm was missing.

Fuck!

Sputtering wild streaks of muted lightning shot out of the stump at his shoulder. There was no pain initially, only surprise.

Is this real? Am I still blurring nightmare and reality?

He shook his head in disbelief.

We need to get out.

"Make the call," he said to Nneoma, shaking large drops of blood loose from his face. His voice was hoarse and barely audible even to himself.

He tried to move, to rise to his feet, and that was when the pain crashed onto him like a wave.

He let out a cry that threatened to rip out his throat.

Nneoma reached for him but he shook his head.

He bit back another cry, pressing his teeth against each other like he was trying to weld them together.

Nneoma was a brown and blue blur as she fumbled around on the floor around her, searching for the phone. The heaving body of Gog lay several feet away, a reminder of the still present danger. When she found the phone, she snapped up the brass head of Obalufon, using her wings to steady herself. She engulfed Shigidi in an embrace that felt like a blanket, her wings cocooning them as her spirit particles formed a bright yellow make-shift bandage around his stump, trying to stop both the bleeding and the as-yet uncaged lightning that was leaking from him. She tapped the fractured green call symbol on the cracked screen, and a white ellipse of light exploded into the space in front of them. At its center was a pinpoint of darkness, an absolute void staring at them like an eye. She stepped into it, bringing Shigidi with her. Then its borders fell in behind them. The world dissolved.

When the world returned, it was changed. They were in what looked like the same space but gone were the giants and the gore and the lamps and the shadows. The stone was preternaturally clean, free of dust, and there seemed to be a faint light everywhere even though no source was immediately visible. It seemed like it was radiating from everywhere at once. Everything around them seemed to have lost some sense of rigidity and gained an aura. They were spirit-side. Stretching ahead of them, now visible beyond the elevated center slab, was an upward sloping walkway leading into a corridor.

"It worked," Nneoma said as she adjusted the grip of her arms around his torso to let him know that she was going to lift him. The brass edge of the thing they had come for dug into his side, but he didn't even feel it. Not really. She gave a gentle flap of her wings and elevated them into the air, gliding forward and upward, almost parallel to the slope as they drifted into the corridor, toward the exit.

Shigidi looked up at her, his vision blurry and unfocused. He thought for a moment he could propelled himself forward on his own two feet; believed that he could make it out of London's spirit side, weak as he was. But something about the way Nneoma looked back at him let him know he should be carried. Besides, he wasn't sure how much time they had till sunrise, before the Wærlan-Drýlic's connection to London's spirit-side would be severed. They needed to get to the rendezvous point quickly. He tried not to slump against Nneoma's body so completely, but he could barely feel anything, not even the air rushing past his bare scalp. He tried to will his body to reshape itself, to loosen and rearrange its form, to take what it needed from other parts of him and reconstitute a new arm, but he could not reform himself no matter how clear the image was in his mind. It felt like he was trying to open a door without a key. Like he had regressed to the time before he met Nneoma, impotently trapped in a form he desperately wanted to change but couldn't. Some aspect of his new self had been lost completely. Annihilated.

So, is this what Shango's final blow would have done to me if Olorun hadn't intervened?

He surrendered his diminished body to her. He was not sure if she understood what it was costing him in pride, but she had already saved him once that night, just before he'd saved her. Partners. The word seemed to settle on a new meaning for him. Besides, it was his love for her that had made him put himself at risk again, to almost destroy himself from within, and so he thought he might as well let her return the favor.

Nneoma's voice shook as she murmured, "Shigidi . . . I don't know what to . . ."

And then, a sound like the grinding of stone against stone erupted before she could complete what she wanted to say. Still drifting backwards, upslope, she spun them around mid-air to look in the direction the sound had come from. The elevated slab at the center of the chamber was shaking, throwing off fragments of loose stone. A faint circle of pale blue light had formed around it and was intensifying, pulsing in time with the vibrations.

No. Not again.

Shigidi knew what it probably was and what was coming after them. He barked out a sound that was meant to say "Faster, we need to get out now," but came out as little more than a series of inaudible groans.

Luckily, Nneoma didn't need words to understand his sentiment. She lifted a knee, flapped a wing and pirouetted back around before shooting forward in a flash, flying as fast as she could for the exit that Olorun's schematics had told them would be there.

The grinding sound continued, getting fainter as they put distance between them and the spirit-side version of the Museum substructure's main chamber of the. The corridor narrowed as they ascended until at last, they could see the gate at its end. An imposing wrought iron and wood barrier that looked like it had been built hundreds of years ago and unopened since.

Nneoma decelerated her flight and stopped just inches away from it, dropping to her feet and setting Shigidi down on the ground beside her. There was no visible handle or keyhole or lock or latch. Nothing except an uneven brown and black barrier. She banged at it wildly with her fists and the tips of her wings. "Aleister! Are you there? Aleister! Open the gate!"

In the distance, over the noise, they heard a soft, sharp snap, like the breaking of bone. And then the quaking of footsteps. The same footsteps that had stalked them from the darkness when they first fell into the substructure. Shigidi knew the giant had finally herniated into London's spirit side and was in pursuit.

For a moment full of perfect physical and emotional exhaustion, with the stump throbbing where his arm used to be and his legs slowly turning into what felt like bags of cement beneath him, Shigidi allowed himself wonder if Aleister had betrayed them. Left them trapped in a secret section of the city's spirit side where they could never escape. It was not inconceivable. Magicians were not the most trustworthy group. And one way to get rid of a debt is to make sure your creditor can never collect. He almost laughed at the thought, but the thing that came out of him was not really a laugh, it was only a muffled choke as his throat dredged up bubbles of blood, froth, and saliva.

Nneoma was shouting louder, "Aleister! Open this gate!"

The footsteps were getting louder too but they seemed to be slowing down.

The narrowing space.

Still, it wouldn't be long. The walkway was tight, but if the giant could follow them through the spirit-space barrier, he probably wouldn't be stopped by stone. Shigidi wondered if he could channel another killing blow through his other arm, regardless of the cost. The effort would probably kill him, but if that's what it took, then so be it. At least Nneoma would survive, maybe even escape. He kissed his teeth and sucked in a deep breath. He tried to gather enough concentration to loosen some of himself and use his own clay body to at least cover his stump, to seal it, but he couldn't, there was just too much of him gone. Too little potency in his imagination. And too much pain to focus.

More banging on the gate. "Aleister Crowley! Open this fucking —"

She stopped when the gate creaked. She took a step back. Shigidi's breath quickened as the gate creaked again, louder this time as the hinges flexed and then rotated. Air rushed in as a gap finally appeared, sundering the gate vertically along its middle.

"Ah!" Nneoma cried out as she pulled her wings in tightly behind her like theatre curtains. She bent over and hoisted Shigidi's arm over her shoulder. He groaned. She stepped through the gap, keeping him in a half embrace while her other hand cradled the brass head of Obalufon. Standing there, on the other side, was Aleister, a look of mild amusement plastered on his face and what looked like a black cab parked across the street behind him.

His cheer became a look of horror in one single brushstroke of realization.

"What the bloody hell happened to you two?" he exclaimed.

"We need to get out of here, now!" she commanded, almost screaming.

He pointed over his shoulder at the cab. "Get in then."

She made for the vehicle, holding Shigidi as she retracted her wings, pulling them into the flesh of her back effortlessly. The street looked normal, rows of tightly packed houses, streetlights, cars. But there was the constant light, and all around, a few ghosts of Londoners past walked down the middle of the roadway, conducting the business of their afterlife, apparently oblivious to the bloody and battered intruders . Above, the sky was a bright, cloudy orange. It looked like a strange storm was coming.

"Shut that gate!" Nneoma cried.

Aleister did as he was told, throwing his weight against the two halves of the gate and forcing them back together like once-estranged lovers. The loud scrambling and scraping sounds coming from within were making him visibly uncomfortable as he tried to focus on getting the gate closed.

"Umm, Nneoma . . . I don't think I want to see whatever did *that* to Shigidi," he said.

"Then just shut up and shut that door! We need to go, now. To the rendezvous point at the Nigeria high commission. That's where Olorun said we should meet him."

Aleister grunted and set to the task. But just before the two sides of the door could come together completely, a bloody finger the size of a man's forearm jammed itself into the space between them. A dirty, claw like fingernail dug into the wood. Aleister screamed. The single finger became eight, with four on each side, and the door began to swing back the other way. Aleister stumbled backward, turned and fled, in wide strides, diving into the driver's seat of the cab just as Nneoma managed to set Shigidi down in the back beside her with her arm still around him, his head resting on her shoulder.

"What the bloody hell is that?!" Aleister shouted as he revved the engine to life.

"I think it's called Gog," Nneoma said quietly, as they watched the gates fly open and the head and arm of the giant poke out, struggling to squeeze the rest of its hulking body through the narrow space.

"A giant! You pissed off a fucking giant?! Where in the hell did you even find one of them to piss off?"

Shigidi groaned again. He could barely talk anymore, his head felt like it was made of stone.

"The substructure in the bottom of the museum," Nneoma answered.

Shigidi wondered how Section Six had revived the long dead giants of Albion and, even more impressively, assigned them to some sort of security job beneath the museum.

"There were two of them. Shigidi was hurt badly when he killed the other one."

The giant was out up to his torso now and wriggling to free his bottom half from the gate that was too small for someone of his size, slamming his fists wildly into the asphalt and bellowing as shocked ghosts and spirit entities fled the streets.

Aleister let out a long whistle, floored the accelerator and swung the ungainly bulk of the vehicle out onto the road, rear tires smoking. "Fucked, luv. This is fucked."

"Yes. I am aware. Just drive as fast as you can so we can unfuck it."

"Yes ma'am," Aleister obliged, and floored the accelerator, steadily revving it up to what the speedometer announced as seventy miles per hour. The top half of the raging giant was receding and becoming a speck in Aleister's rear view mirror as the wind blew wildly through the windows. Aleister barreled down the spirit side of Bloomsbury Street and then swung right, hard. When they lost sight of the giant, Nneoma exhaled the breath she had been holding, and Shigidi felt her torso deflate under him. His head sank into her shoulder and she turned so that they were back in a half embrace. She placed her palm to his face and whispered, "I'm sorry my darling. I'm so, so sorry I blamed you for getting us into this mess with Olorun even though it was not your fault. I'm sorry. Please hang on, I don't want to lose you."

Shigidi heard her voice, even though it was muffled. There was a rising pressure on top of his head, pushing his consciousness down, further down. He was fighting to keep focus, but he was barely able to. The bright night lights of spirit-side London's West End had been transformed to a streak of kaleidoscopic lines against the windows by both the erratic motion of the vehicle and his swimming vision. Still, he could just about make out shapes of buildings and signs and statues and spirit entities and ghosts, so many ghosts.

Nneoma kept whispering to him. "Listen to me. Focus on my voice. I'm sorry, Shigidi. I should have told you how I felt instead of fighting my own emotions. I was afraid and angry, and I . . ." Her voice fell even lower. "I know I have been afraid since I lost my sister, since I lost Lilith. When I saw how love changed her, changed us, it scared me. I couldn't understand it at the time. In a way I'm not sure I do yet, not completely, but I understand a lot better than I did before. Besides, I've never been good at accepting love and care and kindness. Being loved has never been part of my story, you understand? Being lusted after, for my flesh, my power—that has always been my story. Ever since The Fall. And I've embraced it, used it to my advantage, learned to play within its parameters. It is who I am, who I was. Nneoma the pretty serpent that toys with the hearts and minds of men and demons and gods." She pulled him gently closer. "I've been playing that role for so long, it felt natural, and I could not imagine any other kind of relationship with anyone. Until you. I feel things for you that I have never felt for anyone else, and I resented you for making me feel those things. For making me feel like I would do what you did. Risk my own life for you. I know it doesn't make sense. I know . . . but it's how I felt. You've done something to me. And now I can't imagine living without you, so don't you dare die and leave me you fucking nightmare god. You can't leave me now. I love you and I need you to stay with me, okay. Stay with me."

Shigidi's mind, clouded as it was by pain, fluid loss, and the obscuring fog of imminent unconsciousness processed her words slowly. He had never heard Nneoma speak so much before. And she'd said her sister's name. *Lilith.* He didn't even know her sister's name was

Lilith. At last, it seemed like they were fully open to each other, as open as they had instinctively known they could be, that first night in the hotel when they'd caught the sadness in each other's eyes. Why had she waited until he was literally broken? He was about to croak something out in response when the road seemed to suddenly become bumpy and uneven. The vehicle vibrated like a child that had been left outside in the cold.

"Oh, fuck me!" Aleister shouted, turning slightly to throw his voice back while keeping his widened and panicked eyes on the rearview mirror. "Shit!"

Nneoma angled her neck to see what Aleister was panicking about. She did not get a chance to complete the motion.

They slowed down for a fraction of a second, and Shigidi could feel the inertia of all four thousand pounds of steel and carbon fiber slam into him as Aleister veered the taxi off at an impossible angle, into a side road. He fell into Nneoma's lap as his vision became a whirlpool of lights punctuated by darkness. An arc of pain lanced through him, like every nerve in his body had been touched by fire. He let out a hollow, hoarse cry that he didn't recognize as his own. It sounded like a broadcast from far away. And then he felt the hysterical urge to laugh when he realized it was coming from him, because it meant his brain and his body were so uncoordinated that they couldn't even orchestrate a cry of anguish properly. But even that was too much effort, and the laugh remained stuck somewhere in his mind, obstructed by pain. He could tell that he was dying by inches. He hadn't just lost a critical aspect of himself, he was losing still more, unable to maintain the bonds of the physical and spirit particles that held him together. Soon there would not be enough of his essence left to maintain him as coherent entity.

The road beneath them was still shuddering. He lifted his head up slightly with Nneoma's help and peeked up, turning his neck as far as it could until he finally saw what had sent Aleister into a panic as he urgently navigated toward the rendezvous point. Gog was behind, almost beside them, holding onto rough lengths of rope that had been tied around the necks of four metallic horses, their eyes aflame.

What the . . . Are those the bronze horses of Helios?

The horses of Helios were a quasi-famous London landmark he'd seen in pictures and travel brochures, and it looked like Gog had brought the statues to life, taken them from their place at the corner of Piccadilly and Haymarket, fashioned some kind of makeshift chariot from the carcass of a car and was using them to give chase, wrecking the road in his wake. Shigidi managed to see that the brewing orange storm in the sky had finally broken, and the sky was at war with itself. Clumps of asphalt lifted beneath the bronze horses like angry piano keys, throwing off a kaleidoscope of spirit particles. The denizens of London's spirit-side were fleeing blindly, running off the road in a hurry. Some of them were too slow, their collisions throwing off even more bright bursts of damaged spirit particles.

The horses were getting closer, eroding the little distance between them and the vehicle.

Aleister made another sharp turn into another side street and then staggered them down a flight of steps. The descent was rough and rattled Shigidi's head, bouncing it against the roof and back into Nneoma's knees.

"Careful!" Nneoma shouted.

"I'm doing my best here, love," Aleister shot back. "But in case you haven't noticed we are being chased by four living statues and one fucking furious giant."

"Hold on my darling Shigidi. I love you. Do you hear me? I love you. Just hold on. Everything will be okay. We are almost at the high commission. We will hand over the brass head to Olorun and this will all be over, just hold on," she whispered but he couldn't hear her clearly anymore. The echo of his own thoughts had become loud and pounded against the walls of his mind. He could no longer resolve the shapes from the lights in the window. He tried to reach for the brass head of Obalufon that was digging into his side, to hold on to it at the end, feel some small, final connection to the old god who had supervised his creation, abandoned him, then saved his life and sent him off to foreign lands to do his dirty work.

Olorun.

I'm always returning to you, in the end, aren't I?

He tried, but he could not feel his fingers. He could not feel his anything anymore.

Nneoma's whispers evaporated when the horses finally crashed into them. The giant had run the heavy bronze horses right into their side, fishtailing the vehicle into a wild spin. There was a loud metal scream, an inhuman cacophony as the violence battered the vehicle, peeling off metal pieces, powdering the glass of the windshield and knocking in the right-side doors. Nneoma was staring at him, her eyes full of emotion as the world spun around them in what seemed like slow motion, fragments of glass suspended like so many stars. They held each other's gaze for what seemed like a small slice of for-ever and then, they shut their eyes together, just like good partners would, as the world came to a screeching halt.

Darkness.

    Let there be . . .

    Light?

I am. I am . . .

An impossibly large black and red rooster at a dusty crossroads, crowing.

Red clay pouring out of a large white shell into an endless ocean.

A generous offering of yams, palm fruit, palm oil, and ogogoro sitting on a railroad.

A train made of chains, machetes, and machine guns approaches.

Six babalawos wearing white flowing robes, their faces covered in white chalk marks, chanting in a forgotten dialect.

A waterfall of blood crashing down onto a corpulent seven-tentacled mermaid as she breastfeeds a baby.

A crocodile eating a hurricane as it drowns in a muddy river.

Two streaks of angry lightning wrestling each other against a pitch-black sky shaped like a fist.

A horned water buffalo charging a dam made of old bones.

An old man in bright silver armor sitting on two clouds, the sun in his left hand and a spear of pure light in his right.

A chorus of screams and the clash of metal against metal.

I see. I hear. I feel.

I understand.

I . . . I don't understand.

And then

Darkness.

CHAPTER 15

Northumberland Street, London (Spirit side), England

JULY 5TH, 2017 | 04:43 AM.

Shigidi was not expecting it when his eyes flew open and his mouth sucked in a desperate lungful of air. His heart was beating so fast, he could not keep up with it. An immense amount of some sort of undomesticated energy was suddenly flowing through his veins, exploding the life back into him. He felt like someone had injected the essence of a young, raging star directly into his heart. He jerked up in his seat and looked around.

He was in a womb of metal and smoke and fire, but he felt no discomfort. All the agony of losing his arm was gone, replaced by a kind of abstract numbness. Glass lay scattered everywhere like lethal confetti and he could tell that some of it was inside him too, fragments lodged in the clay of his skin by impact. The hard edges of the cab had yielded to forces beyond them and twisted into strange new shapes. The driver's seat in front of him was empty.

He blinked rapidly, eyelids fluttering like the wings of a moth near a flame. He could not tell if it was because of the smoke and the hazy heat of the flames around him or if something had happened to him to damage his eyes but everything seemed so much brighter than it was before, like there was now a lamp buried beneath every surface, like he was seeing new wavelengths. The aura of everything in London's spirit-space seemed heightened.

The thing that felt like a star in his chest drew his attention with an almost insistent pulsing and he looked down at his own torso. His eyes widened with shock when he saw it. The brass head of Obalufon was broken, the face it depicted now split by a jagged fissure from forehead to cheek. Bright white light was spilling out of the fracture with such intensity that he could not actually see the edges where it had separated. He could only see the light gushing out of it like a vandalized pipeline and he could see that the larger half was still attached to the beaded headdress. But what surprised him even more was that the plume extending from the headdress had penetrated him, deeply. He took in a deep breath and felt it move with his heaving chest.

What is happening to me?

He coughed out blood and spirit particles. Some of the light was flowing into him in wide, strange arcs, like a miniature cosmic river. It reminded him of a video he had seen once, of the aurora borealis. Not the near-stationary aurora that you get when what is left of the ancient Roman goddess blows a quiescent solar wind steadily past the corporeal earth's magnetosphere, but the true aurora borealis, the spectacular display you get when the goddess Aurora is desperately trying to remind humanity of her presence and power, to reignite some faith in her followers by using an enhanced solar wind to create a geomagnetic storm. That was what it looked like around his chest, at least in the nature of its swirling motion and form, despite the pure whiteness of its color. It was a divine light show centered around the thing in his chest. He needed to get the thing out. He tried to pull it out of him with his remaining arm, but he couldn't. It held firm in place, almost as if the vengeful fist of Shango, still lodged in his chest, had grabbed onto the new foreign thing and did not want to let it go.

Not again. It's getting crowded in there.

Shigidi wondered briefly if he'd also be able to absorb anything from this new thing in him, but then he started to hyperventilate, struggling to keep up with the growing surge of energy inside him.

Too much. It's too much.

His sensory perceptions were different, but focused. It was similar to the way he'd felt just before he killed Magog with a surge of power that he couldn't control. But this wasn't just a single spike, it was perpetual now, continuous and unrelenting and scary. He tried to weave the fear that was creeping into his mind into a vision of something more confident, more in control, but he couldn't focus. Strange and unfamiliar images flashed through his mind intermittently like cut ins in a movie.

I don't even know what's real and what's a dream anymore.

Giddy with all the new sensations, his head was floating and his heart was beating twice as fast as it ever had just to keep all his thinning blood and overstimulated spirit particles flowing. The smoke and fire made it all worse, but he barely even noticed them. He was still entranced by the sight of the thing stuck in his chest and by the feeling that was invading his body when he remembered . . .

Nneoma!

In a panic, he realized that she was lying unconscious beside him, her head resting on the bright yellow armrest of the broken passenger door. Her wings were fully retracted, her shoes were gone, and her dress was torn across the back and belly. Black blood and bright yellow spirit-particles were running down the side of her beautiful face, her smooth skin radiantly illuminated by the glow of fire, her eyes shut tight against the world.

Through the window, he saw that the giant who had chased them had dismounted his makeshift chariot. The untethered horses of Helios were fleeing, turning back in a tight circle, about to gallop back in the direction of Trafalgar Square. Gog was approaching the wreck of the cab with long strides, each half the length of a house, his face a mask of grim menace. There was a trail of broken asphalt, skid marks and assorted destruction behind him.

Shigidi grabbed onto the impaling plume of the headdress on the brass head of Obalufon that was in his chest and broke it off cleanly with a short, sharp, snap. It took much less effort than he had anticipated. Another explosion of swirling white light erupted from the point of the break. He wrapped his arm around Nneoma's body and jammed his shoulder into the burning cab door, smashing it out of its place, off its hinges, and sending it skidding several feet away. They tumbled together onto the hard asphalt road and rolled twice, his stump scraping on the jagged ground each time. He ended up on top of her and waited for pain to come, but it never did.

"Wake up!" he said, shaking her at the shoulders. "Nneoma, wake up!"

The giant was almost upon them, but Shigidi's focus was on the only person in the world who mattered to him, the person he loved more than he loved himself.

"Nneoma!" he shouted as he cupped her face with his hand, shaking her head from side to side with his bloodstained fingers. He felt a chill of moving air, like exhalation, on them, but he couldn't tell if those were her shallow breaths or just eddies in the morning breeze. His own fingers tingled with wild new sensations, so he wasn't sure if he was actually feeling what he thought he was feeling, and it was that uncertainty that spiked his panic.

"Nneoma! Wake up!"

When she sucked in a breath and let out a deep hacking cough, he nearly cried out with relief.

She is alive.

She was alive. She wasn't dead. The confirmation hit him in the chest harder than he thought it would. He knew deep down that it would take far more than a motor accident to kill her. But it had been a strange night full of unwanted surprises, and he needed to see her moving and conscious, there to face the rest of the night with him. And now that he knew she was, all his fear and uncertainty and worry began to spontaneously distill into a singular, all-consuming emotion: anger.

It purified and fractionated and concentrated as it rose through him, stripping itself of all the excess emotions, of all other things that were on his mind until it was the only thing left.

Pure. Fucking. Anger.

It tasted like iron on his tongue. Like blood in his throat. Like fire on his skin. Like lightning in his veins.

There was a tightening in his chest and in that moment all he knew was that he wanted to hurt the giant. Hurt him very badly.

And then, it took over.

He didn't completely realize it when it happened. Not really. It came as a kind of a contraction in his consciousness, as though the connection between his mind and body had loosened, become less tightly coupled. Like someone or something had reached into him and was weaving his actions as easily as he wove nightmares in the subconscious.

He was still there. Still aware. He could feel the pressure of the ground and the crunch of debris beneath his knees when he stood up and stepped away from Nneoma as she started to sit up on her own power. He felt the grind of bone against bone when he gritted his teeth and stared down the incoming attacker. He was aware enough to be confused when a flurry of horrifying images flitted by like memories that didn't completely belong to him. Images of broken bloody bodies piled in a heap, of machetes and spears cutting into flesh, spilling blood and spirit particles. Cut ins. So many cut ins. Random visions flashing. It all made him feel like he was partly possessed by someone or something else at their most bloodthirsty and vicious and powerful, yet calm. He had become a passenger in his own body, aware and observing himself from within as something else took the reins.

Saturated. I'm saturated. I've absorbed too many things and now those things are taking over .

Whatever it was, he didn't fight it.

As long as it hurts this bastard.

Na condition na im make crayfish bend.

Gog slowed as he tended toward them. Shigidi saw his own feet stepping forward to meet the giant, and he watched them curiously, almost enjoying the strangeness of the out-of-body sensation. Right foot. Left foot. Right foot. Left.

When they were close to each other, Gog lifted his arm to launch a punch and threw his weight forward, screaming, "You killed Magog!"

Shigidi observed as the thing controlling his body calmly lifted his remaining arm, positioning it at an upward angle to intercept. His sense of time seemed to slow down too, as his hand went up. Even the turbulent orange skies above appeared to decelerate in their discordant display as Shigidi watched the lightning turn into a network of crisscrossing lines that flickered and morphed and shifted slowly from one point to another across the sky.

Is my body really moving that fast, or is everything suddenly slow?

The two fists crashed into each other and the world around Shigidi lost all its sound in one clean break, as if some supreme and bored elder god had just turned it off. The ground beneath them developed a network of fractures that propagated itself in every direction, radiating from their feet and mirroring the lightning above. He watched with a kind of detached curiosity as a luminous white, green and blue ball of displaced spirit particles erupted where their fists met. Shigidi watched the giant's face as a look of shock and horror evolved across it, rounding his mouth, bunching up the folds of skin between his brows, and widening his eyes to saucers. Every little twitch and movement that coursed through it was visible as he was racked with what Shigidi was certain must be an avalanche of pain. And then the ball expanded, and Shigidi saw that the giant's hand had disintegrated into tiny pieces.

An arm for an arm.

Or maybe more.

Gog fell back as a powerful blast scattered spirit particles, blood, and bone but Shigidi's body held firmly in place, as if resisting nothing more than a light breeze.

Time suddenly seemed to regain its usual velocity. Sound returned to the world. The skies resumed their roil, thin fragments of coming dawnlight starting to peer through angry clouds.

The white and green and blue wave of disintegration followed through from Gog's hand to his arm and shoulder, consuming the giant like a plague of invisible locusts. Gog was only about half of himself by the time he hit the ground with a thud, like several bags of rice. The giant was screaming or, at least, he was trying to scream, but the sounds were so muffled they were little more than a mewl, because he was missing not just his right hand, his shoulder, and a chunk of his torso but also about half of his neck and lower jaw.

Shigidi sensed his feet take another two steps, coming up to his defeated foe. He stared into the giant's eyes, large and black and wide. He saw nothing but fear. Far more fear than he had ever seen concentrated in one place when he'd been the active god of nightmares. The anger in him subsided and as it did, a sense of control returned to him. He tried to wiggle his fingers and he was surprised when they responded.

I am still here.

I can control this.

I need to control it.

I can end this and get out of here.

He took in a deep breath and, as he exhaled, the sense of control grew. He thought himself loose, exercising every technique he knew for manipulating the clay of his body as he became more aware of his own will inside it, despite the resistance of the foreign power that was steering his mind. The power that had possessed him was coming from his chest, from the place where the brass head of Obalufon had pierced him, where Shango's hand was still buried. He knew because as he pushed back against it, he could feel the tightness in his chest concentrate there. But he would not let it take over again, whatever it was.

I am in control. I have this power; it does not have me.

He raised his hand up to the sky and harsh white lightning screamed down from the raging dawn sky into his fist as if it were a lightning rod. It was exhilarating, the feel of it riding his body, wrapping itself around him like a trained python at his command. More and more and more of it flowed down from above, crashing into Shigidi like he was standing in the plunge pool of a waterfall of electric discharge, and he started to wonder if he could empty the heavens, in this spirit side of the city, of all its power without destroying himself—if this new power in him was as potent as he suspected. Lightning continued to flow down. When he felt the power peak, he swung his hand down and let it all go, pointing his finger at the giant's shocked face to release it all, concentrated from a single location. The lightning struck Gog square in the forehead, and he exploded into a million meaningless flesh and spirit particles.

Spent, Shigidi fell to his knees as the fading remnants of what used to be Gog the giant floated all around him like a field full of fireflies.

I didn't lose my hand this time.

I controlled it.

He hung his head for a second before turning back to see Nneoma back up on her feet, a strained smile on her face despite the obvious confusion in her eyes. Aleister was with her, standing in the middle of the road, his clothes ripped and charred, his face bloody from cuts. The Wærlan-Drýlic was still in his arms, held tightly to his heaving chest like the most precious thing in the world and right then, perhaps it was, because they absolutely needed to get out of there. But he could see that Aleister was staring off eastward, into the distance and shaking his head softly, his eyes wet and shiny like he was about to cry. Following his gaze, Shigidi saw what Aleister was looking at and instantly wished he hadn't. He closed his own eyes to shut out the light that was erupting over the horizon. His shoulders slumped with the weight of the realization.

Too late.

We are too late.

He didn't know how long he had been kneeling there before Nneoma's hand touched his shoulder. "Shigidi, my love."

He opened his eyes to take in her face. She was kneeling right in front of him, and with his heightened vision he could see every pore, every hair, every inch of her perfect brown skin. He could take in every reflection on the surface of her wet eyes, every spirit particle that danced along her body, every puff of gas and water vapor in the breaths that came out of her nose. He could see her completely, and he knew with an unclouded clarity, free of the primal compulsion of instinct, that he loved all of her with all of him. No matter how much damage he sustained, or how many transformations he underwent or how many conflicting powers he absorbed that wrestled for dominance within him, clinging to the absorbent particles of his body, he loved her and that would never change. It didn't even matter where they were or what they were doing or what side of reality they were on, he knew that he loved this beautiful demon he'd met by chance in a hotel while trying to kill a woman for pray-pay. He loved her completely and truly, and he knew she loved him too. That was all that mattered. Shigidi fell into her for a kiss as deep as a dying breath, embracing her as closely as he could without allowing the glowing tip of the headdress that was lodged in his chest to harm her. The scarf of light around his pierced chest adjusted its flowpath on its own as though it were aware, parting and shifting behind her until it had wrapped itself around them both in what looked like the shape of an infinity symbol, its nexus at his heart.

When they separated, he opened his eyes and stared into hers, which were full of something like hope or determination but less clearly defined. He held onto her, taking in the place where they were now, apparently, trapped. A few ghosts, deities, and assorted minor spirit entities stared at them from open windows of the surrounding buildings but, largely, the spirit side of London seemed empty. And then he saw it in the distance, almost directly in front of them but at a slight angle: a white stone building hugging the intersection between Northumberland Avenue and Great Scotland Yard. The familiar green-white-green flag blew lazily in the morning air, and the words "Nigeria House" were embossed in gold above a dark plaque which he could not read clearly. He couldn't hold back the smile.

Maybe we made it after all. Maybe it's not too late. Maybe we aren't stuck here forever just yet.

"Nneoma . . ."

"Yes darling." She cooed.

"I think we might still be able to make it."

Her eyes widened in response as she spun around. She shot up to her feet like a gymnast when she realized what it was, using one hand to pull down her torn, dress which was riding up her thigh.

"Aleister!" she called out, pointing frantically as she sprouted and spread her wings. "The High Commission! If that book is still in your hands then doesn't that mean it's not yet sunrise?"

Aleister looked confused for a moment as his eyes swept from Nneoma to the eastern horizon to the Wærlan-Drýlic and back to the horizon again as he slowly came to realize what Shigidi and Nneoma already knew; that the lights in the sky were only refractions. The upper edge of the sun's disk was still not visible.

"Come on," Nneoma shouted. "It may be dawn but it's not yet sunrise!"

She took off, up into the air in a straight line like a rocket, and then slowed, folded her wings, and dove downward, spreading them again on the descent so that she could glide smoothly toward the building that was supposed to be their rendezvous point. Shigidi stood up and ran swiftly back to the still-burning black cab. His movement was awkward, each step almost throwing him over to one side since he was not used to moving with his increased speed nor with a new center of mass, now that his arm was gone. Barely noticing the heat and haze, he retrieved the two remaining fragments of the brass head of Obalufon that were not already lodged in his body from inside the cab. His hand was smoky and black when he extracted it, but there was no other effect of the fire on his body except a kind of tingling that was almost . . . pleasurable?

He handed the pieces over to Aleister who had approached as close as he could and was staring quizzically at the trail of light around Shigidi's chest. Shigidi gave the magician a slight nod and a shrug.

Yeah, I don't know what that is either.

They followed Nneoma's lead toward the high commission building, racing against the sun.

At the entrance, they pushed against the thick brown door, but it didn't budge. Shigidi placed his palm on it, channeling some of the wild energy he could feel flowing through him into the reinforced wood. With a calm thought, he tried to release a little bit of the energy, suppressing the surge of images and sensations that tried to take over his body again, but it was like trying to carefully open a valve on an overpressurized gas cannister. A blast of lightning escaped, and the door shattered into splinters. Aleister staggered back and almost fell over. Nneoma, hovering above, shot him a look like surprise mixed with concern.

"Sorry," he said.

No time.

They entered.

Immediately Shigidi set foot in the building, the images flooded his mind again, and he could not hold them back. Black and red roosters. Horses. Smoke. A train. Yams dipped in bright red palm oil like blood. Machetes. Spears. Men in white robes, their faces chalked over with symbols. A stagger of bloody waterfalls as high as the heavens. A giant crocodile rolling in the mud.

What are these? Nightmare fragments? Vagrant memories? Visions?

I don't understand what any of this means.

What is happening to me?

He blinked rapidly until, thankfully, the images cleared from his head almost as quickly as they had entered. When they left, a bone-deep emotional vibration pulled at the glowing hole in his chest, like homesickness. Weak light was starting to peek into the building through the windows. The thing vibrating in his chest nudged him to move, like it was a kind of compass.

Up. Upstairs. We need to go upstairs.

"Follow me," he said as he allowed the vibrating sensation to guide him upstairs, bounding up the steps half a dozen at a time. They swept past the rows of ugly white walls and cream-colored office doors until he felt the tug of a heavy pulse behind one of the doors. He touched it, and Aleister took a cautionary step back. Shigidi tried again to channel more of the new power in him into the obstacle without pulverizing it. He failed and the door exploded inward, disintegrated almost to a fine powder. Nneoma gave him the same surprised and concerned look again but with more intensity this time and he simply said "sorry" again because what else was he going to say that would make any sense?

They entered a large, empty office with a large woodgrain executive desk in the corner and a picture of the President of the Federal Republic of Nigeria hanging above it like a curious micromanager. Shigidi pointed to the center of the room where the tug of the vibration in his chest was strongest. "This is it. The connection is strongest here, so there should be a tension site or whatever you call it, that you can use. Quickly!"

"I don't think I have enough time to properly anchor the particles to the sockets," Aleister protested. "The sun is almost up. If we lose the Wærlan-Drýlic mid-transit we could end up in a worse situation than being trapped spirit-side."

"Just do it!" Nneoma insisted.

Aleister nodded, tucked the two pieces of the brass head under his arm and took his phone from his jacket pocket. He drew symbols quickly with his stylus as he chanted something new that Shigidi could not really distinguish from the strange hodgepodge of words he'd used before. Light like the one swirling around Shigidi's chest but more well defined at its edges—like the beam of a powerful flashlight—erupted from the phone screen and began to pulse weakly. Aleister kept chanting as Nneoma gestured with her fingers and used her spirit particle pressure to remotely pry open the only window in the room. They could both see the golden edge of the solar disk peeking above the horizon, its light scattering more steadily into the maelstrom of clouds above. Shigidi's breath caught.

It's almost here. It's almost here.

Aleister placed the phone on the floor and threw the sacred text of the Wærlan-Drýlic onto it, stepping on top of the book immediately, barely giving it time to settle over the phone.

"Get in!" he cried.

Nneoma and Shigidi took each other's hands, interlocking their fingers, and stepped on top of book with him, struggling for balance just as an eye of light flared beneath it, opening the breach between worlds. The light beneath them wobbled but its borders held as they started to sink into it. The intensity of light in the window exploded just as their line of sight fell below the ground and the eye above them began to close. Shigidi felt the familiar tingle of the wind between worlds as it blew in and took them away from the spirit-side of London.

And then, there was nothing.

They were in a bubble of absolute dark, absolute silence. The only thing that Shigidi could perceive was the feel of Nneoma's and Aleister's bodies pressed against his; the touch of their feet packed tight, almost atop one another. He tried to say something, to call out to Nneoma, and his lips made the motions but he could not hear himself so he could not tell if he was actually making sounds or if the sounds were just not going anywhere. He squeezed Nneoma's hand, grateful that he could still feel that, at least. He began to wonder if Aleister's warning had been right. If they were lost in the space between worlds, if it was indeed too late, if the sun's edge had truly risen above the city's horizon before they made their escape, if the sacred text had faded away just as they slipped out of London's spirit-side . . .

What if we are lost?

It was true. The only thing he could think of that was worse than being trapped spirit-side in a foreign land was this—being lost in the space between worlds. He steeled himself and focused, trying to play back the images that had been flitting in and out of his mind since the brass head impaled him because they had guided him before. Perhaps they would again. They came freely once he let them, as freely as the rush of air from the other side of a shattered door. Black and red roosters. Red sand. Chains. Machetes. Palm fruit. Horses. Smoke. Yams. Palm oil. Lightning. Bones. Spears. The men in the white robes with chalked faces. Waterfalls. Crocodiles.

What does it all mean?

I don't know.

I know.

Are they . . . me?

I don't know. Do I?

Shigidi felt like he was teetering on the edge of understanding something profound but being constantly reeled back. About to grasp some new realization that was always just a hair's breadth out of reach. And then he felt it. The familiar vibration in his chest, like a beacon.

Home.

I am going home.

CHAPTER 16

Nigeria High Commission, Northumberland Avenue,
London, England

JULY 5TH, 2017 | 05:08 AM.

The world returned around them suddenly.

The leather-bound Wærlan-Drýlic beneath them dissolved to nothing, leaving only a wispy trail of grey smoke and the faint smell of sulfur in the air as they fell and hit soft carpet. Shigidi barely noticed its disappearance as they struggled to their feet. It seemed like Aleister was the only one to acknowledge it with a groan, although that could have been caused by something else, as he stood up holding the two glowing pieces of the brass head of Obalufon, one in each hand.

Shigidi took in their surroundings. They were in the same office, that much was obvious, but it was also different. For one, there was no longer a light-edge to everything even though Shigidi could still perceive things with far more clarity than he was used to. The window was open, and a solid beam of young daylight had stabbed its way into the room at a hard angle, throwing a cluster of linear shadows around the entire office. The walls were still cream-colored, but they were now covered with chalk drawings of icons and symbols and images—some of which Shigidi recognized from his past life in the Orisha Spirit Company and some from the more recent visions that had plagued him since the headdress of the brass head had pierced his chest.

There was no watchful picture of the demure Nigerian president here, but the large executive desk was still in the same corner. Atop it were an assortment of things Shigidi was intimately acquainted with: a small calabash of water, some pieces of tortoise shell, an old laptop computer, some cowrie shells, a stack of documents, dried frog skin, kolanuts, and gourd of what he presumed was palm wine set on a mound of red clay that reminded him of the old Oyo palace grounds in Ile-Ife, the spirit side of which was directly linked to Orun. The items on the desk were all tools of the trade for an acting Orisha Spirit Company employee. And sitting calmly behind the desk with his eyes closed, was the company executive, Olorun.

He was wearing a white, flowing agbada, and his neck was saturated with an assortment of beads and cowrie shells and brightly colored precious stones. His eyes flew open, blazing white and hot like twin stars. The moment they settled on Shigidi, the aurora around Shigidi's chest streaked out like pulled rubber and clamped onto Olorun's hand so rapidly, Shigidi didn't notice it happen until it was over and the extended end of the light stream had formed something like a knot in Olorun's open palm. He gripped it and tugged. Nneoma and Aleister were knocked to the ground as Shigidi was dragged chest-first across the room, bumping past them. He scudded forward along the ground as if the light was a rachet. Then he crashed to his knees in front of the desk before Olorun.

"You've failed," he said, his voice sounding like an earthquake but edged with disappointment, "You were supposed to bring the brass head to me intact."

Shigidi tried to explain. "There was an accident, we were—"

But Olorun was already shaking his head before Shigidi could finish. "No. No. No Shigidi." Each repetition sent an even more intense vibration through him, like he was at the epicenter of the old god's earthquake voice.

What is he so upset about?

It's bad, I know but it can't be that bad. Can it?

Nneoma must have sensed the gravity of the situation because Olorun's typical jovial tone was completely absent, and so she jumped in, continuing where Shigidi had been cut off. "There was an accident. We were attacked. Section Six probably, but we made it out. I know it's broken, but we brought it back. All three pieces of it." She turned to indicate Aleister with a jut of her lips, and he hastily dropped the other two brass pieces on the carpet. "See. It's all here. We brought it back. That was the deal. That's what matters in the end. Isn't it?"

"No," Olorun said. "It would have been better for it to be lost, left over in London spirit-space than this thing you have done."

Confused, Shigidi asked, "What thing have we done that the great Olorun cannot fix?"

"What thing indeed?"

And that answer, more than his twin star eyes or his earthquake voice or anything else, chilled Shigidi to his core.

Olorun's star-white eyes flashed sharply, and Shigidi began to convulse, seized by the flow of power through the light that connected him to the supreme orisha. The strange images that had been trickling into his mind now came in a flood that overwhelmed him as he saw it all so clearly, as clearly as though he was *in* them. They coursed through his mind with every spasm, and they looped and looped and looped until he could no longer see Olorun's face in front of him. The images were no longer images but had taken on the more complete texture of experiences. And he experienced them in rapid succession, each making more sense to him than they had before.

Lightning streaked across pitch black sky, and he knew it was the first spark of light that had strained against the primordial void of the universe because the hand that painted the lightning across the sky was his. Red sand was poured into an endless ocean and piled up high until it was an island, and he knew it was the first tectonic plate that had been willed into existence because it was by his will that it was done. A black and red rooster was set down from the heavens on that first mound of red earth, poured out from the white shell (the same original red clay that Shigidi now realized his body had been molded from) by a careful hand he knew was his own, and it scratched away at the sand until it was a continent, each scratch of its feet a fulfillment of his own commands. The images, memories, experiences continued to come. Bleached bones from a variety of creatures. A ram. A purple swirl of nebulae. Water buffalo. Red, mud-capped mountains. Flags of stiff white cloth burning with blue fire. The sun pierced by a spear. An ancient man in silver armor sitting on two clouds. These were Olorun's divine memories. Shigidi was inside them, and now he understood them all completely. Olorun was the principal agent of creation. Every member of the spirit company had been created at his command, all of them aspects of his original form—brought into existence by the faith of the first Yoruba people. Their stories and their beliefs. All the orishas, their symbols, their wars, their rituals, their petty squabbles, all that mattered to them were little more than the fragments of the original Olorun, imbued with different parts of his ashe, his divine energy, like the various wavelengths of light, simultaneously in conflict and harmony with each other. From the abundance of his first form, he had instigated them all.

Shigidi continued to convulse on the floor as he came to realize what was happening to him: Olorun had bound up a small aspect of himself in the headdress of the brass head of Obalufon, a piece full of aggression and thirst for war, his conquering aspect. It was the aspect which had once been completely embodied by Ogun, the god of war—until it was recalled and given to Obalufon Alayemore. That aspect was now merged with Shigidi. The merging of two aspects of the original Olorun had triggered the visions that saturated Shigidi's mind. Olorun's wartime essence was now embedded in Shigidi's blood, his clay, his imagination, all of that divine potency now entangled with his spirit particles by accident.

In a burst of clarity, Shigidi understood how he had come to be in his previous life as a lowly minor god, delivering nightmares on request.

I am nothing more than another aspect of Olorun.

A unique expression of elemental divine energy, his ashe.

I am his creative and formless essence, his flexibility and adaptability.

I am the fullest expression of the divine subconscious.

Shigidi had journeyed far and suffered much only to finally return to the source of his own existence—the one who had distributed himself into the entities that now loved, hated, fought, honored, resented, betrayed one another.

But I am more than . . .

The thought was cut off before Shigidi could complete it as he suddenly stopped convulsing and his blurry vision slowly came back into focus, stabilizing just like the light bond between them. He was face to face with Olorun, Olodumare, Olofin-Orun, Chairman of the Board of the Orisha Spirit Company, first of the orishas and ruler of the Yoruba heavens in all his revelatory glory. Shigidi could now see him clearly for the first time in his truest form with true understanding. Understanding of who he was, where he came from, why his war aspect bonded to Shigidi so completely in that accident but perhaps, most clearly, Shigidi understood what separating it would now do to him.

Sundering.

"Do you see now?" Olorun said.

"Yes," Shigidi croaked. His throat was raw like it had been rubbed with sandpaper, and he was still a bit dizzy.

"You understand?"

"Yes."

"Then you know that I cannot take what is mine without destroying this version of you," Olorun said with sadness in his voice. "When my essence leaves you, it will break you apart. The sundering must occur at the sub-spirit-particle level. It is the only way to collect all of my war aspect that is bonded to you. It is unlikely you will ever be whole again, not in this form. There is no other way to separate."

"No!" Nneoma's cry came from behind Shigidi, piercing their conversation like a spear. It was full of pleading, but anger too. "We did everything you asked of us! There must be another way to extract it. We almost died because of you." She paused to buttress her point by indicating the stump where Shigidi's arm used to be with a jut of her jaw. "There must be something," she continued more frantically. "There must be something you can do, once you get back to Orun, surely you can do it. Your creation, your spirit-side, your realm. I can even help you. Tell me what you need, and I can help you."

"It doesn't work that way. There is only one way to obtain it from him now. Only one process." Olorun's voice had gone gentle, like a tremor, but his gaze was still focused on Shigidi.

"If you could make him and I could remold him, then surely we can find a way to take out your essence without destroying him or his memories."

"I created him a long time ago. When I was far more potent, far more complete. The source that sprung him no longer exists. And what is left is even less complete without that war aspect which is in him now. I'm sorry Shigidi. But you should not have let it come to this. It was contained. The essence was contained. All you needed to do was bring it back here like I told you. In one piece." Olorun shook his head. "It's a pity. You have both done a lot for me since I came out of retirement, and we have had a fruitful business relationship. But it ends now, because I need as much of my war aspect intact as possible in order to accomplish what I have set out to do. To completely oust Shango and bring order and stability and progress back to the company, I must have the will for war and the completeness of power for battle. Do you understand?"

Shigidi did. And he could not think of anything to say so he remained silent.

How do you respond appropriately to the one who created you when he says he must do something that will destroy you?

He reached into his own mind, trying to sort out the threads of his life so far, to select the memories that and emotions that had mattered most. There were precious few of them with true value. Almost of them included Nneoma and Olorun.

So much of my time was wasted.

Olorun shook his head again and the beam of light between them oscillated laterally before resolving back to its straight-line form, like a once-weighted tightrope or a plucked guitar string. There was something bitterly ironic about the situation that made Shigidi crack a thin, bloody smile.

Shango and I are both aspects of Olorun.

I am only here now because Olorun saved me when Shango was about to destroy me.

Now I am about to be die because Olorun must destroy me to get the thing inside me that he needs to destroy Shango.

The bitter smile didn't last long on Shigidi's face. He turned around and caught the forlorn look in Nneoma's eyes, the shock and frustration and sadness hanging in the corners of her mouth like rusty fishhooks.

I think I know what she wants to say because I want to say it too.

But neither of them said anything. The moment had moved beyond words.

Aleister had retreated to the corner of the room, and was sitting there, hugging his knees like a scared schoolboy, completely silent. It was probably for the best; he had reached the extent of his usefulness to them and the situation was far beyond his knowledge or his magick.

"I am sorry," Olorun said.

The piece of brass headdress embedded in Shigidi started to slide out, and he could feel it grind against his chest. It didn't hurt, which didn't surprise him because he no longer felt any pain at all, not even the leftover pain of losing his arm. Besides, it hadn't hurt on the way in either. Although it was a strange sensation, like being awake and fully conscious during your own surgery. The white light between Shigidi and Olorun intensified, brightening until it was almost blinding. And then it erupted with new colors, becoming a kaleidoscope.

I was right after all; it looks just like the aurora borealis.

Olorun's wartime aspect began to leave Shigidi's body in a slow release of pressure, like the end of a long embrace. Weight descended on his shoulders and his arm. So did the throbbing pain pulsing through his stump. The weakness he had felt back in London's spiritside had returned, and for the third time since he met Nneoma, Shigidi was certain that he was going to die. He bit down on his tongue to stop himself from crying out.

Don't draw this out, just get it over with, he wanted to say, but he was suddenly too weak to muster the words.

His body sagged as if it had been anchored.

"No!" Nneoma said in voice so low it was only a little more than a whisper.

She scrambled to the floor until she was beside him and held his head in her hands. She was slowly shaking her head as she pulled his face into her chest. She felt warm and tender, and the heaving of her chest was almost soothing. It distracted from everything else. He could feel her heart beating like a dundun drum beneath her sternum. Wet drops hit his head, and it took him a while to realize that they were tears. She was crying. Shigidi had never seen Nneoma cry. Her hands were shaking, and it took him even longer to realize that the hand he had left was shaking too. But he was not shaking from an overabundance of emotion like she was, he was shaking because he felt cold. So very cold.

"No. This is not going to happen. I'm not going to let you die," she said.

She lifted his head up so that they came nose to nose and forehead to forehead. Nneoma was careful not to let the light that bound Olorun's hand to Shigidi's chest make contact with her skin.

Shigidi inhaled her breath as she said, "I don't care what Olorun said, I am not going to let you to die."

Shigidi did not know what to say and even if he had, his tongue would not have been able to form the words. He was already depleted and weakened, even more than he had been when his lightning-gloved arm shattered in Magog's neck.

They stayed there for what seemed like hours even though Shigidi knew only a few seconds had passed. But his receding mind had made a cocoon of the moment because they were together. Truly together. That's all he'd wanted since he first realized he loved her. He didn't know when it happened. There had been no grand moment, no sudden elevation of feeling. Instead, it had built up in the small moments until existence had become noticeably warmer when he shared it with Nneoma. It was everything, all coming together. The fact that she'd given him the gift of a new body and freed him from his contract. That ever since he met her, he'd felt good about himself for the first time since his creation. That she saw something special in him. That she laughed with him and kissed him and consumed spirits with him. That he'd felt free when he was with her, and he felt able to do so much more than he could before, capable of taking on any challenge and able to go through anything. Even his own impending destruction.

And then, suddenly, she pulled away, "Wait!"

Her eyes were full of excitement.

"Olorun, wait please!" She turned and looked him right in the eyes like they were equals. "You said there is only one way to do this and that once it is done it is *unlikely* that he will ever be whole again. So, does that mean it's not impossible?"

Olorun's twin sun eyes flashed again but his palm stayed up. The river of light continued to flow but the current of it slowed. "No, it is not impossible," he confirmed. "Just extremely unlikely."

"And what could make it possible?" Nneoma asked.

"Faith," the old god said after a short pause. "The same thing that initiated us all, that gives all of us sustenance. The same thing that created the orishas in the first place. Faith. Belief. Absolute certainty in a thing, as impossible as it may be. Absolute faith in his own existence and form and memories and abilities and relationships as they are now." Olorun's voice had changed, it was still a tremor that made Shigidi's jaw feel like it was in the grip of a grinding machine, but the impact was reduced, slowed. And there was a change in tone too.

Is that . . . admiration?

"If there is enough faith in him, enough for every spirit particle component that constitutes him to be focused on the same thing with such absolute certainty that when I am done distilling my essence from him, he can spontaneously return to the same space and time and form in the same configuration with all his memories intact. If there is sufficient faith, then perhaps he can survive," Olorun continued. "You must understand. This is not a matter of conscious control. If it were, I would simply will it to happen. Faith is not a god-thing, it is a human-thing. We did not will ourselves into existence. Do you realize what I am telling you, Nneoma?"

"Yes, I do." Nneoma nodded, wiping the tears from her face. "He needs an anchor belief."

"Indeed," Olorun agreed. "Something he believes in so deeply that is not just known, it just *is*, in every element of his being. Something that is so certain that every particle that makes him what he is will gravitate back towards it and crystalize around it after the sundering."

Olorun twisted his fist and the light between them vibrated, gaining strange new colors at the edges where it dipped in and out of the surrounding air in unsteady arcs. "Do you have such a thing?" he asked, finally turning his question and his gaze to Shigidi. "Do you believe in anything so deeply?"

Nneoma turned to face Shigidi. Her eyes were telling him what she was thinking before the words left her lips, and he understood completely. The gentle arcs of her eyelids were telling him to trust in what they had developed between them, as shaky and uncertain as it had seemed only a few hours ago. The wet filminess that glazed her eyes was asking him to have faith in the love that she had refused to acknowledge until he was half a step from death's door under the raging London spirit sky. "I love you Shigidi. I have never loved another like this—god or man." She paused as tears began to roll down her cheeks again, like lovely liquid pearls. "And I know you love me too. I believe you love me enough to find your way back to me. So, focus on that love, focus on me, hold on to me, and don't let go."

She was shaking. The tears continued to fall. It was the most vulnerable and open he had ever seen her, and he wanted nothing more than to fall into her and swim in her outpouring of emotion.

"Hold on to me," she pleaded.

But there was no need to plead. Shigidi had decided to do it the moment the first tear fell, because he knew that he loved her and of that, there was absolutely no doubt in his clenched, pierced, but unbroken heart.

He managed to nod once and that was enough.

Together they turned to Olorun and answered the question he had left suspended in the air like a feather. Nneoma mouthed the word, "Yes."

"Hmm." Olorun grunted, considering for a moment. Then he tilted his head to the side, and his face almost creased with a smile. "You are sure?"

"Yes, we are," Nneoma said, taking Shigidi's hand.

"We are," he echoed, finally finding enough strength to make the words. As they left his lips, the warm certainty of her love rushed to his head like a gust of warm air, filling him with hope that it could, would, work.

No, it's more than hope. It's certainty.

"Very well. So be it." Olorun closed his eyes again and the kaleidoscope of light binding his palm to Shigidi's chest tightened like a rope before coruscating into a dancing rainbow-colored stream of solid light. Shigidi's fingers went numb. The piece of brass in his chest resumed its slow sliding-out motion, the pressure against insides steady but still not painful, like it was a natural process, like he was giving birth to a fragment of the divine. As it exited, he slumped again, his body stripped completely of the power that had artificially animated it since his battle with the giant. He felt light-headed and nauseated, the image of Olorun behind the desk blurred until it was impossible to tell what he was looking at. He tried to say something, but he could not hear his own voice. Around him, bright green spirit particles floated about like fireflies. That was when he noticed that his entire body had loosened without his willing it, the clay that was used to mold him had liquified, and his knees were sinking into the ground, forming a muddy pool. He was not afraid, but he did not like the feeling. From the first time he had been embodied in that squat ugly body, to Nneoma's remolding, to his own manipulations of his form, to Shango's strike and the fragment it had left behind, to the unconstrained explosion of power into Magog's neck, and now to this, he realized that his body had never truly been in his control.

I'm really getting tired of being changed, of being broken apart.

But he hoped, no he *believed* that this would be the last time. After this final sundering, this final and complete separation, he would take control. He knew what he was now. He would put himself back together, collect all of himself and scaffold it around his love for Nneoma.

When he could no longer feel her hand in his, he spun around to take one final look before his body was completely lost from his control. Nneoma. Her face was the last thing he saw before he collapsed into a wet, brown muddy mass, and his consciousness was swallowed whole by the most complete darkness he had ever known.

I fall into the nothing.

I am nothing.

. . .

CHAPTER 17

Outside space | Beyond time

The first conscious thought Shigidi formed was this: *Nneoma, hold me.*

How much time had passed? Seconds? Minutes? Days? Years? He couldn't tell. The ends of his thoughts clashed with their beginnings. His sense of time was gone. He simultaneously felt like he was just arriving in that non-place and that he had been there for a long time. In some sense, he felt like he was trapped in an endless instant that was going on forever, all at once, overlapping. He was floating in a bubble of reality where there was no sense of time or direction.

But what matters is that I am.

I am not gone.

I am.

Where am I?

He wanted to scream but he had no mouth. He wanted to see but he had no eyes. He wanted to grab on to something, anything, but he had no sense of a body. He was just a disembodied consciousness floating in an ocean of emptiness. Fear seized him, deep and abiding and pure, and he could not conjure enough of himself to weave it into anything new, to control it. The fear settled in. It was worse than being lost in the space between worlds. At least there, there had been a sense of mass and energy and time and enough embodied containment of himself to hold on to Nneoma and to push against the dark.

Now, I just am.

But at least I am.

Focus on that.

I know who I am, and I know at least one thing with absolute certainty.

Nneoma.

Shigidi focused on everything about her that his mind could summon—the sound of her voice when she said his name, her lovely brown eyes that glazed over when she consumed a spirit, her thick lips, the way her heart beat when she was sleeping in his arms, her lovely and dangerous laugh, her silhouette against the moon when she flew through the night sky, her moans of pleasure when they made love, the dance of her feet through fine sand on the beach, the heat of her tears falling onto his skin when she finally told him she loved him. He focused on it all until he started to feel the flowering within him of a potential for something like a sense of direction, a sense of time. Like something vaguely magnetic was pulling his raw, exposed consciousness toward it. He allowed whatever sense of consciousness he had to follow the feeling because even though he could not see or hear or sense where—or even how—it was moving him, he knew with every fiber of his being, that it would lead him back to her. He had faith. He believed.

He followed it and followed it and followed it until the flowering became a bloom. He could finally tell that time was going by in a steady direction even though he could not tell how much of it had elapsed.

Time.

I am tending towards time.

He continued to follow the potential that was guiding him until his consciousness hit what appeared to be a barrier of unreality. It seemed thin and elastic and uneven, like a membrane. He pressed ahead, pushing against it with a singular, focused thought of her. It gave. When he broke the surface of the unreality membrane, sensations rushed in to fill the vacuum. Space and time themselves had finally been let in, and his consciousness could finally take shape within them, like water flowing into a vessel. He felt everything, too many things all at once. Sensory overload. But he kept his focus on her. And then suddenly the chaos ceased, and his consciousness achieved clarity. He felt the familiar weight of presence in his own body settle on him, but it was lacking . . . something.

Breathe. Breathe. Remember how to breathe.

Shigidi opened his mouth and swallowed a clumsy gulp of air like he'd been drowning. The retreating sense of nothingness still weighed his body down to the ground, but he could now feel and move, a little at least. He opened his eyes and there, staring down at him, was the face of what had to be the loveliest being in all of creation. She was crying.

Nneoma.

I am back in the world.

I am not lost.

I found Nneoma.

Or perhaps she helped me find my way back.

He heard Aleister finally break his shocked silence from the corner of the room. "Well, I'll be fucked . . ."

Me too.

Shigidi took stock of himself as his breathing finally caught a rhythm. His arm was still missing, there was barely a crackle to his spirit particles, and the beating of his heart was slow and sluggish. The blurriness of Nneoma's visage as she leaned in to kiss him let him know that he was not yet whole, that he was still broken, perhaps more broken than he was before Olorun withdrew the broken headdress which contained Olorun's wartime aspect from his body, and even then, he was barely hanging on. But at least he was not destroyed. There was still a faint vibration in his chest, though, like something remained of the power that had gone out of him, a kind of energy echo, making him yearn for a fight even though he knew he was not in any shape to survive one. The muted vibration was pulling at his emotions, making him miss Orun more than he ever had before, even while he had worked for the spirit company. He was not sure what it was or if it was even real. And if it wasn't, perhaps it would fade away with time. But none of that mattered in the perfect moment of reawakening. What mattered was this: He was alive.

I am alive.

He threw all of himself into the kiss of the woman for whom he had reconstituted himself. For whom he would wage war against gods and giants. The woman he loved and believed in completely. The kiss subsumed the world until it was the most real thing he had ever felt, fully anchoring him back in reality. Their love tasted like cool wine on his lips.

"So, it worked. You found your way back," Olorun said.

It seemed less of a question and more of a statement intended to pry them apart and force them back into conversation.

Shigidi saw that Olorun's white agbada was glowing intensely like there was a fluorescent bulb woven into the fabric. The glow matched his eyes and contrasted spectacularly with his dark skin, making it look recently polished. The beam of light that had bound them was gone, leaving nothing but an extremely faint glow around Shigidi's chest, which he doubted was even real. It had the quality of an after-image, or a mirage, and Shigidi's eyes were still adjusting to being back from unreality so he wasn't completely sure of anything except that Nneoma was with him. Atop Olorun's head, the brass headdress of Obalufon sat like a crown. It was glowing too.

"Yes," Shigidi finally managed to croak out. "Thanks to her."

Nneoma disengaged and sat up, placing her palms on her knees as though she were about to say a prayer, but instead, she pulled his head into the softness of her lap and held him there like a sick child.

"You still feel it, don't you?" Olorun said.

Realization fell on Shigidi with shocking suddenness.

Yes.

Fear and guilt and uncertainty alchemized into a tight knot in the pit of Shigidi's stomach as he tried to suppress the vibration in his chest. He was afraid to answer the question, to admit that he still felt it. Afraid that if he did, it would turn out to be true. Afraid that it had been a mistake. Afraid that perhaps Olorun was referring to something else when he had asked the question: *You still feel it, don't you?*

What if Olorun was merely talking about the disorientation, the remnants of the sensation of being lost in unreality, of being out of space-time, and not about vibration in his chest, the hint of blood-thirst in the back of his throat, and the persistent longing for Orun that he felt? If he answered wrong, perhaps Olorun would realize his mistake and decide to take whatever little of himself was still left in Shigidi. And whatever was left could be the spark of animation he needed, the only thing that was still keeping him alive, that helped hold enough of himself together to find his way back.

No. Please.

Shigidi's shallow breathing became labored.

"I . . ." He stuttered.

"Don't worry, I'm not going to take it back," Olorun said before twisting his head and flashing a playful smile. "Besides, it will fade. Or perhaps it won't. Who knows?"

Ah! Olorun you lovely bastard. Shigidi smiled.

You didn't take all of it, did you?

You left some of your war aspect in me, a small spark to keep me from dying, from being completely lost. You gave me a chance to find her.

"Consider it a hazard pay bonus," Olorun said. And Shigidi ex-haled a lungful of fear. Nneoma must have realized what Olorun was implying too, because she squeezed Shigidi to her even tighter. She looked up into Olorun's bright star eyes and mouthed the words, "Thank you." Over and over and over again.

Thank you, kaabiyesi.

They remained motionless for a moment, and Shigidi let every-thing that had happened settle on him like rain. He acknowledged the gift . . . and the risk that Olorun was taking. Now that he truly understood who he was, who Olorun was, Shigidi understood. It was a small risk, but a risk, nevertheless, leaving some small fragment of his wartime aspect within Shigidi, out of his direct control as he went up against the most powerful of his fragments, Shango.

So why? There had to be a reason, something to make Olorun think it was worth leaving some of his power behind.

Shigidi thought back to the moment when he'd reconnected to the source, when he'd felt just on the verge of some further, final revelation.

I am the fullest expression of the divine subconscious.

But I am more than . . .

The connection had been severed just before he could grasp that final piece of understanding.

What are you not telling me?

The brass head of Obalufon on Olorun's head began to fade, slowly and unevenly, like it was being digested by some invisible creature, until finally it disappeared. When it did, so did the glow emanating from Olorun's clothes and skin. But the white-hot metal glare of his eyes remained. Slowly, with a stately manner, he rose to his feet.

He spoke as he approached Shigidi and Nneoma on the floor. "Hmm. I must admit, I did not think that you would be able to reconstitute yourself. Even though I left some of my wartime ashe in you, I still had to sunder you to extract most of it. All I gave you was a chance, a chance to find your way back. But even with that, it should have been near impossible. And yet, somehow, you did it. You believed yourself back into existence. It's truly rare to have so much faith in anything, even for a god." He paused and ran a finger along his thickly bearded chin before adding, "Especially for a god."

Olorun tapped his foot on the ground. "Perhaps it is because . . ." he stopped himself and shook his head. "Anyway. It doesn't matter. Even with a belief in yourself and in a love that is as strong as yours seems to be, it is still a near impossibility—the recollection of oneself after being sundered, especially in your physical condition. You have always had potential to be more, Shigidi, and I expected that your time would come. But it seems fate has led you on a different path from the plan I envisaged for you and has twice forced you to be tested much sooner than I anticipated. And twice, you have far exceeded my expectations."

Shigidi squinted in confusion.

Potential? Test? Expectations? Plan? What is he talking about?

But he didn't want to stop the flow of words coming from Olorun, so he didn't interrupt because it seemed Olorun was talking to himself almost. Trying to convince himself of something.

"Perhaps there is more to the value of formlessness and flexibility than even I originally foresaw. Perhaps it was a waste of your talents to hide you in corners of the spirit company weaving petty nightmares in that ugly shrunken form for all those years. I thought it was necessary at the time but perhaps I was wrong. Perhaps if I had made difference choices, the company would not be in the state it is now."

Olorun leaned forward. "You are a strong one Shigidi, stronger than I expected you to be when I first made you and yielded a portion of my ashe to you. And full of far more potential."

For the first time since Shigidi met Olorun face to face, he could hear something in the tone of the old god's voice that sounded to him a lot like pride.

Shigidi gripped Nneoma's hand tighter.

She'd said it too when they'd first encountered each other in that hotel room. *Potential.* So she, too, had sensed something in him, and she'd even reminded him of it, even when they were in the car being chased by Magog.

Nneoma fixed her gaze intently on Olorun. The lines of her face deepened.

What is everyone seeing in me that I can't see in myself?

Perhaps, as he had come to find, it was just like everything else about him—easy to read but formless and poorly defined, its shape unclear and difficult to pin down, even for himself.

"Potential for what? What plan did you have for me?" Shigidi asked.

"I will tell you both, when the time is right," Olorun said.

Shigidi wanted to ask more, so much more but every question that his mind constructed felt like broken glass when it reached his tongue, so he didn't ask any of them.

Nneoma pouted but didn't press either, and they allowed the silence to settle.

From the far corner of the room, Aleister stood up and interrupted the silence with a muttered question, apparently directed at Nneoma: "Uh . . . can I go now, luv? I think my debt is paid in full."

Shigidi had almost completely forgotten he was still there.

Olorun turned sharply and stared at the anxious magician. Aleister started to shake visibly. He tried to hold the gaze, but he couldn't and eventually he wilted and sat back down in the corner, hugging his knees like he was trying to fold himself into the tiny space and disappear.

Olorun broke out in exuberant laughter, folding his arms in front of him. "Don't give yourself a heart attack, oyibo," he said as he returned to his desk and settled heavily into the plush leather chair. He closed his eyes and put his hands to his temples, deep in thought.

Nneoma leaned over and kissed Shigidi again and then she rose, laying his head down carefully on the floor. He stared at the plain white ceiling, pockmarked with small holes in the plaster, like missing information, and then he turned his head. Nneoma was with Aleister, who was still shaking. She extended her hand to him, he took it, and she helped him up from his fetal position in the corner. She gave him a light kiss on the cheek.

Shigidi was surprised to find that he didn't feel even the faintest hint of jealousy anymore.

"Yes Aleister, your debt is paid in full," she said.

"Umm . . . what just happened? What does oyibo even mean?" he said, lowering his voice and leaning in. His voice, like his hands, was shaking.

"It's just a slang term for a white person. He doesn't know your name."

"Good," Aleister said, allowing his voice return to its normal level. "I don't think I want him to. Demons and magick I can handle, but gods make me uncomfortable."

"Me too," she said. "And yet, look at me. I know this is not how you expected your night to go, but I'm glad we found you. And thank you, for everything."

"I'm not sure I even understand what happened tonight. Weirdest heist I've ever seen or heard of," Aleister replied. "I am just glad it's over, and we are all alive and here."

"Me too," Nneoma echoed.

"Will you be okay?" Aleister asked, staring over her shoulder at Olorun's pensive face.

When Shigidi heard the question, he found himself wondering the same thing: *Will we be okay?*

"Yes," Nneoma told Aleister. "I have Shigidi with me. I will take care of him. We will take care of each other. We will be okay. I hope *you* will be okay."

Aleister nodded. "I hope so too. And I think I will be. But I think I'll be avoiding London's spirit-side for a while. First, I have to go back to the Temple. Make sure the Wærlan-Drýlic is back where it belongs and buy old George a drink to apologize. You know."

She nodded. "Yes, I know. I'm sorry about all that."

"It's alright luv, he wasn't hurt." Aleister scratched his head. "Well, maybe his pride was, a bit."

"Yes, probably. But you humans have too much to begin with." She smiled.

"Will I see you again?" Aleister asked, dropping his voice again. There was a hint of something like hope floating atop the question.

"Probably not, Aleister, and you should be happy about that. We no longer owe each other anything, and I hope we never will. It took almost a hundred years, but our transaction is completed. So, enjoy the rest of your . . . life. I hope you finally find what you've really been looking for all these years and through all your lives. I think I have."

She glanced in Shigidi's direction, and Shigidi could feel his heart soar. *So have I Nneoma, so have I.*

"And maybe consider changing careers," she said to Aleister, still smiling. "I don't know if this emo-teen-rockstar thing you have going on right now is really working for you. I preferred you when you were the great beast, brash and arrogant with a bit more belly on you and less hair too."

"Ah, well. Everyone is a Satanist these days, I wouldn't stand out," he quipped, displaying a thin-lipped smile.

"Then maybe consider the priesthood."

They shared a laugh and then a final lingering hug.

"You know, it's funny, but I'm glad I met you," Aleister said as he took a step back, toward the door. "There's one thing I always wanted to ask you."

"Sure," she said, "Go ahead."

"You're not a manifestation of the goddess Nuit, are you?"

"No." She smiled and placed her finger coated with yellow shimmer on his chest. "I'm so much more."

She pushed gently.

"Goodbye, Nneoma."

Aleister took two steps backward, spun around, and left, shutting the woodgrain door behind him and leaving them in silence once again.

Nneoma sighed and returned to Shigidi's side, kneeling beside him so that her nose touched his. There were pale streaks running along her cheeks where tears had fallen. He took her hand again and squeezed it tight. Her touch was warm. With her other hand, she took the base of his jaw between her thumb and forefinger, pulling down gently.

"What are you still stressed about?"

Shigidi managed a small smile.

She returned his smile and held it for a moment before she looked away, up, at Olorun who was still quietly thinking at his desk.

"So what do we do now that . . ." Nneoma started, before Olorun raised his hand to stop her.

"Please. Just wait, ehn."

She interlocked her fingers with Shigidi's and they remained there, waiting for what seemed like a lifetime, unsure of what to do next, if anything at all. Section Six would probably be looking for them by now, but Shigidi didn't care. He focused on her breath, the steady flow and warmth of it, until they were synchronized, like two halves of the same creature. The cloud-filtered light streaming in through the window shortened the shadows around them as the sun rose up higher in the sky.

Shigidi wasn't sure how much time passed before Olorun finally moved.

When he did, his motions were quick, leaving a trail of his image behind, as if his presence was so intense that he had imprinted onto space itself and it took time for the world to adjust to his absence. His hands left his temples and swiped across the table as he picked up the calabash of water on his desk and tossed in the tortoise shell, cowries, dried frog skin, and kolanuts. The water started to bubble. Shigidi, roused and fascinated, angled his head to get a better view.

Olorun tossed the red clay onto the floor beside the desk and typed something carefully on the old and clumsy computer keyboard before taking a deep swig of palm wine and spitting it out in a wild spray over the calabash. The bubbling became an eruption, its contents leaping into the air and splashed on him like he'd just sprayed water onto hot palm oil. He poured the agitated water over the red clay on the floor, and the floor rippled where they made contact like it, too, had become fluid, taken on the quality of the water.

So, it was a secret gateway after all.

Nneoma was right.

"It's ready," he said to them calmly, "but unfortunately, it's detectable. Once I use this, British Spirit Bureau border authorities will know there has been a breach. They will know there is a backdoor and where it leads, so they will know it was me. They will probably find it and block it in a matter of hours. But I have a follow-up board meeting to attend so—so be it. Teju is in charge here at the Nigeria High Commission so she can deal with the diplomatic fallout. Now I can finally end this business with Shango. Besides, I promised you safe passage back to Orun, free of Shango's wrath, and I intend to keep that promise. But first, we need to go Ogun's workshop."

"Ogun? The orisha of iron and war?" Nneoma asked.

Shigidi shook his head.

No. Not war.

"Not anymore," Olorun clarified. "He chose to retire from that role centuries ago and free himself of spirit company politics, which is why he helped me craft the brass head and embed into it my war-time aspect—which had previously been within him. The process sundered him, as you can imagine, and it has taken a long time for him to reincarnate in a new form with the new ashe I gave him. Perhaps too long. Anyway, he handles only metal work and technology now. He will take care of you. Nurse you back to full strength once you get used to your new constitution."

Nneoma looked confused. "Why him? Why not a healer?"

Olorun paused and smiled in a flash of bright white teeth. "Primarily, because I trust him. I can't say that about everyone in the company right now. But also, because he is no longer a member of the board and Shopona, who would have been my first choice, is dead, taking on a different and abstract form. Besides, Shigidi needs a new arm. Clearly my clay is no longer enough to contain all the assorted powers he has been absorbing and accumulating. So, we will need to make an adjustment."

He faced Shigidi directly, "We want to keep your flexibility and ability to absorb different energies, but we need to increase your overall pure strength and boost your ability to resist great forces, if you are to live up to your full potential. I know Ogun has been work-ing on some new metal-clay admixtures."

Nneoma and Shigidi looked at each other when Olorun asked, "How do you like the sound of steel?"

I like it.

I like it a lot.

Shigidi squeezed out a bloodstained smile.

One more change, hopefully for the better.

"Good, I knew you would. We will reinforce you with it." Olorun nodded and angled his head at the gateway he'd just opened. "Oya enter. Let's go."

Nneoma helped Shigidi to his feet. His stump throbbed with a new and more mature pain when he moved. Every motion sent stabs of it through the rest of his body but he clenched his jaw and pushed past the pain. Once he stood, he could barely keep his feet under him. Nneoma hung his arm around her shoulder, carrying most of his weight, and he was grateful for it. Grateful for her. They struggled over to the place on the floor where the red clay had been. It was now a backdoor portal that shone and rippled and swirled like a red-tinted liquid mirror or the opening to a dream. He stared into it, the gate-way back to Orun, back to the home of the orishas. His birthplace. His home. He felt a tug in his chest like the pull of a treasured memory.

"Are you ready?" Nneoma asked, shifting her bare feet.

"Yes," Shigidi replied.

I am.

I am ready for whatever comes next.

And with that, they stepped into the gateway, together.

ACKNOWLEDGMENTS

I'm really lucky to have been encouraged and supported by so many people along the road to this novel. Some of them are not even aware of the magnitude of their impact. So, thank you to Nick Wood, Tade Thompson, Geoff Ryman, and Lola Shoneyin whose comments and encouragements convinced me to write a full-length novel.

This story has been in my mind for a long time. Nneoma and Shigidi have taken on several iterations to get to this point. From early story sketches in *The Alchemists Corner* with input from Edwin Okolo and Joshua Segun-Lean (thanks guys!) to the first true expression of this story arc that appeared as the novelette "I, Shigidi", in *Abyss & Apex* magazine back in 2016. Thank you so much Wendy S. Delmater and Tonya Liburd for publishing the story and letting the world see Shigidi and Nneoma's potential.

Thanks to my agent Bieke van Aggelen for seeing that potential and championing this story. And thank you Martijn Lindeboom, for helping me shape this novel along the way as I put all my wild ideas together. And of course, Betsy Wollheim at DAW Books for taking a chance on my voice when the story was still being formed and the pandemic was at the height of its powers. The entire DAW team has been wonderful.

I am highly indebted to everyone who helped me with research, and to my beta readers Nerine Dorman and Makena Onjerika, for the early feedback that helped me turn my first draft into a more polished product.

A special thank you to my wonderful partner Rocio Vizuete Fernandez, who has read and discussed so many aspects of this story with me over the last three years; my brothers Seyi and Segun, for all their love and support; and my parents Kola and Sola, who laid the foundations of my imagination. I know they would have been happy to see me finally write a book after reading (and sometimes ruining) so many of theirs.

And finally, thank you to everyone that has read my stories over the years, going all the way back to the days of the *The Toolsman's Blog/TNC* (I troway salute to Olawale Adetula, Pemi Aguda, Tokunbo Aworinde and the crew) when I was still Thinktank/The Alchemist. Thank you, dear readers. Without your faith, these stories wouldn't have their power. I hope you enjoyed this one and all the stories that are to come.